Witchlight

Jessi
Zabarsky

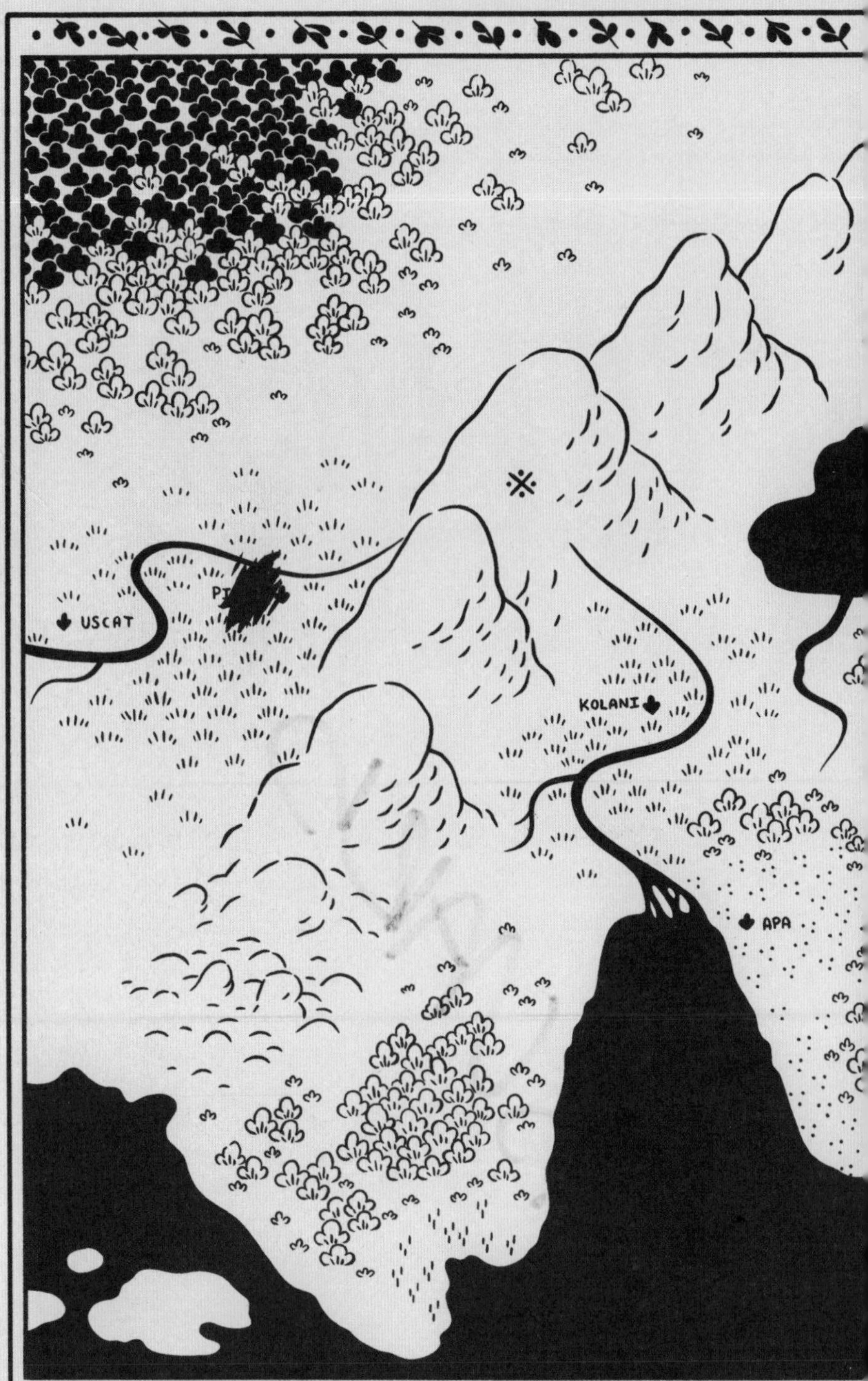
USCAT
PI[redacted]
KOLANI
APA

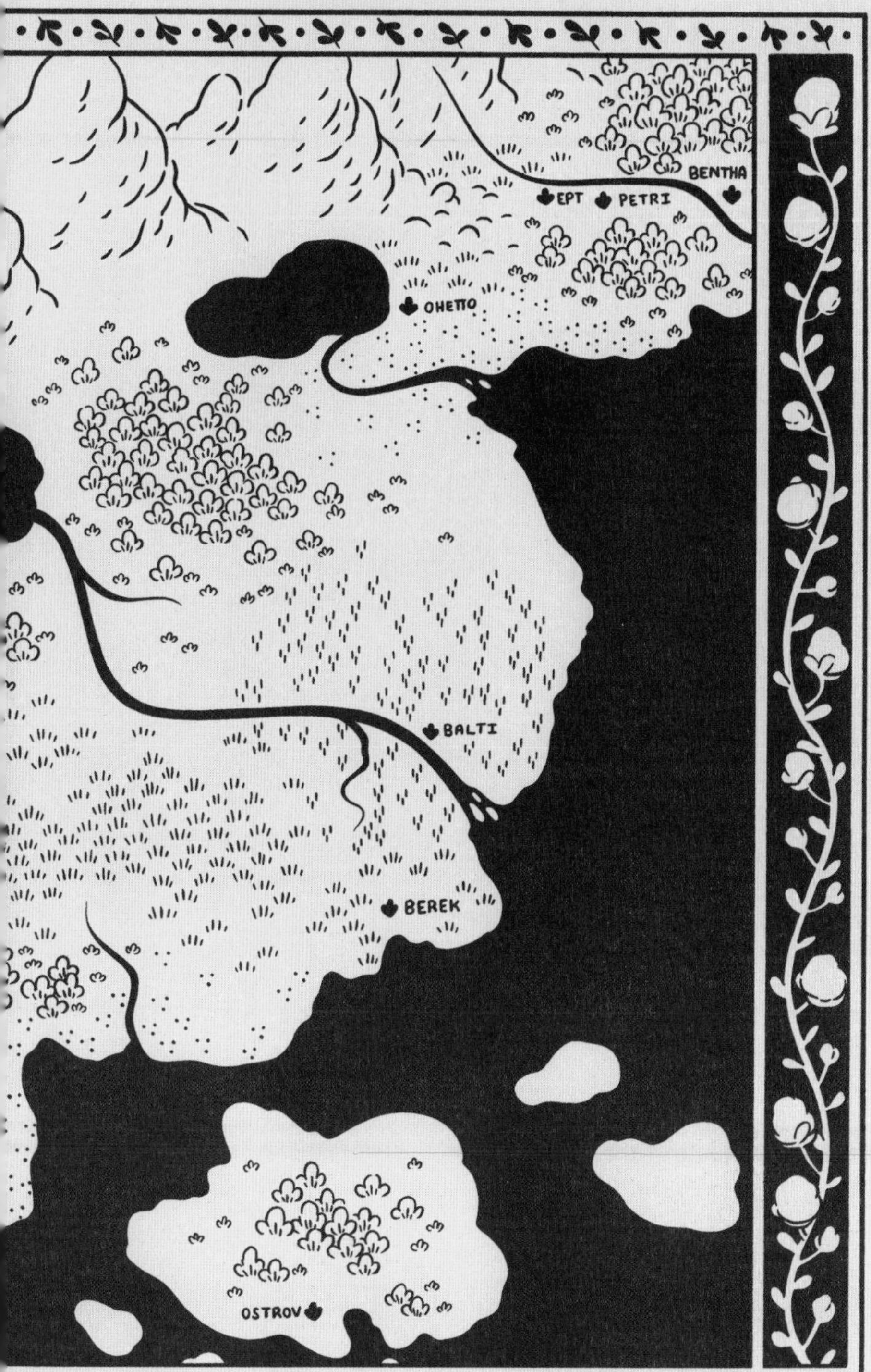
BENTHA
EPT
PETRI
OHETTO
BALTI
BEREK
OSTROV

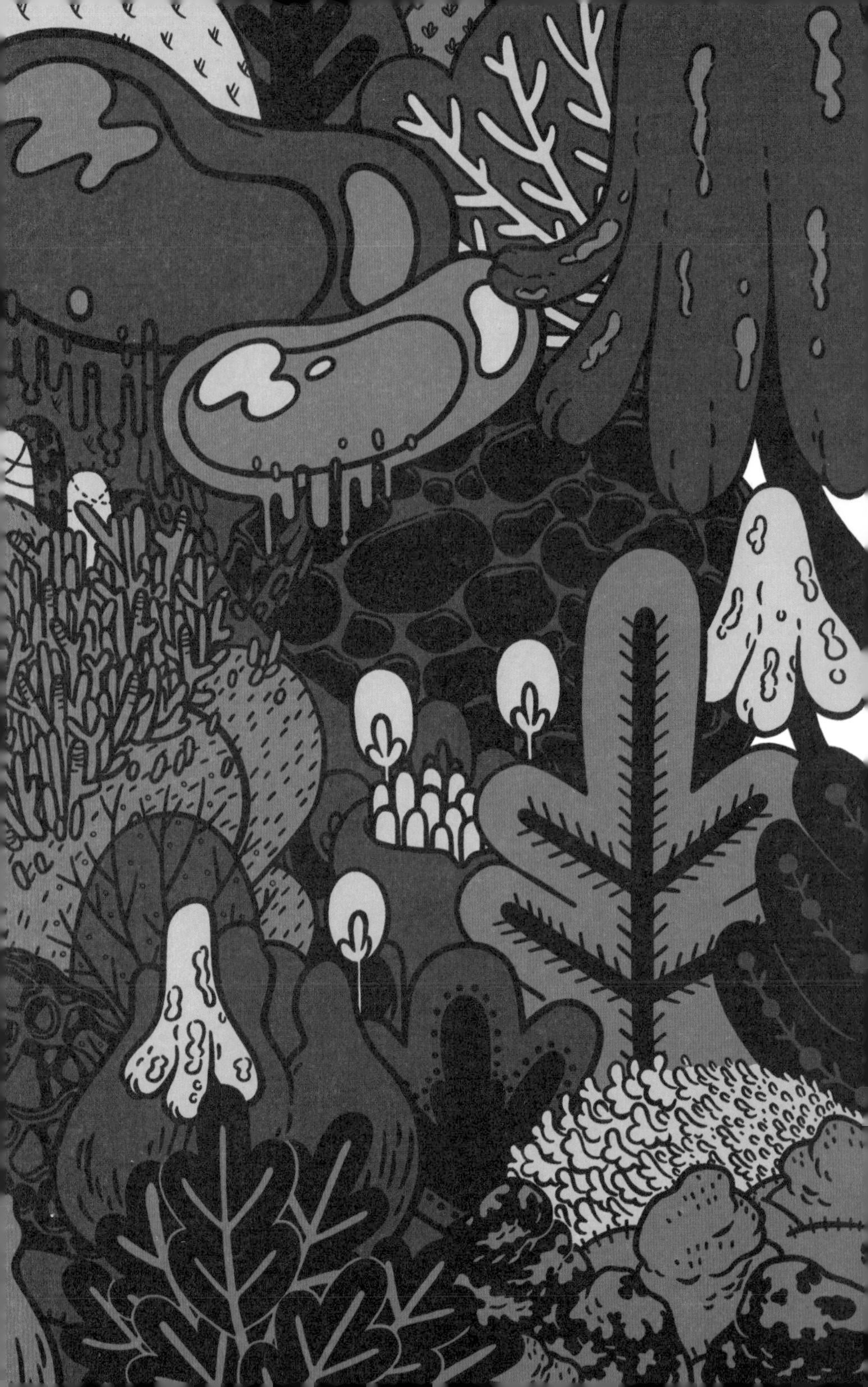

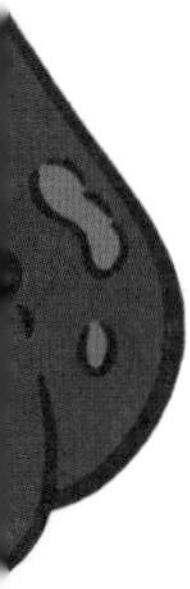

Witchlight

Jessi Zabarsky

with coloring by Geov Chouteau

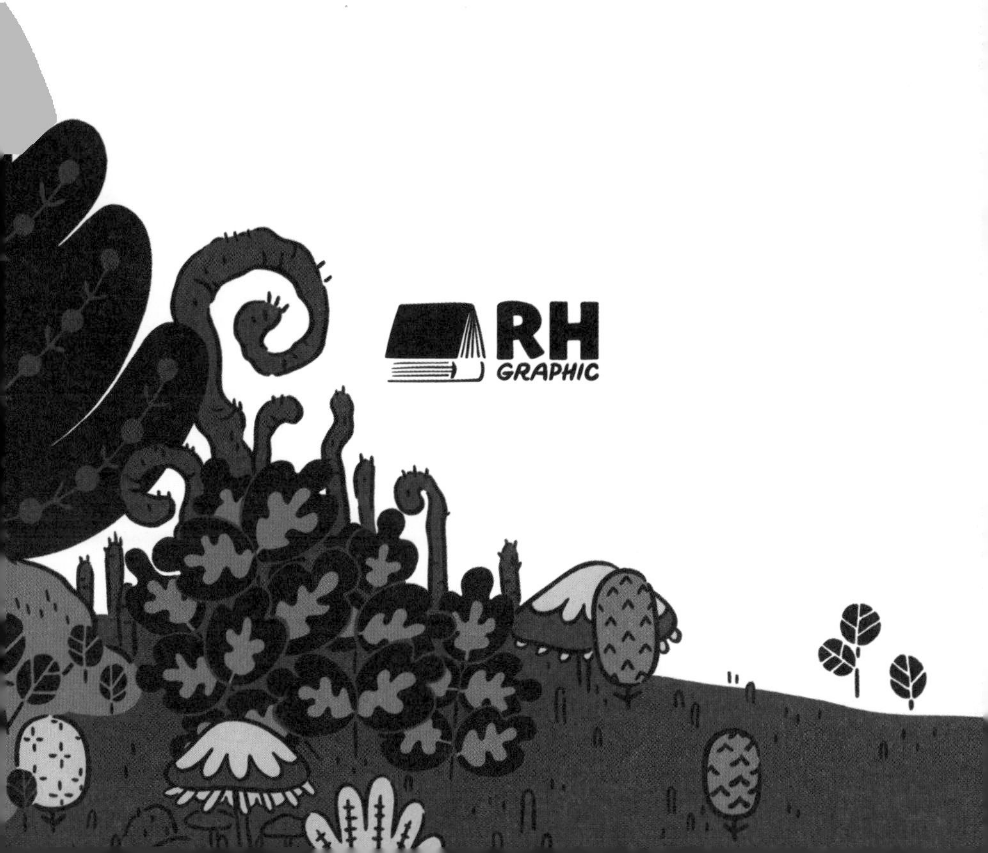

RH GRAPHIC

Witchlight was drawn with ink on paper, then lettered and colored digitally.

Text and art copyright © 2016, 2020 by Jessi Zabarsky
Cover art copyright © 2020 by Jessi Zabarsky

All rights reserved. Published in the United States by RH Graphic, an imprint of Random House Children's Books, a division of Penguin Random House LLC, New York. Originally published in the United States in different form by Czap Books in Providence, Rhode Island, in 2016.

RH Graphic with the book design is a trademark of Penguin Random House LLC.

Visit us on the Web! RHKidsGraphic.com • @RHKidsGraphic

Educators and librarians, for a variety of teaching tools, visit us at RHTeachersLibrarians.com

Library of Congress Cataloging-in-Publication Data
Names: Zabarsky, Jessi, author, artist.
Title: Witchlight / Jessi Zabarsky.
Description: First RH Graphic edition. | New York : RH Graphic, [2020] | Audience: Ages 14–18 | Audience: Grades 10–12 | Summary: "Sanja gets taken by Lelek, a witch, and they find themselves on an adventure to discover the truth about Lelek's powers and each other"—Provided by publisher.
Identifiers: LCCN 2019025813 | ISBN 978-0-593-11999-0 (paperback) | ISBN 978-0-593-12418-5 (hardcover) | ISBN 978-0-593-12001-9 (ebook) | ISBN 978-0-593-12000-2 (library binding)
Subjects: LCSH: Graphic novels. | CYAC: Graphic novels. | Witches—Fiction. | Ability—Fiction.
Classification: LCC PZ7.7.Z33 W58 2020 | DDC 741.5/973—dc23

Designed by Patrick Crotty
Colored by Geov Chouteau

MANUFACTURED IN CHINA
10 9 8 7 6 5 4 3 2 1
First RH Graphic Edition

A comic on every bookshelf.

To the best park in
the Cuyahoga River Valley

Part 1

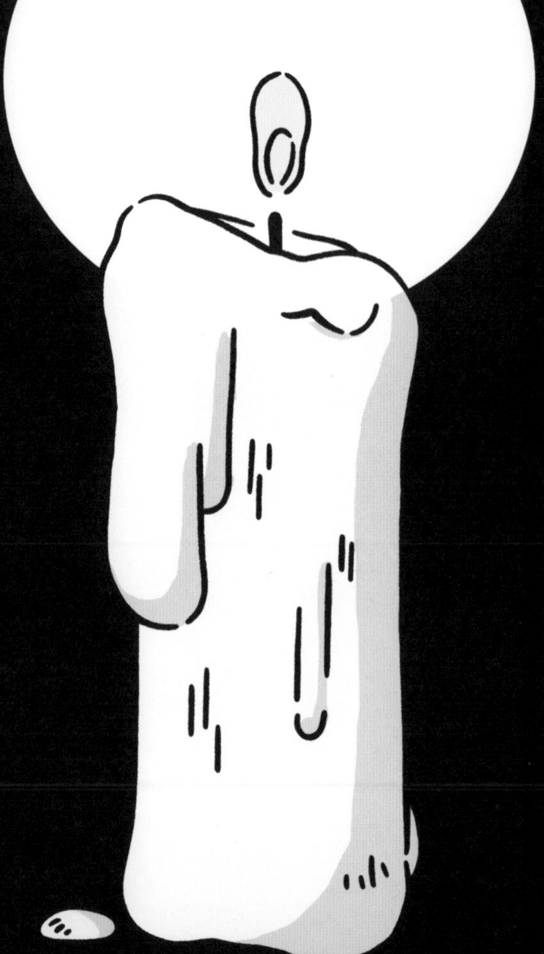

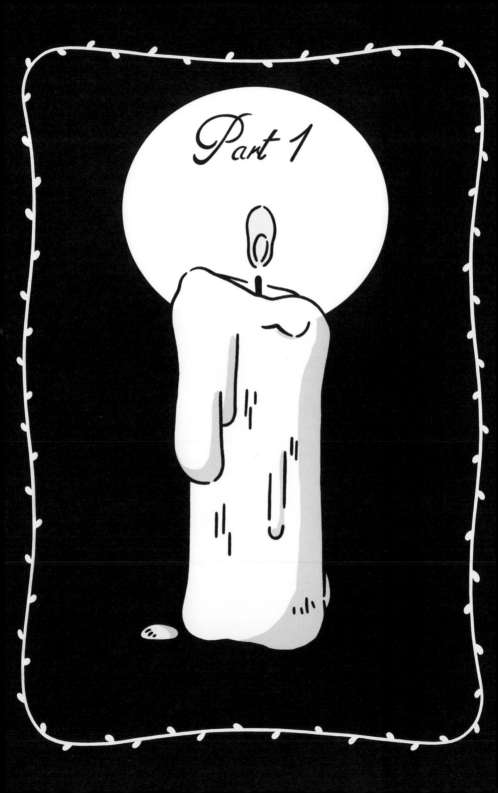

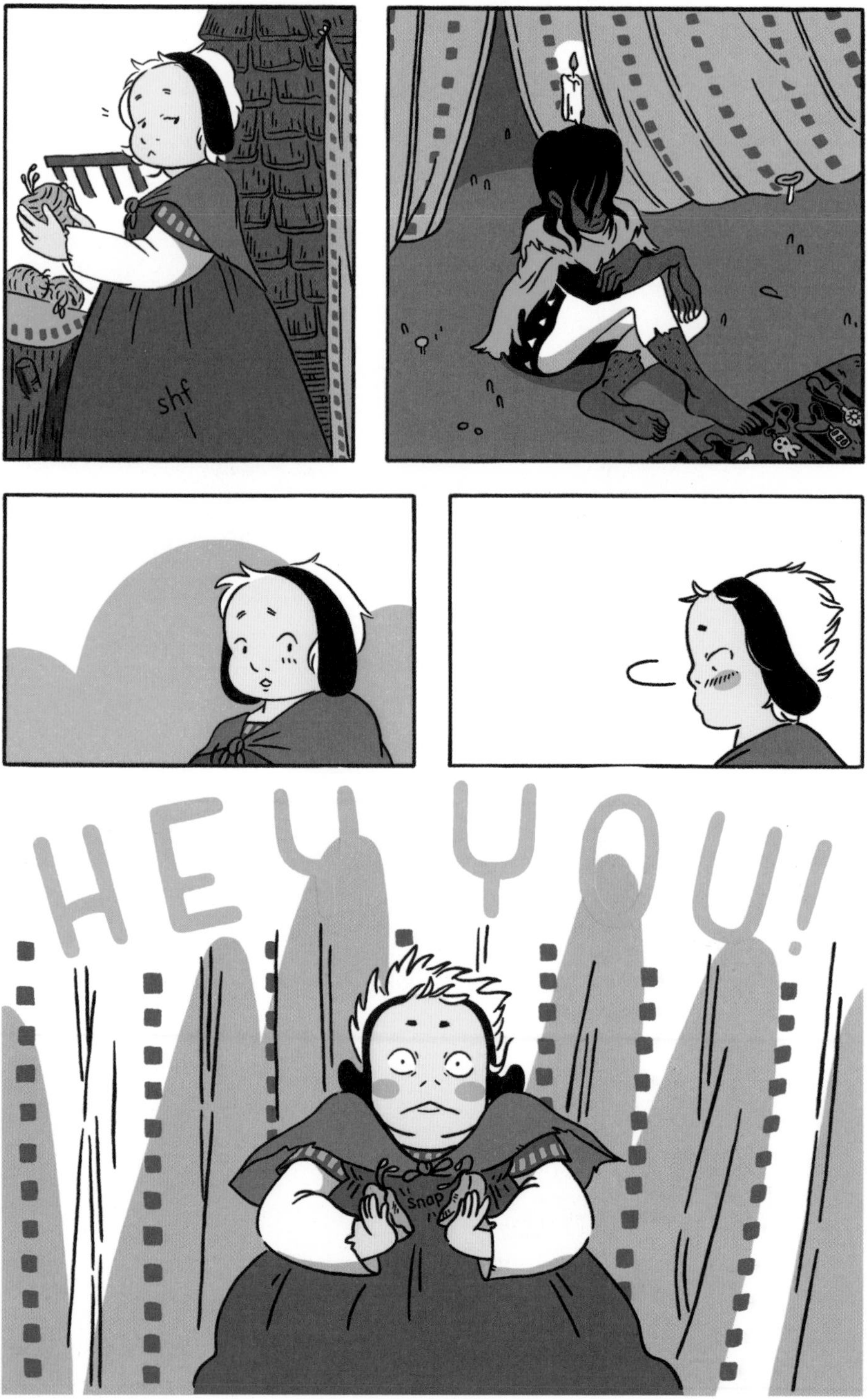
shf
HEY YOU!
snap

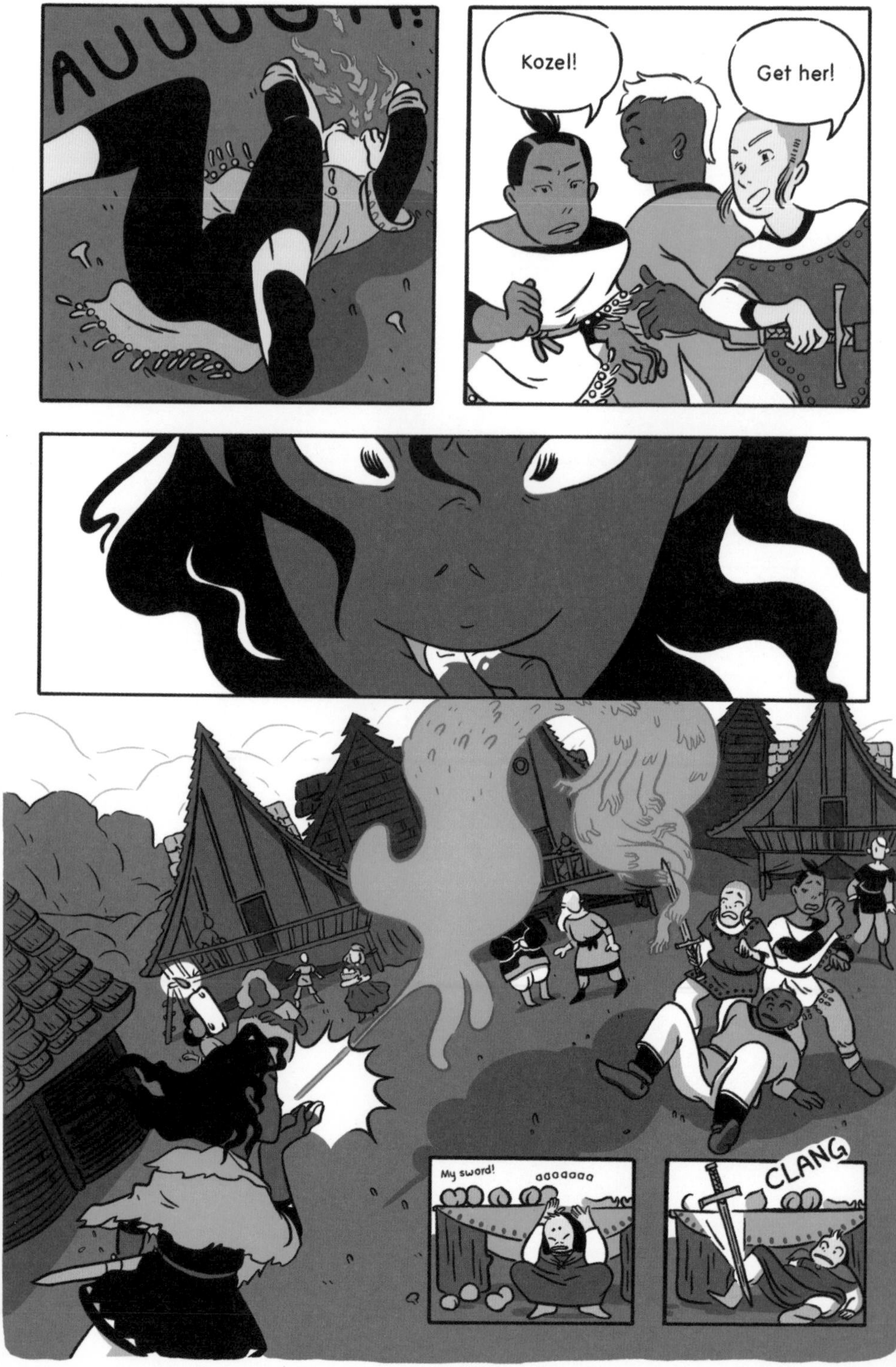
AUUUGH!
Kozel!
Get her!
My sword!
aaaaaaa
CLANG

tmp
tmp
tmp
Blast!
ugh
Kaff
Kaff

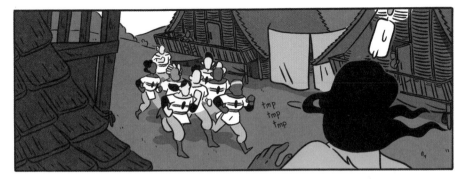

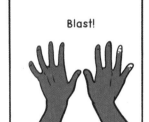

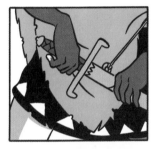

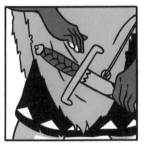

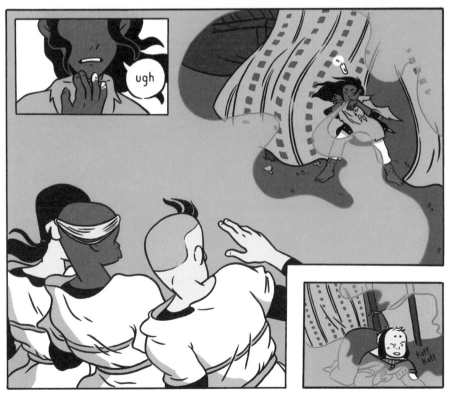

9

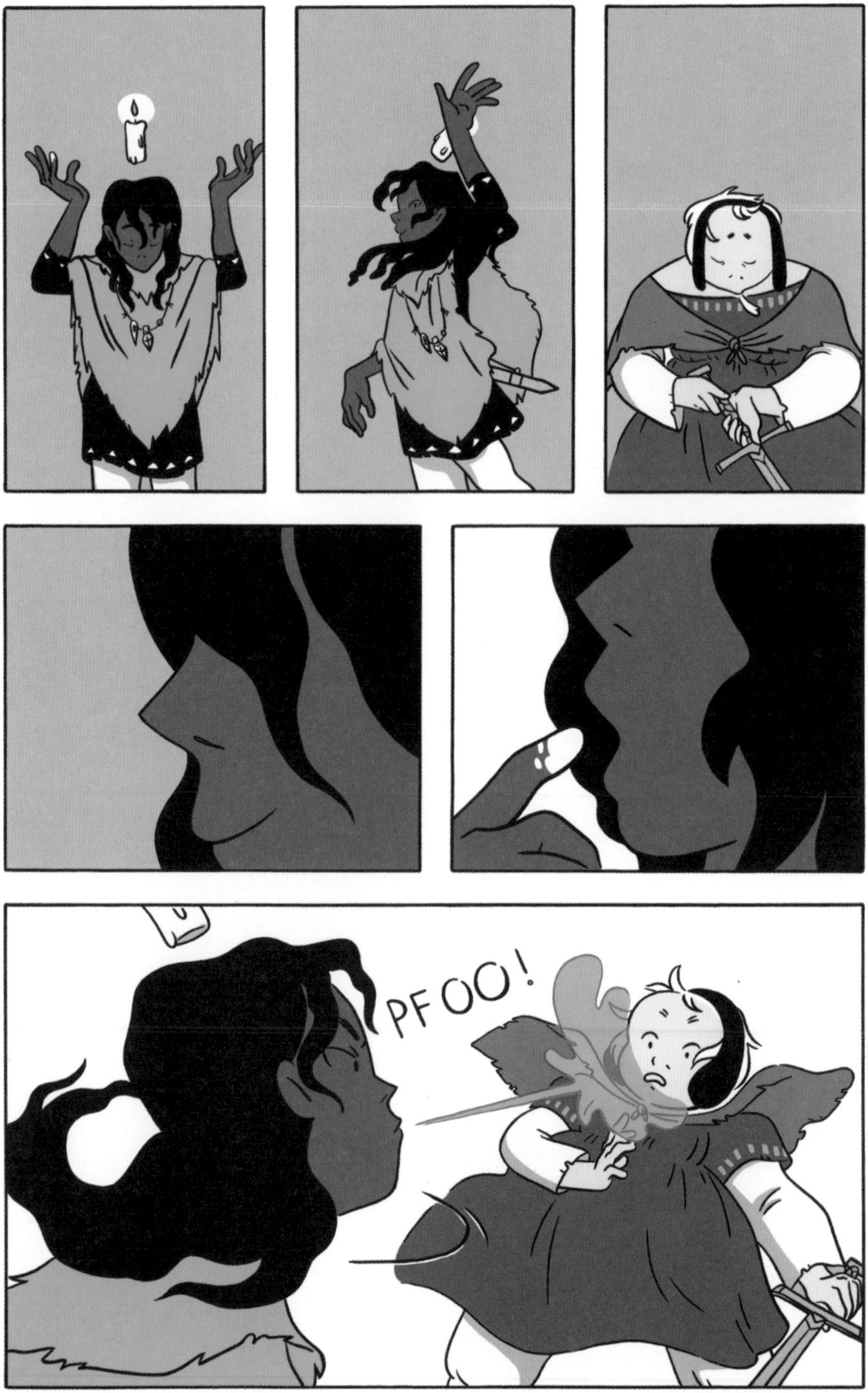
PFOO!

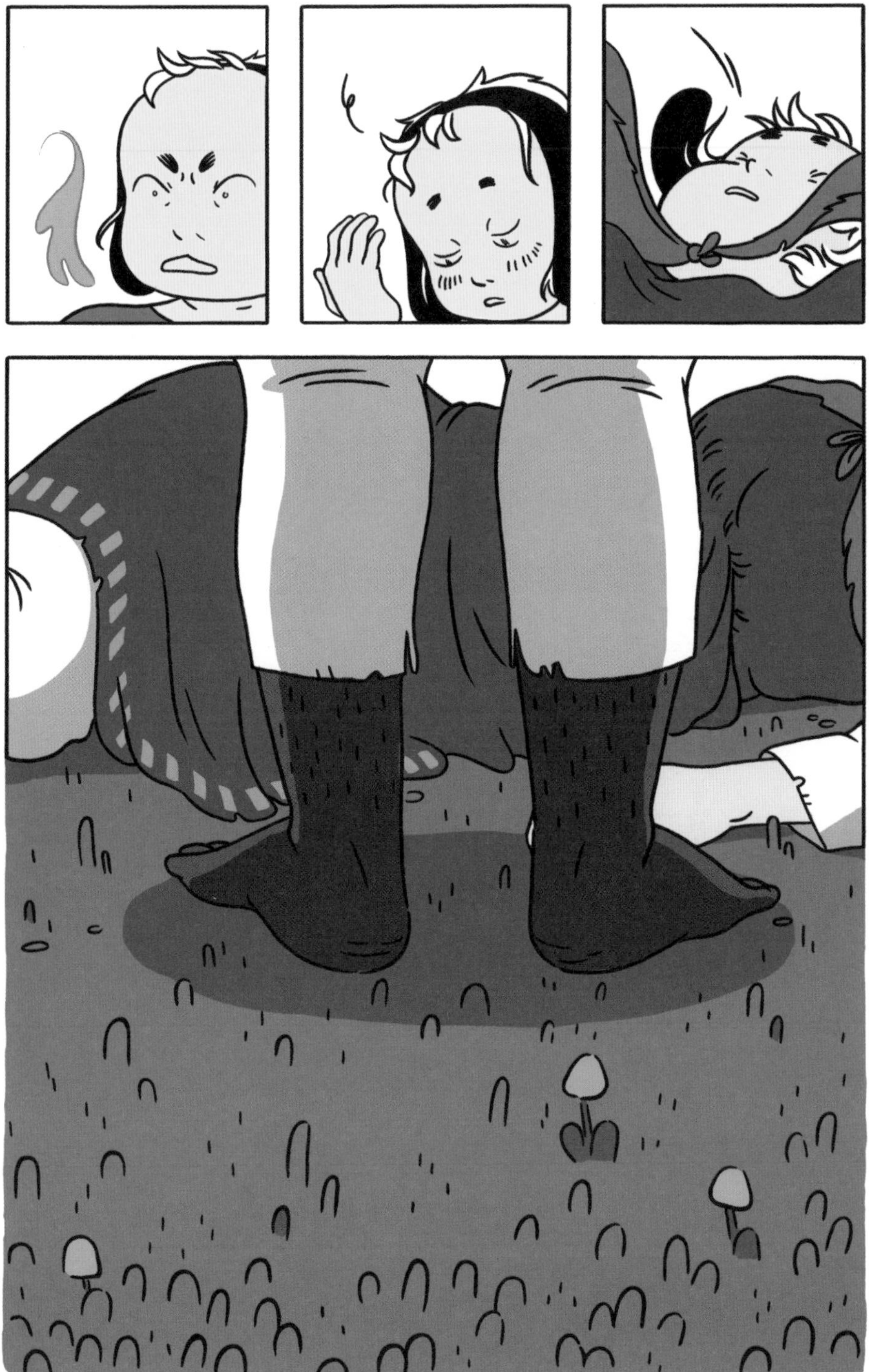

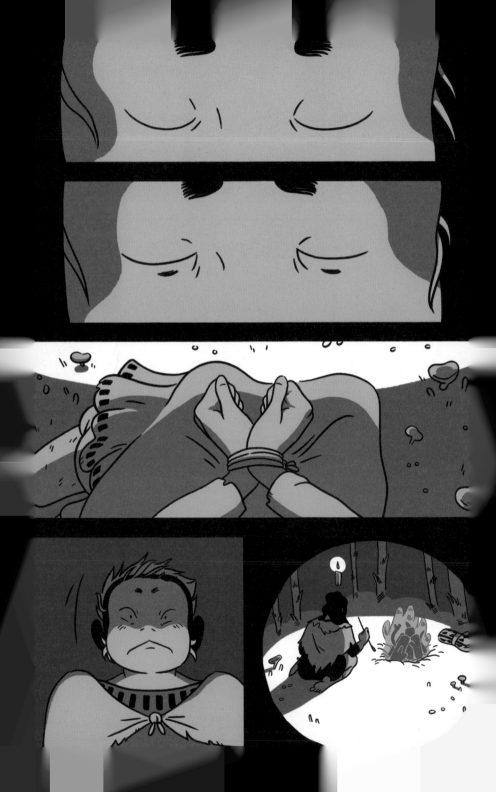

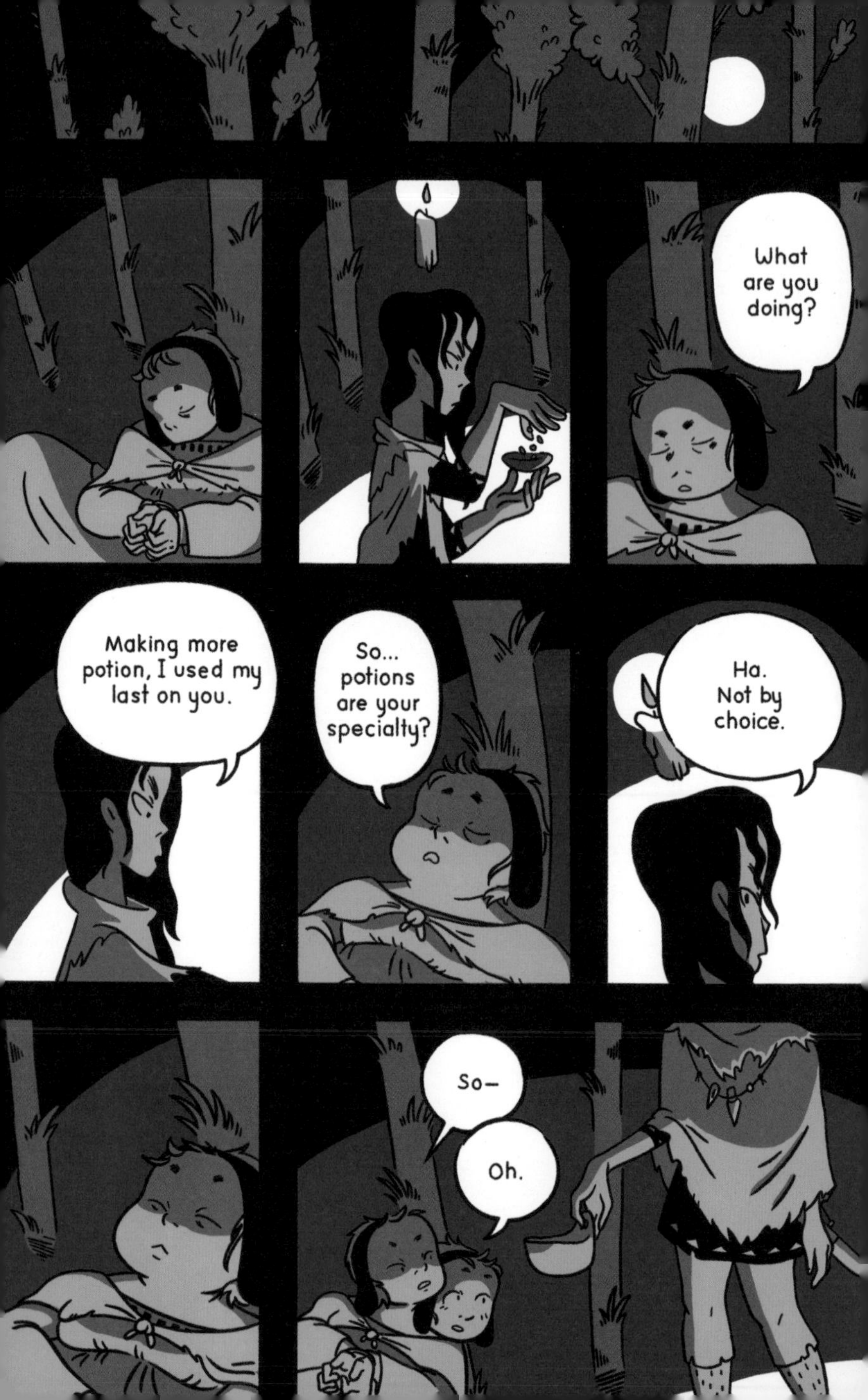
What are you doing?
Making more potion, I used my last on you.
So... potions are your specialty?
Ha. Not by choice.
So—
Oh.

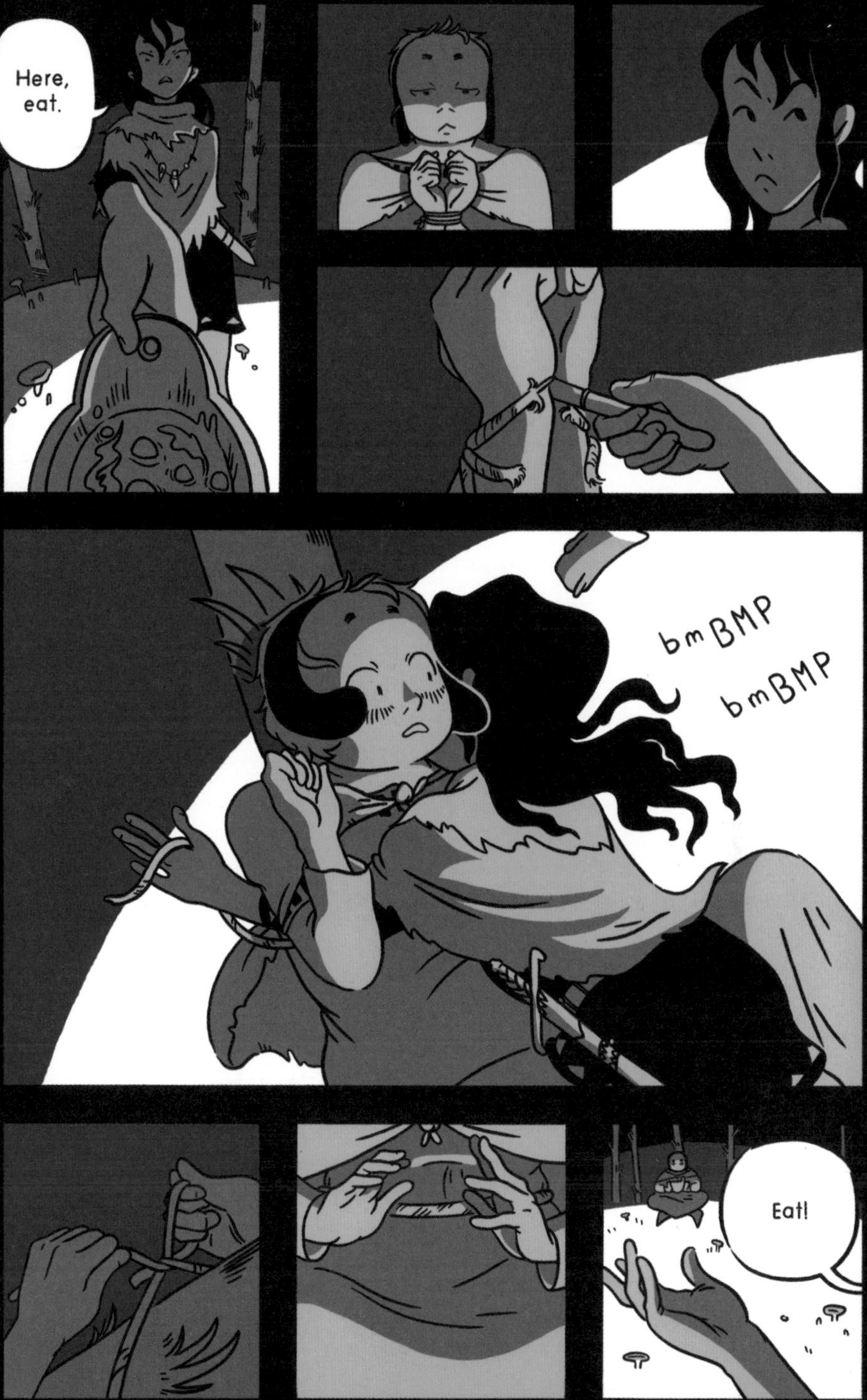
Here, eat.
bmBMP
bmBMP
Eat!

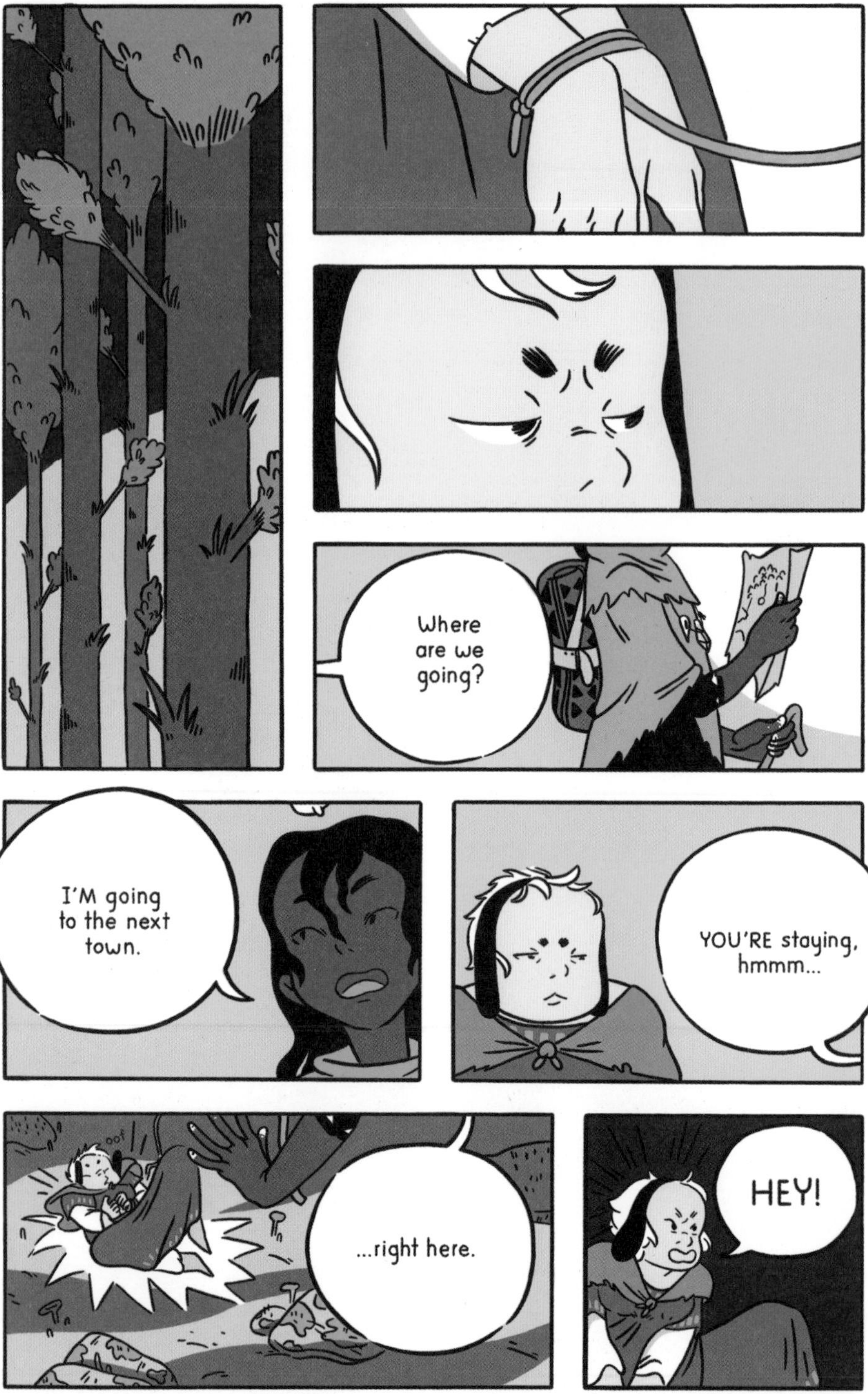
Where are we going?
I'M going to the next town.
YOU'RE staying, hmmm...
oof
...right here.
HEY!

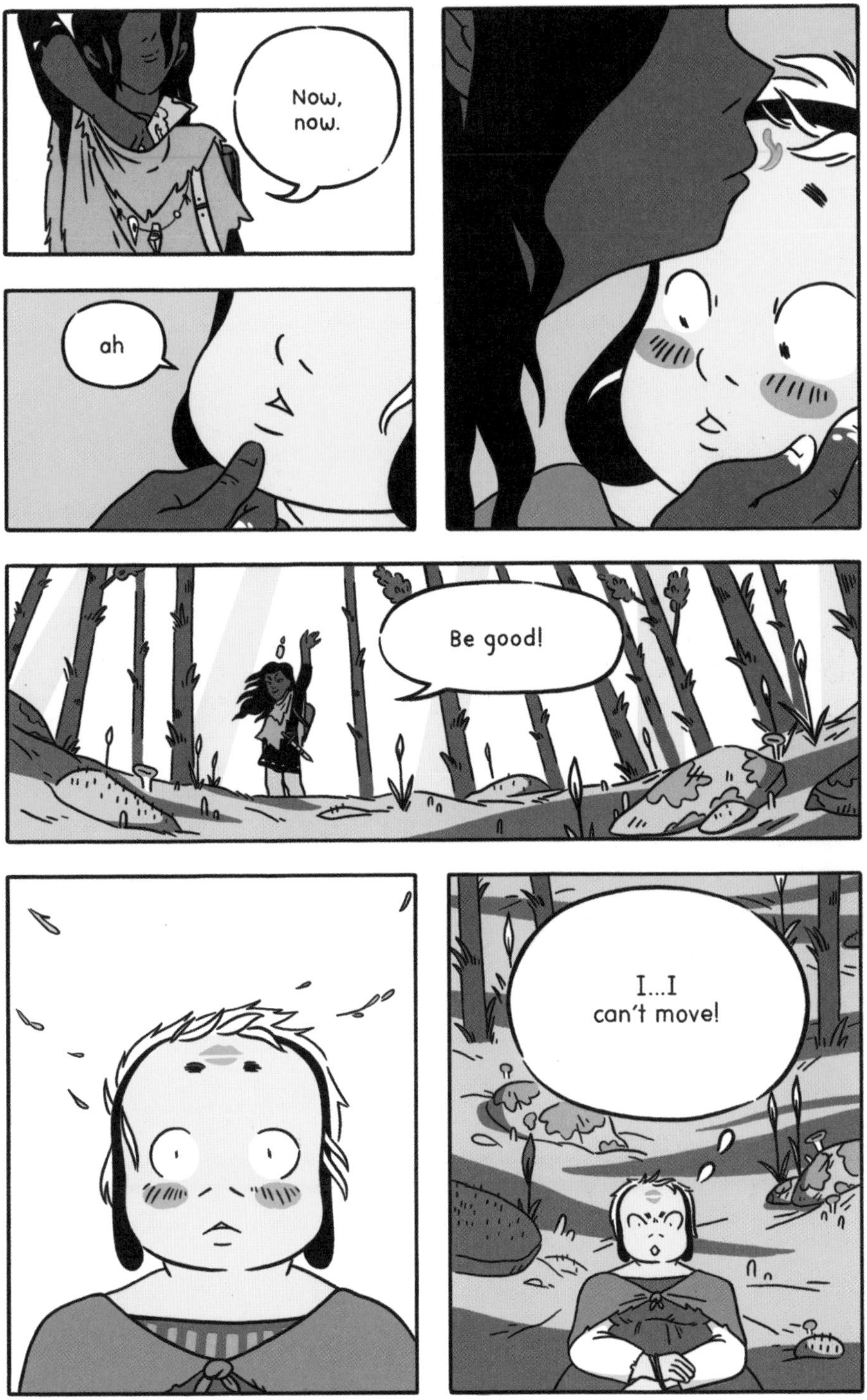
Now, now.
ah
Be good!
I...I can't move!

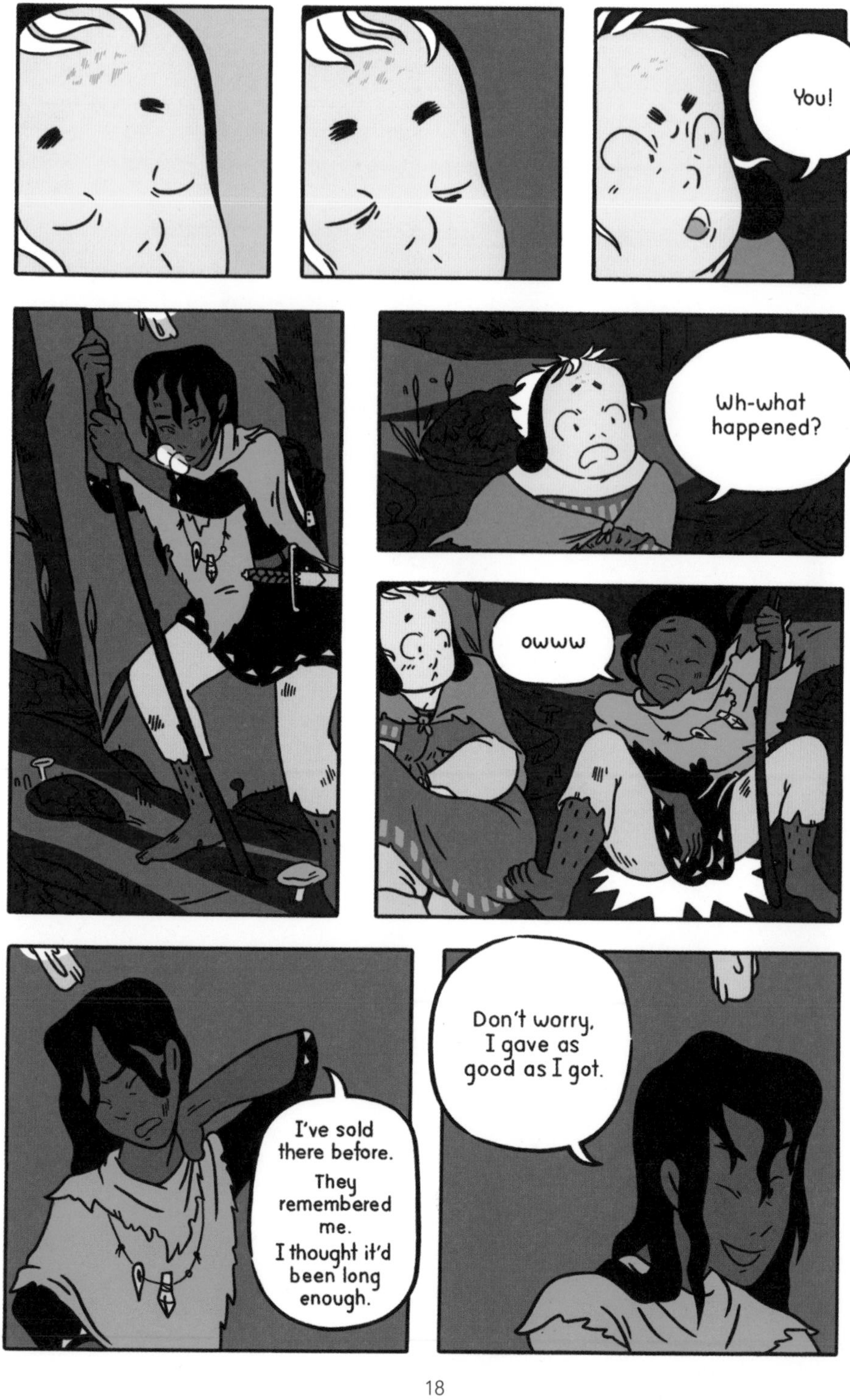
You!
Wh-what happened?
owww
I've sold there before.
They remembered me.
I thought it'd been long enough.
Don't worry, I gave as good as I got.

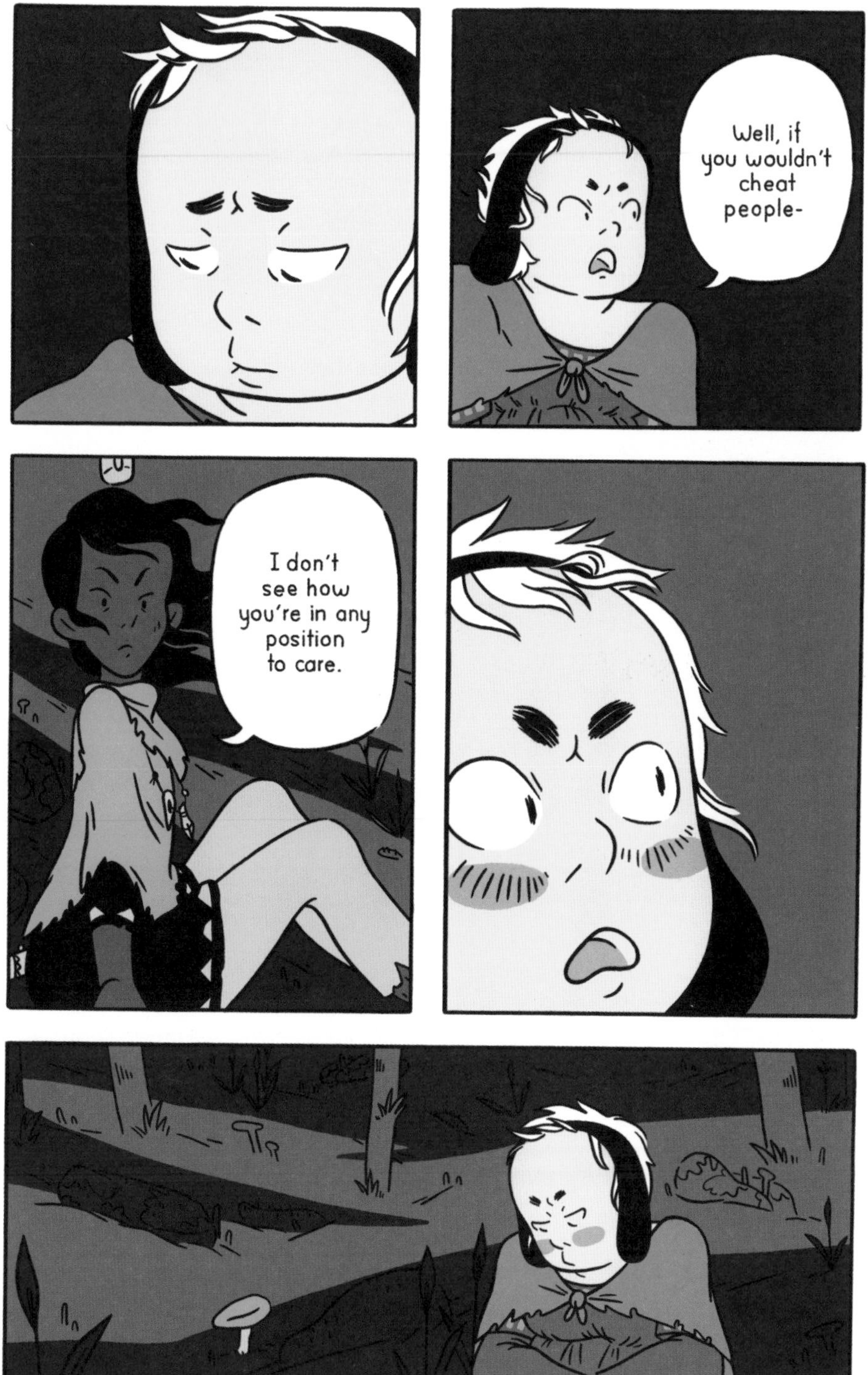
Well, if you wouldn't cheat people-
I don't see how you're in any position to care.

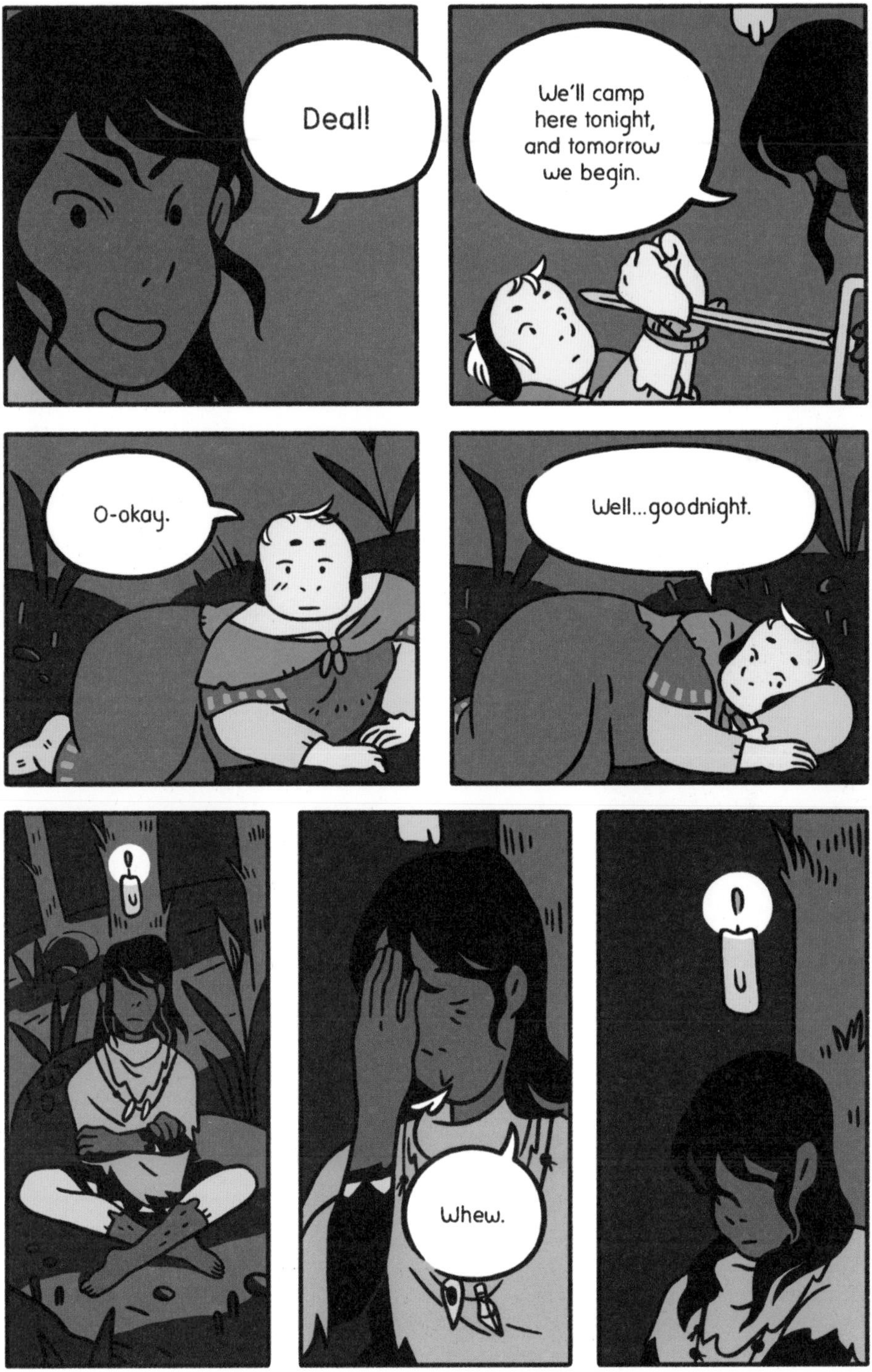
Deal!
We'll camp here tonight, and tomorrow we begin.
O-okay.
Well...goodnight.
Whew.

Part 2

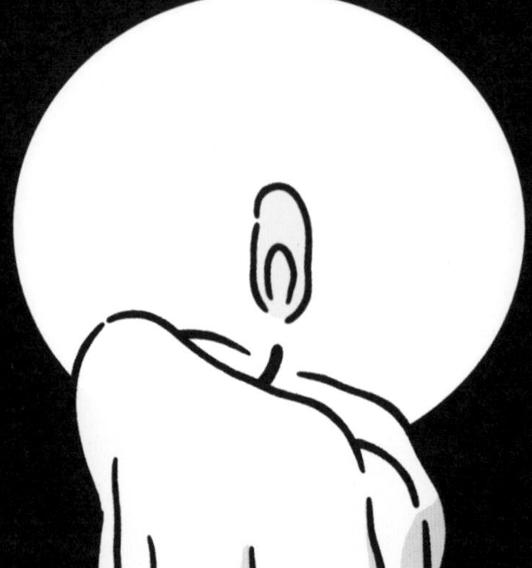

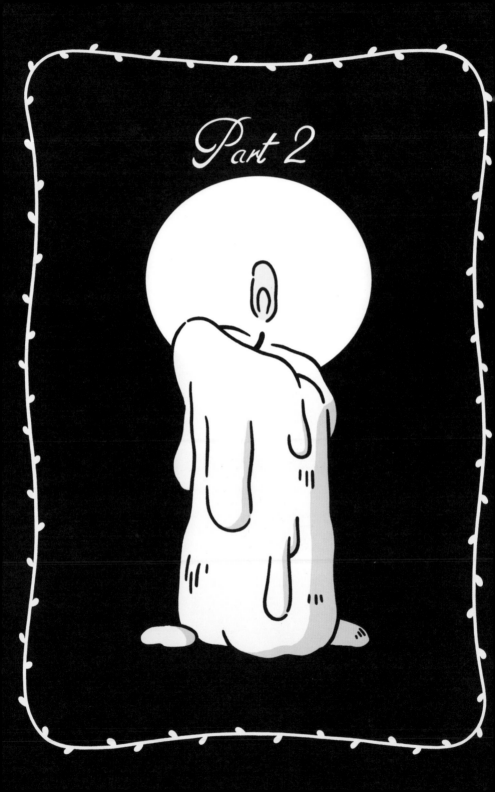

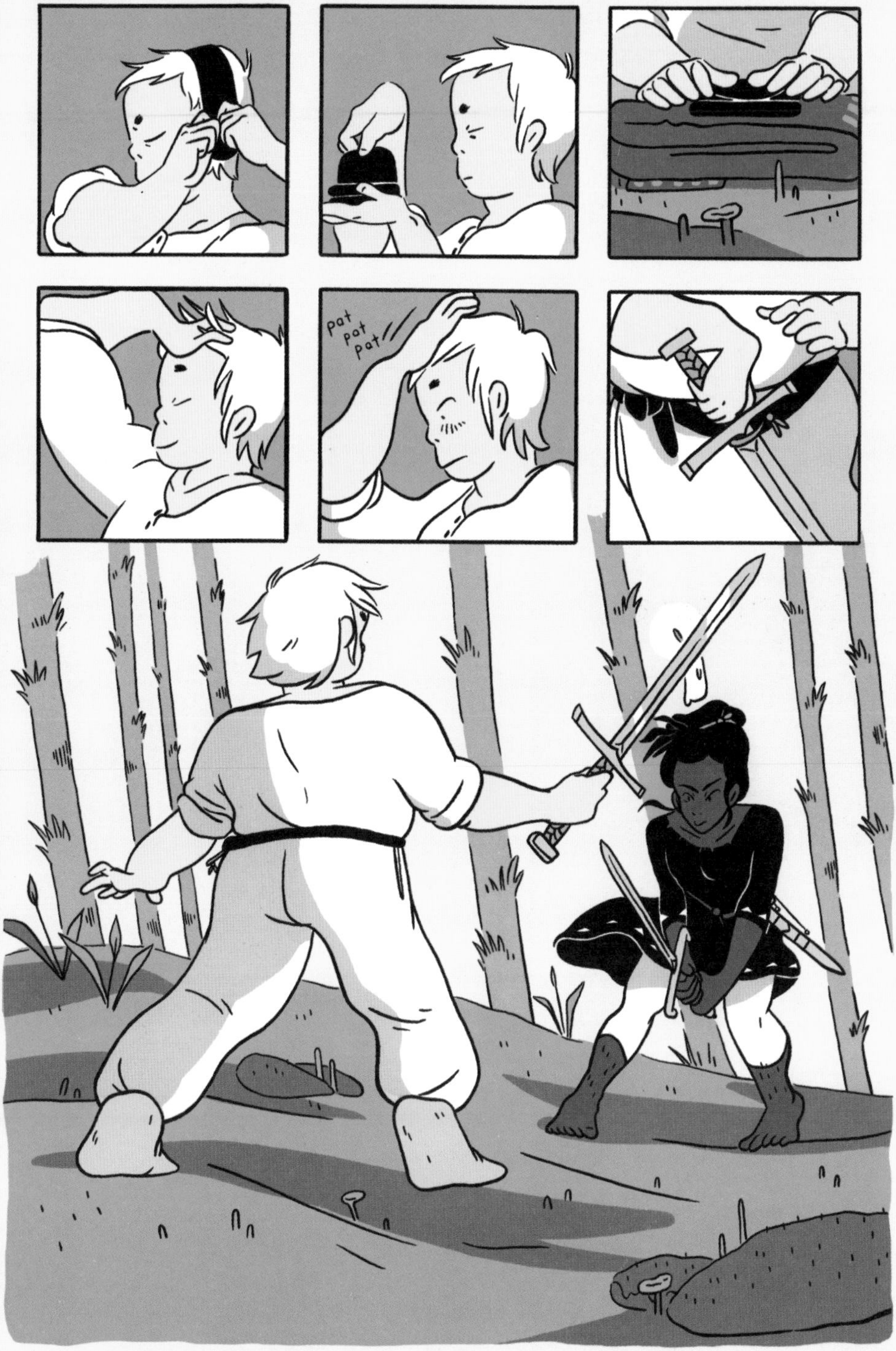
pat
pat
pat

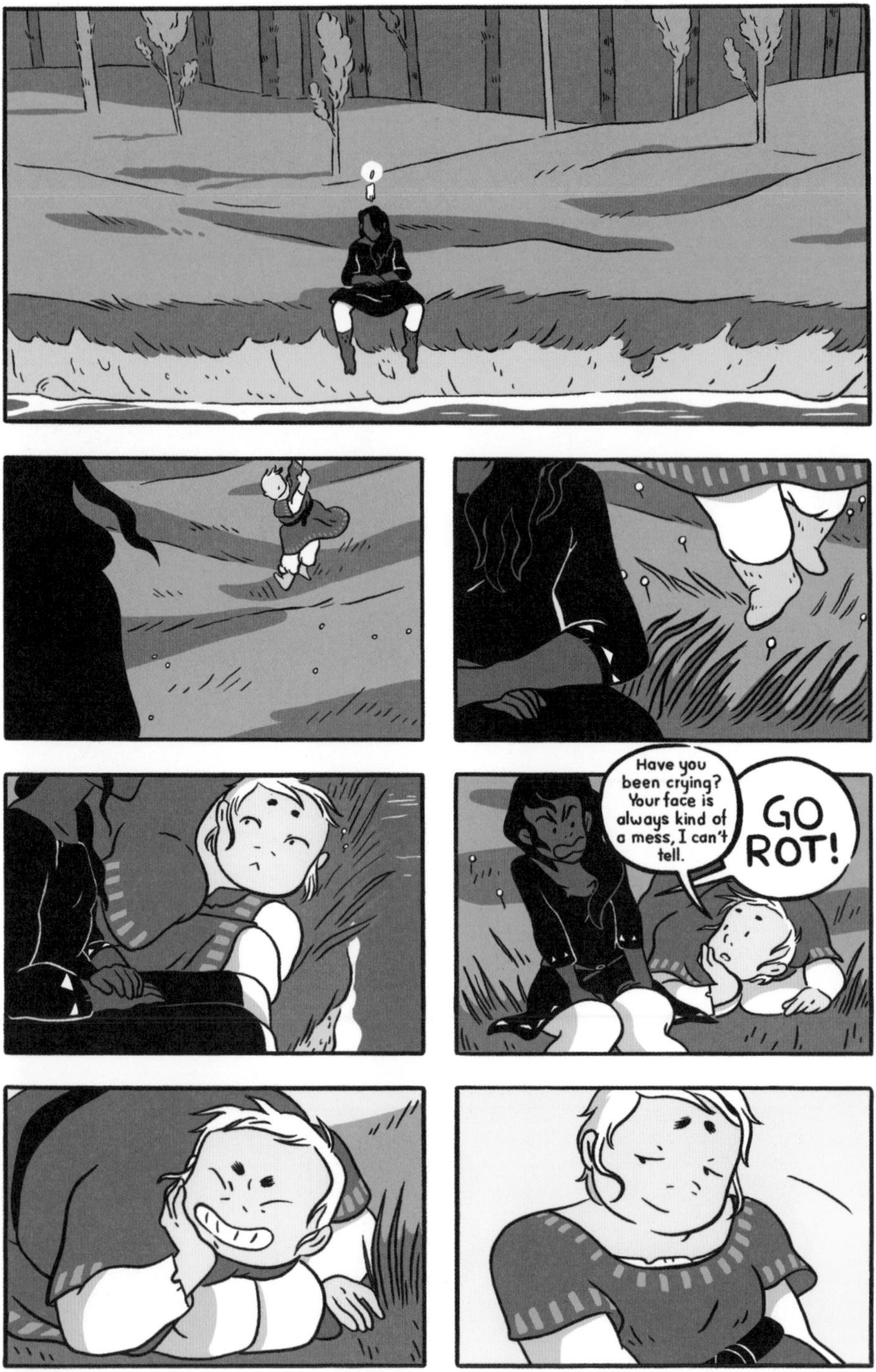
Have you been crying? Your face is always kind of a mess, I can't tell.
GO ROT!

29

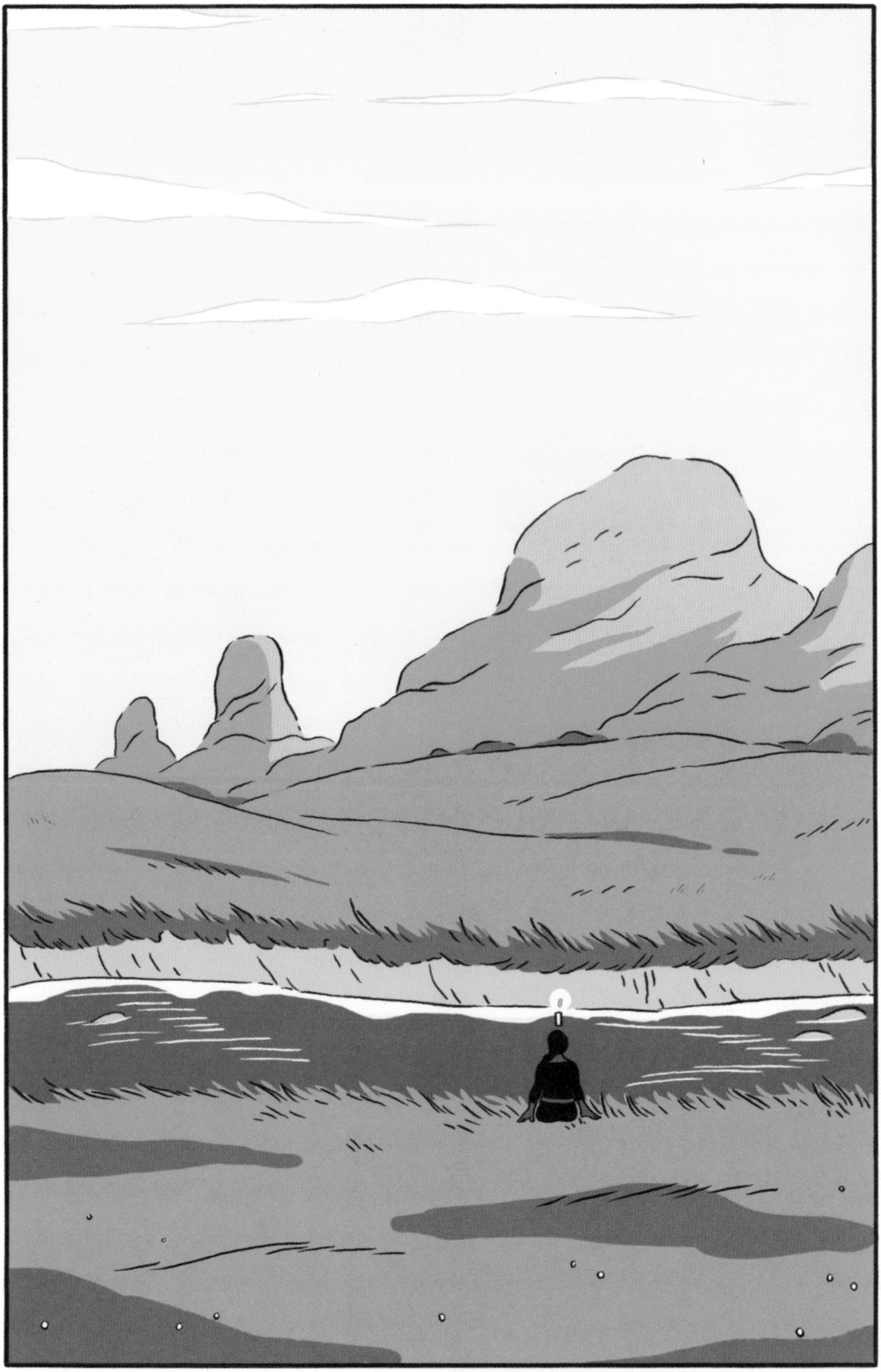

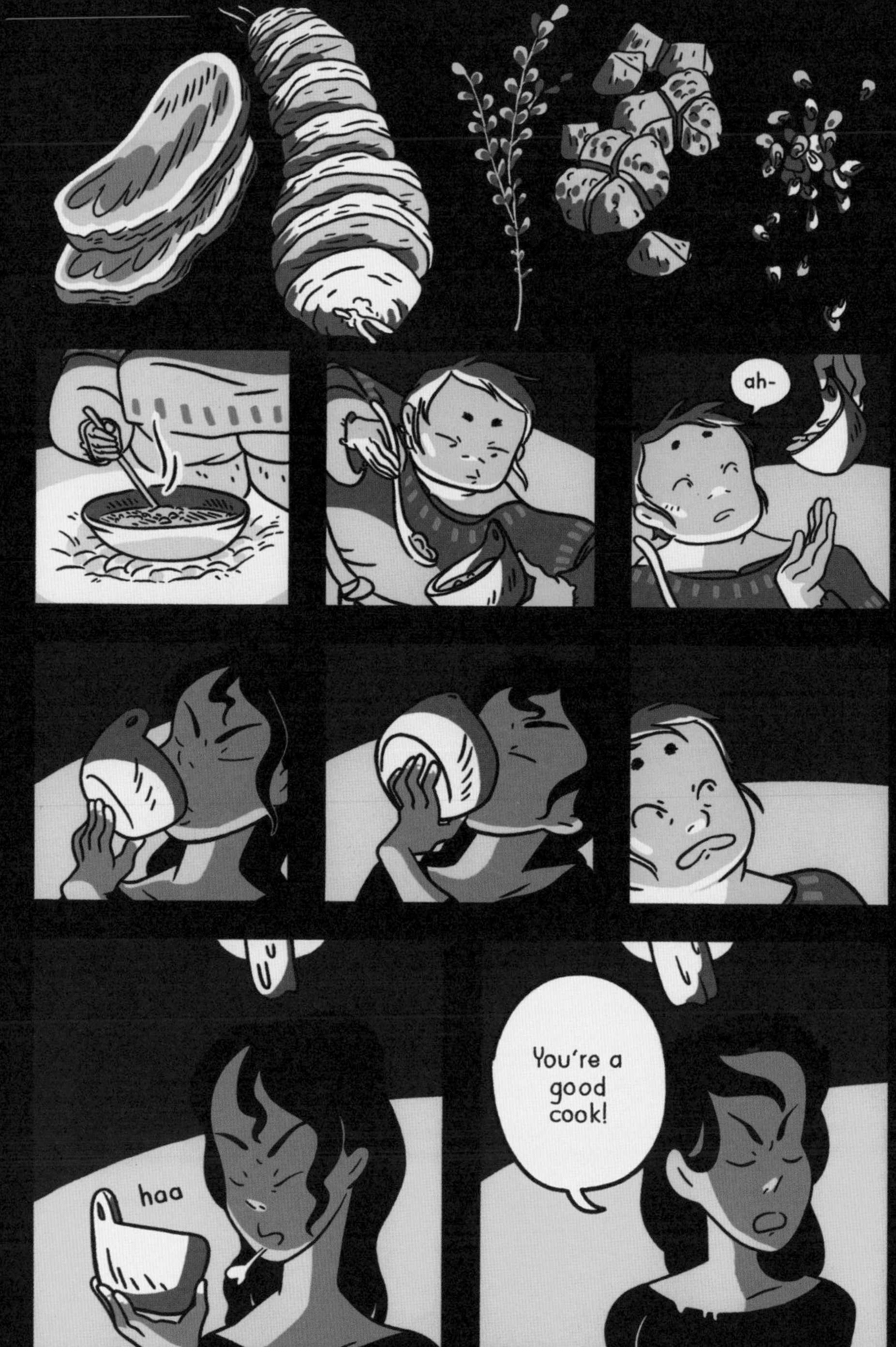
ah-
haa
You're a good cook!

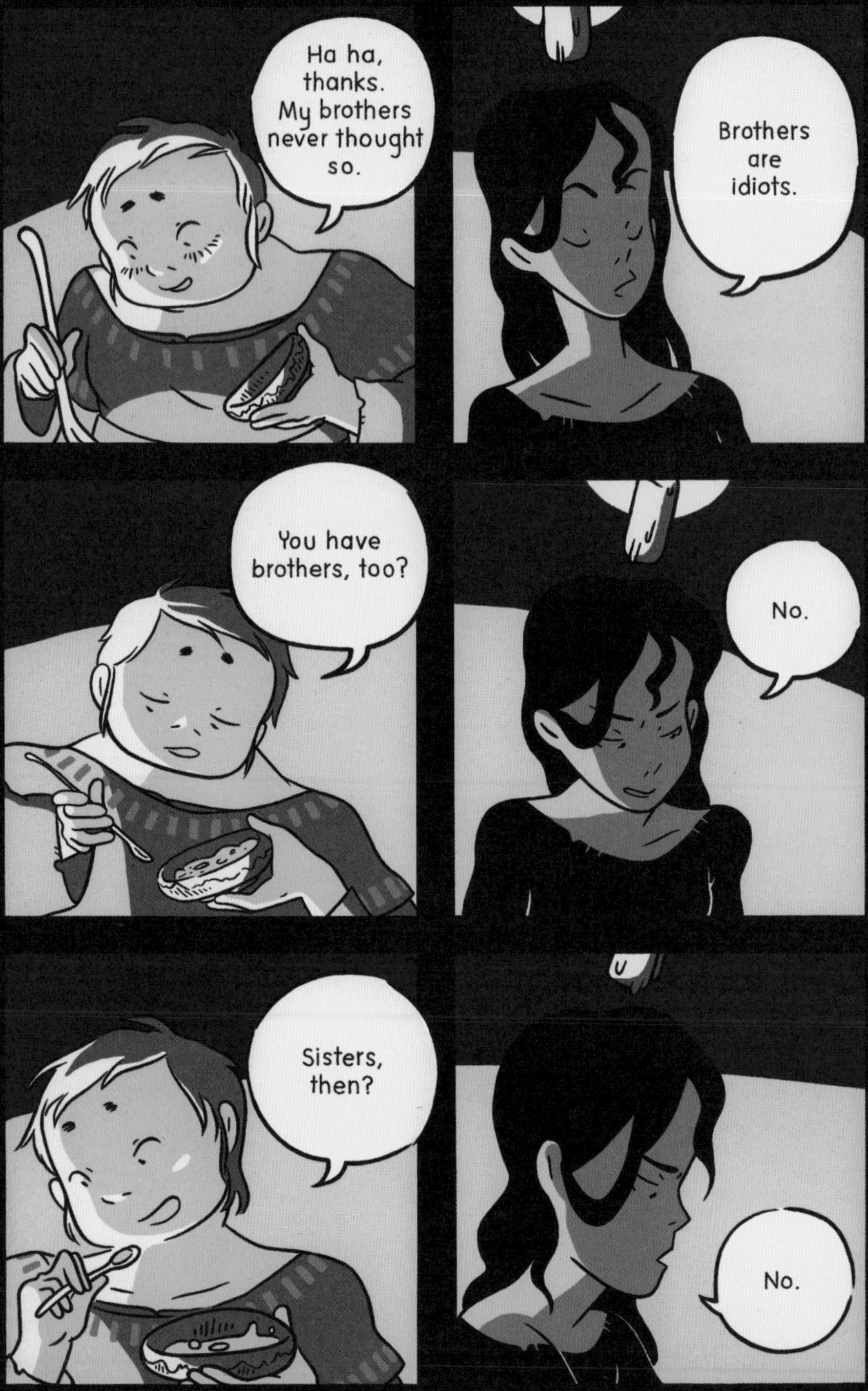
Ha ha, thanks. My brothers never thought so.
Brothers are idiots.
You have brothers, too?
No.
Sisters, then?
No.

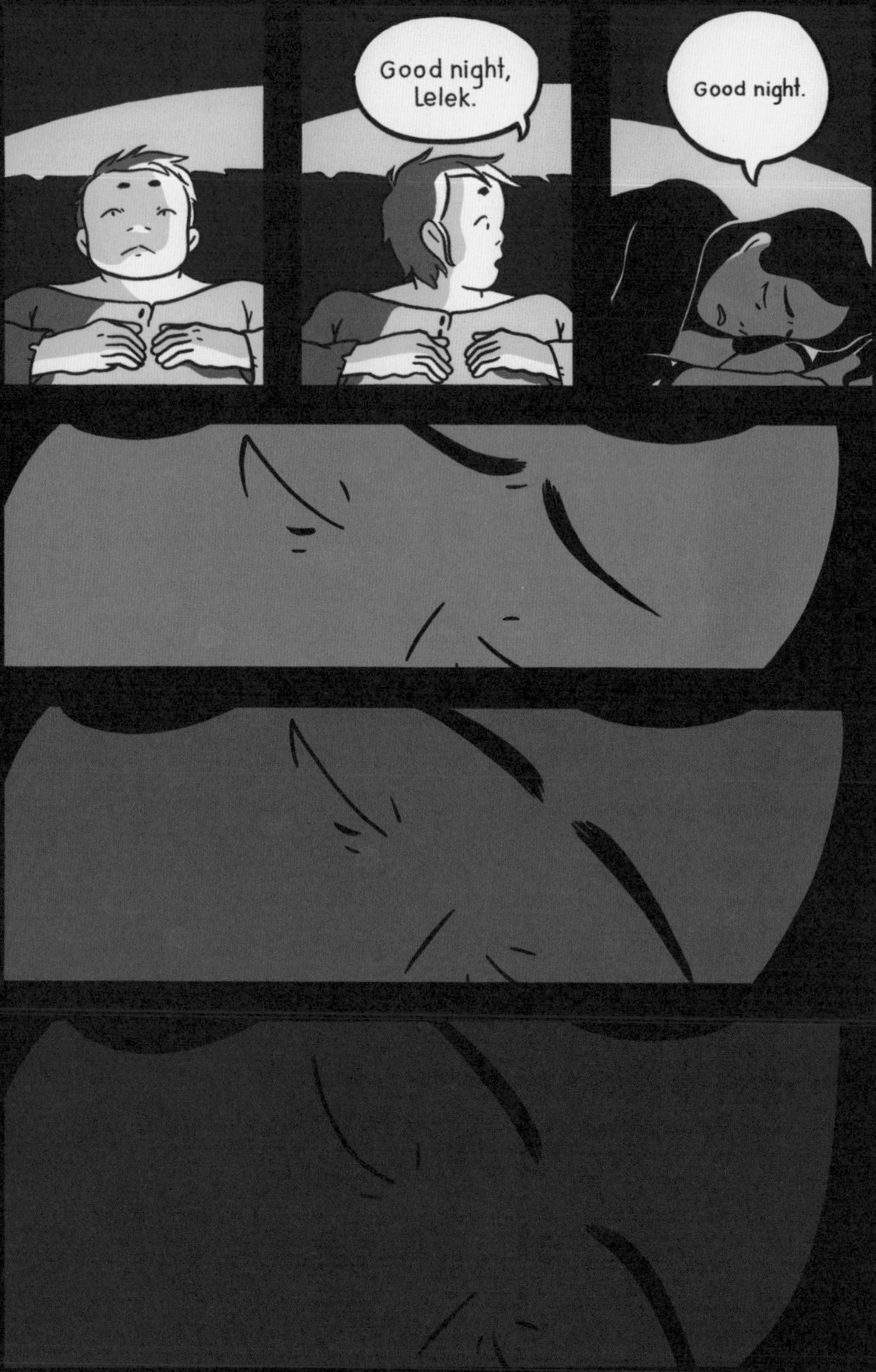
Good night, Lelek.
Good night.

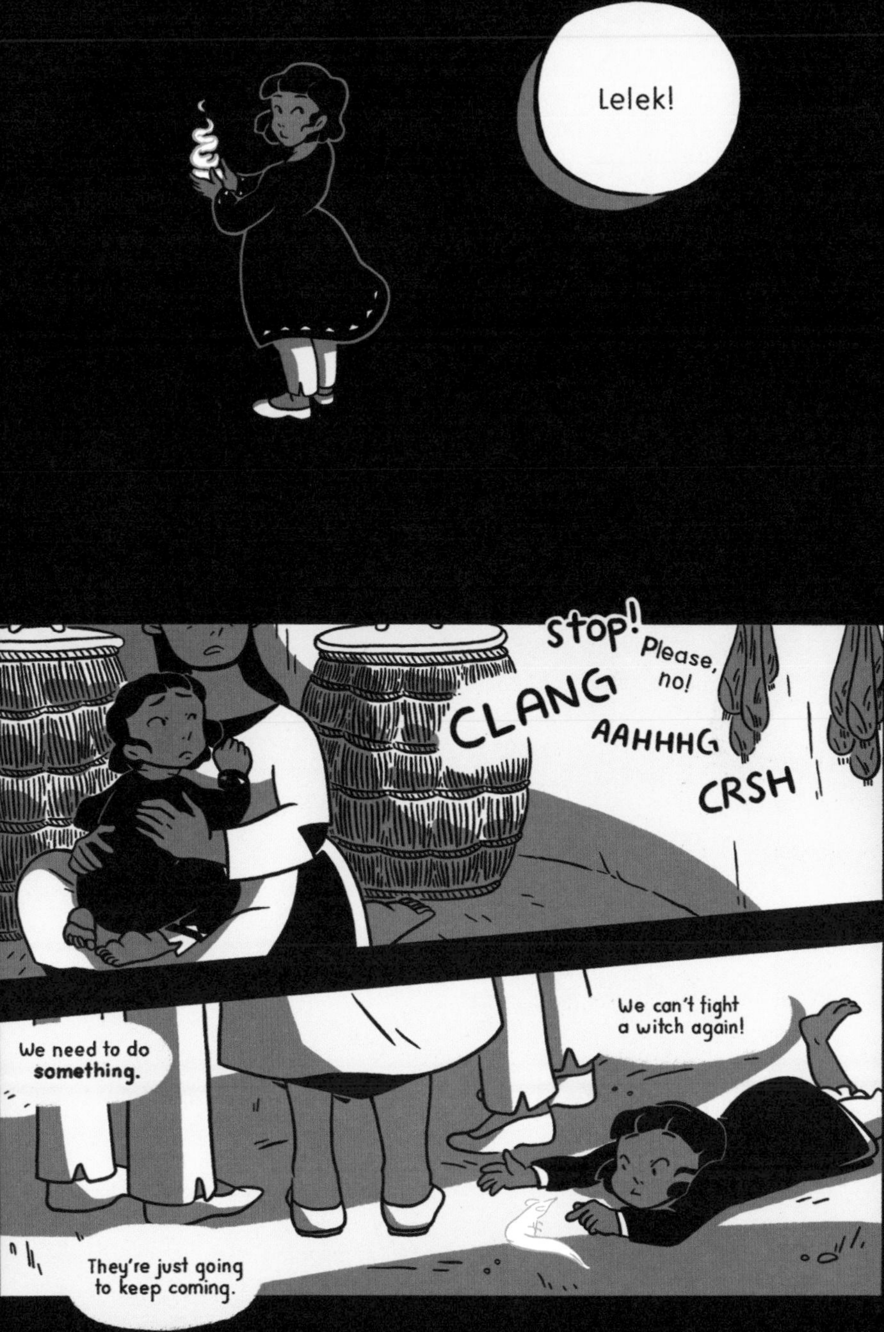

Lelek!
Stop!
Please, no!
CLANG
AAHHHG
CRSH
We need to do **something.**
We can't fight a witch again!
They're just going to keep coming.

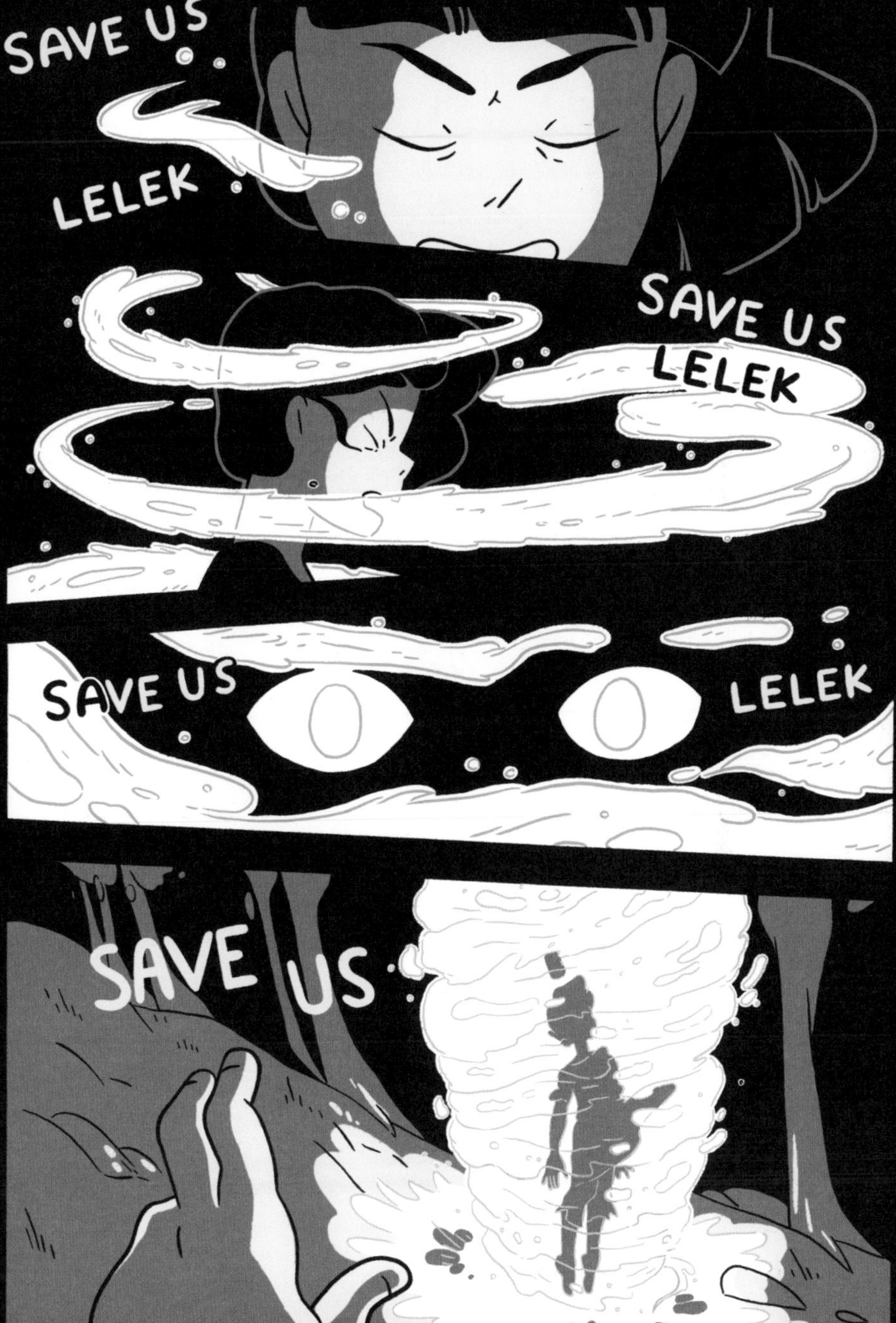
SAVE US
LELEK
SAVE US
LELEK
SAVE US
LELEK
SAVE US

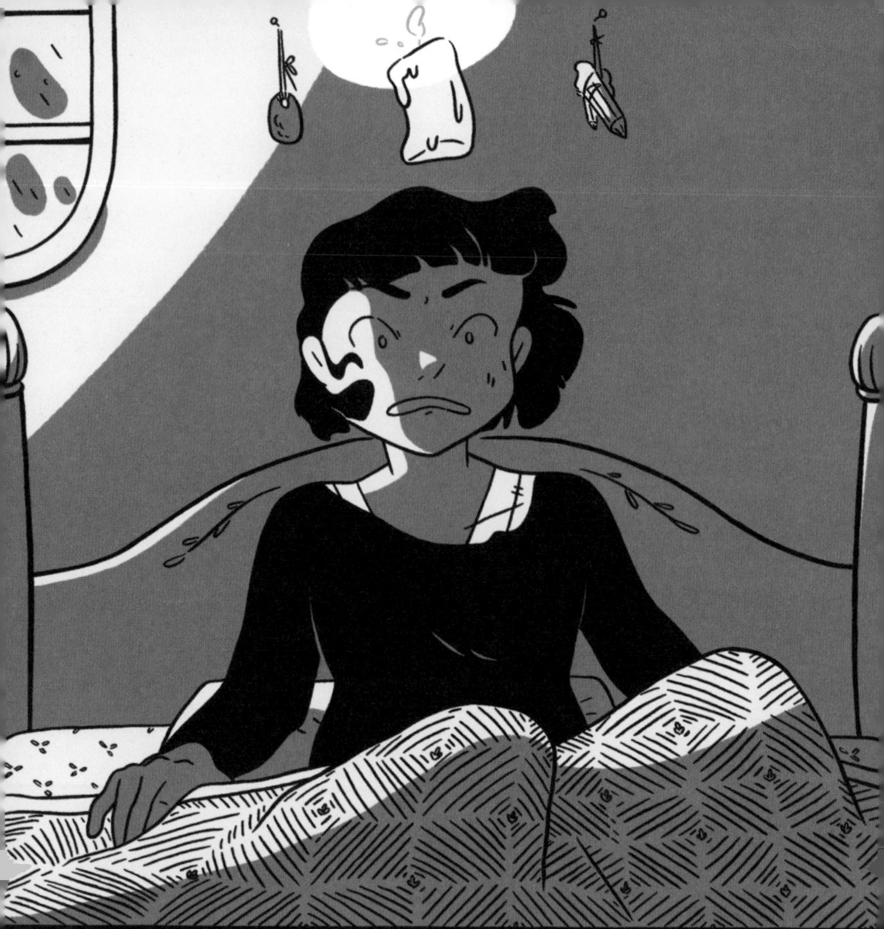
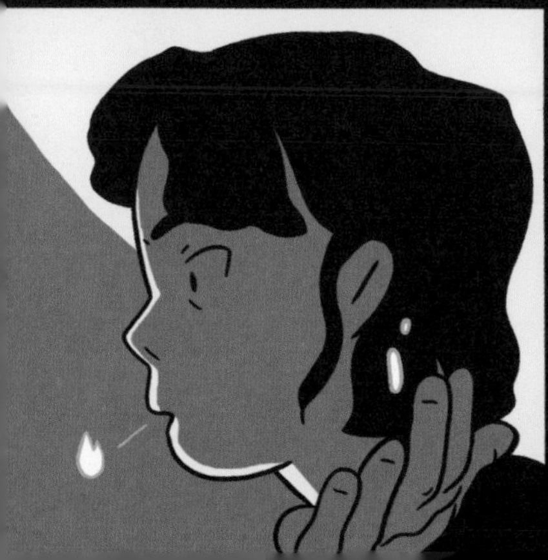
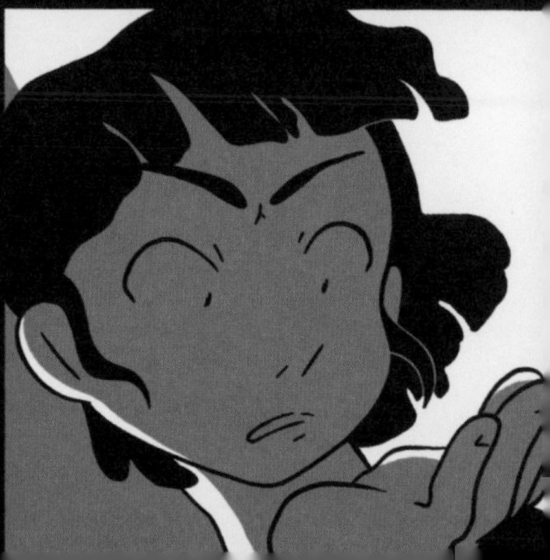

t-tump

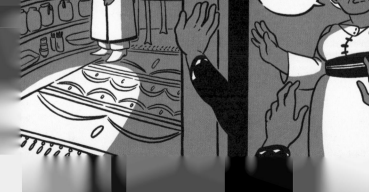

Lelek!

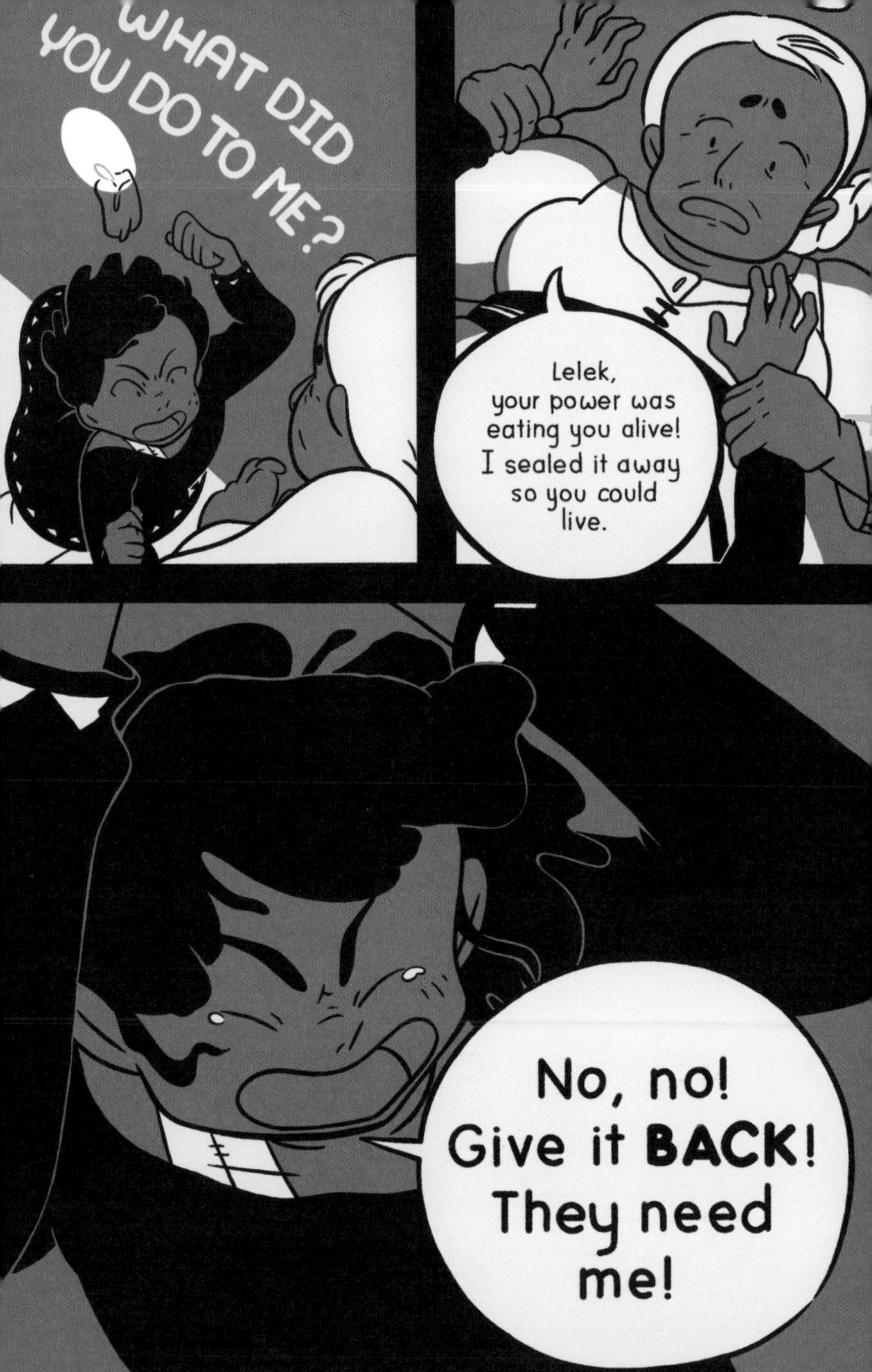
WHAT DID YOU DO TO ME?
Lelek, your power was eating you alive! I sealed it away so you could live.
No, no! Give it **BACK**! They need me!

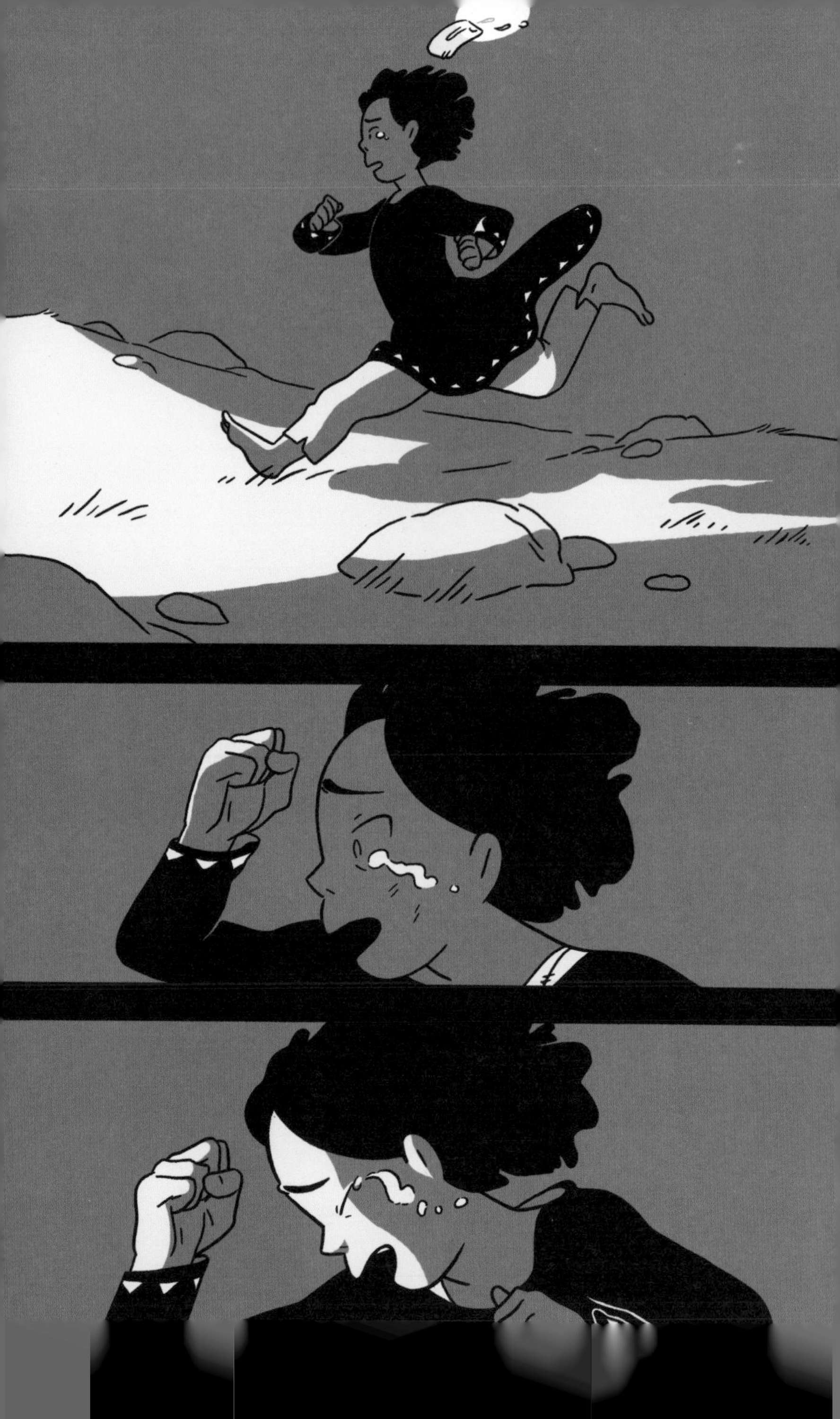

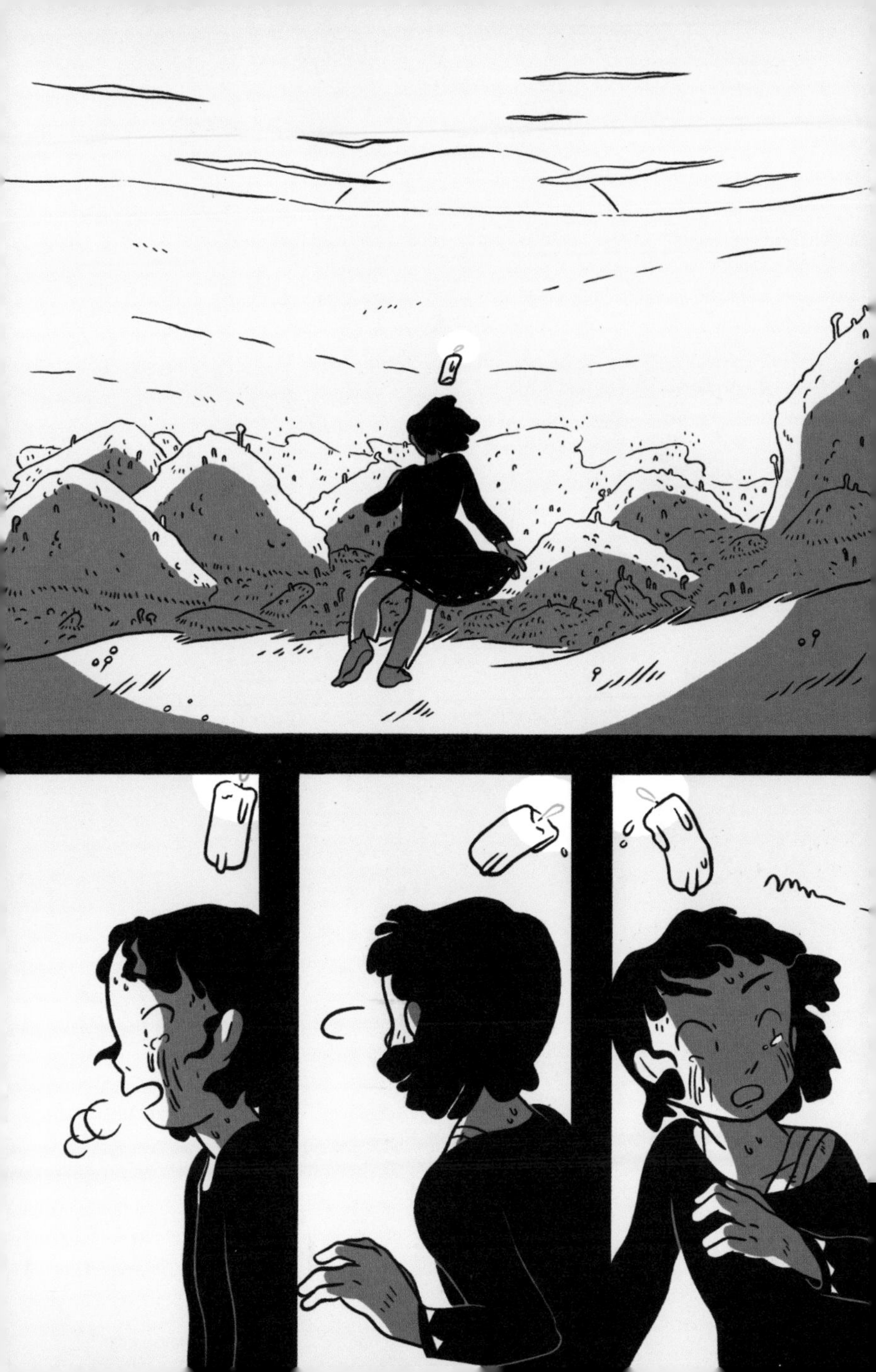

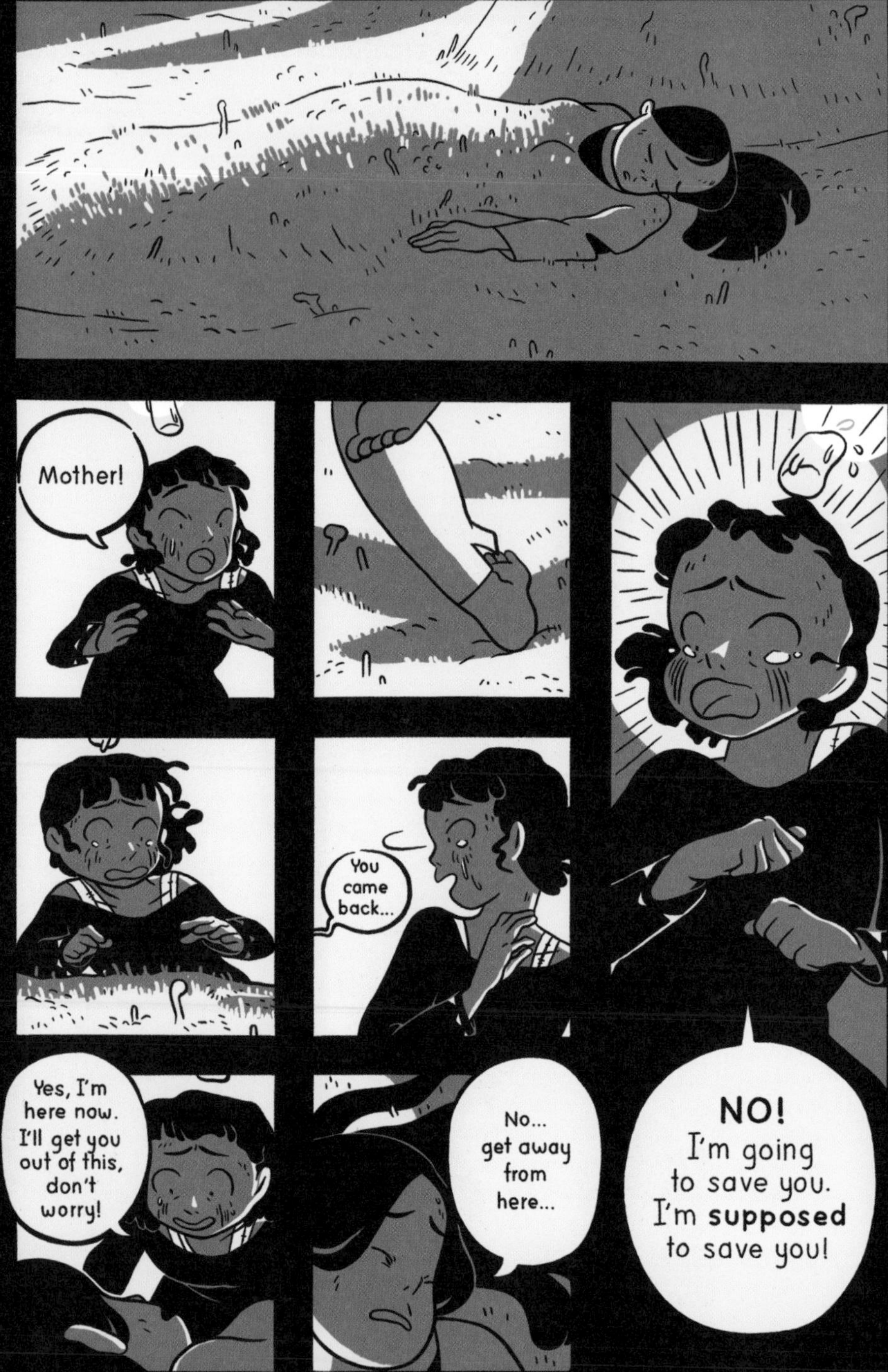
Mother!
You came back...
Yes, I'm here now. I'll get you out of this, don't worry!
No... get away from here...
NO! I'm going to save you. I'm **supposed** to save you!

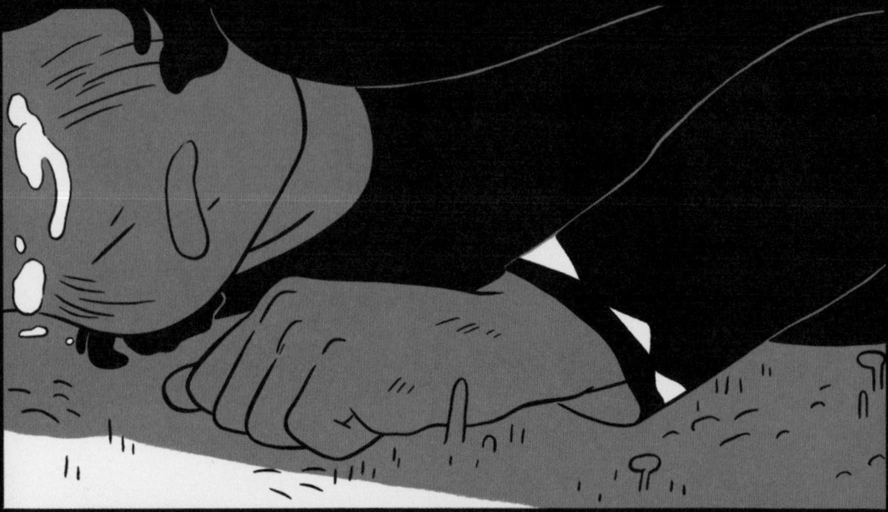
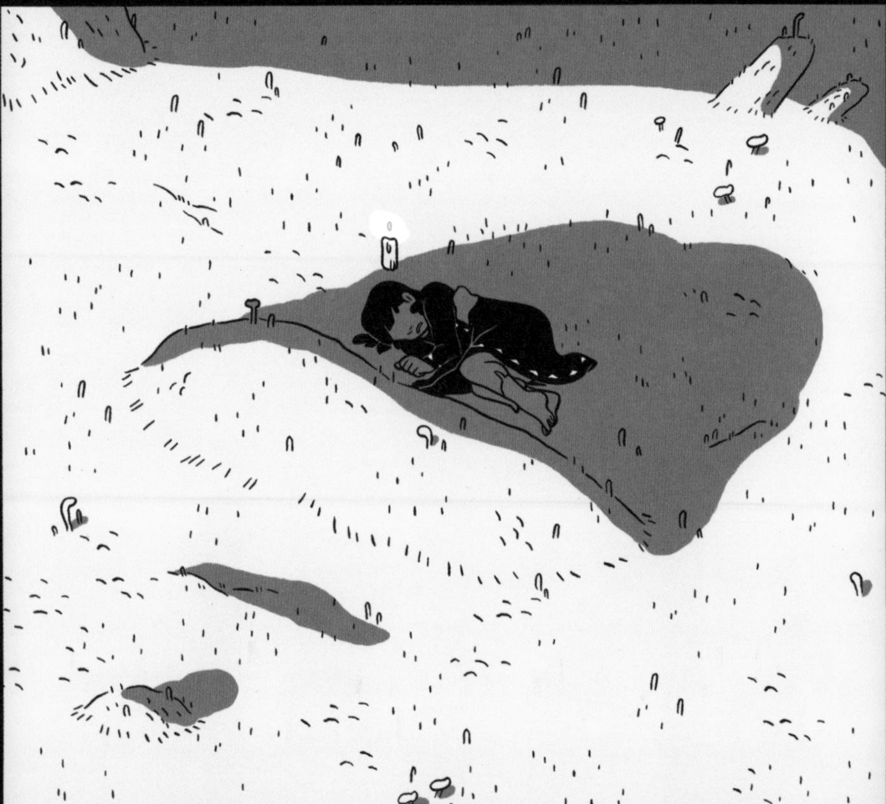

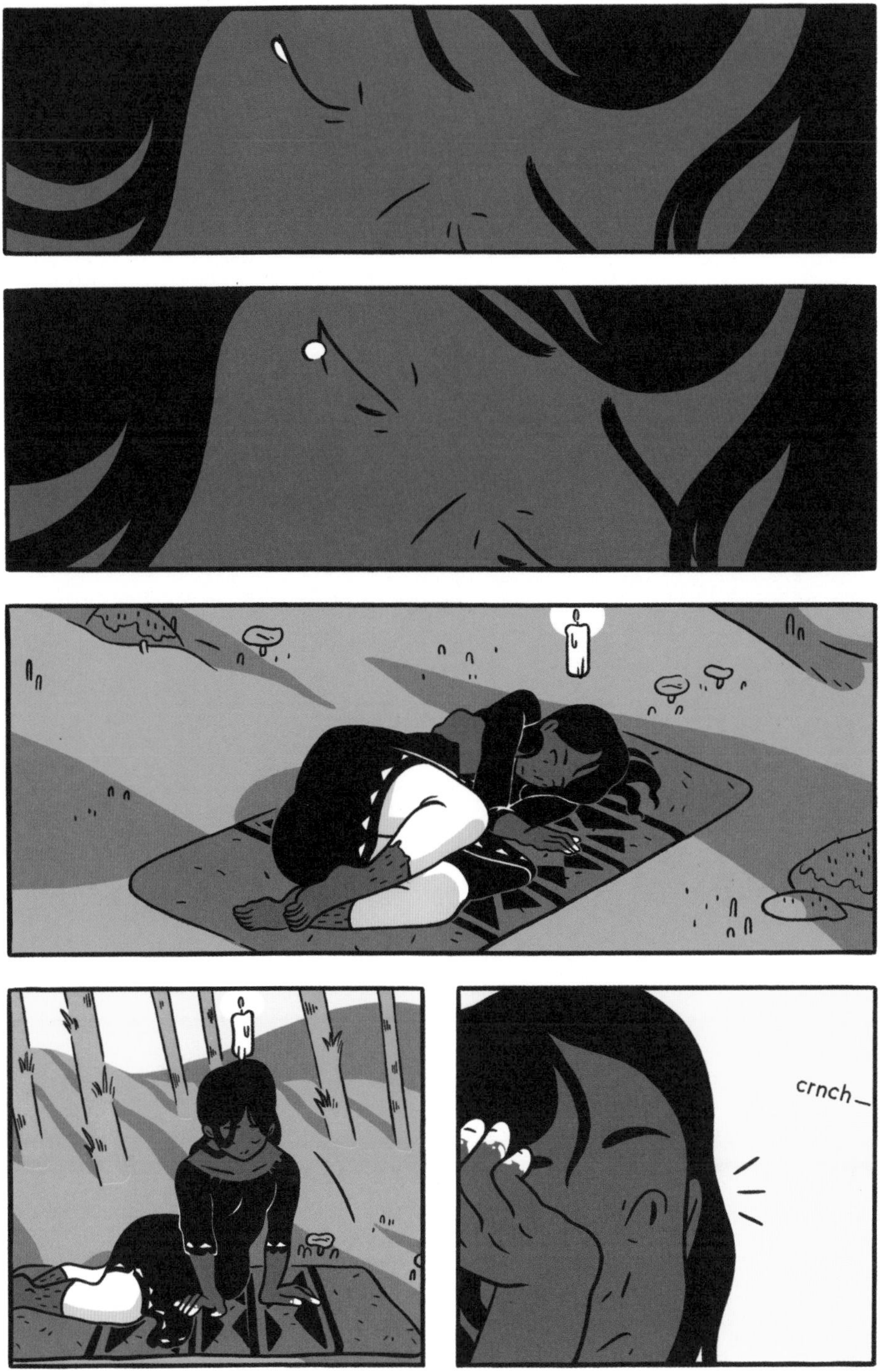
crnch—

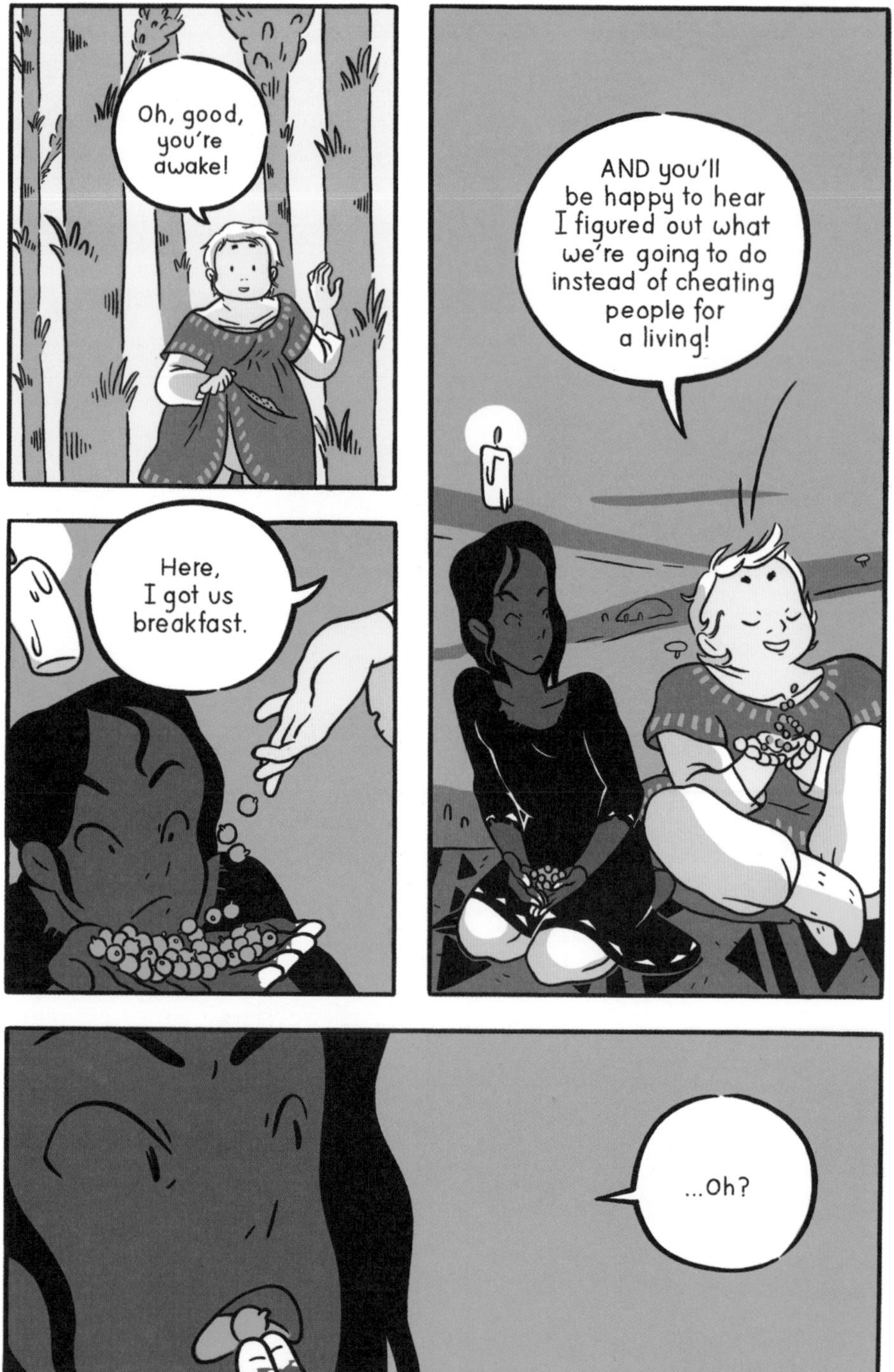

Oh, good, you're awake!
Here, I got us breakfast.
AND you'll be happy to hear I figured out what we're going to do instead of cheating people for a living!
...Oh?

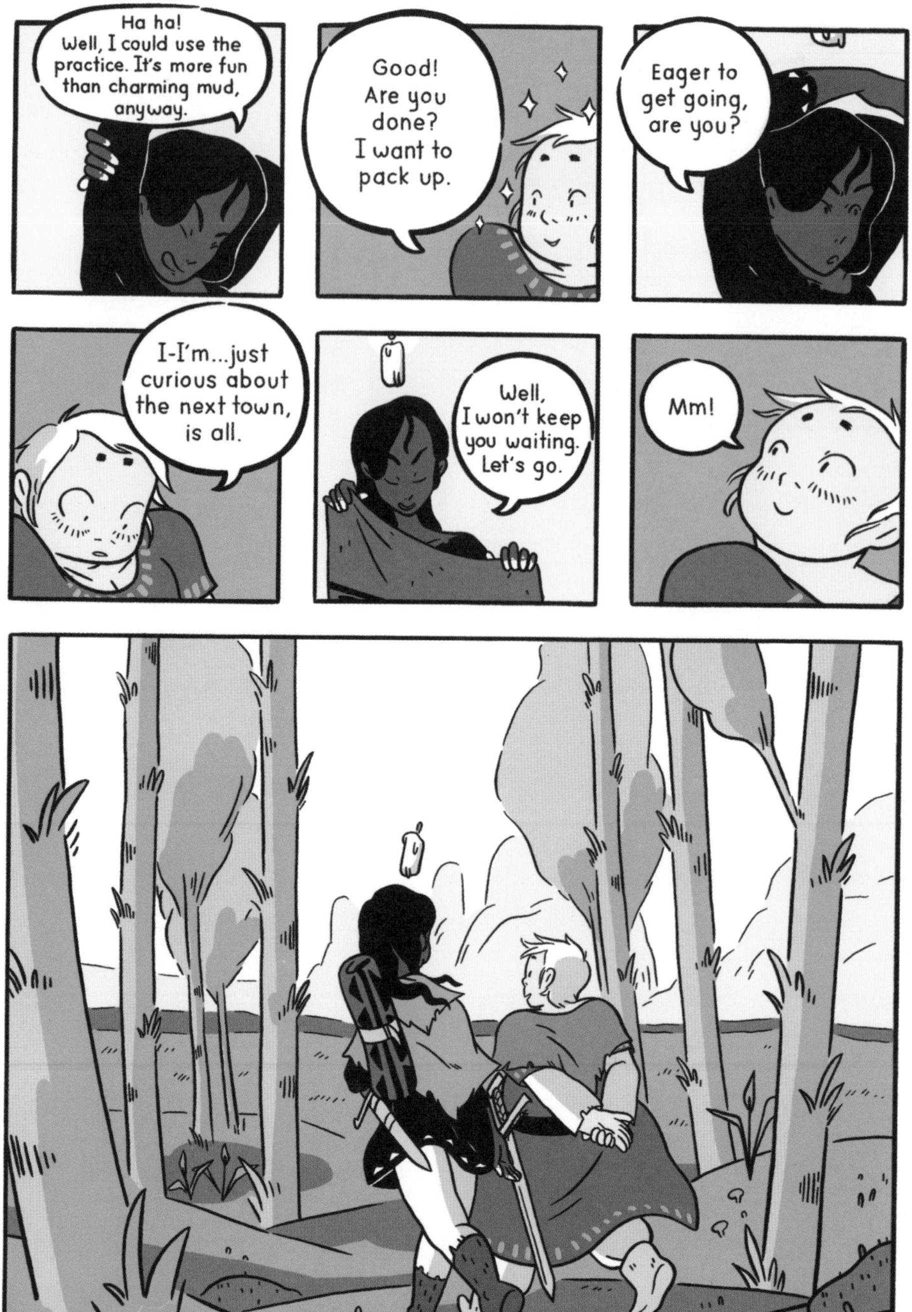
Ha ha! Well, I could use the practice. It's more fun than charming mud, anyway.
Good! Are you done? I want to pack up.
Eager to get going, are you?
I-I'm...just curious about the next town, is all.
Well, I won't keep you waiting. Let's go.
Mm!

Part 3

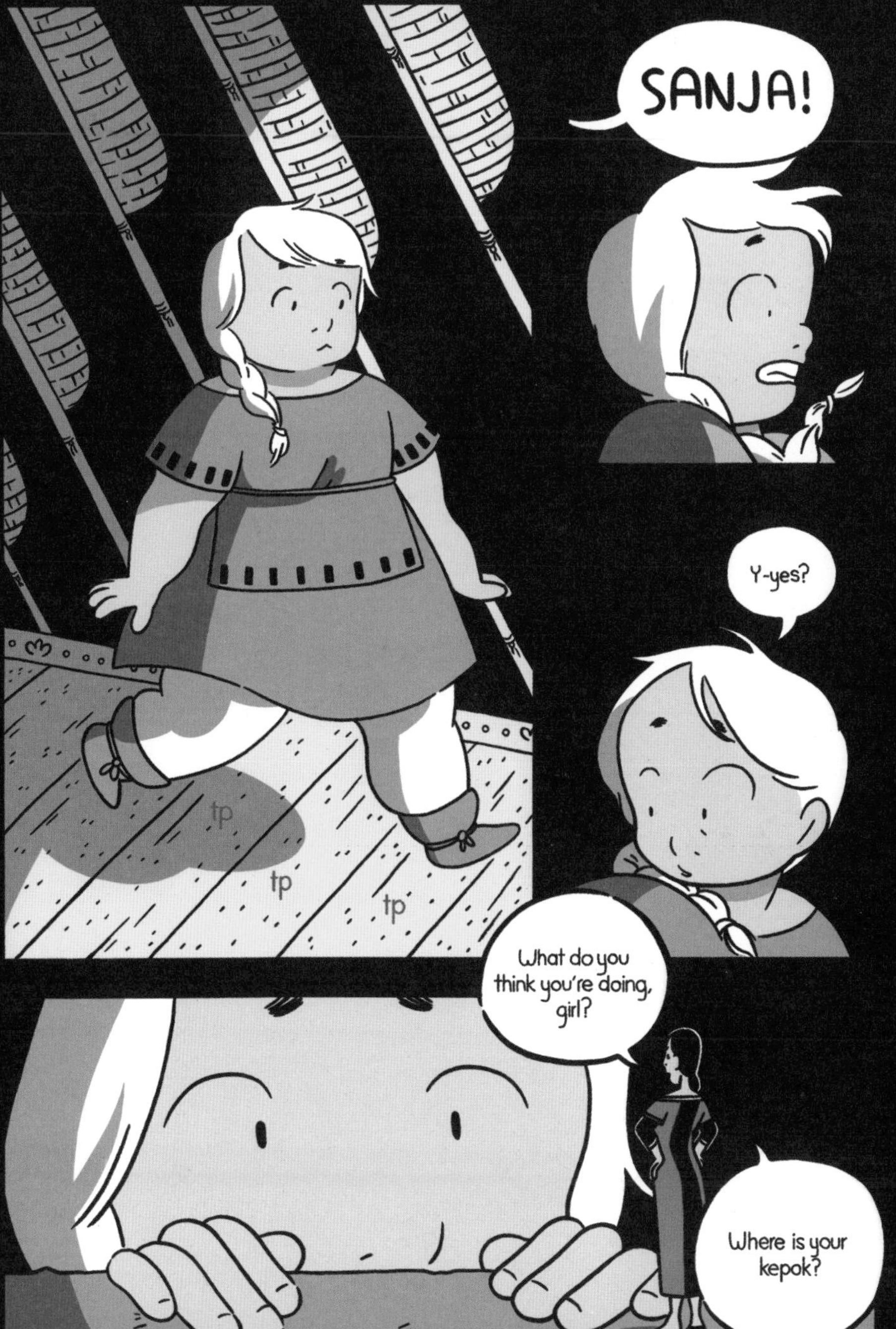
SANJA!
tp
tp
tp
Y-yes?
What do you think you're doing, girl?
Where is your kepok?

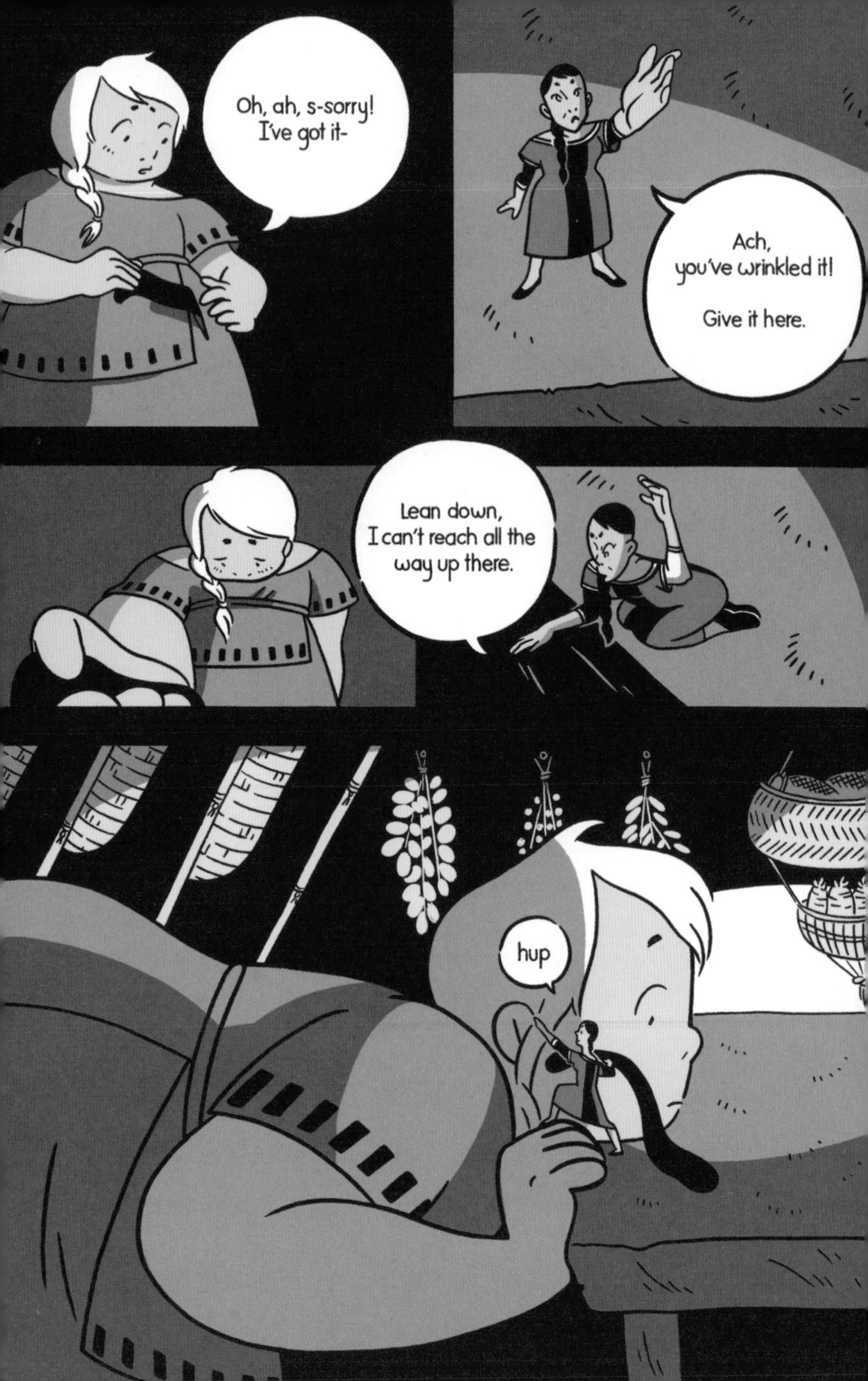
Oh, ah, s-sorry! I've got it-
Ach, you've wrinkled it! Give it here.
Lean down, I can't reach all the way up there.
hup

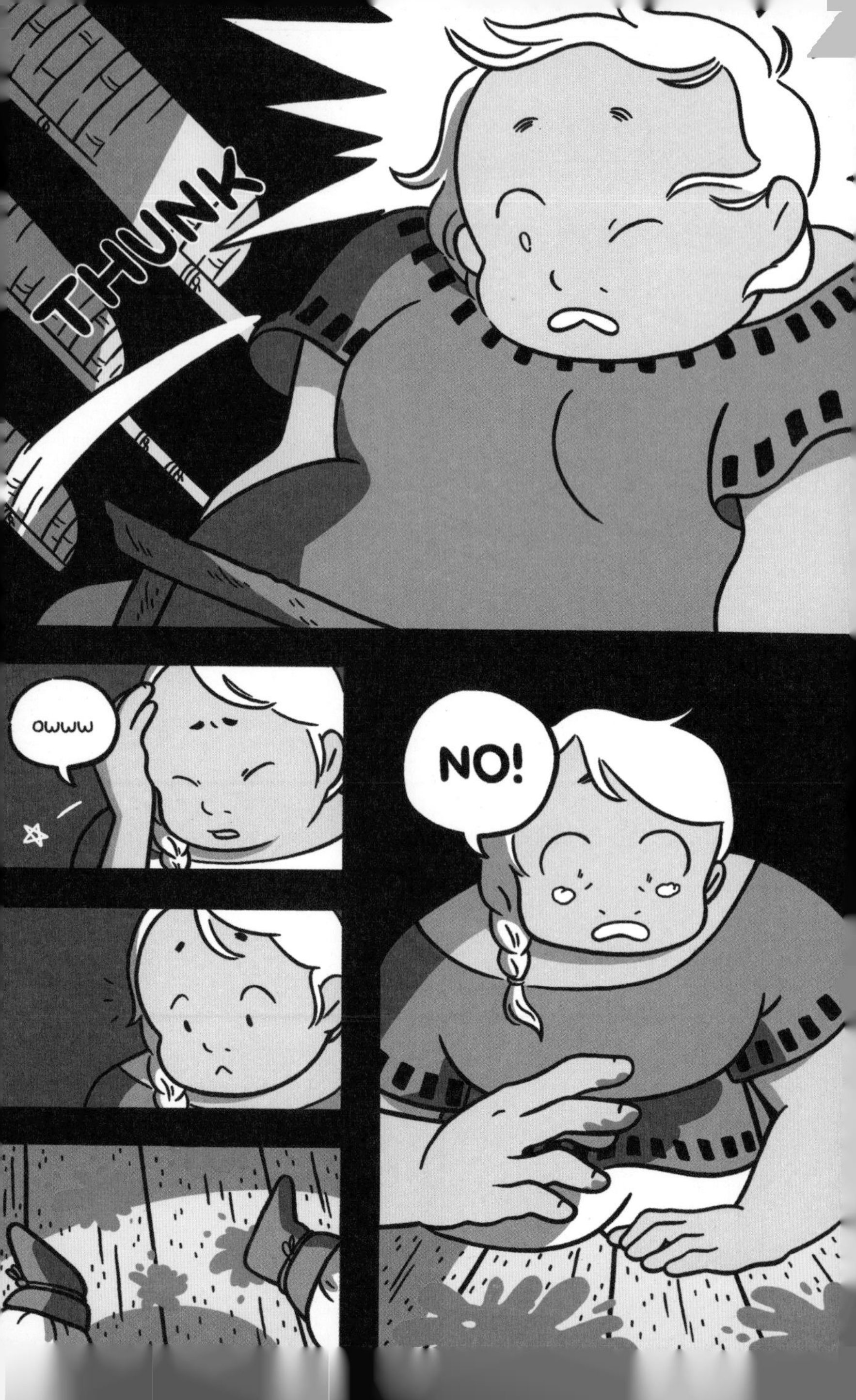
THUNK
OWWW
NO!

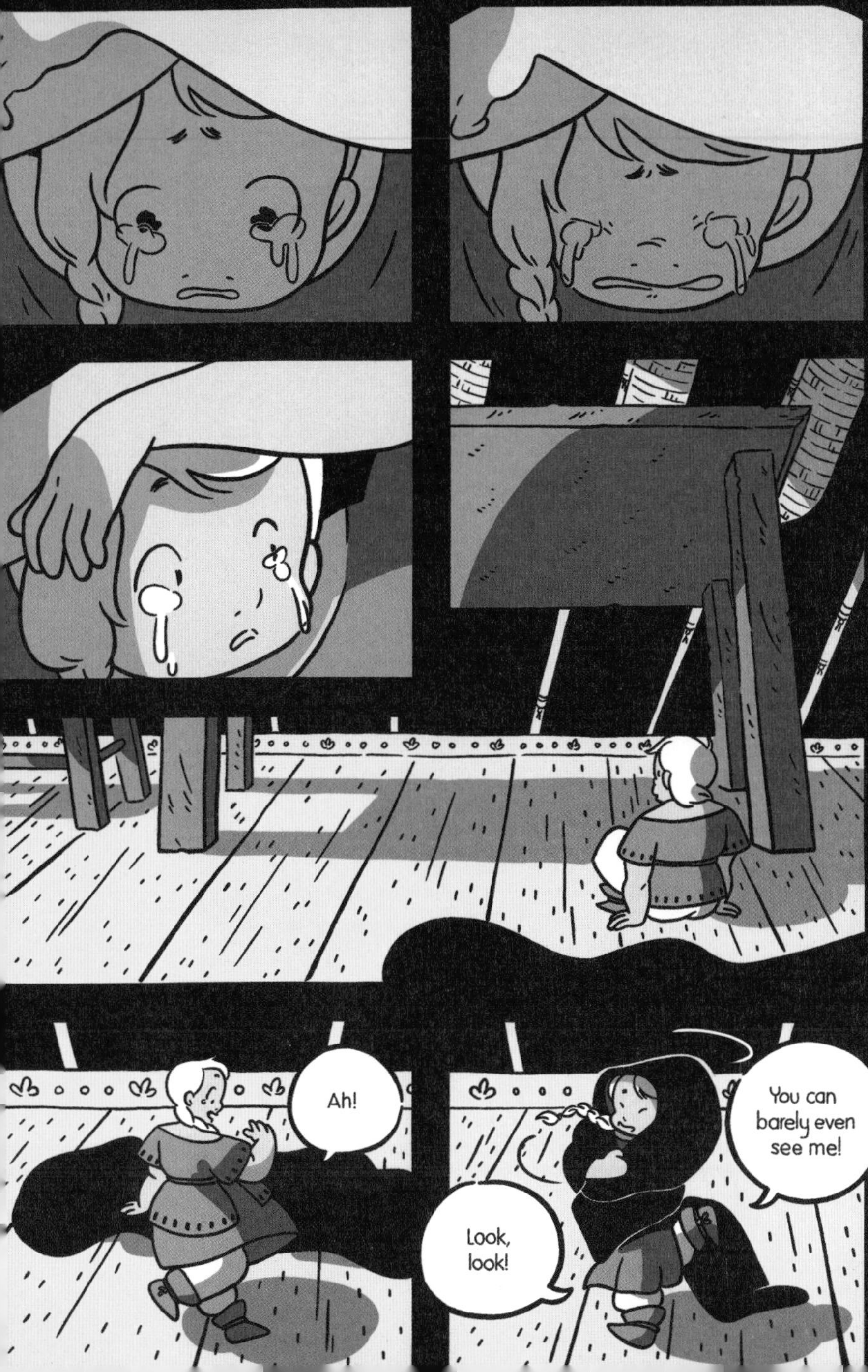
Ah!
You can barely even see me!
Look, look!

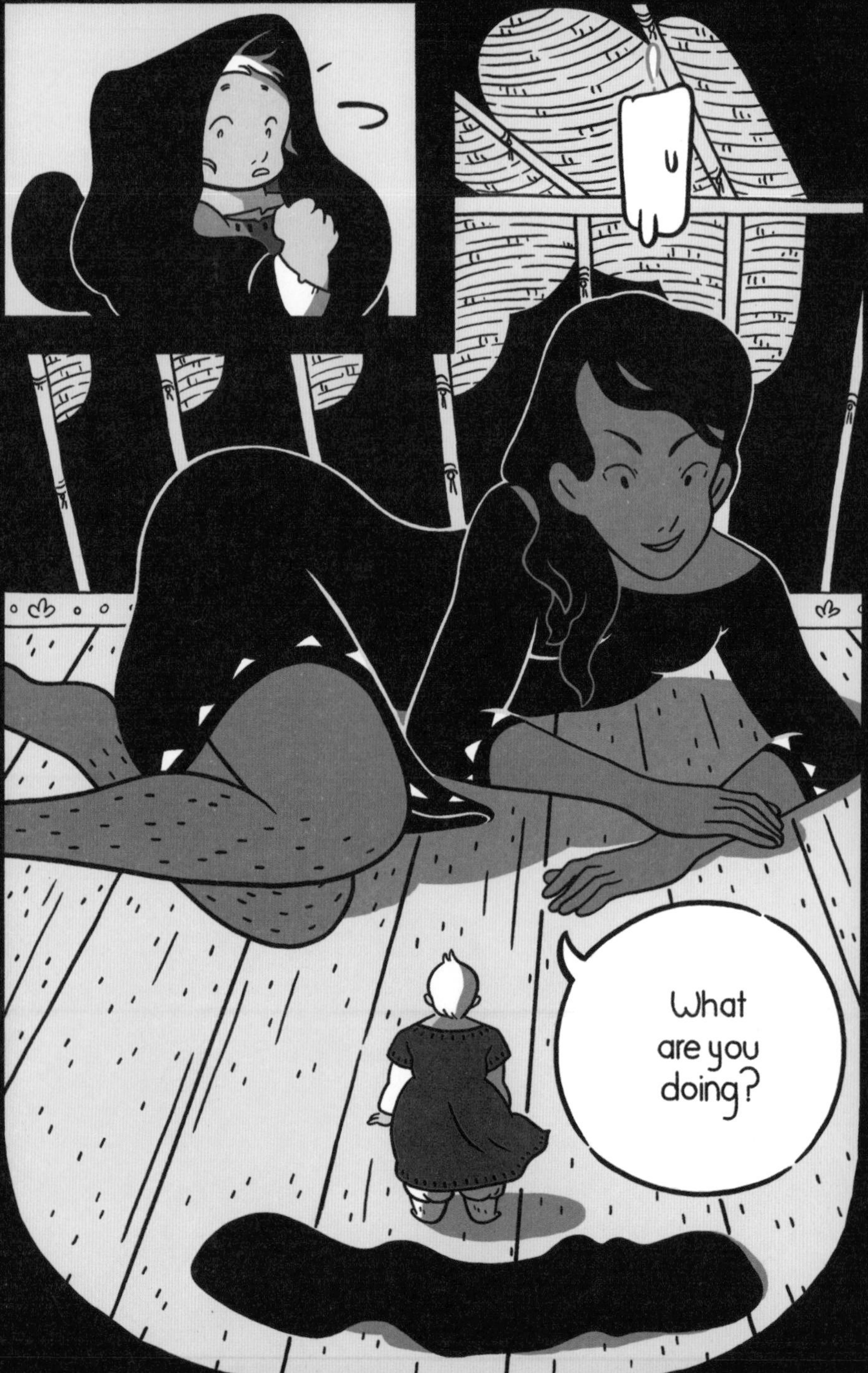
What are you doing?

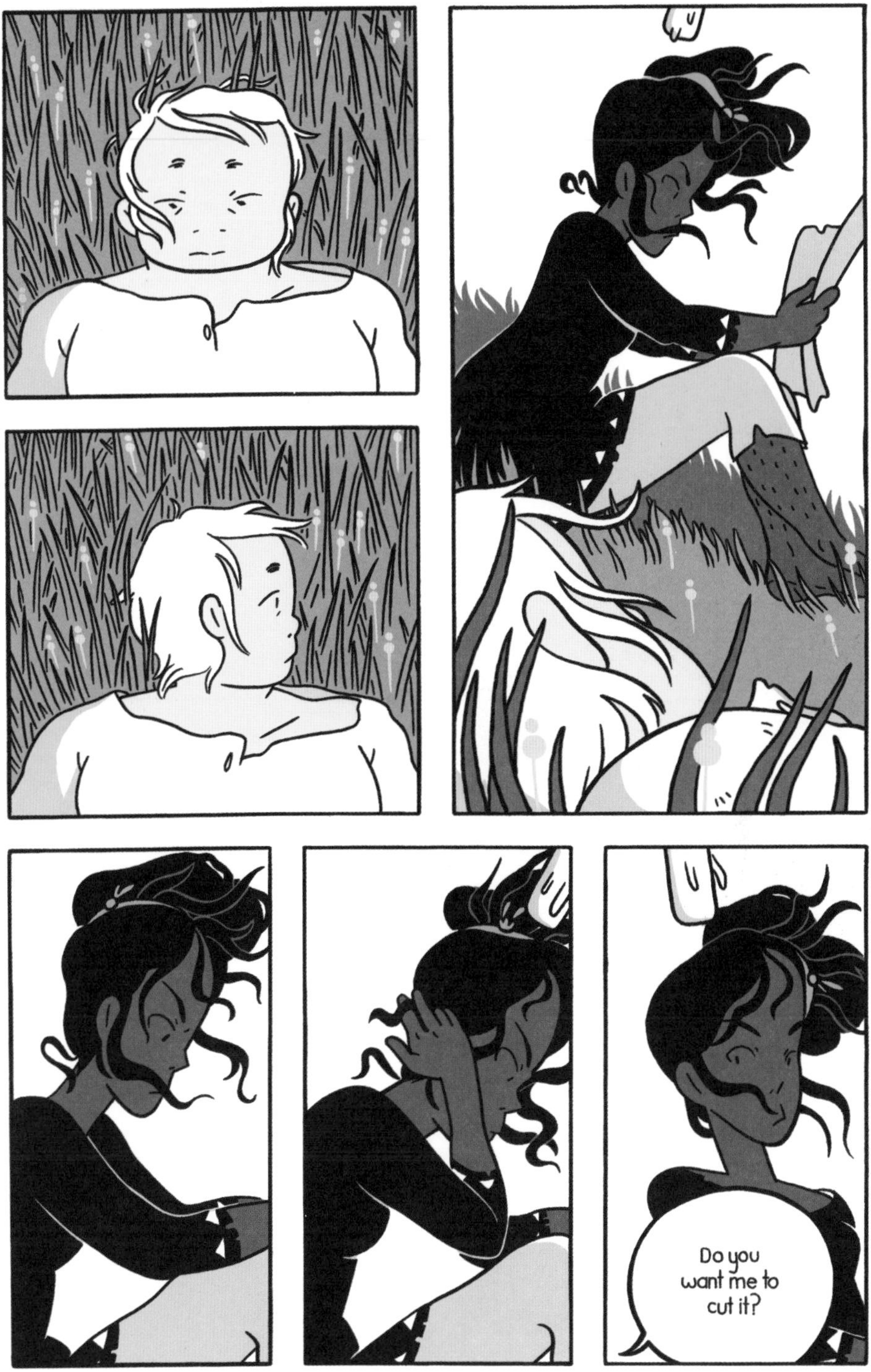
Do you want me to cut it?

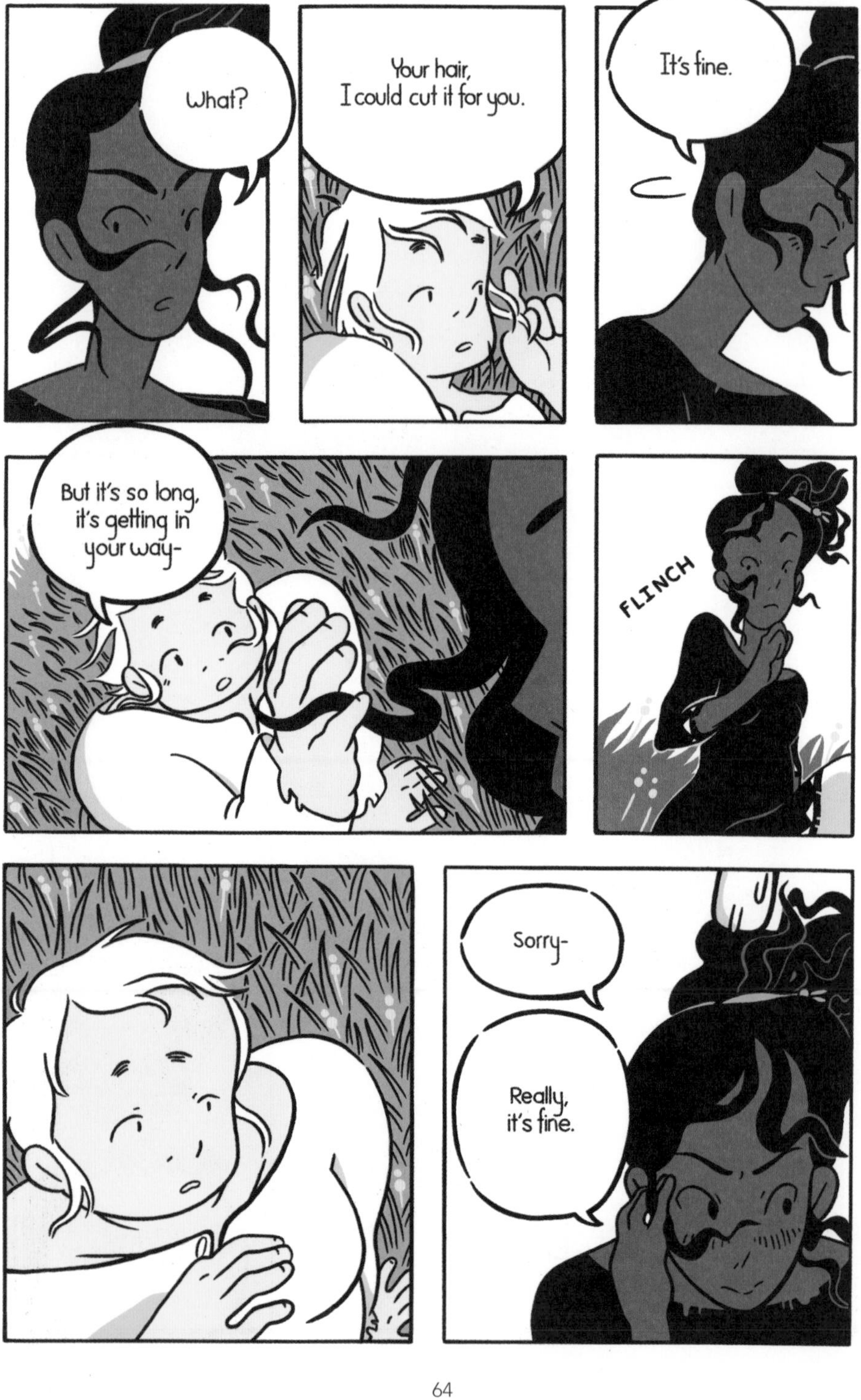
What?
Your hair, I could cut it for you.
It's fine.
But it's so long, it's getting in your way-
FLINCH
Sorry-
Really, it's fine.

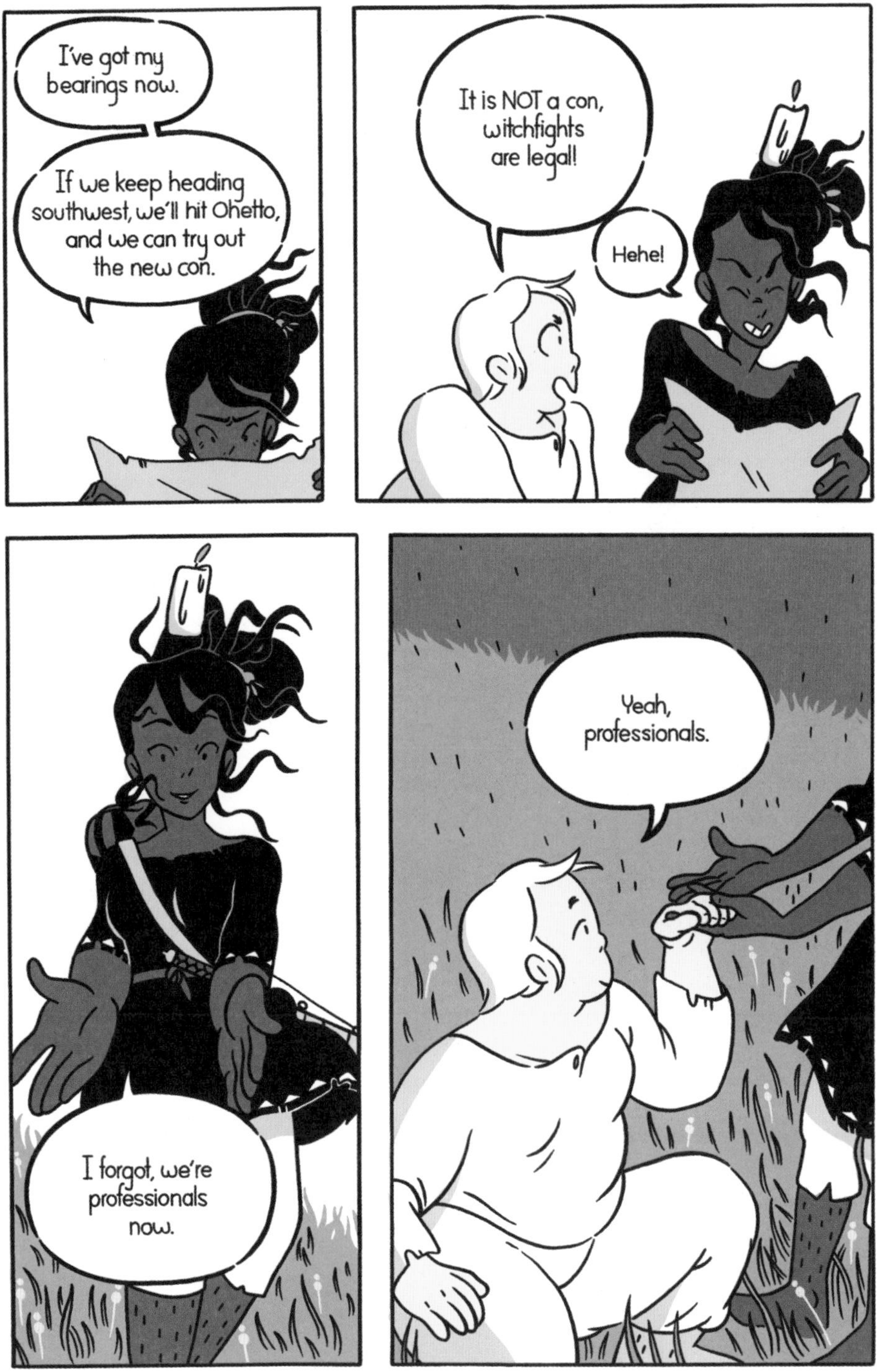
I've got my bearings now.
If we keep heading southwest, we'll hit Ohetto, and we can try out the new con.
It is NOT a con, witchfights are legal!
Hehe!
I forgot, we're professionals now.
Yeah, professionals.

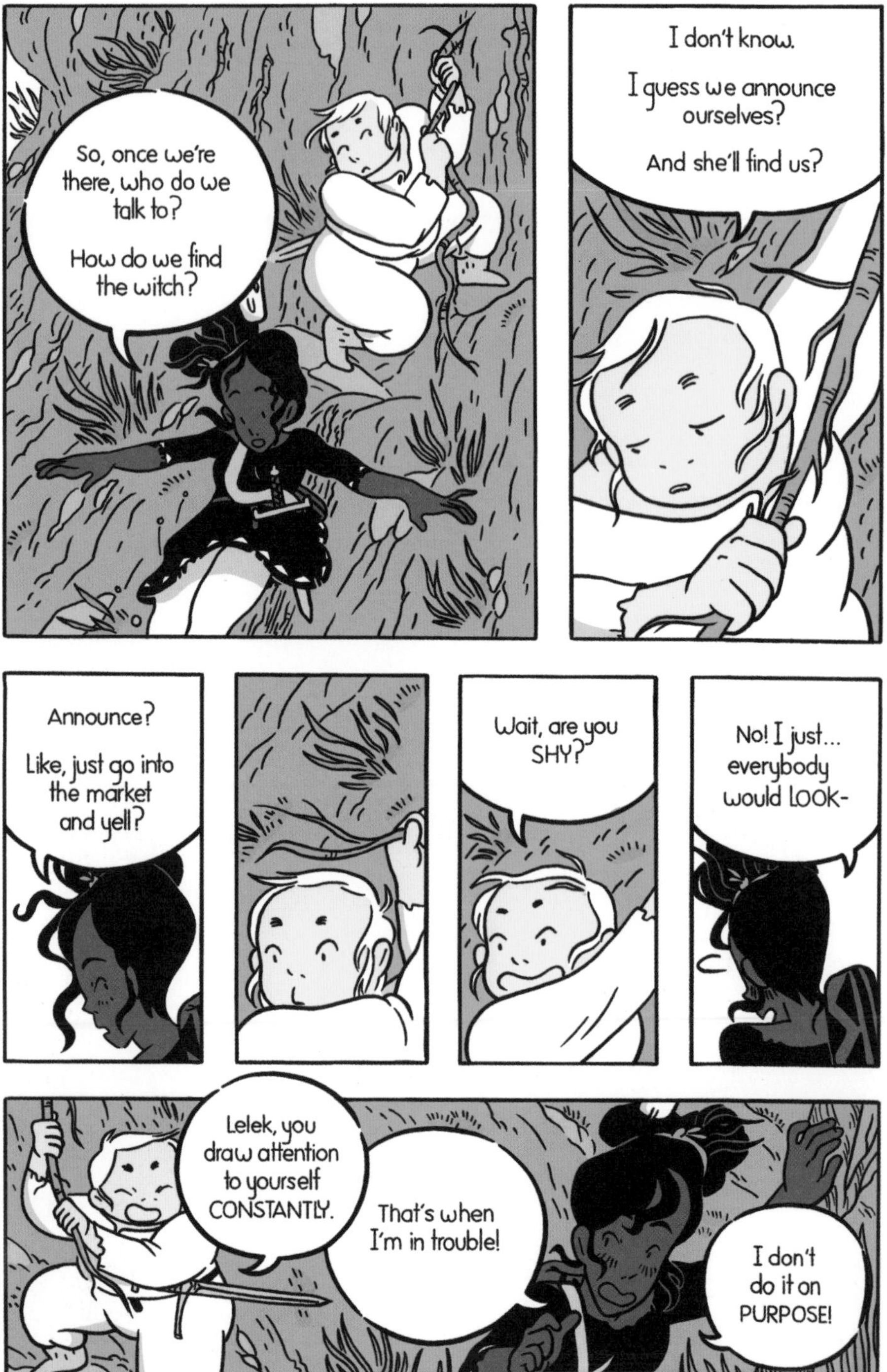

So, once we're there, who do we talk to?
How do we find the witch?
I don't know.
I guess we announce ourselves?
And she'll find us?
Announce?
Like, just go into the market and yell?
Wait, are you SHY?
No! I just... everybody would LOOK-
Lelek, you draw attention to yourself CONSTANTLY.
That's when I'm in trouble!
I don't do it on PURPOSE!

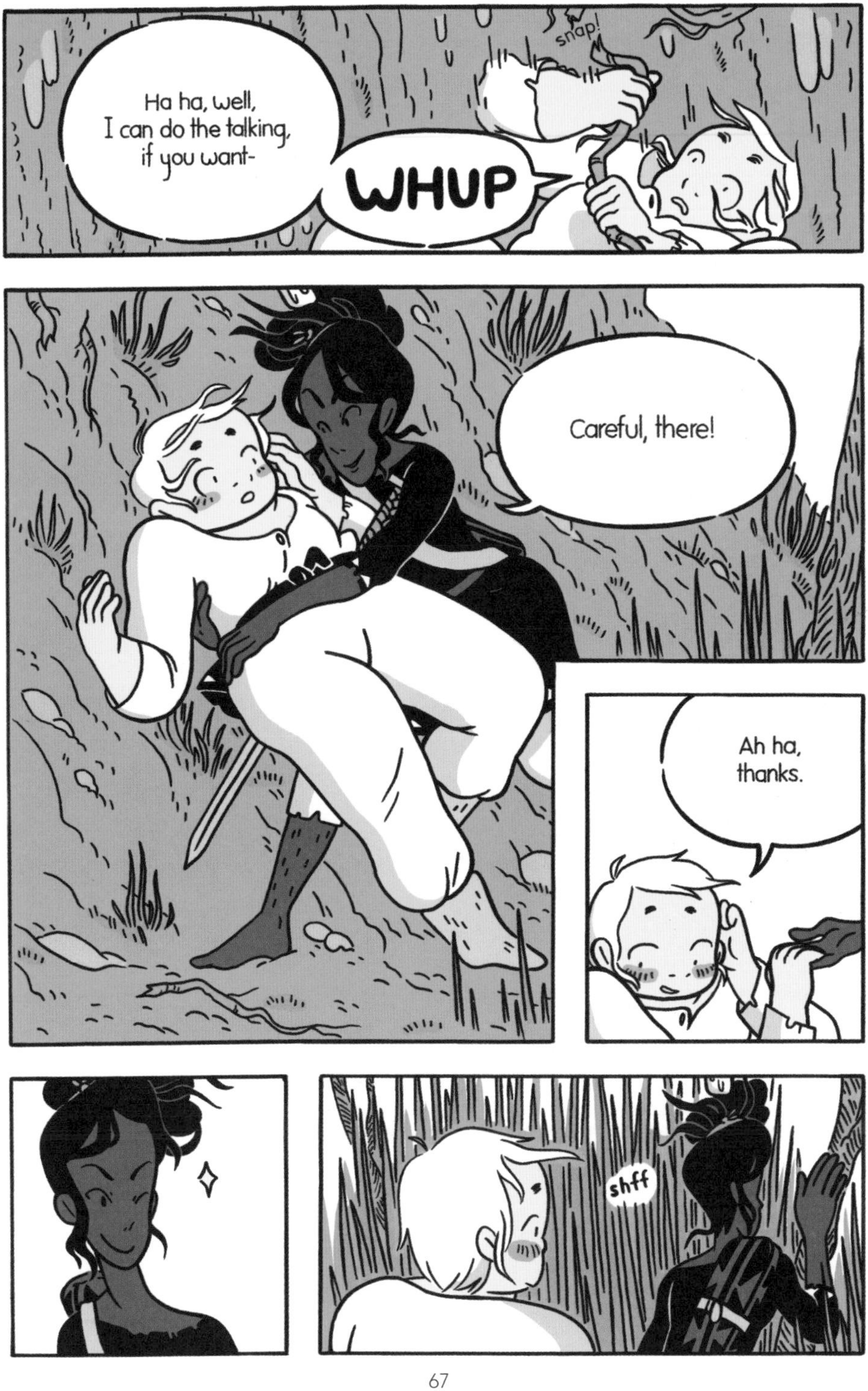
Ha ha, well, I can do the talking, if you want-
WHUP
snap!
Careful, there!
Ah ha, thanks.
shff

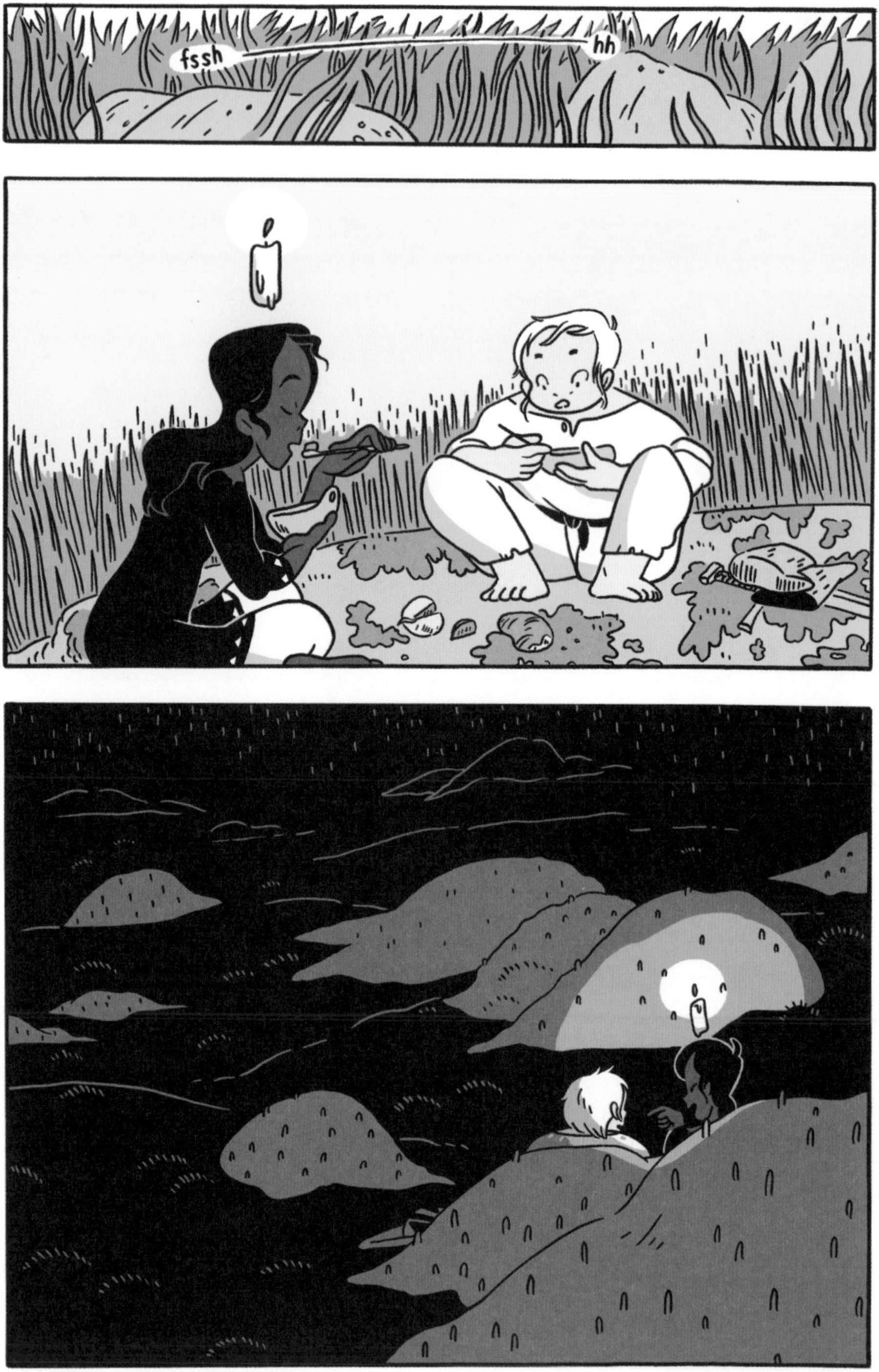
fssh
hh

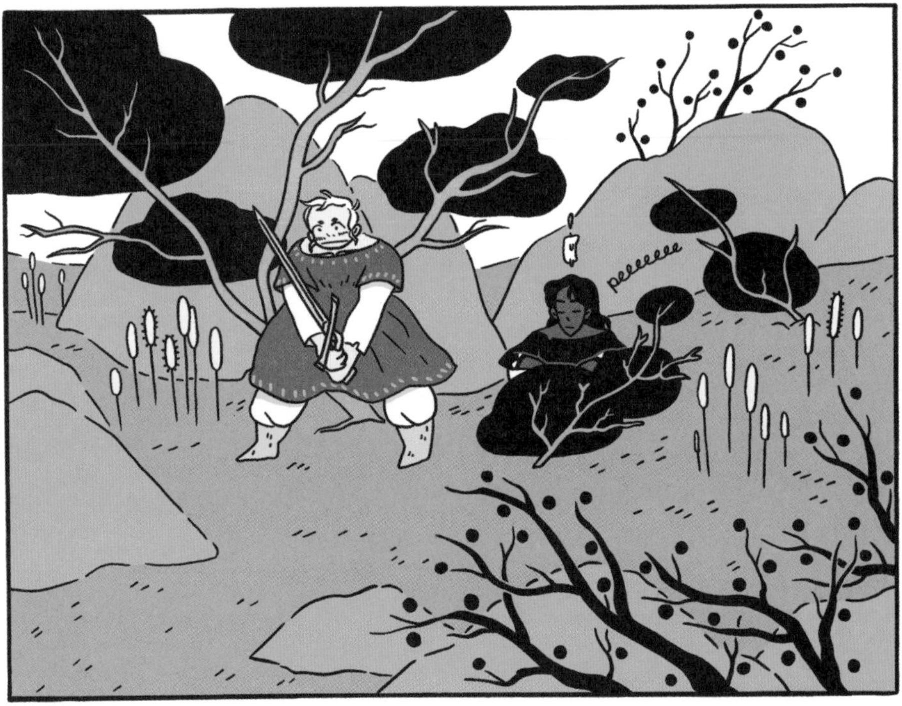
peeeeeee

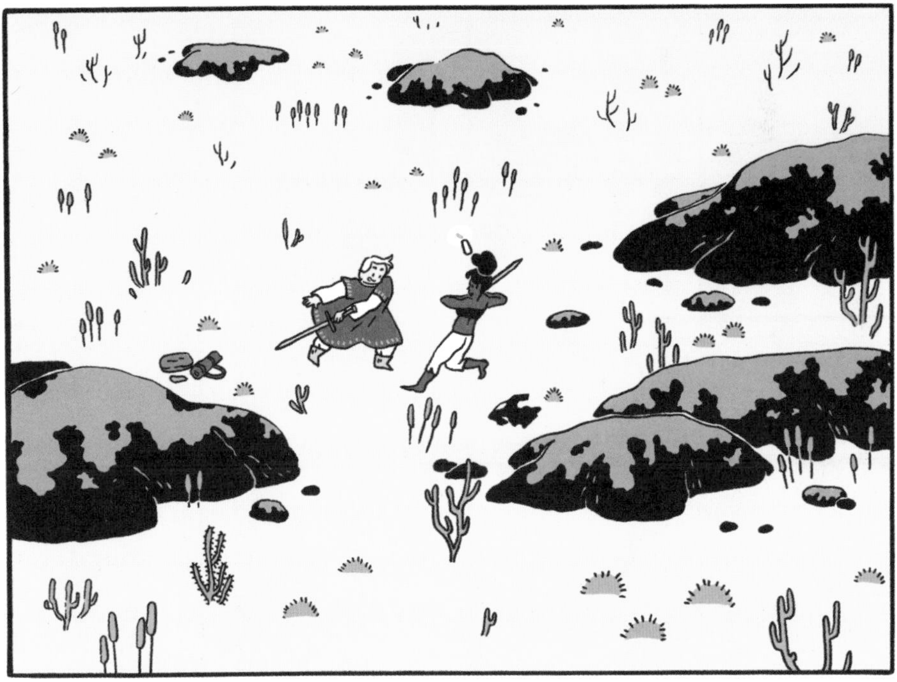

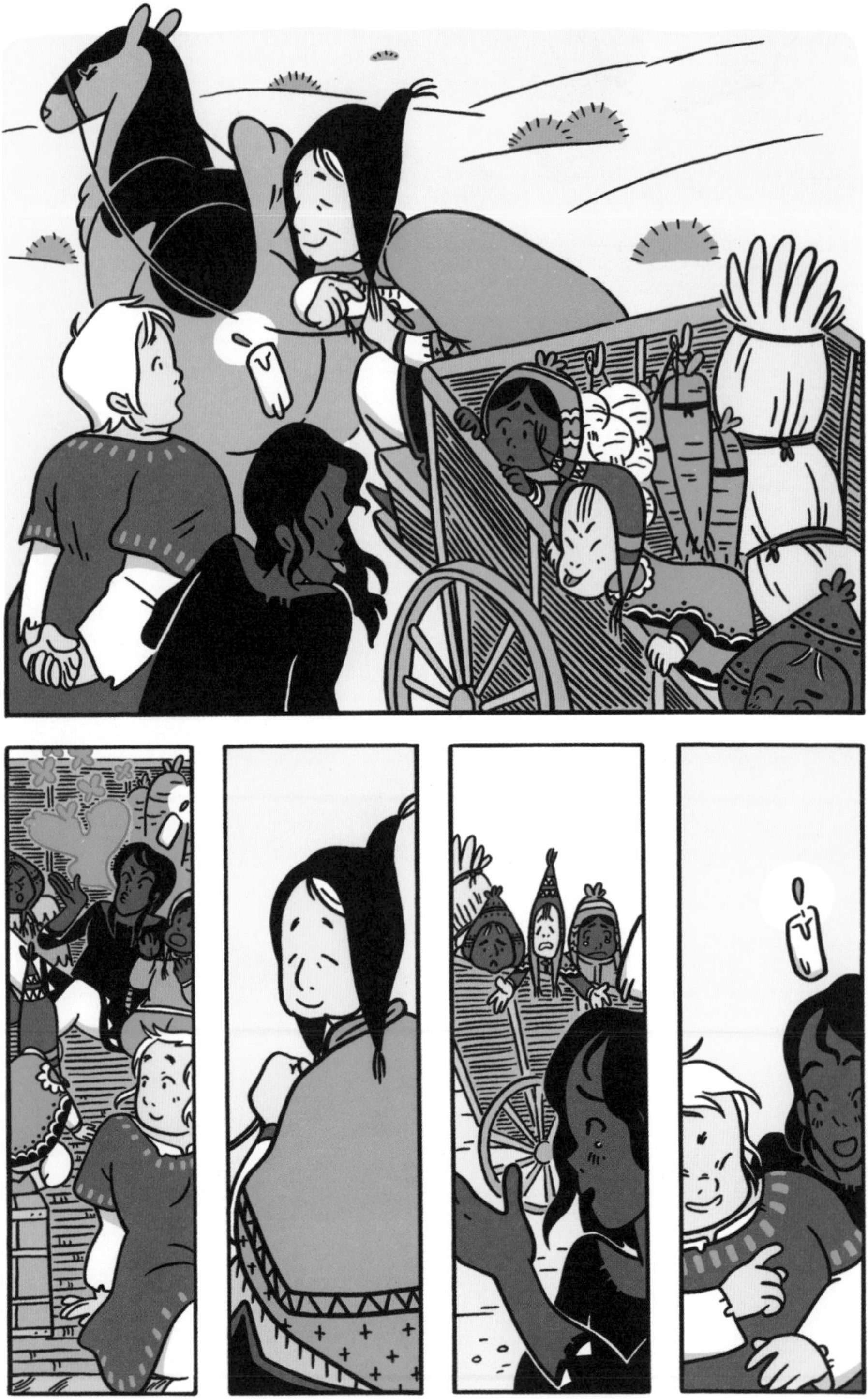

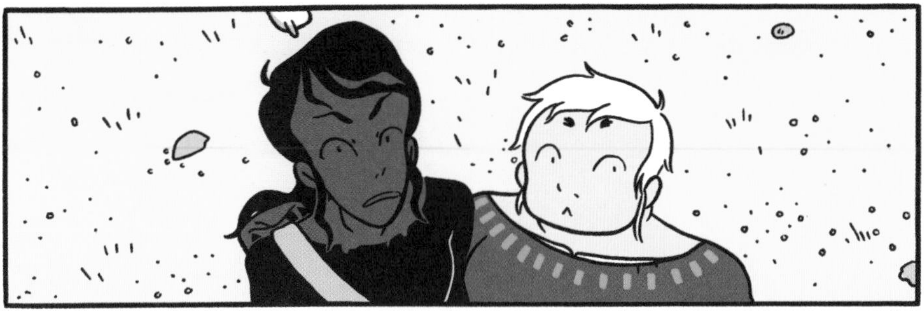

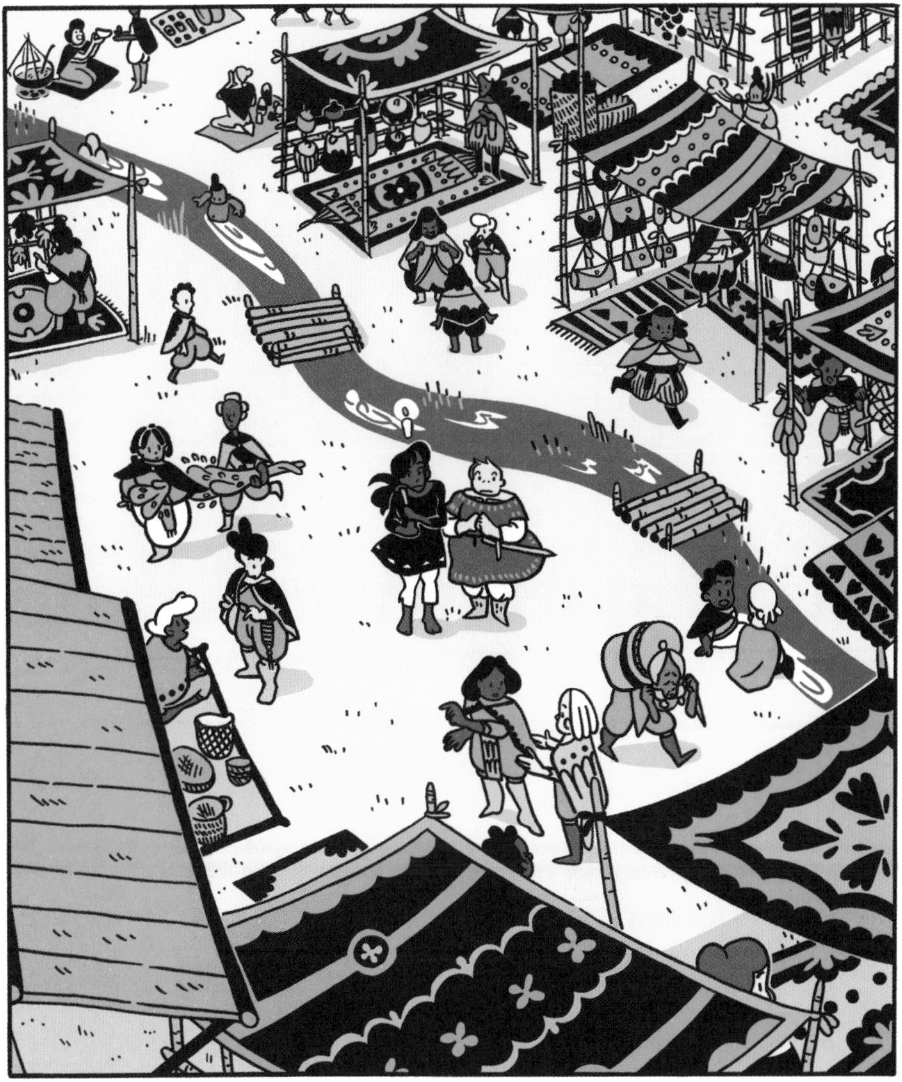

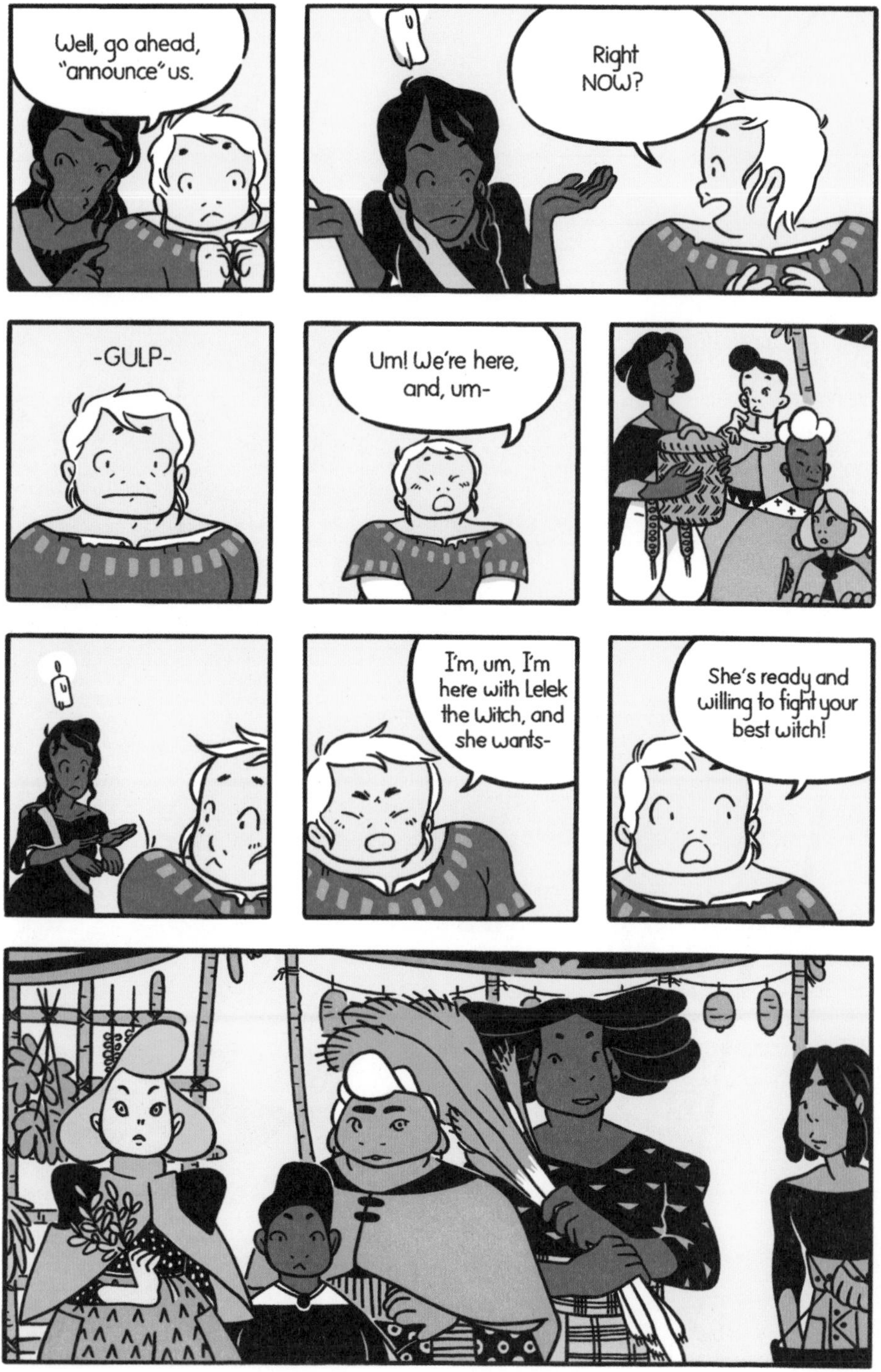
Well, go ahead, "announce" us.
Right NOW?
-GULP-
Um! We're here, and, um-
I'm, um, I'm here with Lelek the Witch, and she wants-
She's ready and willing to fight your best witch!

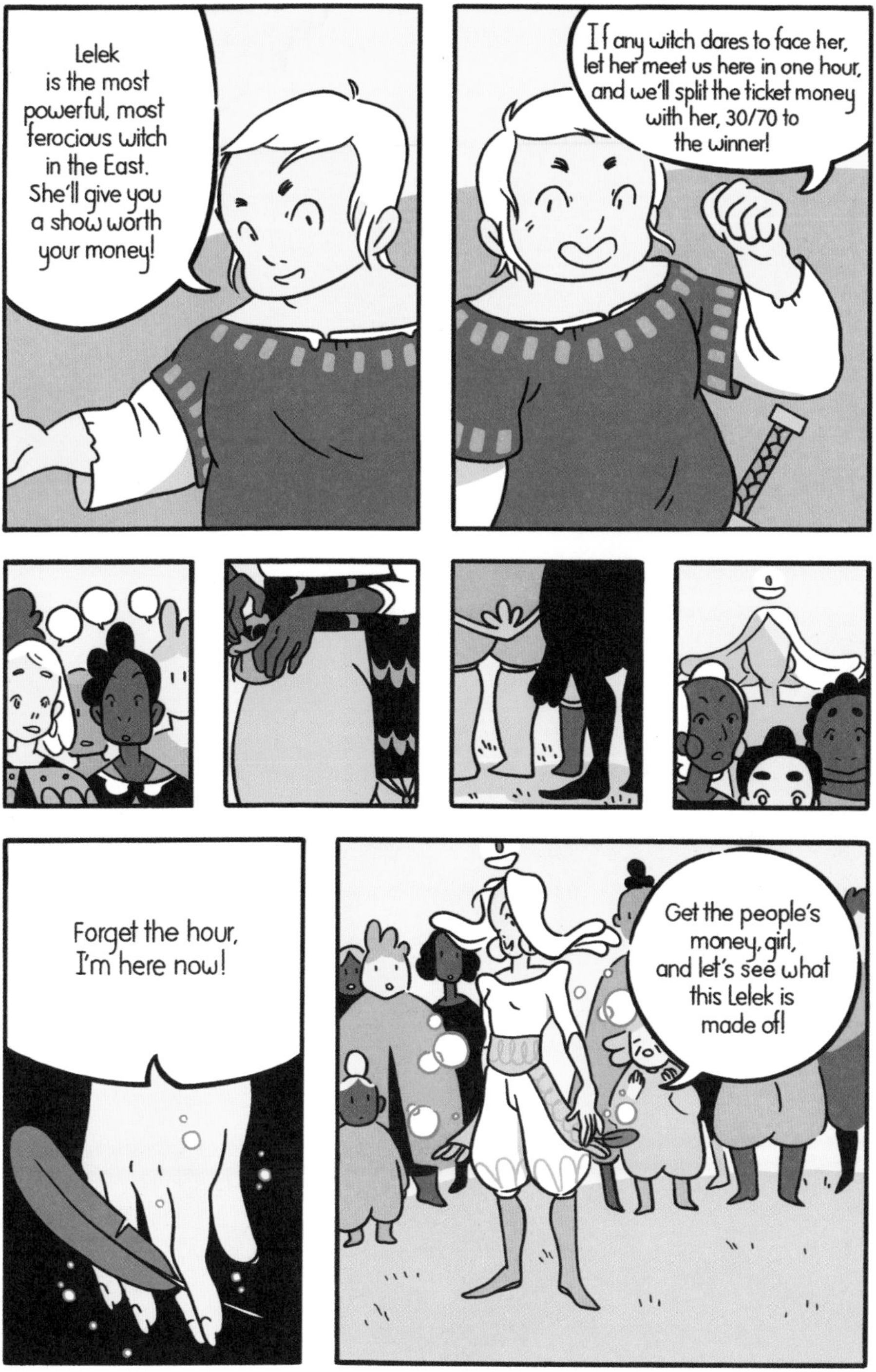
Lelek is the most powerful, most ferocious witch in the East. She'll give you a show worth your money!
If any witch dares to face her, let her meet us here in one hour, and we'll split the ticket money with her, 30/70 to the winner!
Forget the hour, I'm here now!
Get the people's money, girl, and let's see what this Lelek is made of!

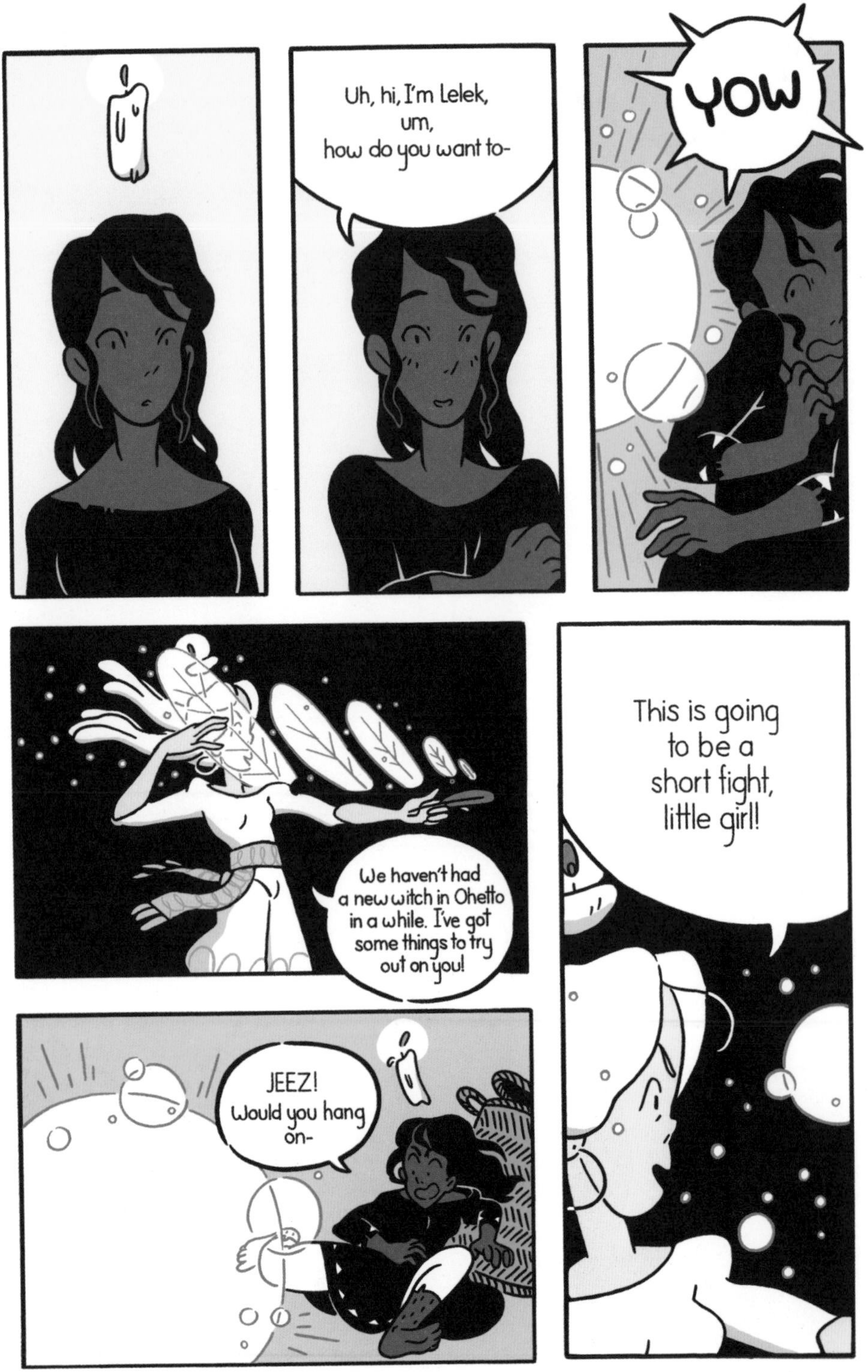

Uh, hi, I'm Lelek, um, how do you want to-
YOW
We haven't had a new witch in Ohetto in a while. I've got some things to try out on you!
This is going to be a short fight, little girl!
JEEZ! Would you hang on-

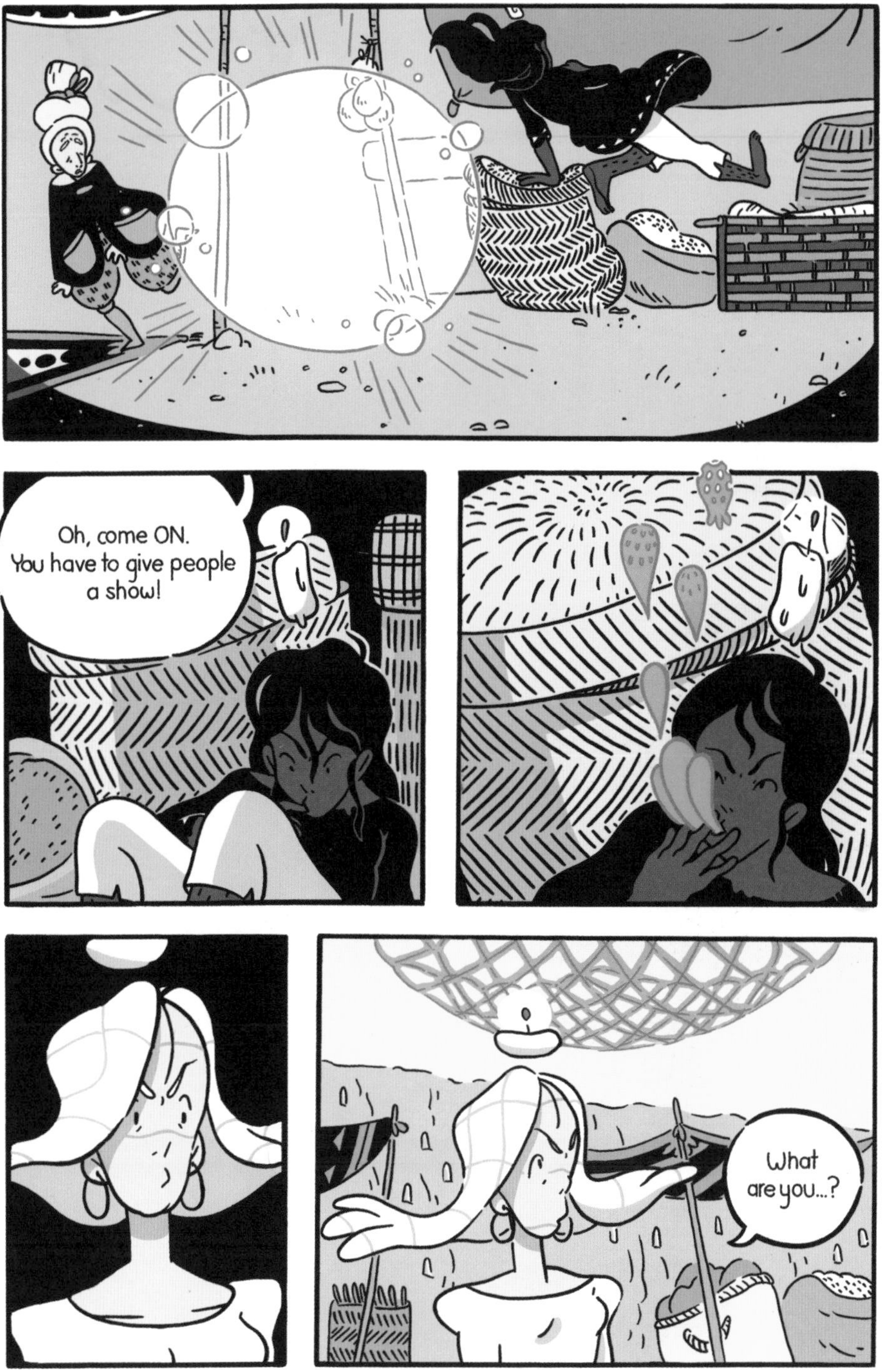
Oh, come ON.
You have to give people a show!
What are you...?

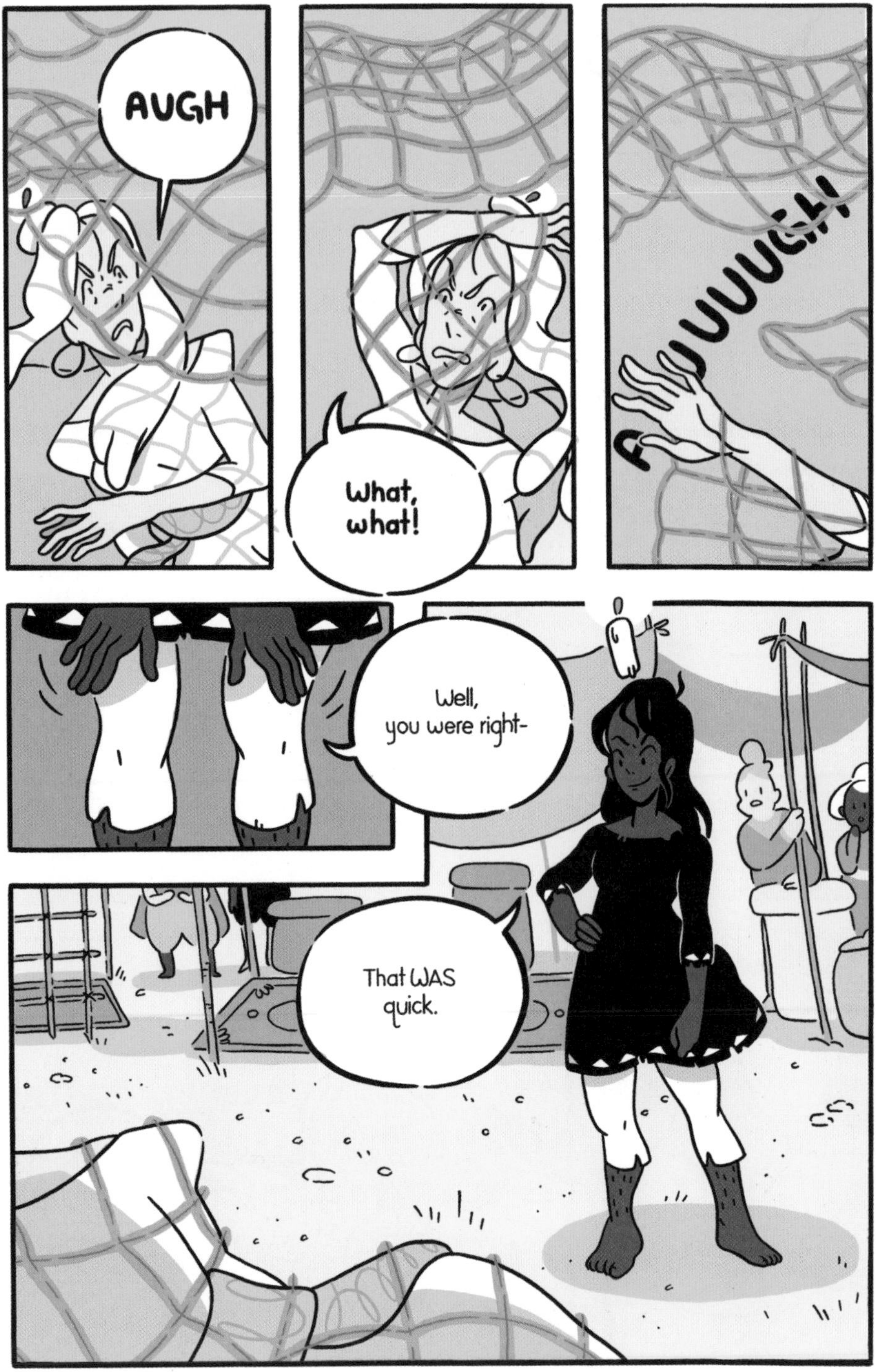
AUGH
What, what!
AUUUUGH!
Well, you were right-
That WAS quick.

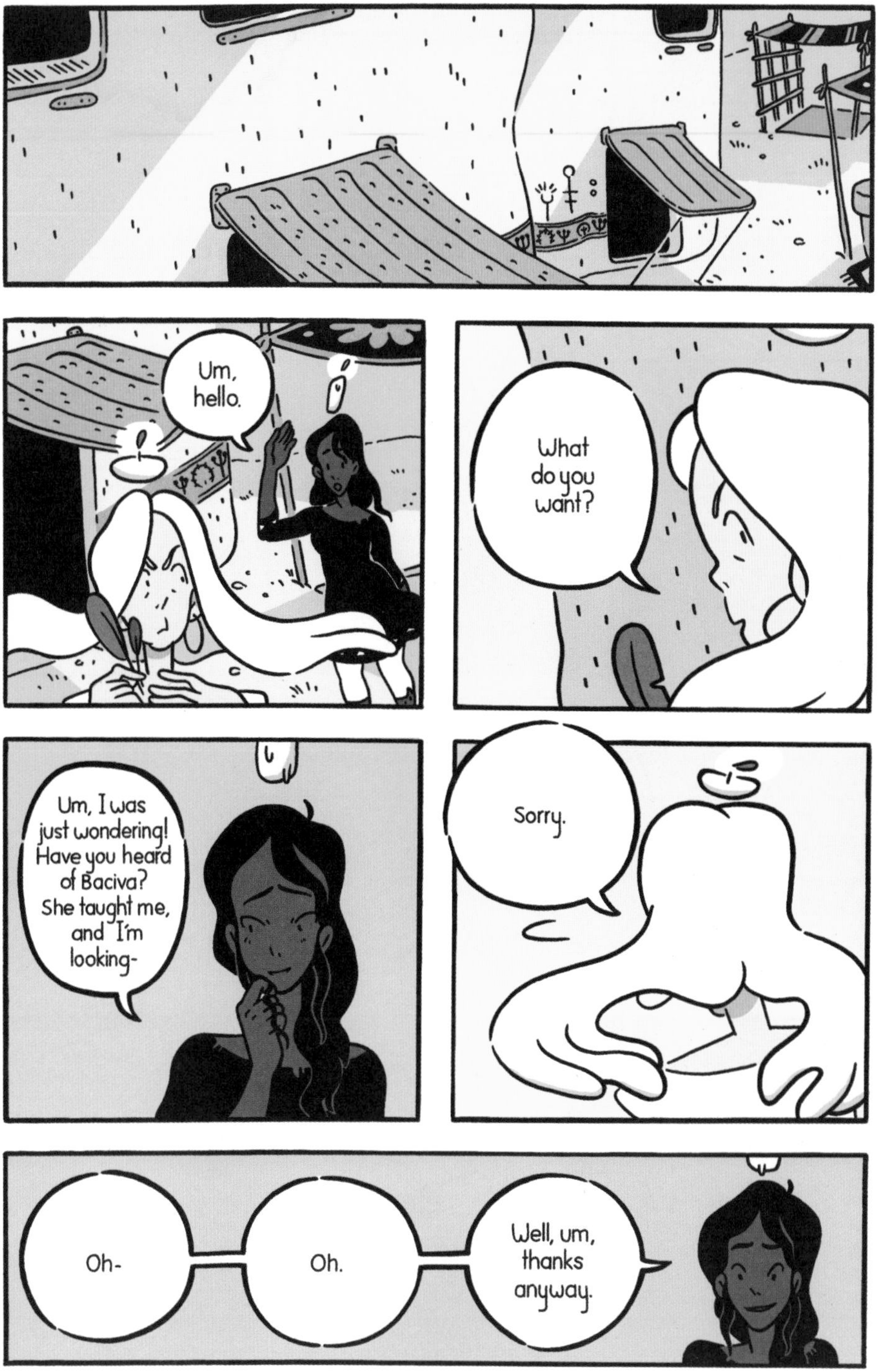
Um, hello.
What do you want?
Um, I was just wondering! Have you heard of Baciva? She taught me, and I'm looking-
Sorry.
Oh-
Oh.
Well, um, thanks anyway.

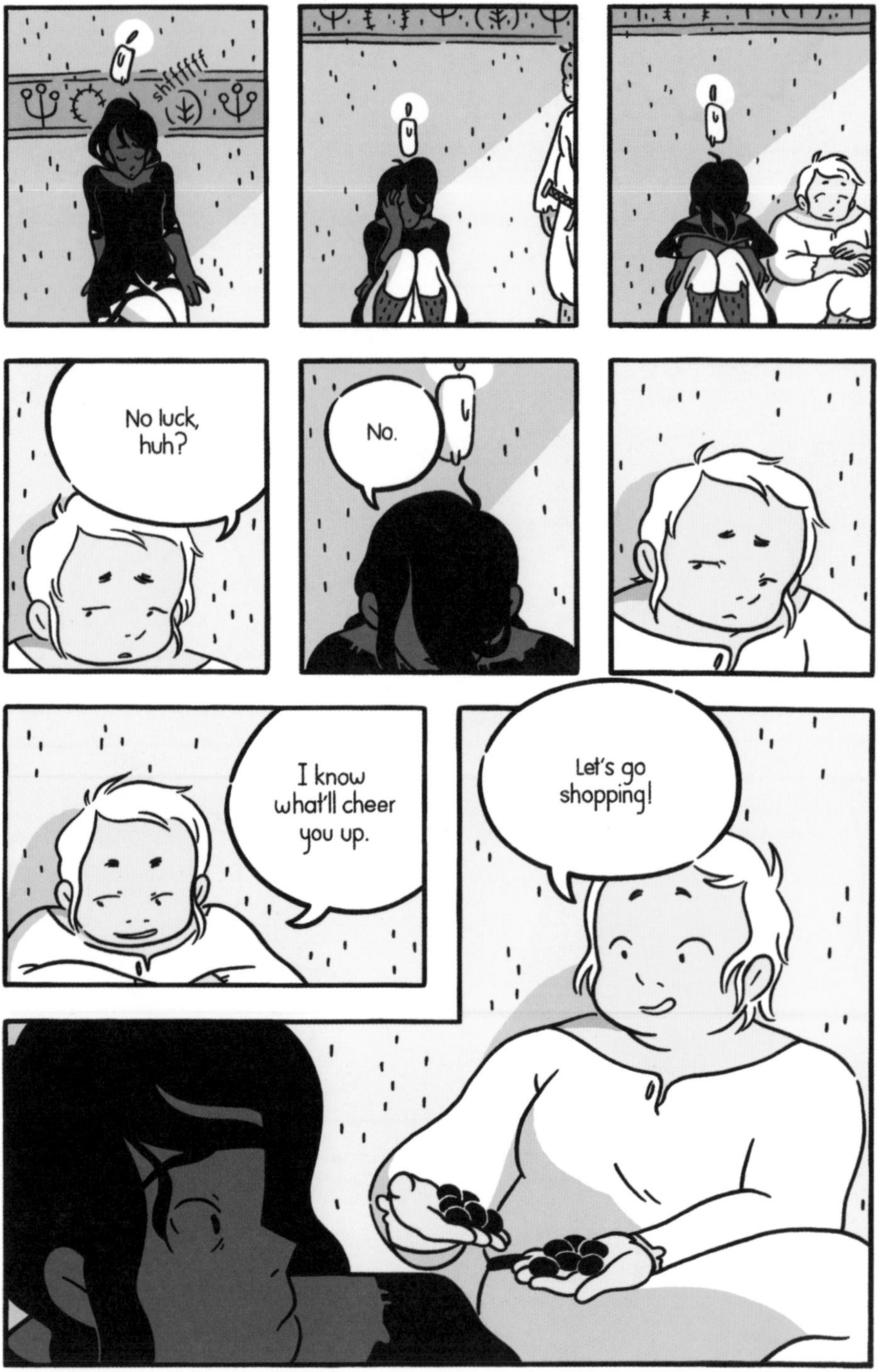
shffffff
No luck, huh?
No.
I know what'll cheer you up.
Let's go shopping!

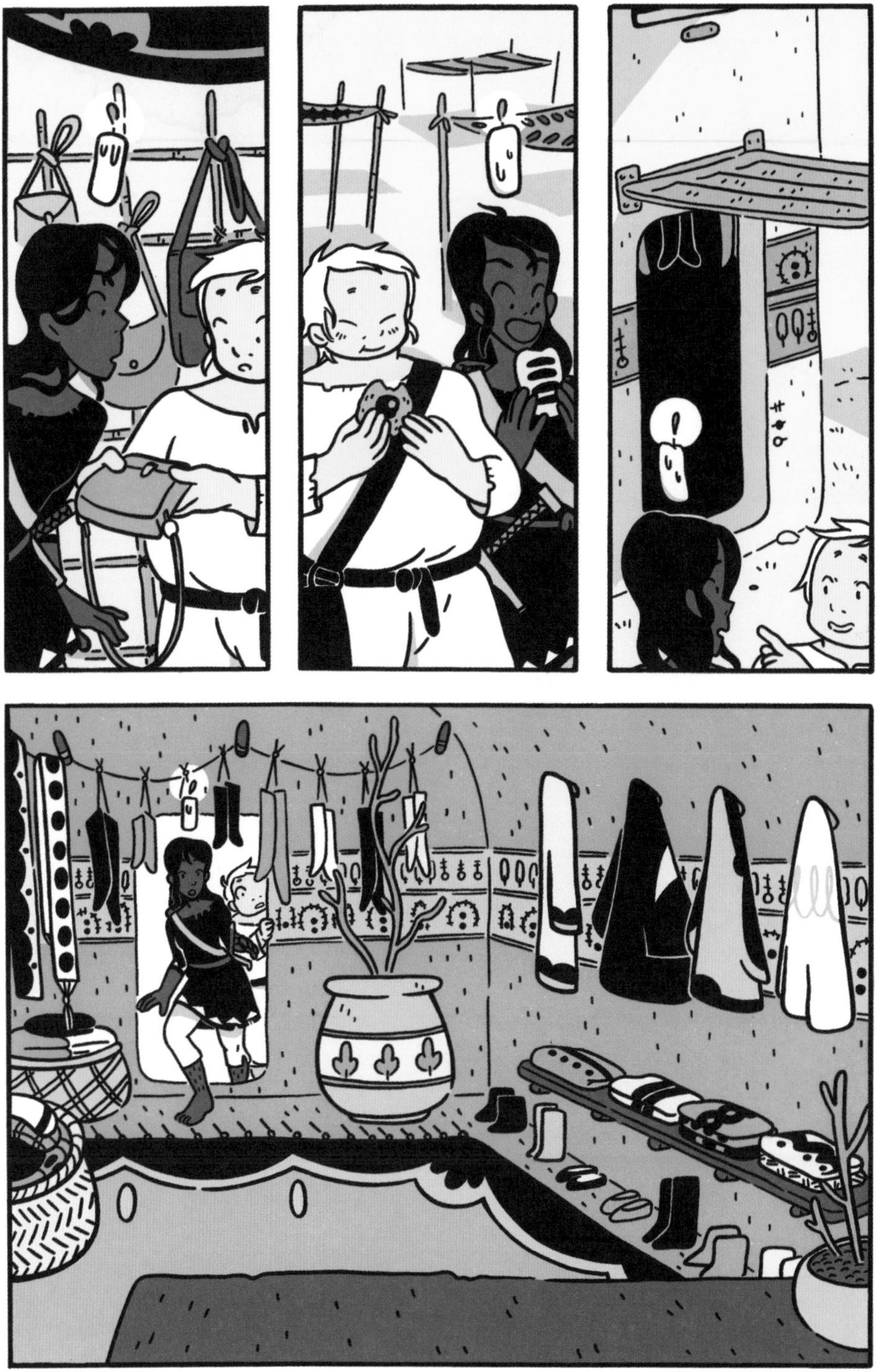

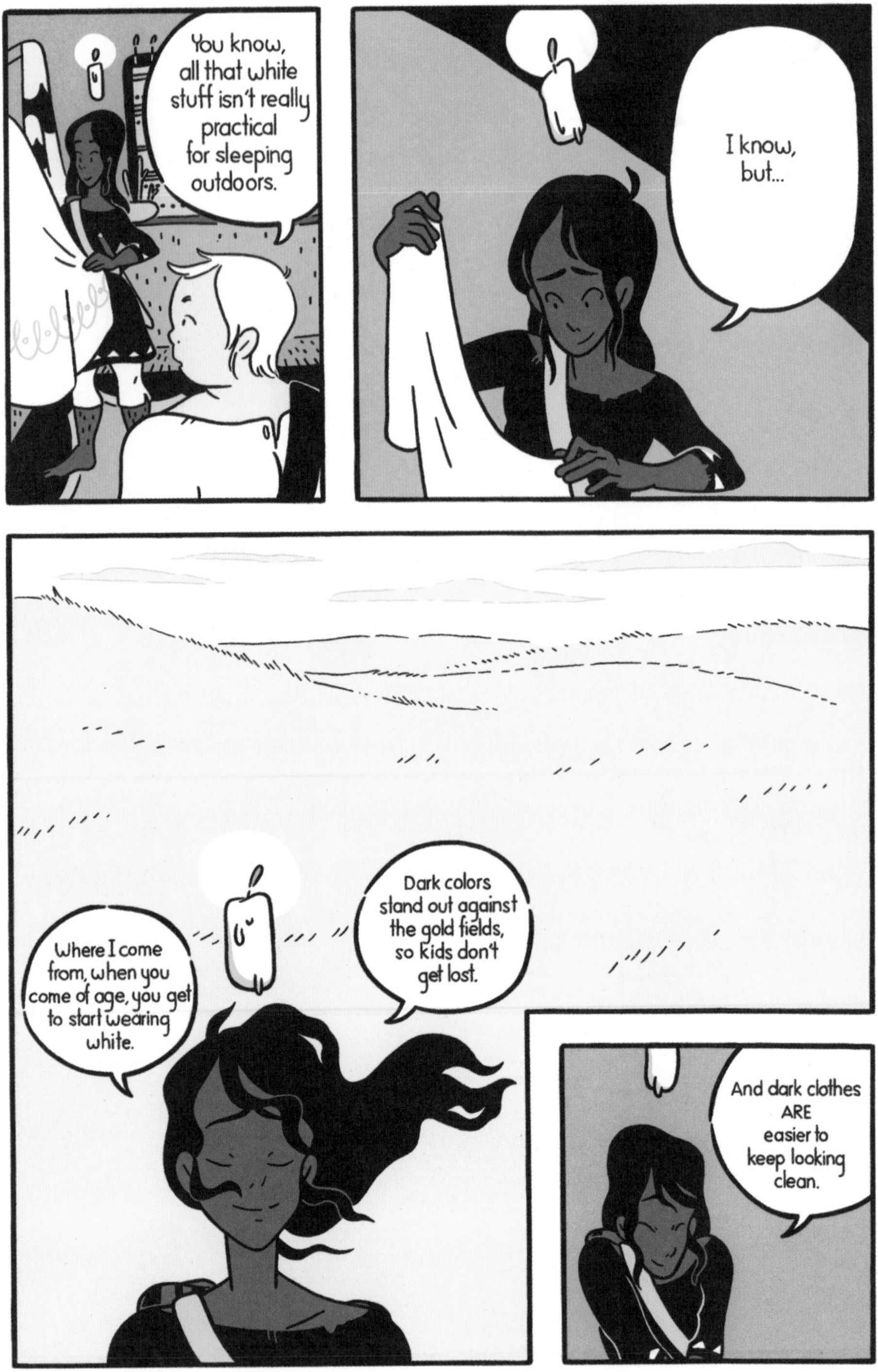
You know, all that white stuff isn't really practical for sleeping outdoors.
I know, but...
Where I come from, when you come of age, you get to start wearing white.
Dark colors stand out against the gold fields, so kids don't get lost.
And dark clothes ARE easier to keep looking clean.

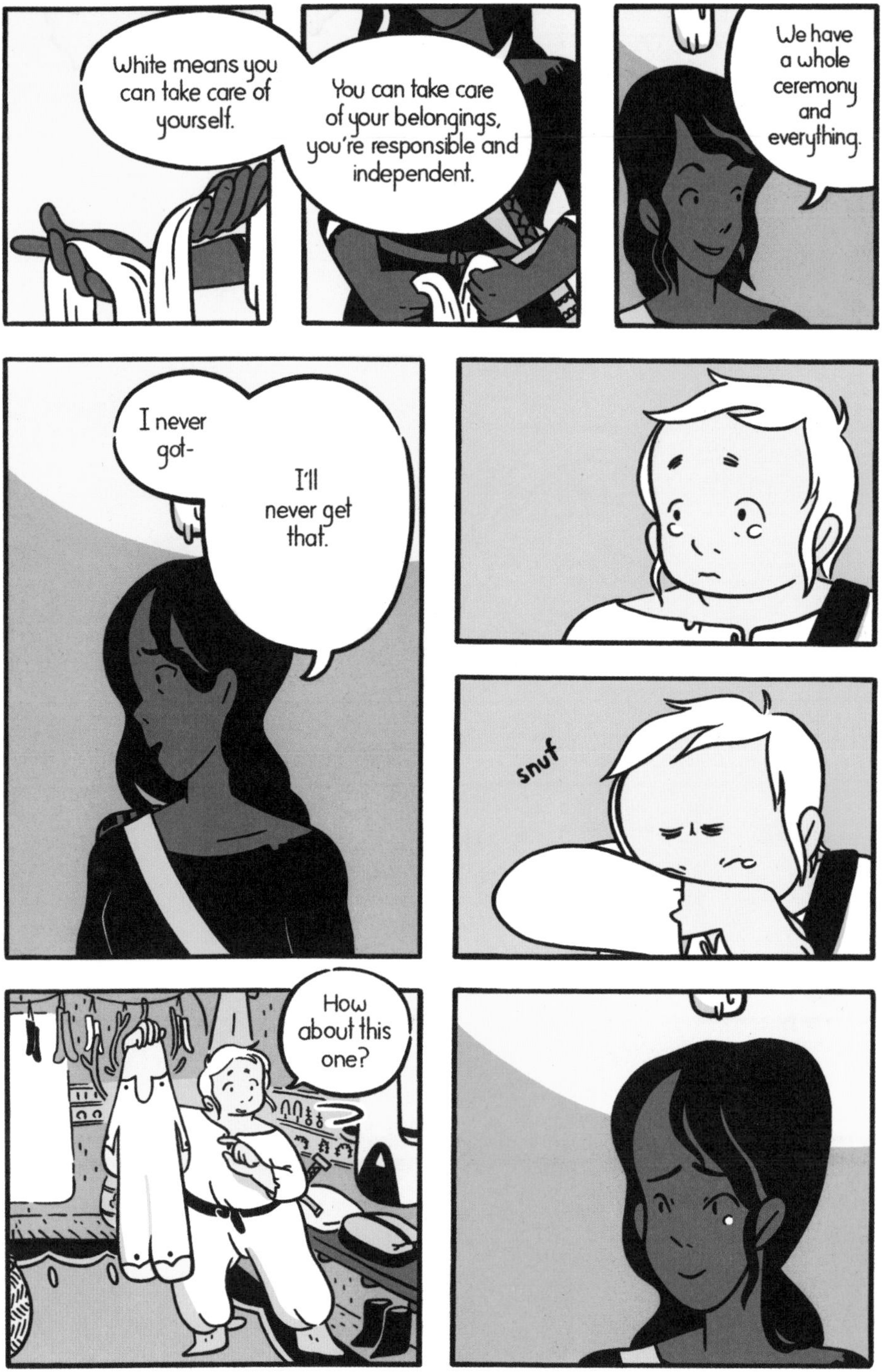
White means you can take care of yourself.
You can take care of your belongings, you're responsible and independent.
We have a whole ceremony and everything.
I never got-
I'll never get that.
snuf
How about this one?

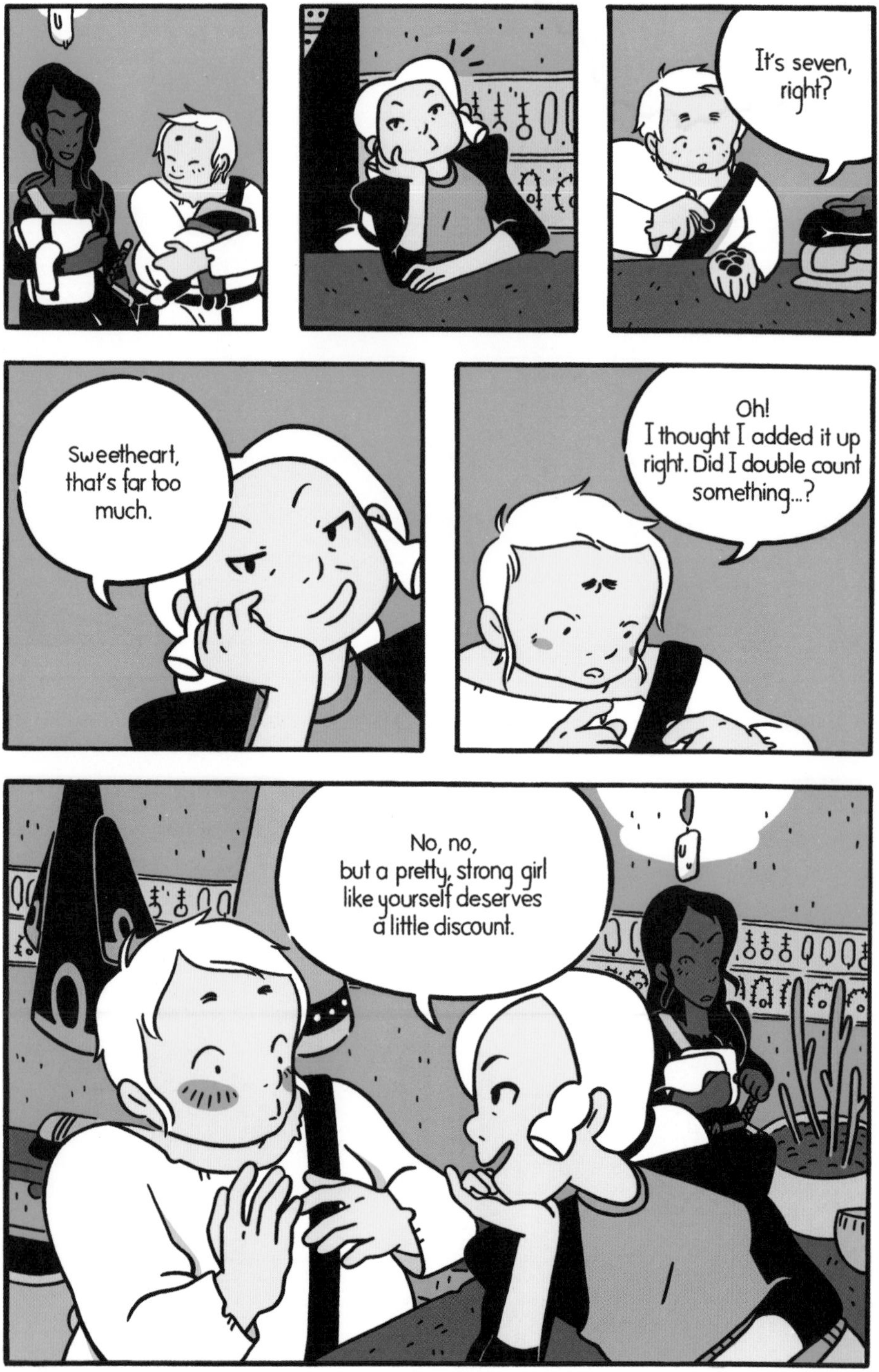
It's seven, right?
Sweetheart, that's far too much.
Oh! I thought I added it up right. Did I double count something...?
No, no, but a pretty, strong girl like yourself deserves a little discount.

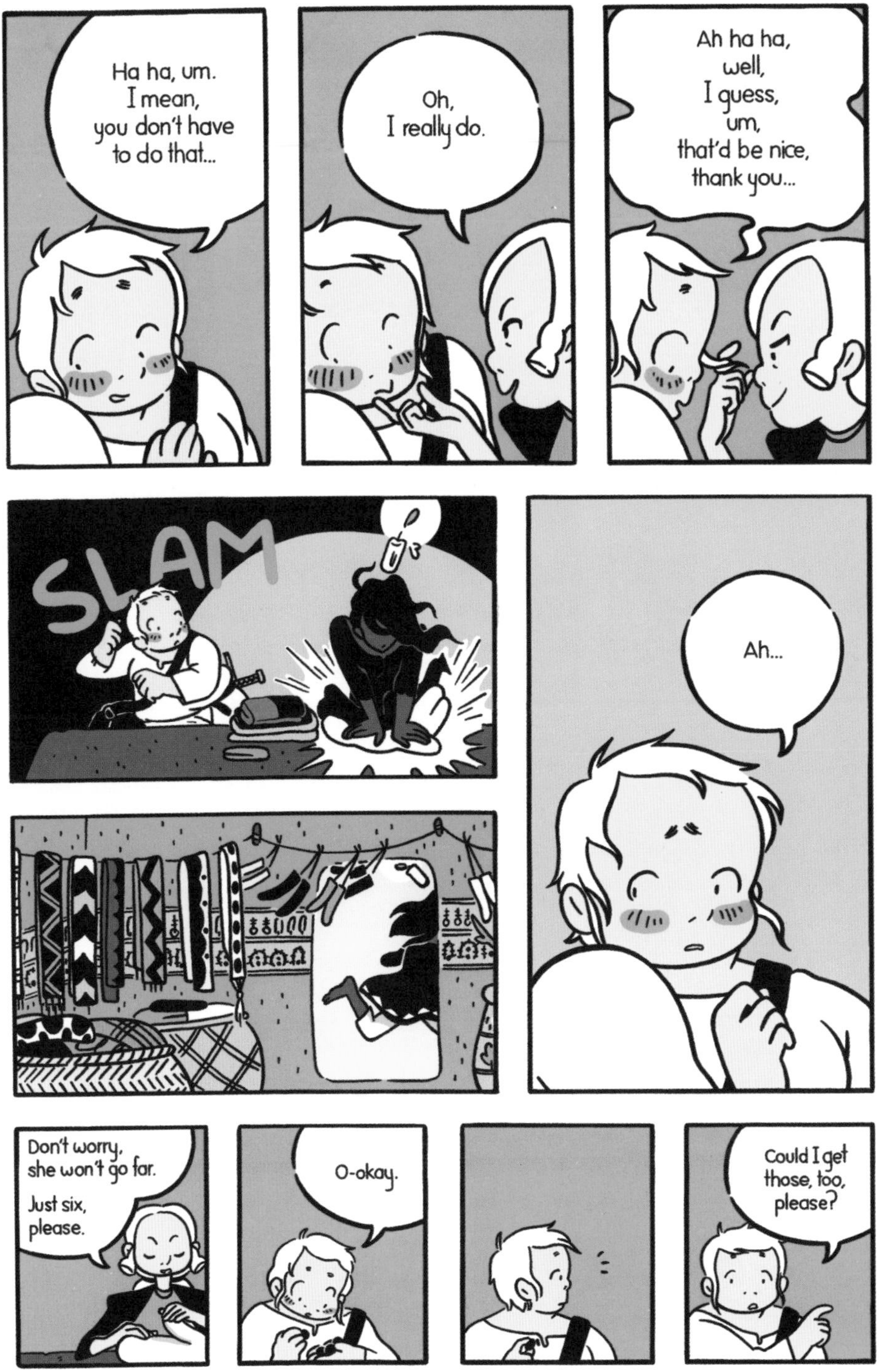
Ha ha, um. I mean, you don't have to do that...
Oh, I really do.
Ah ha ha, well, I guess, um, that'd be nice, thank you...
SLAM
Ah...
Don't worry, she won't go far.
Just six, please.
O-okay.
Could I get those, too, please?

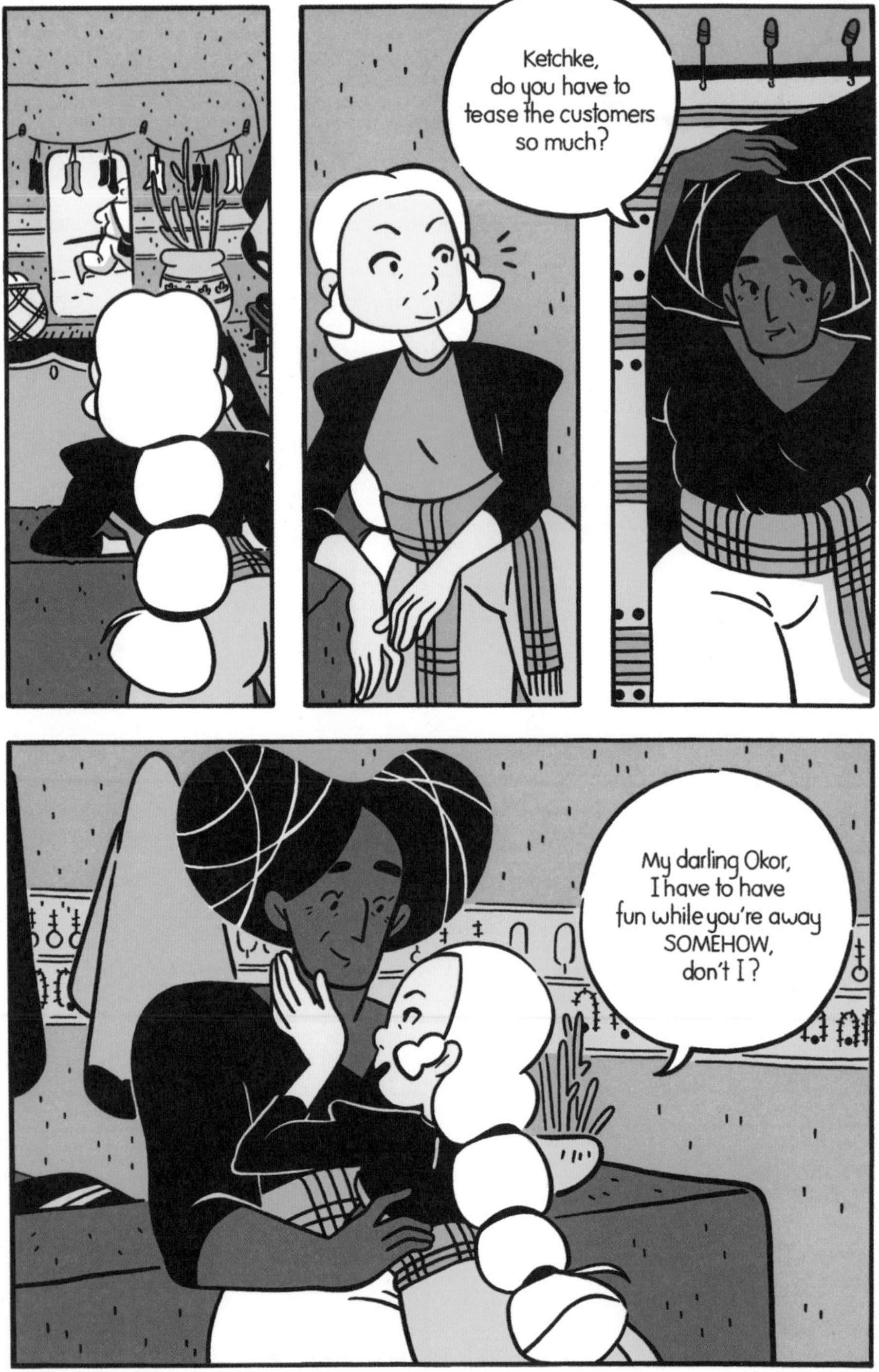
Ketchke, do you have to tease the customers so much?
My darling Okor, I have to have fun while you're away SOMEHOW, don't I?

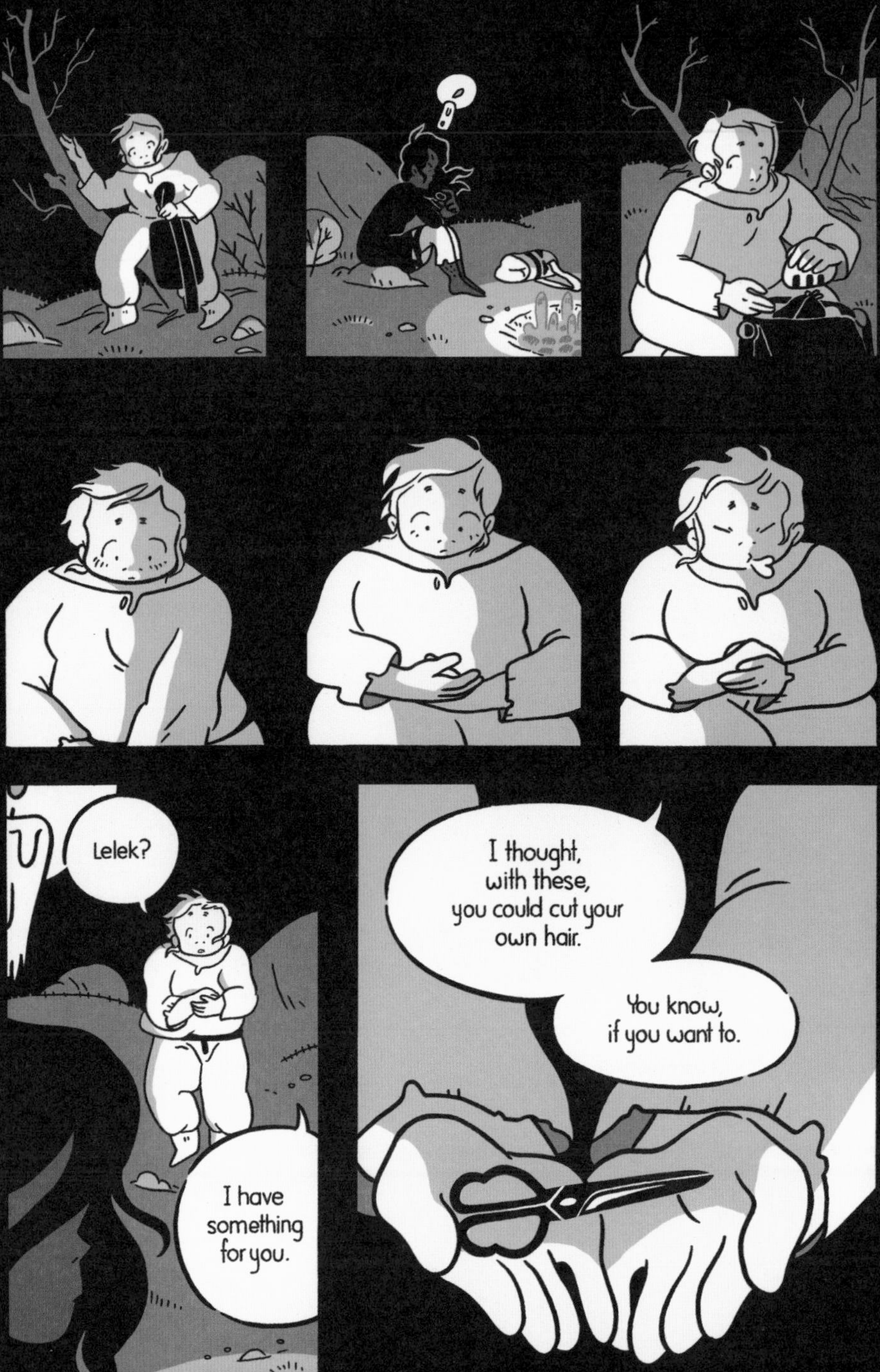
Lelek?
I have something for you.
I thought, with these, you could cut your own hair.
You know, if you want to.

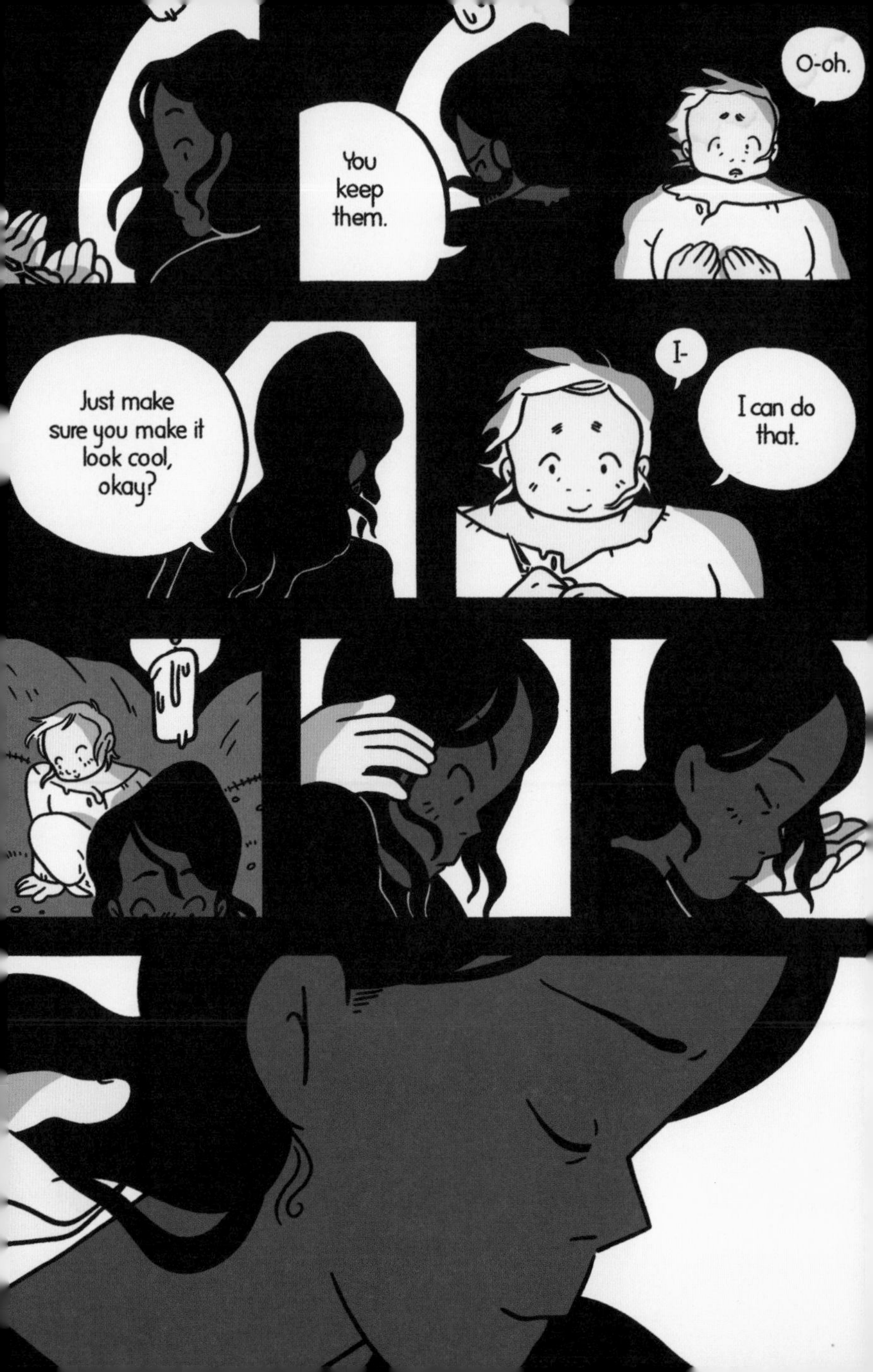
You keep them.
O-oh.
Just make sure you make it look cool, okay?
I-
I can do that.

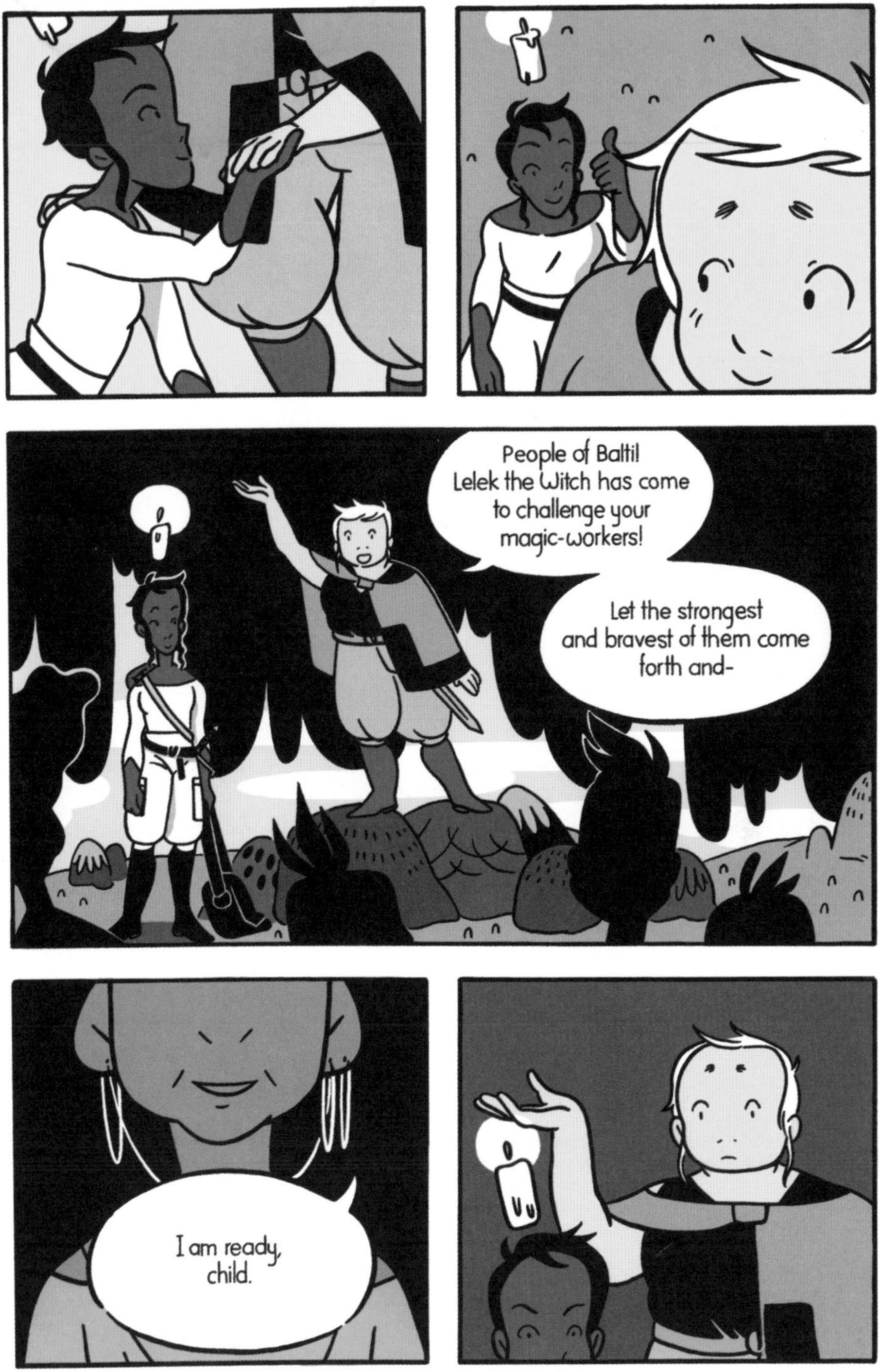
People of Baltil! Lelek the Witch has come to challenge your magic-workers!
Let the strongest and bravest of them come forth and-
I am ready, child.

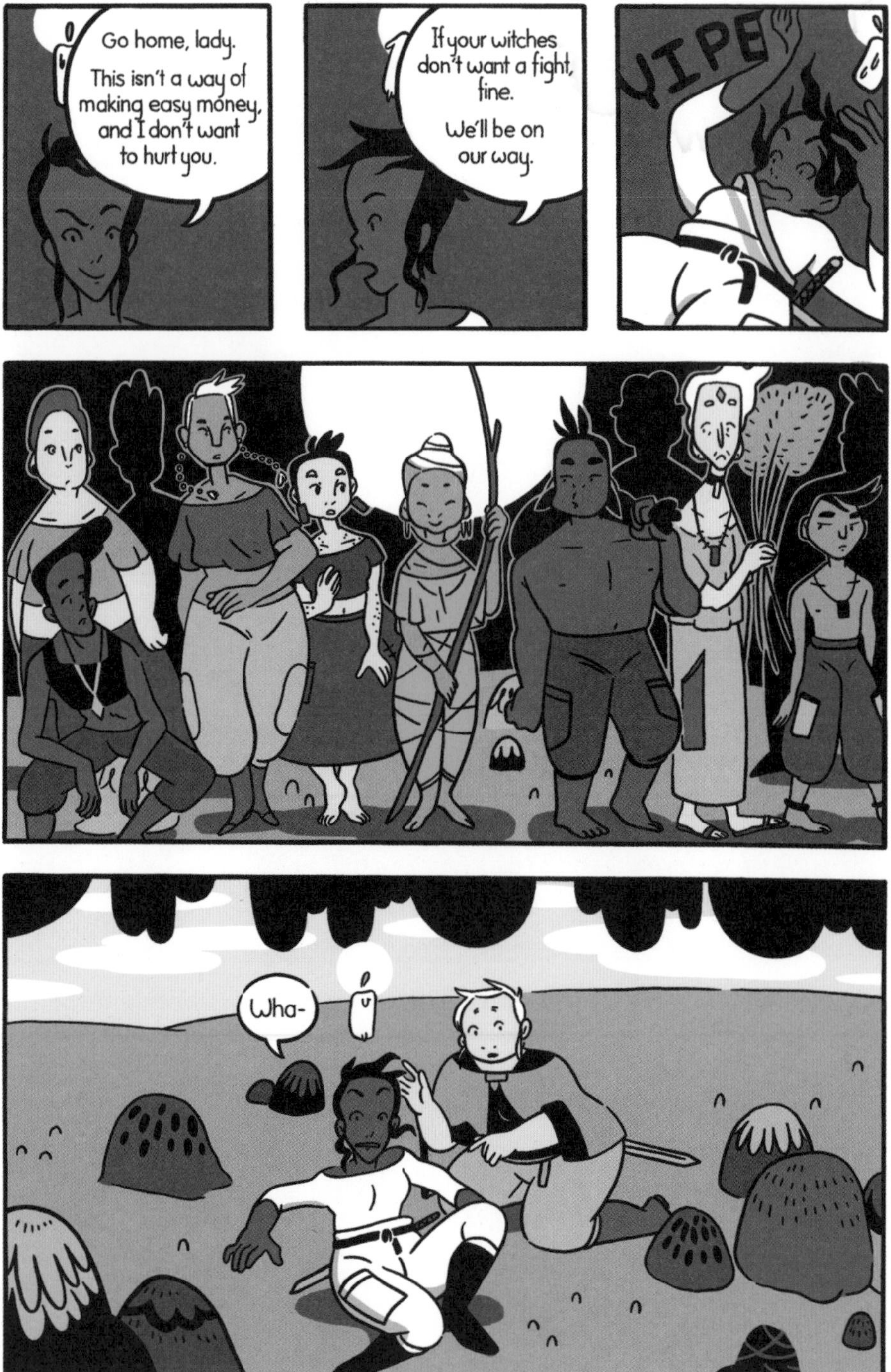
Go home, lady.
This isn't a way of making easy money, and I don't want to hurt you.
If your witches don't want a fight, fine.
We'll be on our way.
YIPE
Wha-

Part 4

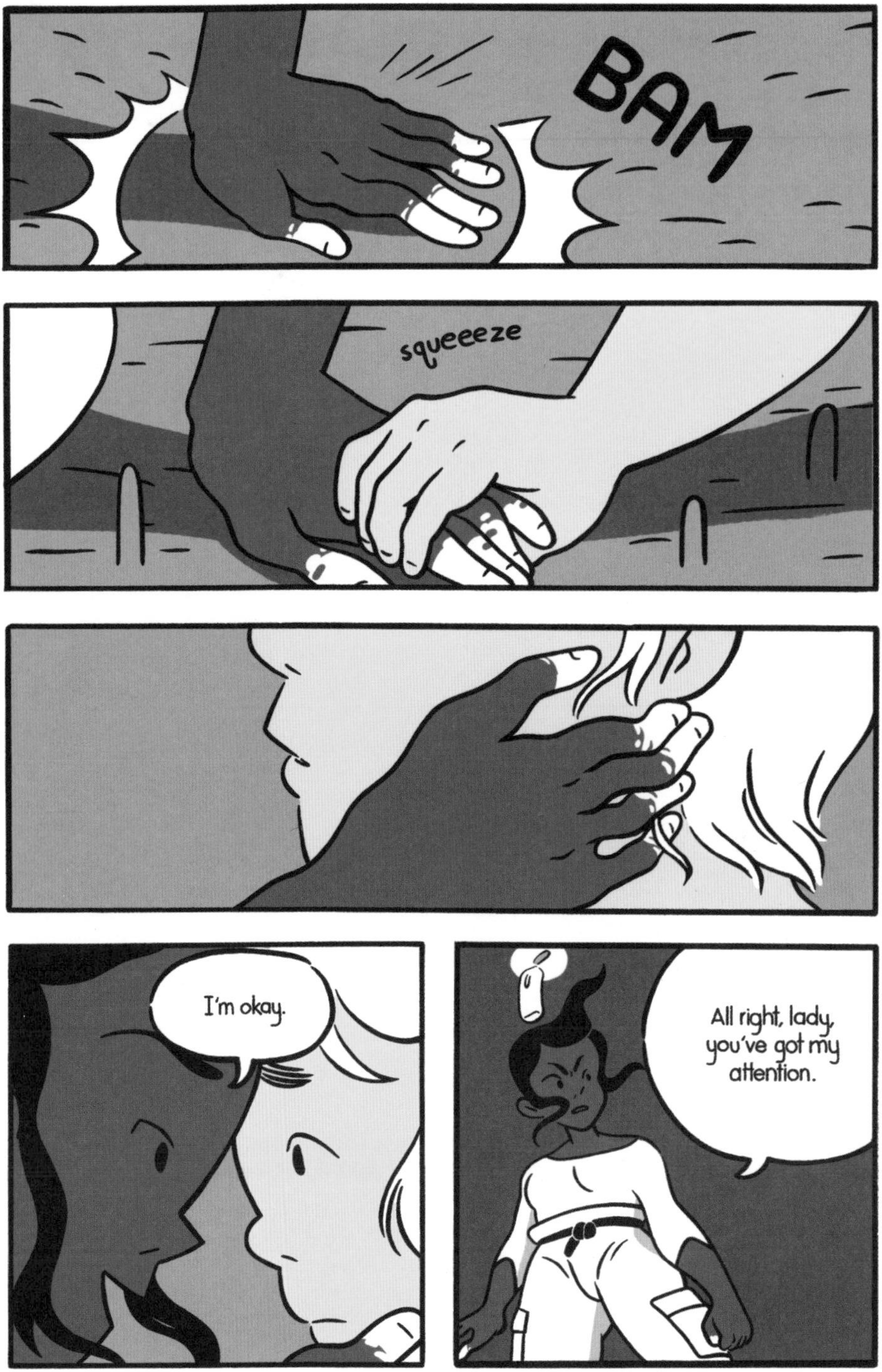
BAM
squeeeze
I'm okay.
All right, lady, you've got my attention.

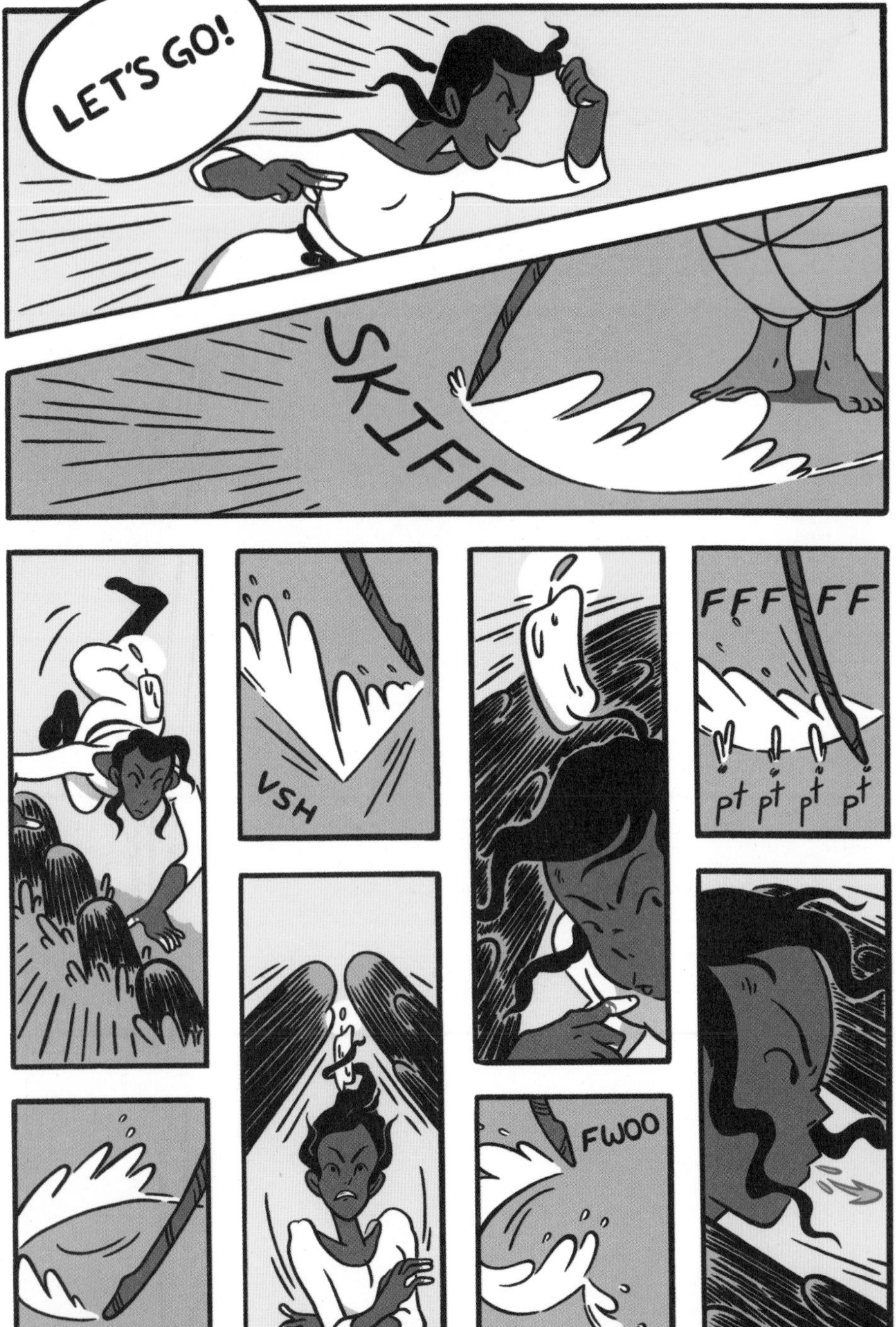
LET'S GO!
SKIFF
VSH
FFF FF
pt pt pt pt
FSHHH
FWOO

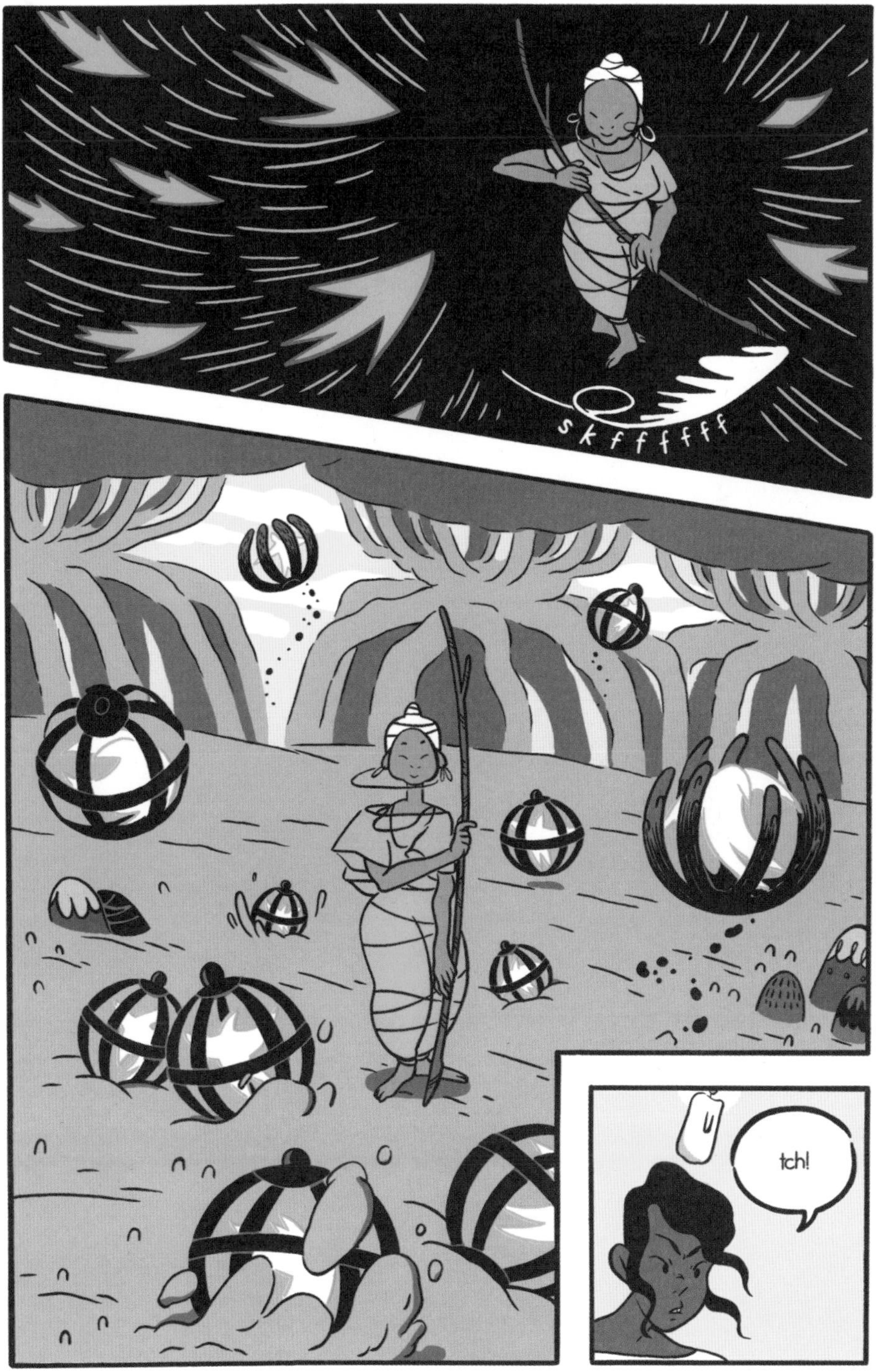
skffffff
tch!

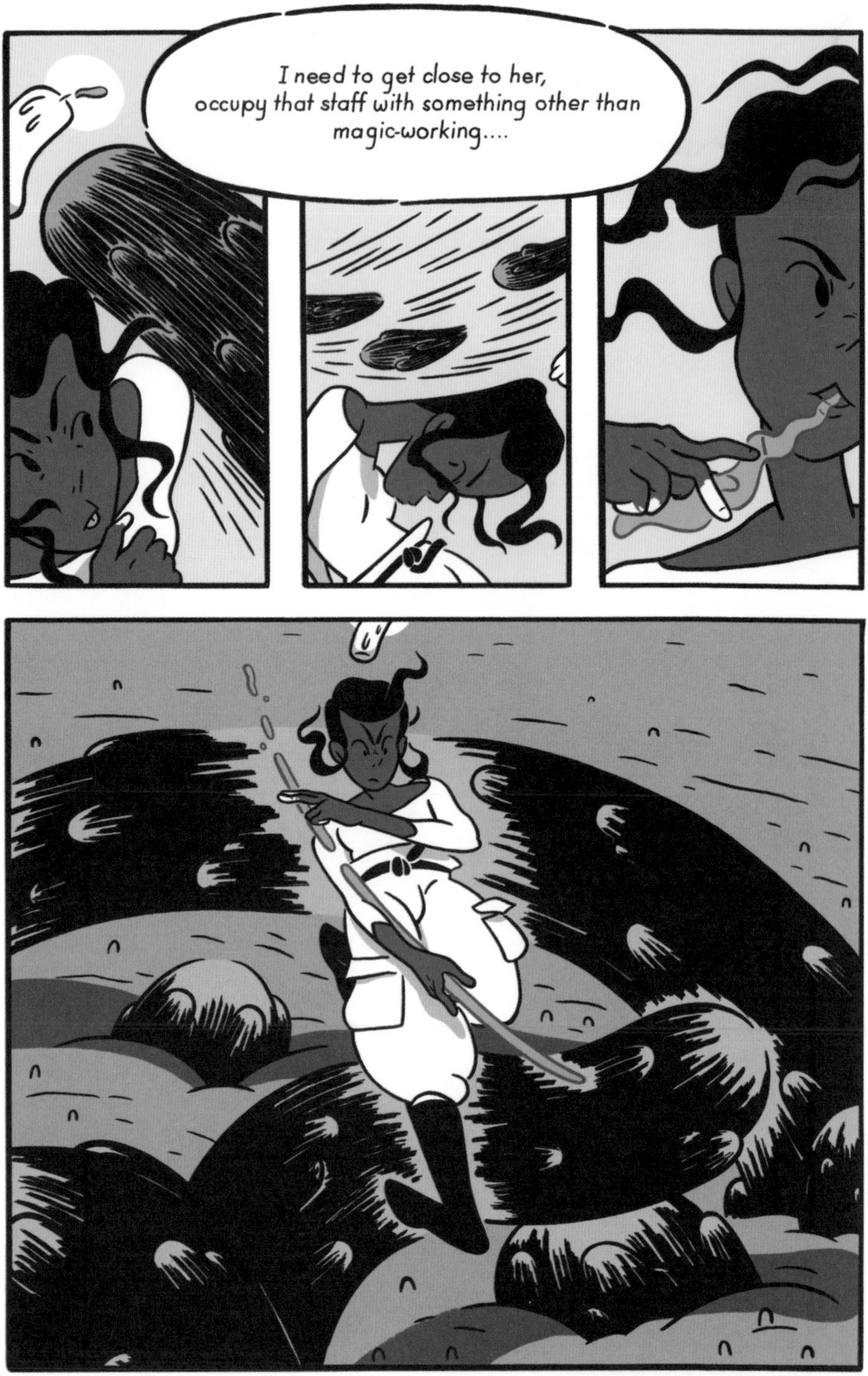
I need to get close to her, occupy that staff with something other than magic-working....

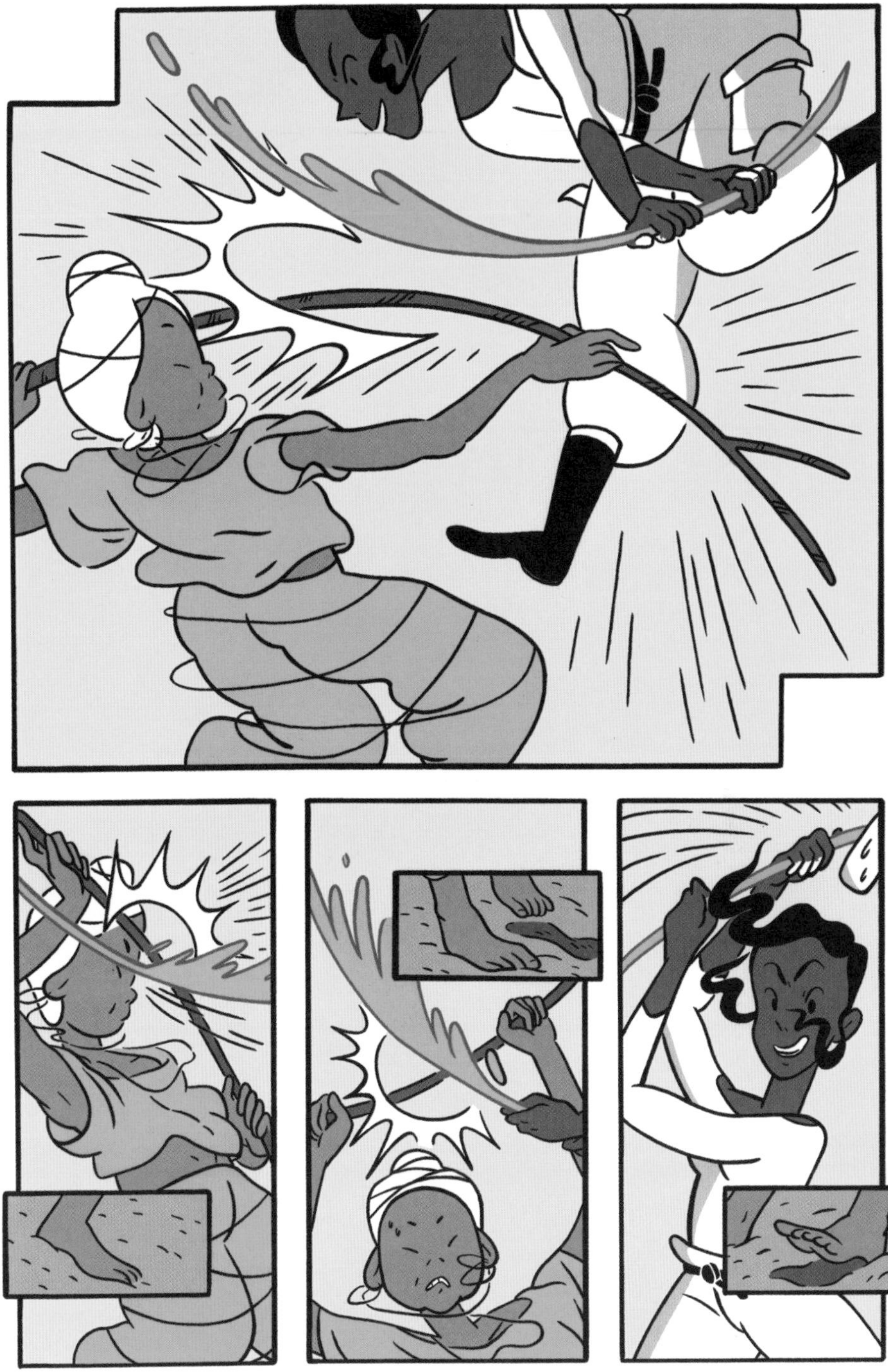

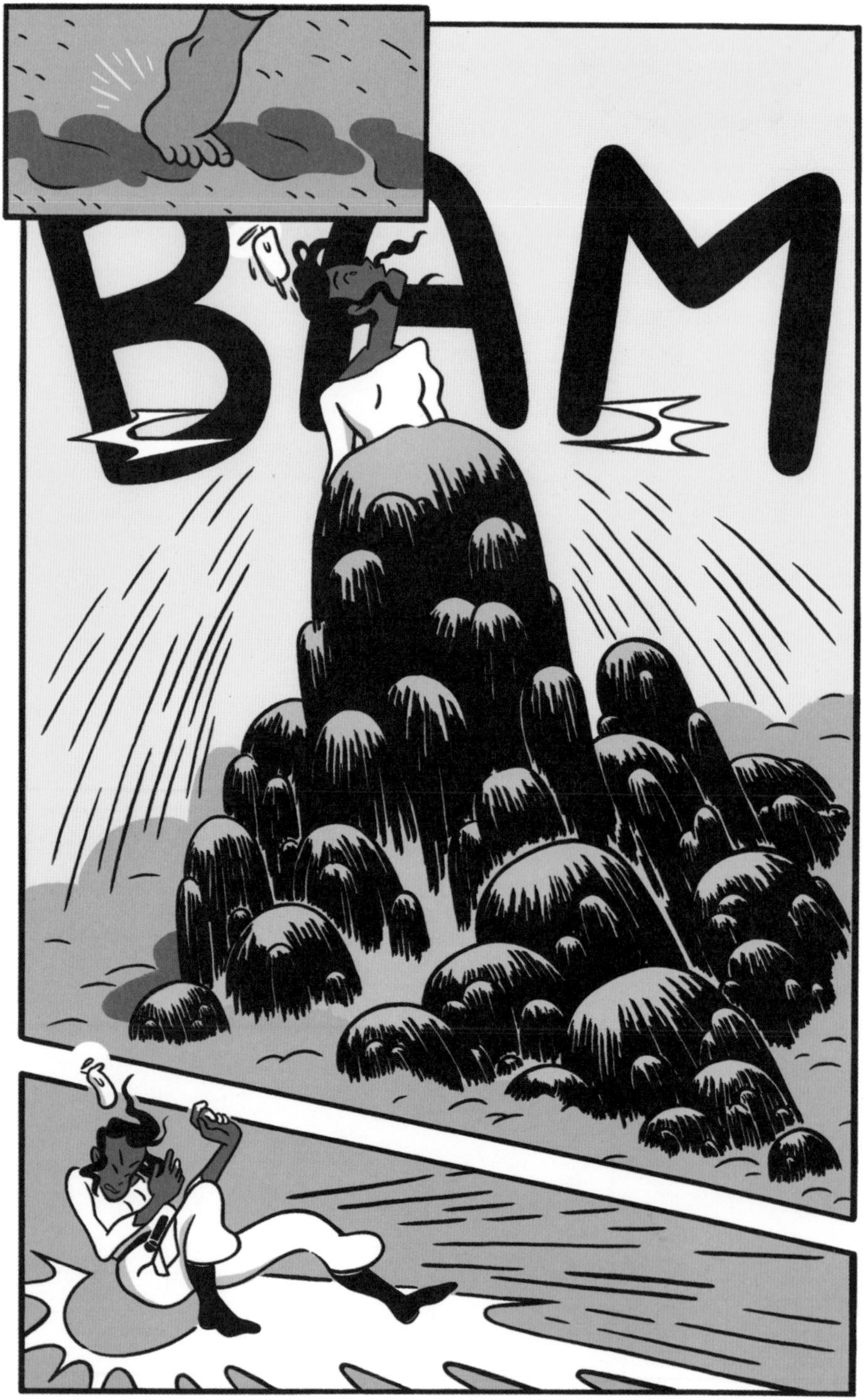
BAM

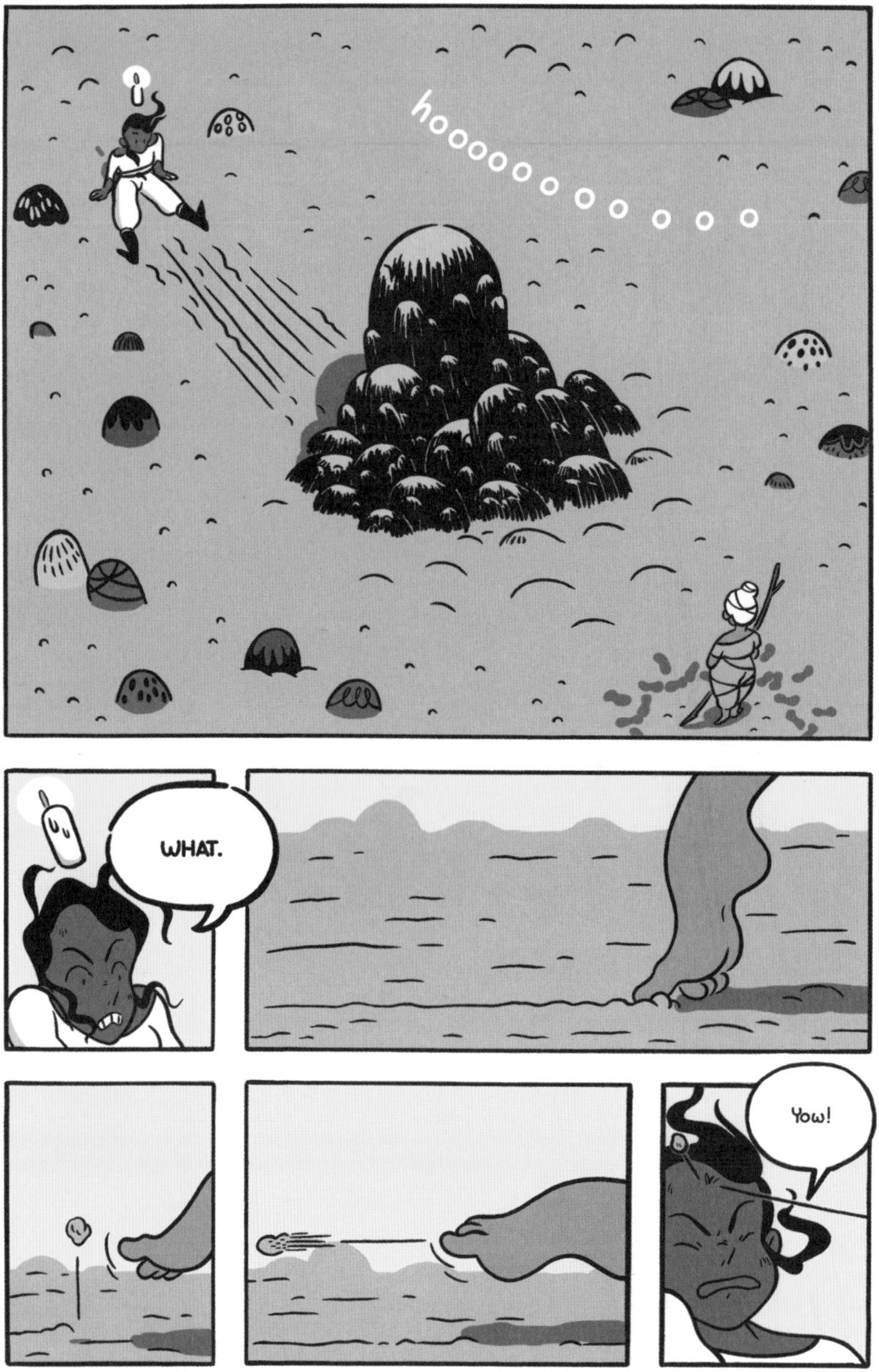
hooooooooooo
WHAT.
Yow!

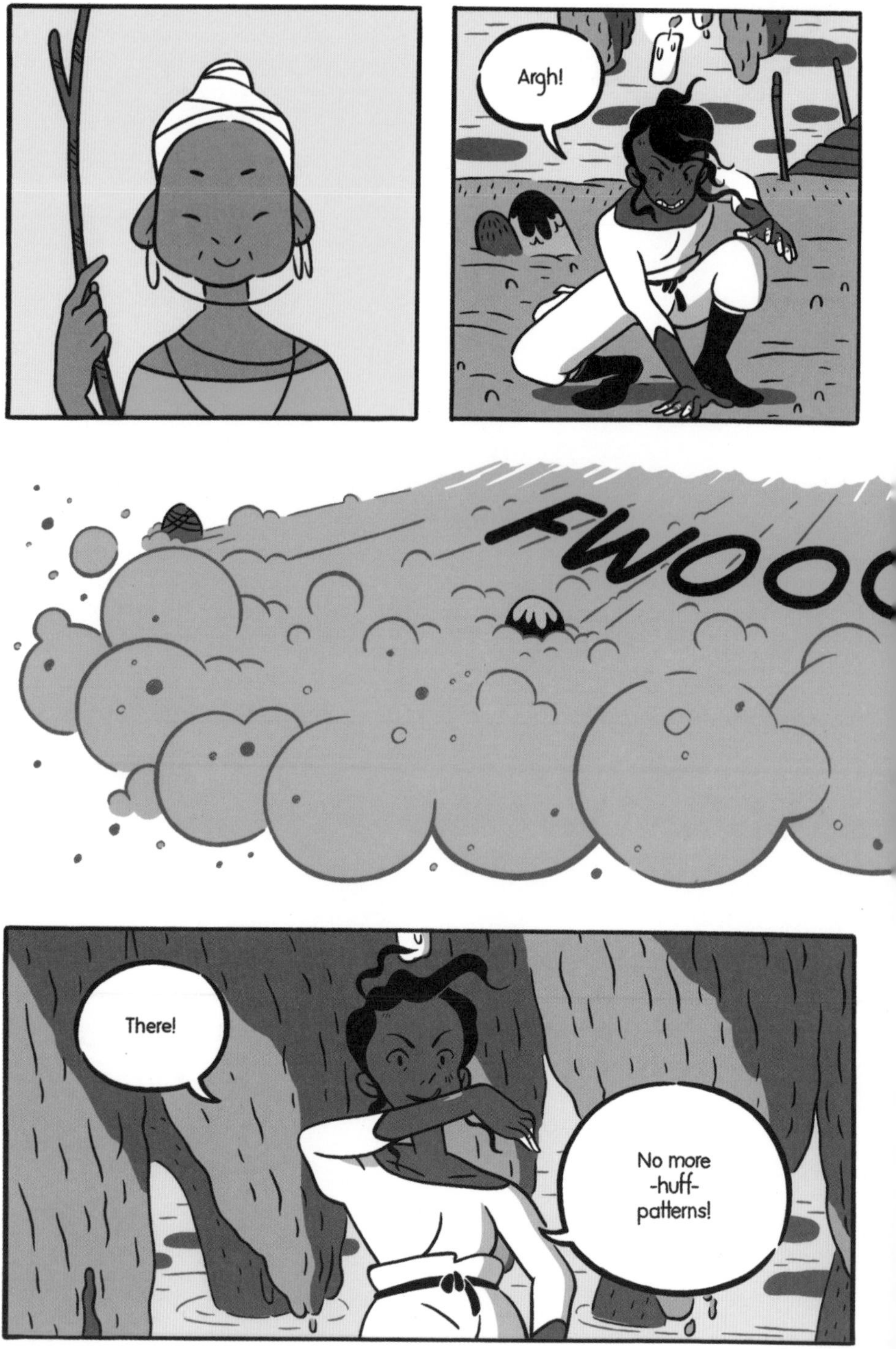
Argh!
FWOOO
There!
No more -huff- patterns!

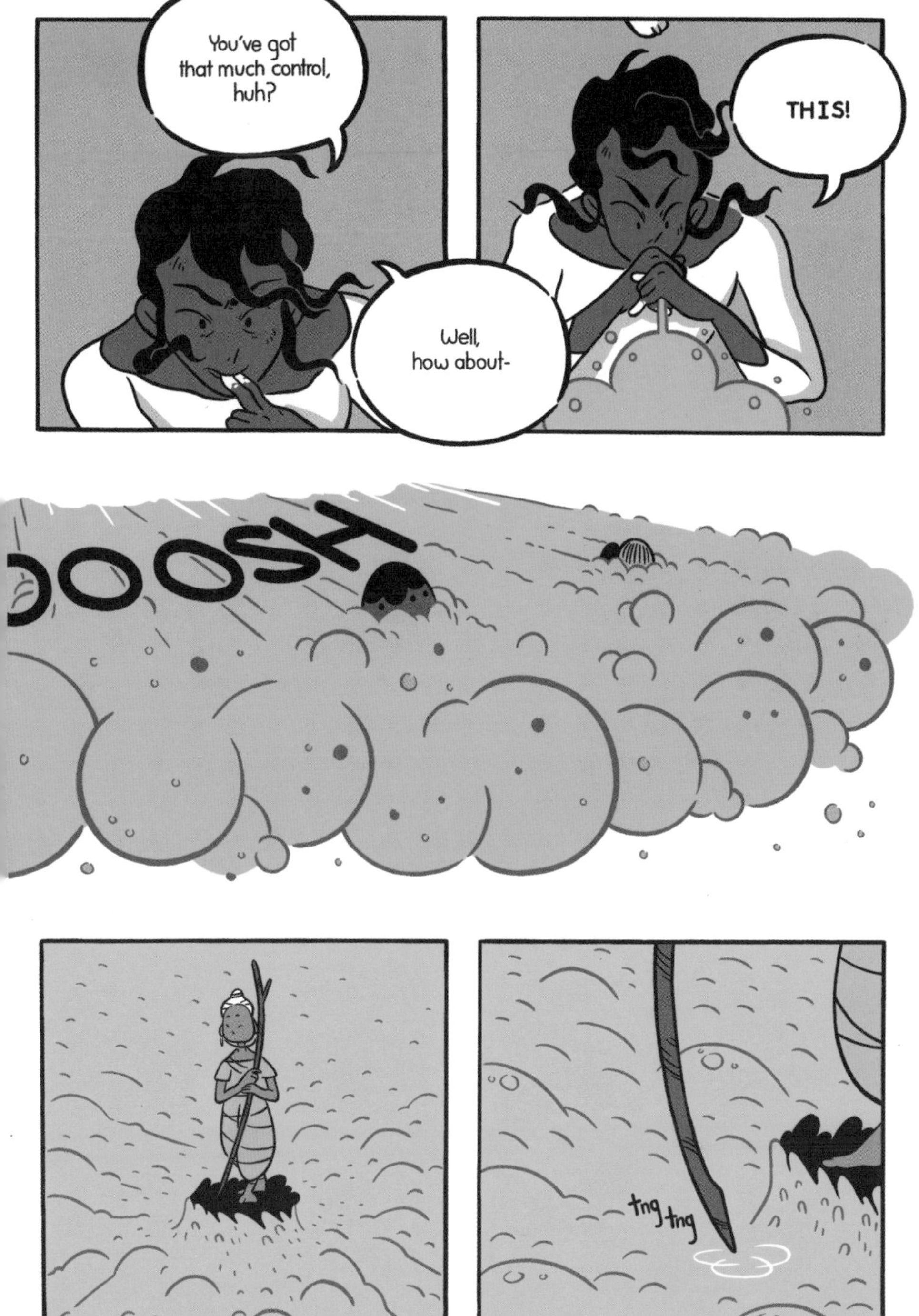
You've got that much control, huh?
Well, how about-
THIS!
OOSH
tng tng

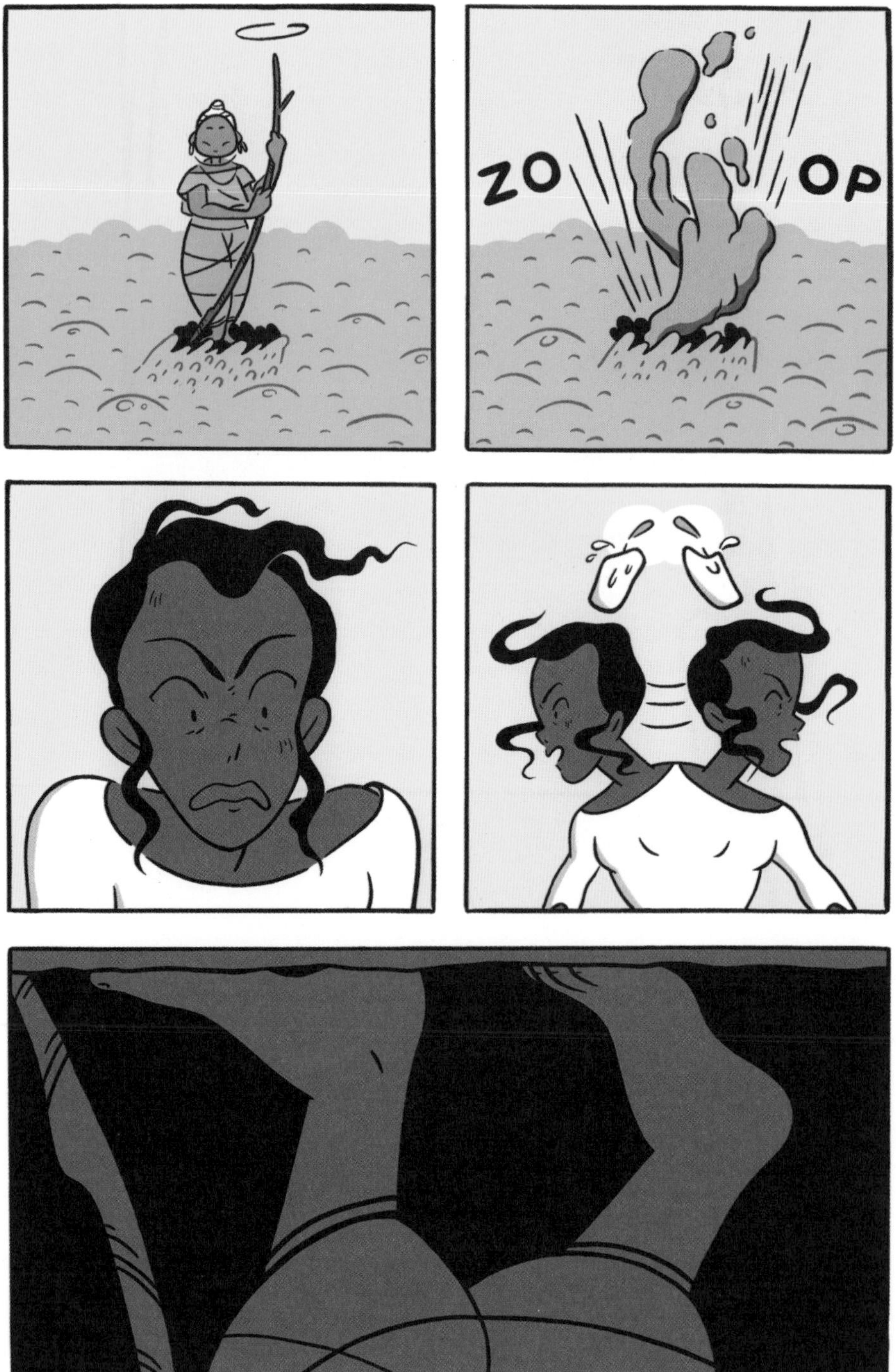
ZO
OP

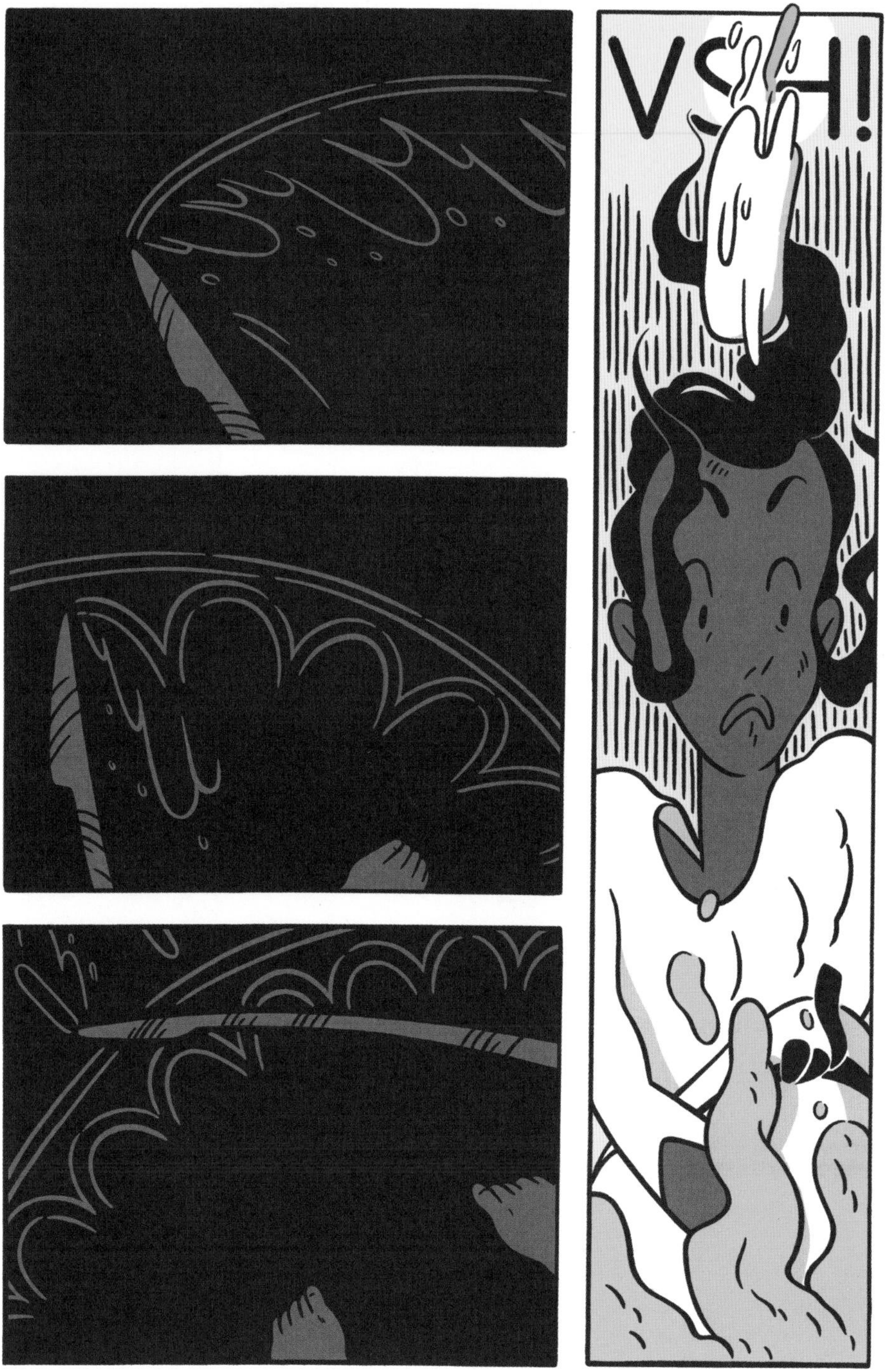
VSH!

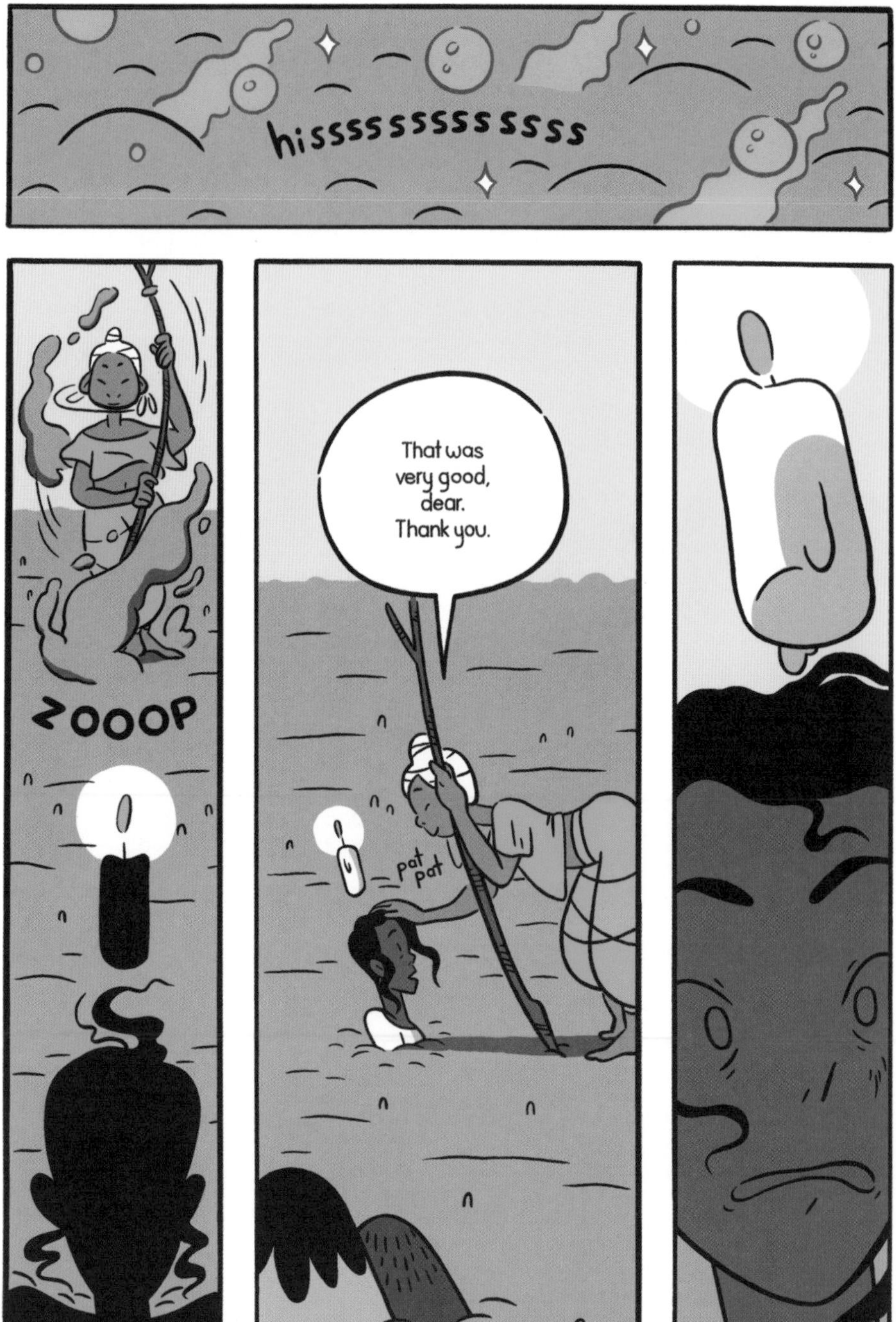
hissssssssssssss
ZOOOP
That was very good, dear. Thank you.
pat pat

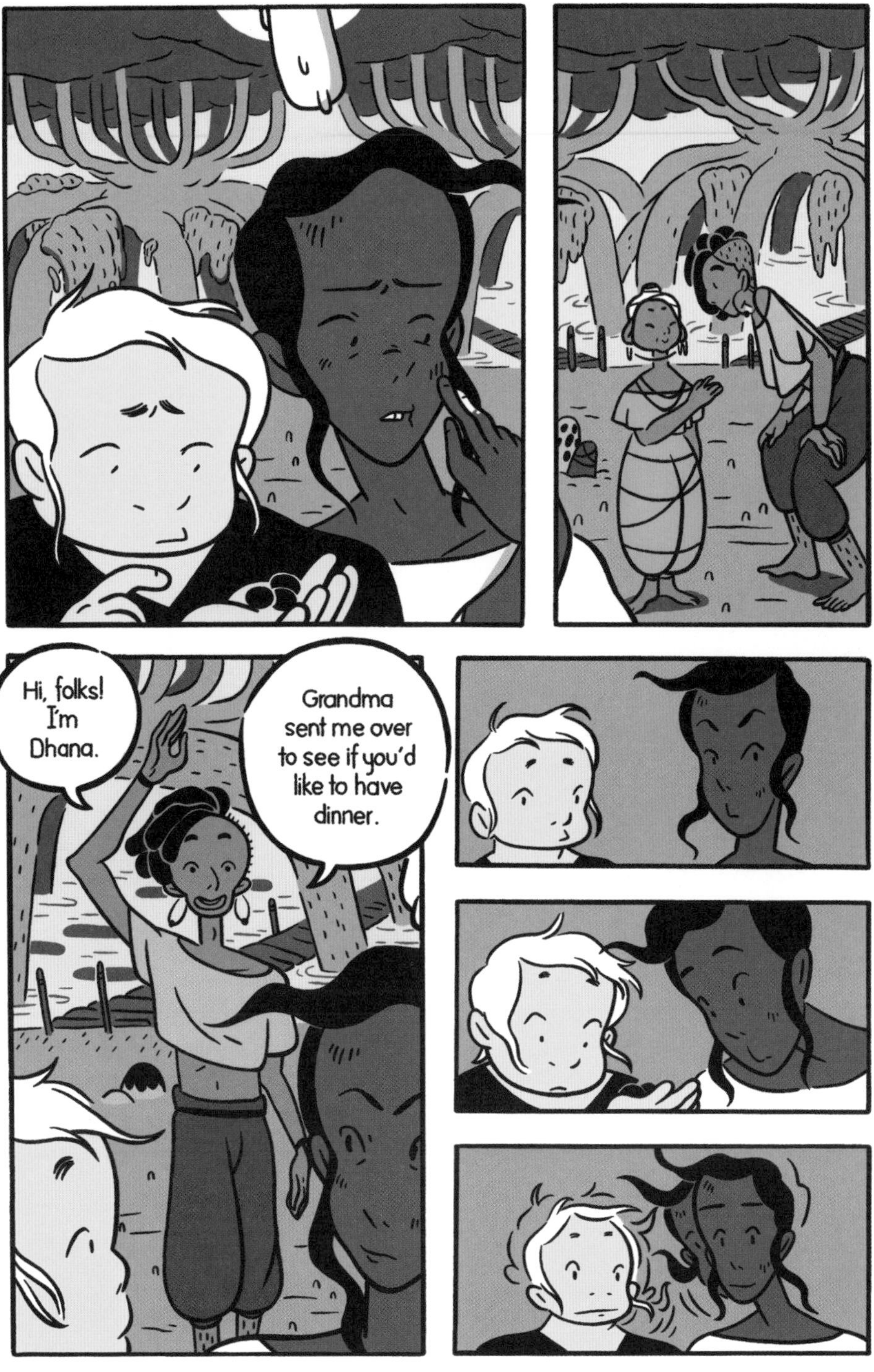

Hi, folks! I'm Dhana.
Grandma sent me over to see if you'd like to have dinner.

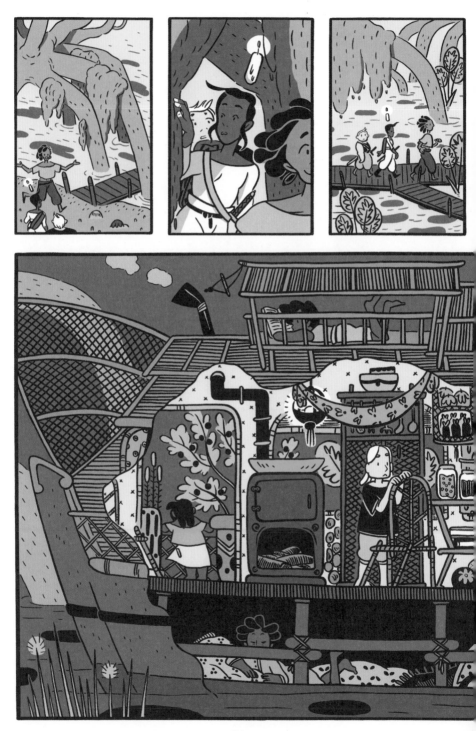

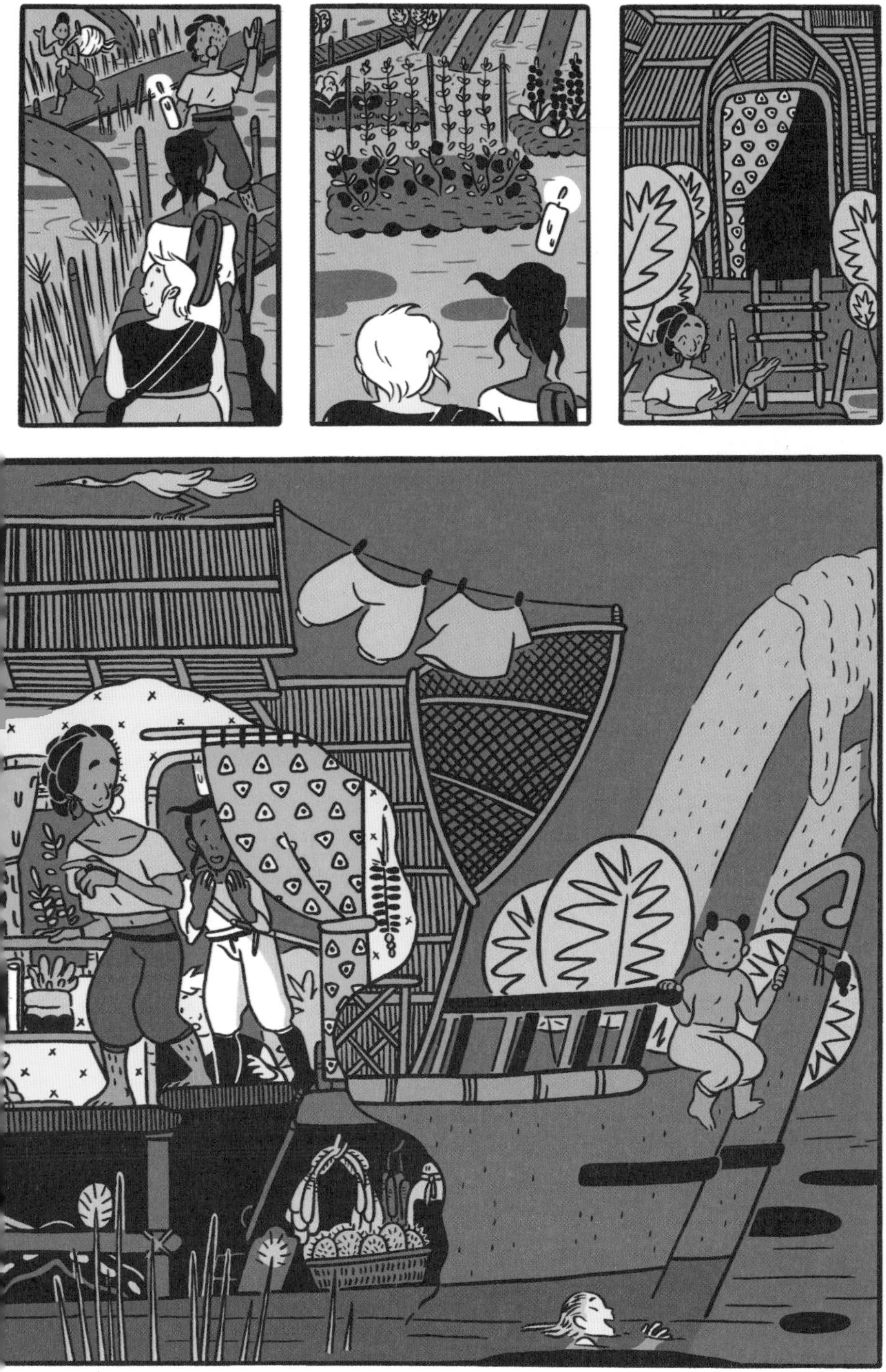

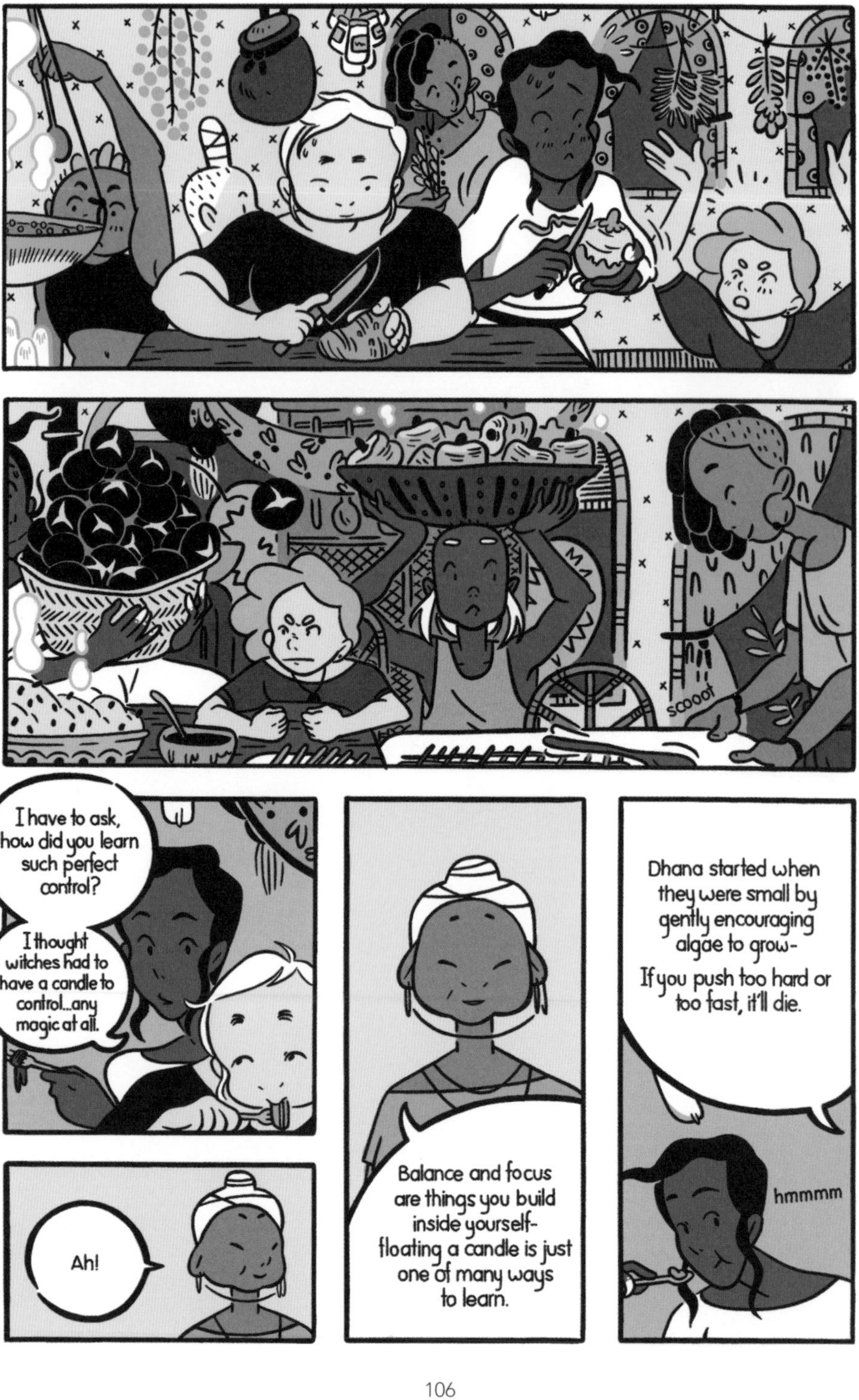
scooot
I have to ask, how did you learn such perfect control?
I thought witches had to have a candle to control...any magic at all.
Ah!
Balance and focus are things you build inside yourself- floating a candle is just one of many ways to learn.
Dhana started when they were small by gently encouraging algae to grow-
If you push too hard or too fast, it'll die.
hmmmm

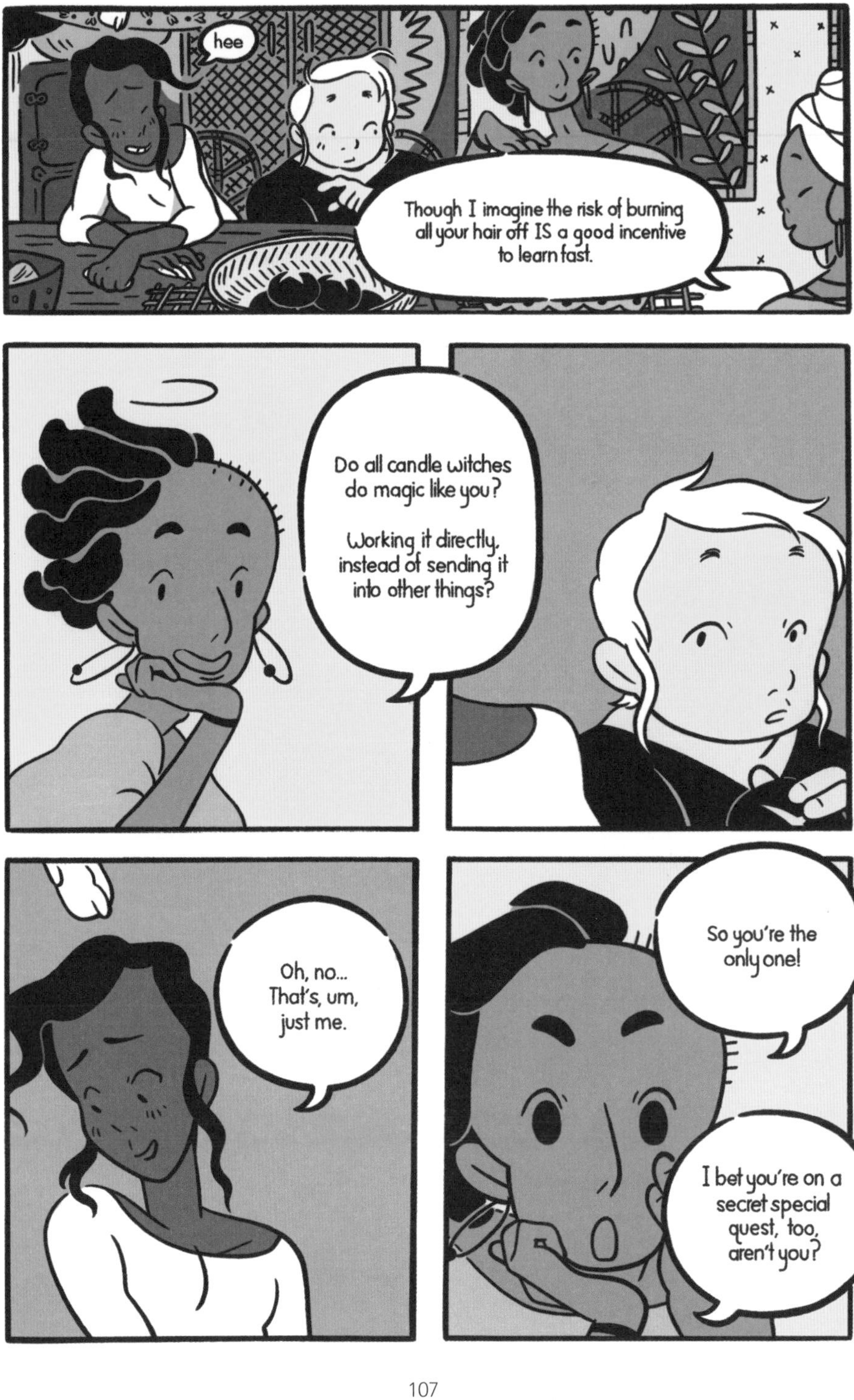
hee
Though I imagine the risk of burning all your hair off IS a good incentive to learn fast.
Do all candle witches do magic like you?
Working it directly, instead of sending it into other things?
Oh, no... That's, um, just me.
So you're the only one!
I bet you're on a secret special quest, too, aren't you?

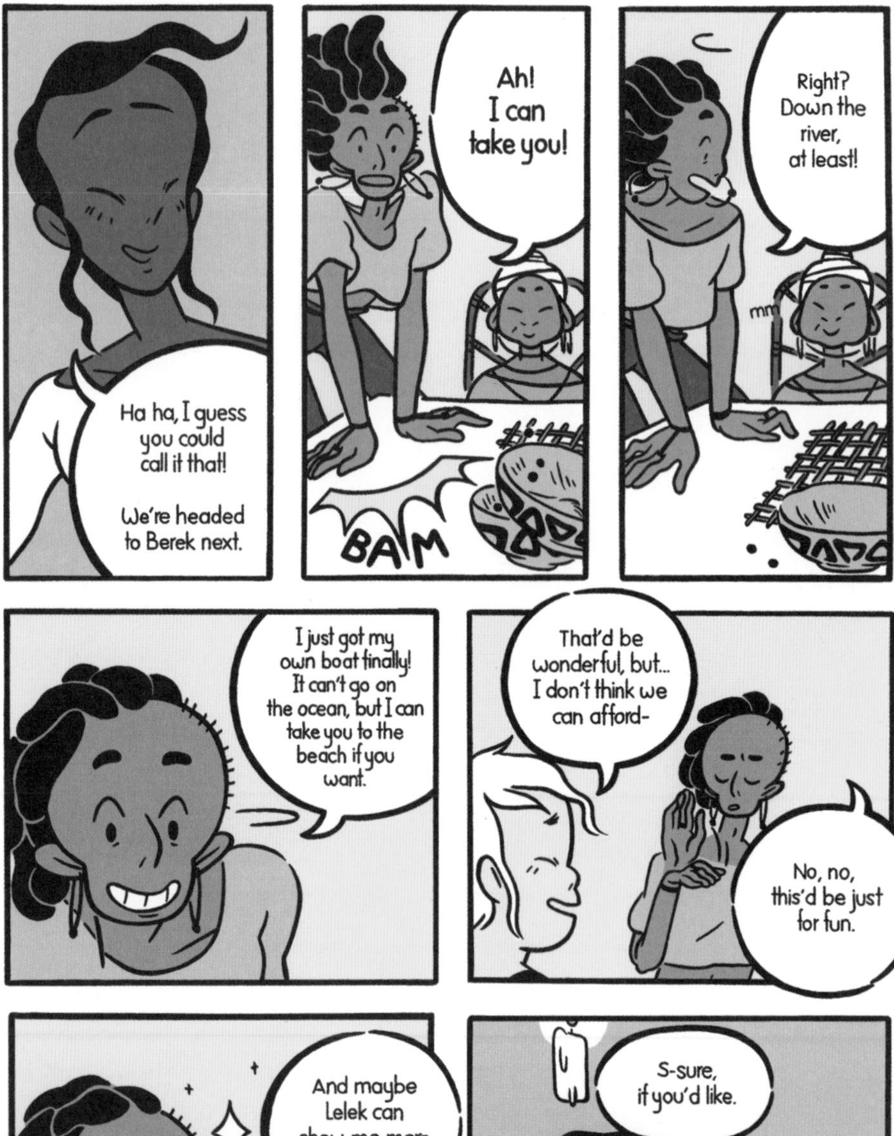
Ha ha, I guess you could call it that!
We're headed to Berek next.
Ah! I can take you!
BAM
Right? Down the river, at least!
mm
I just got my own boat finally! It can't go on the ocean, but I can take you to the beach if you want.
That'd be wonderful, but... I don't think we can afford-
No, no, this'd be just for fun.
And maybe Lelek can show me more candle magic.
S-sure, if you'd like.

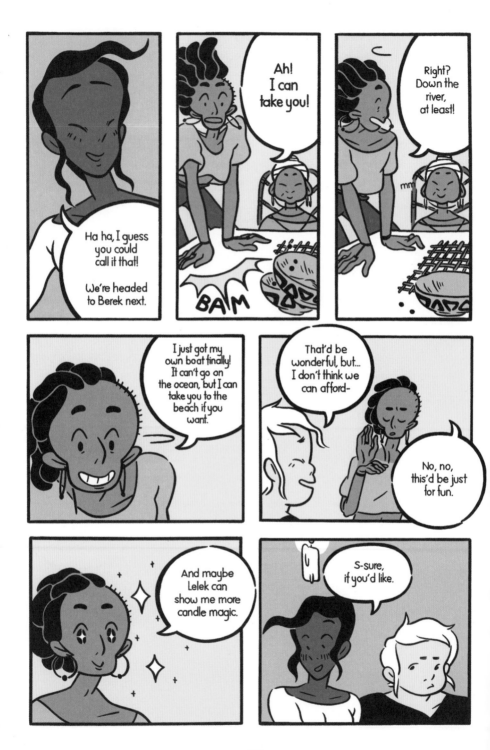

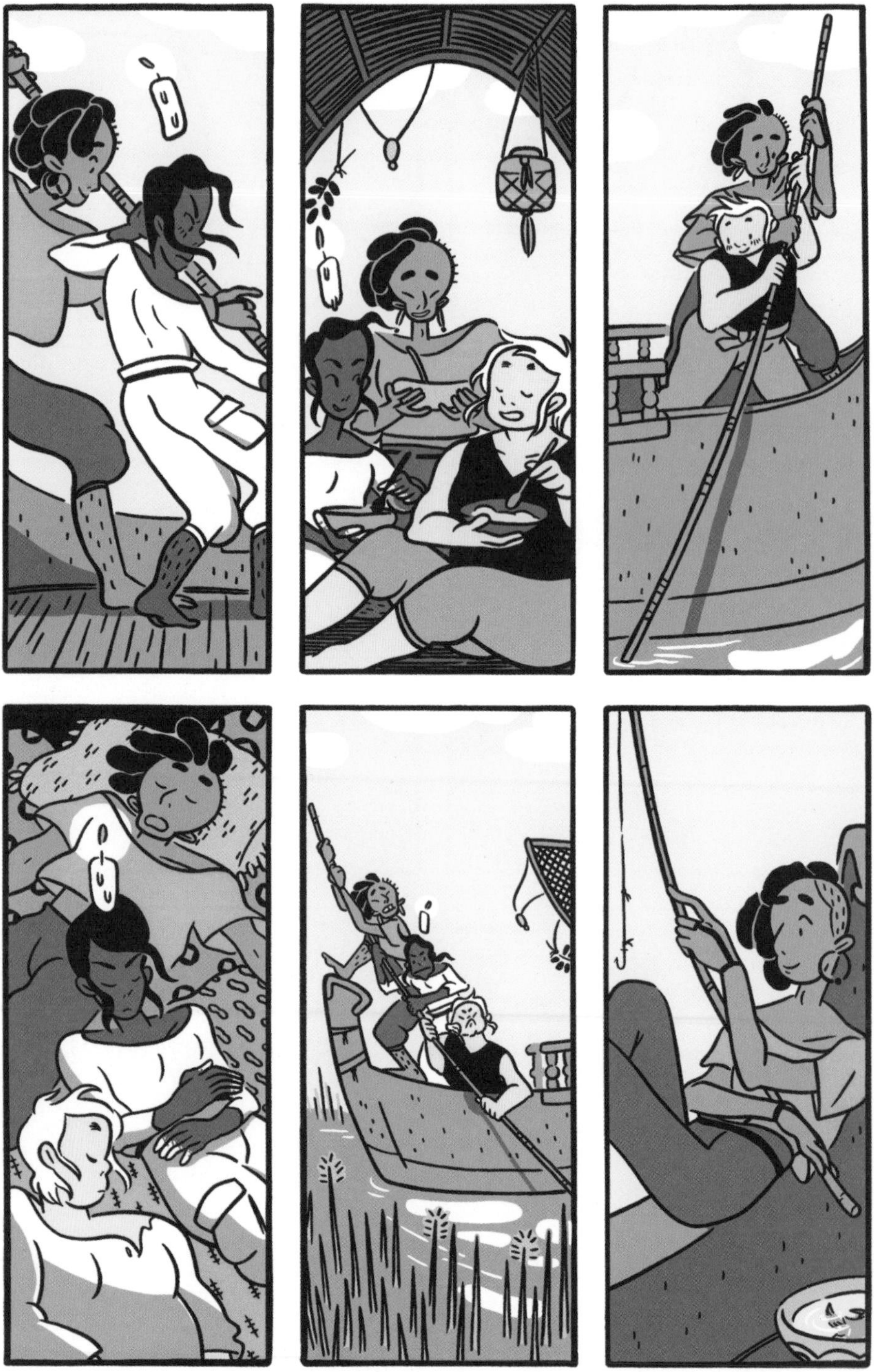

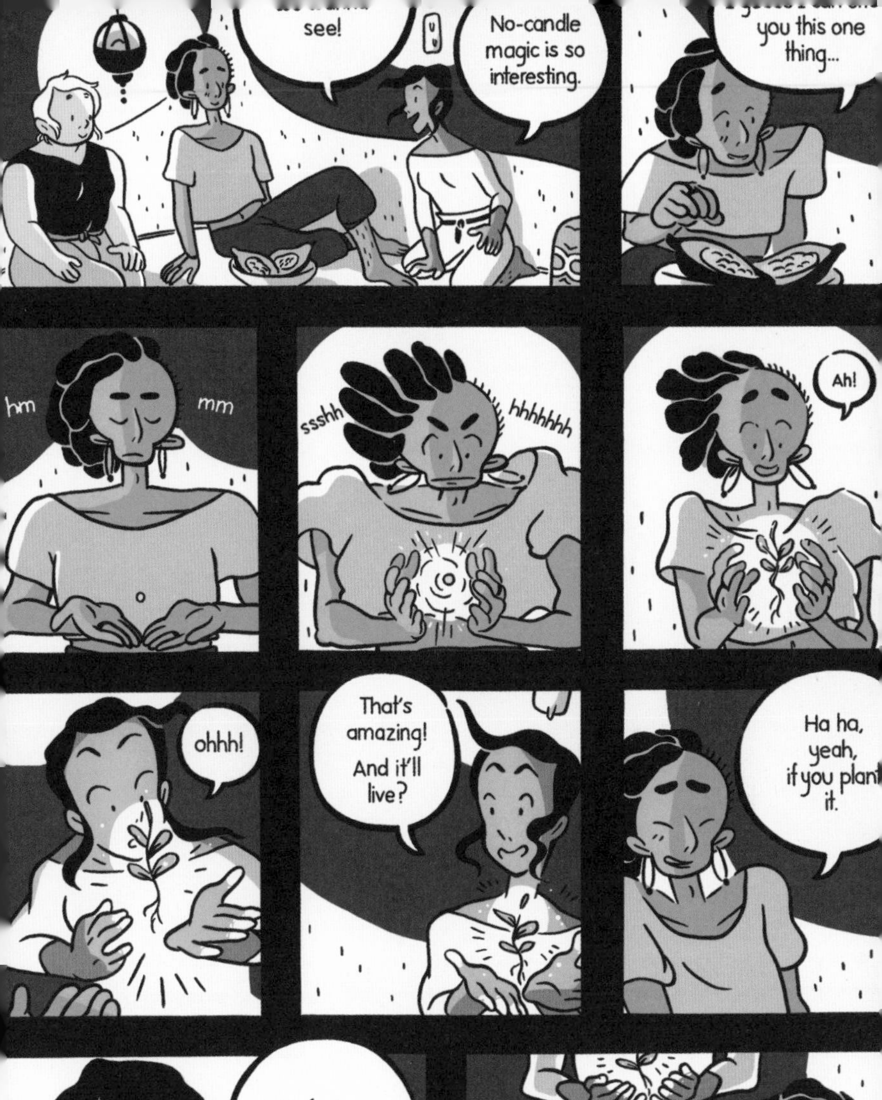
see!
No-candle magic is so interesting.
you this one thing...
hm
mm
ssshh
hhhhhhh
Ah!
ohhh!
That's amazing!
And it'll live?
Ha ha, yeah, if you plant it.
Let's find you a pot, little one.
tp
tp

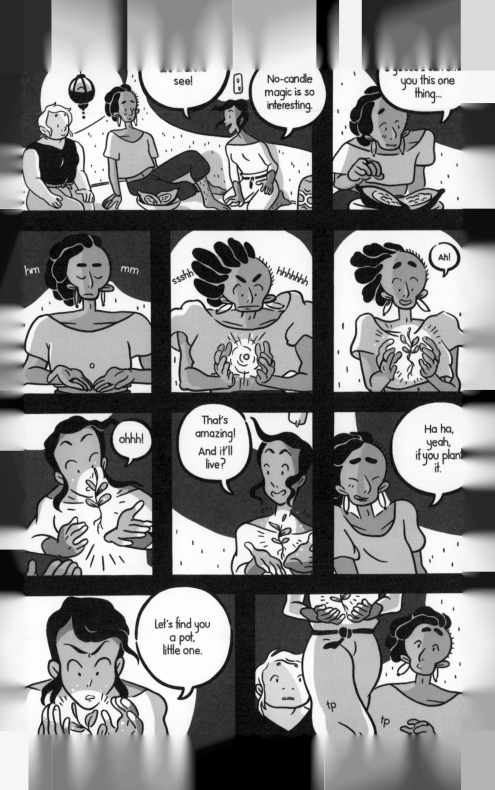

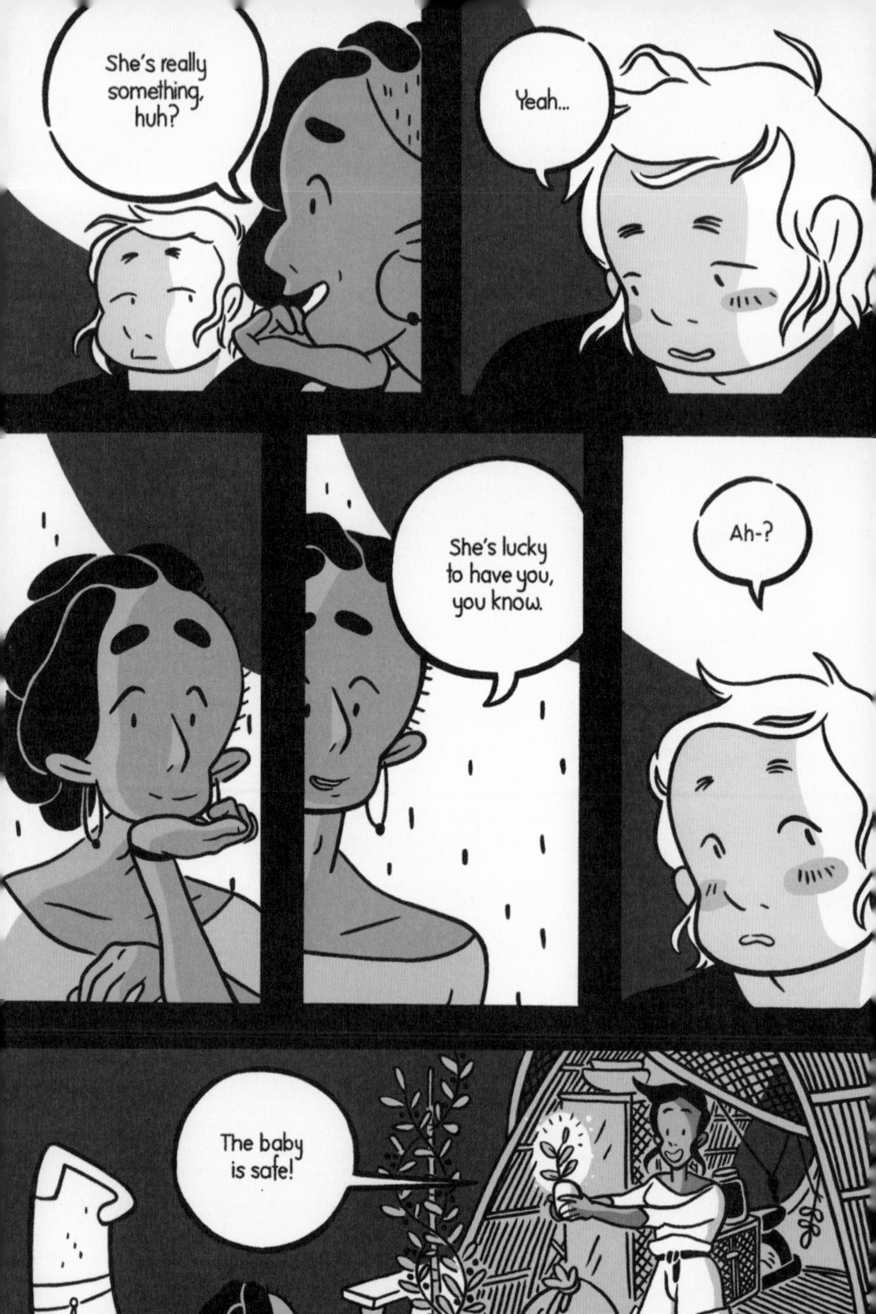

She's really something, huh?
Yeah...
She's lucky to have you, you know.
Ah-?
The baby is safe!

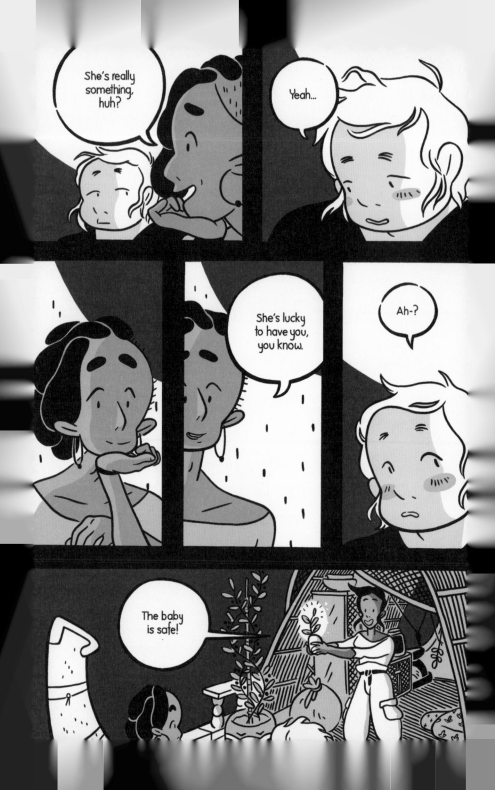

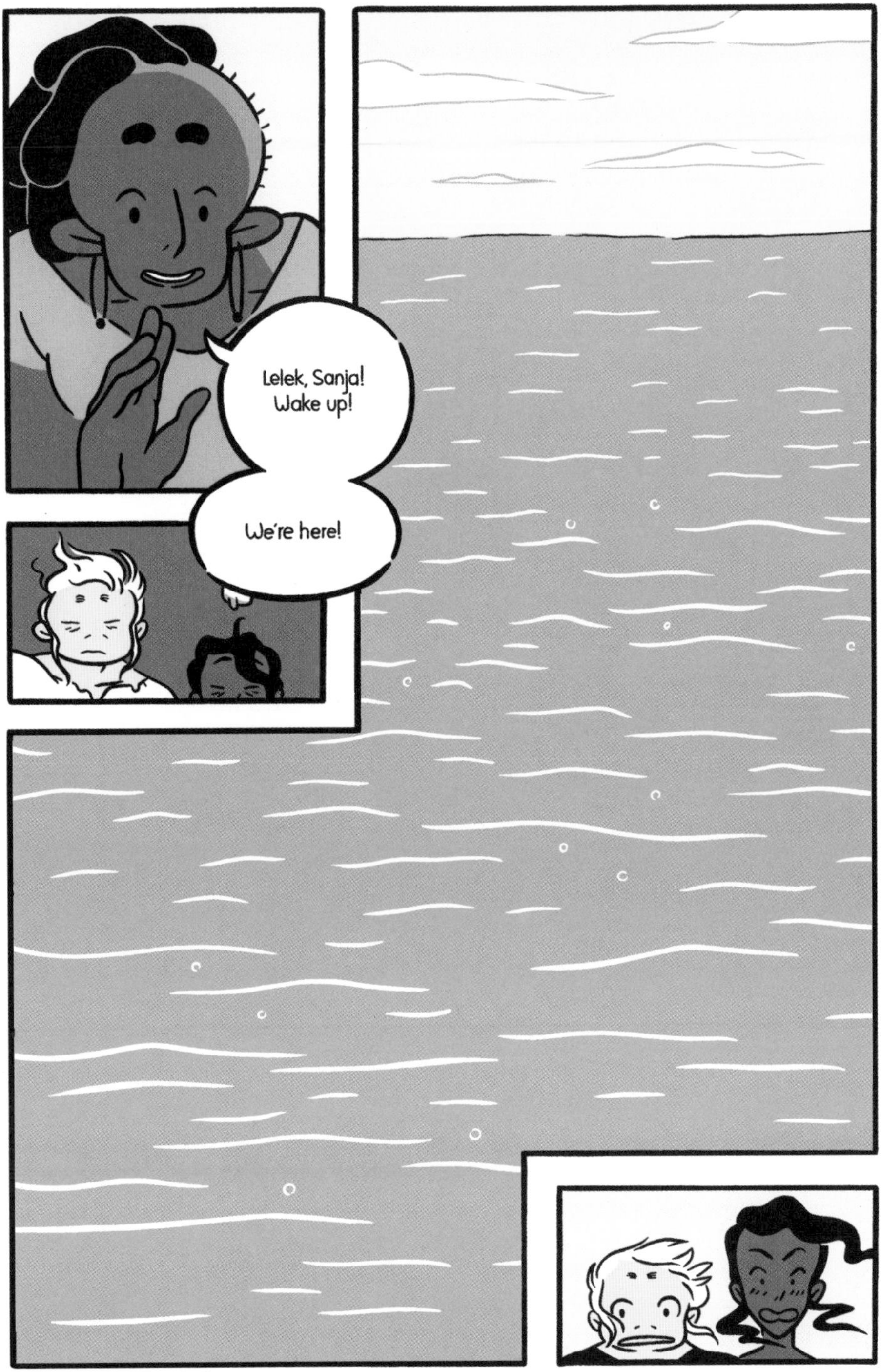
Lelek, Sanja! Wake up!
We're here!

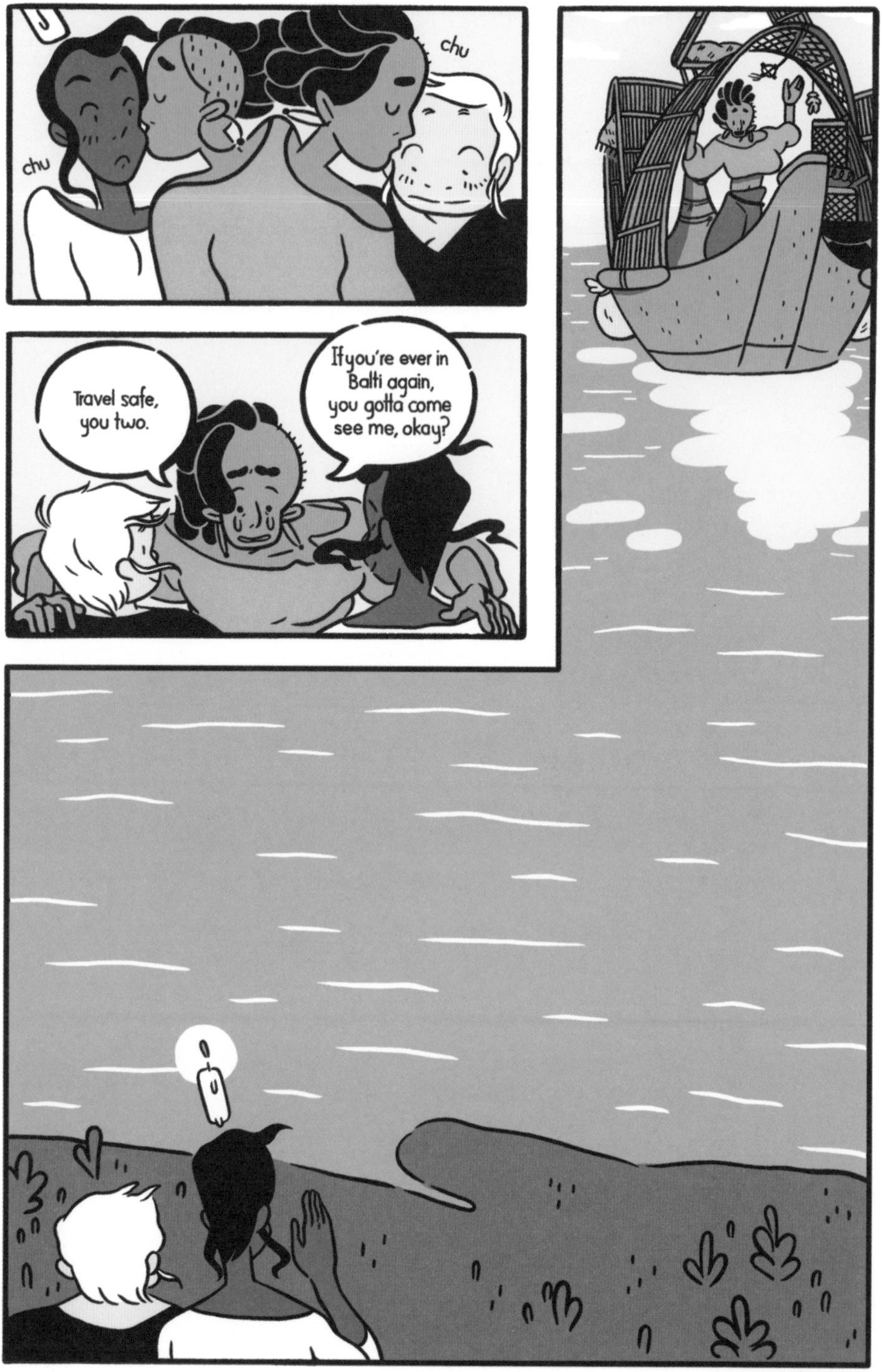
chu
chu
Travel safe, you two.
If you're ever in Balti again, you gotta come see me, okay?

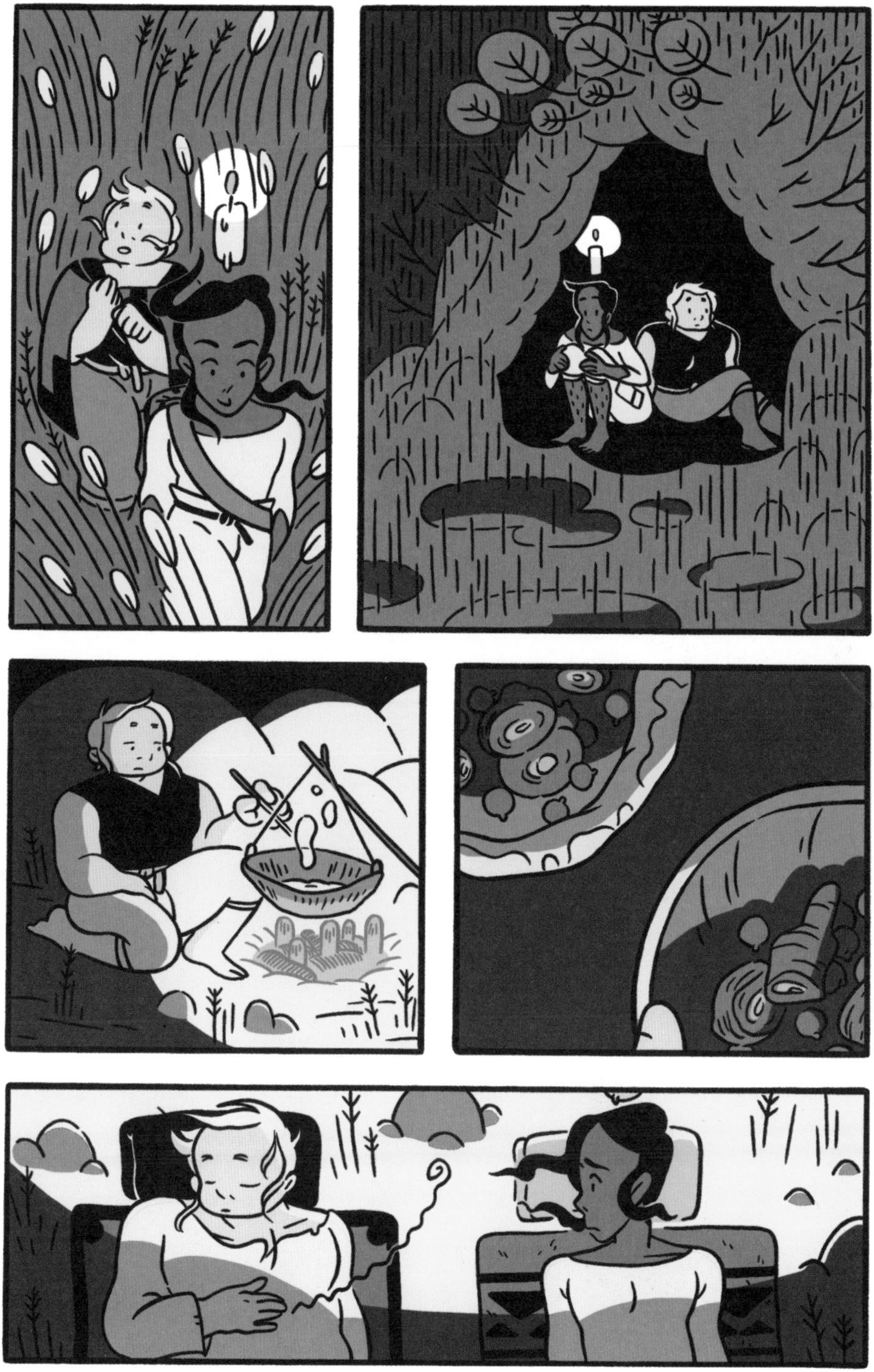

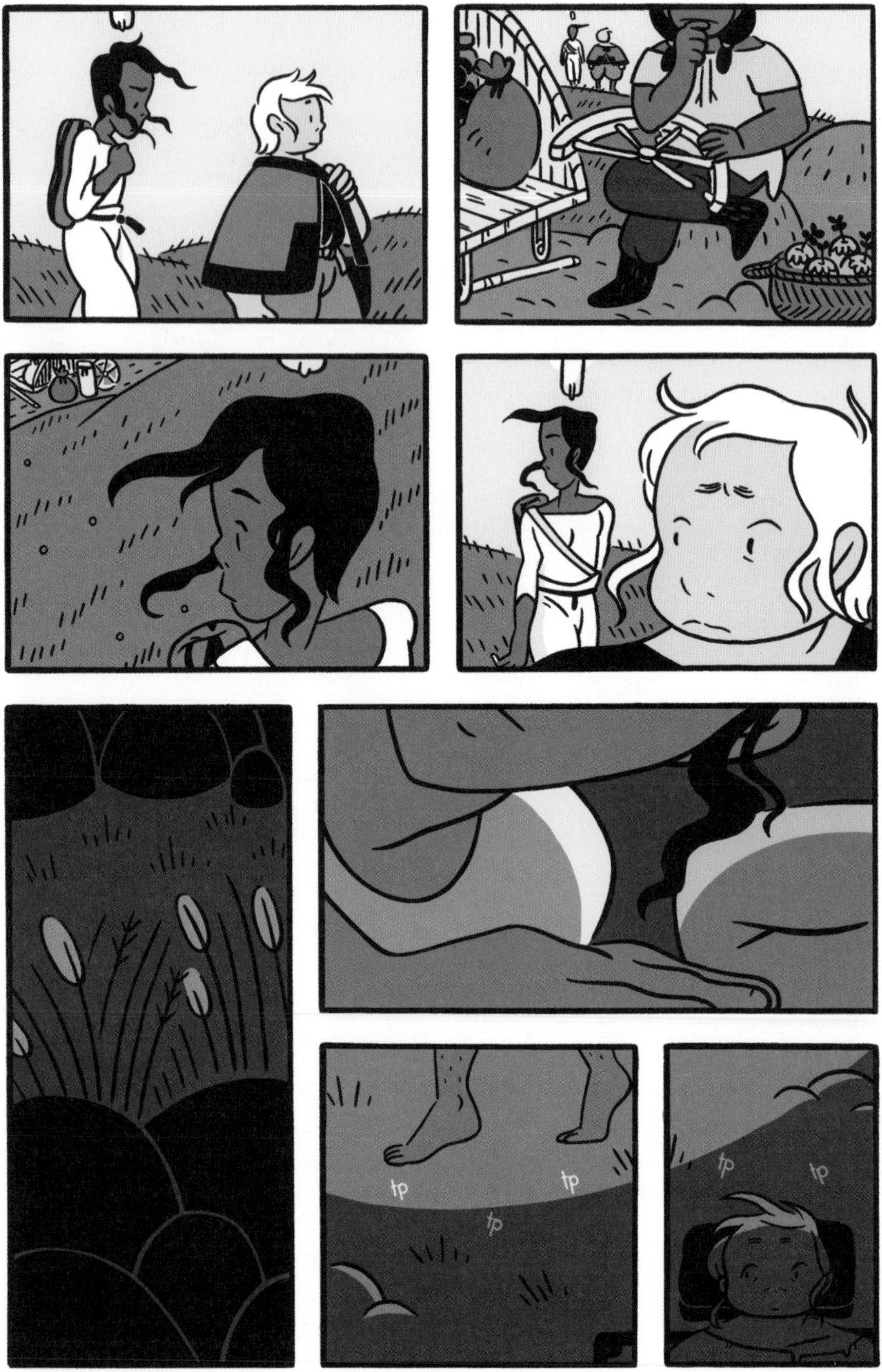
tp
tp
tp
tp
tp

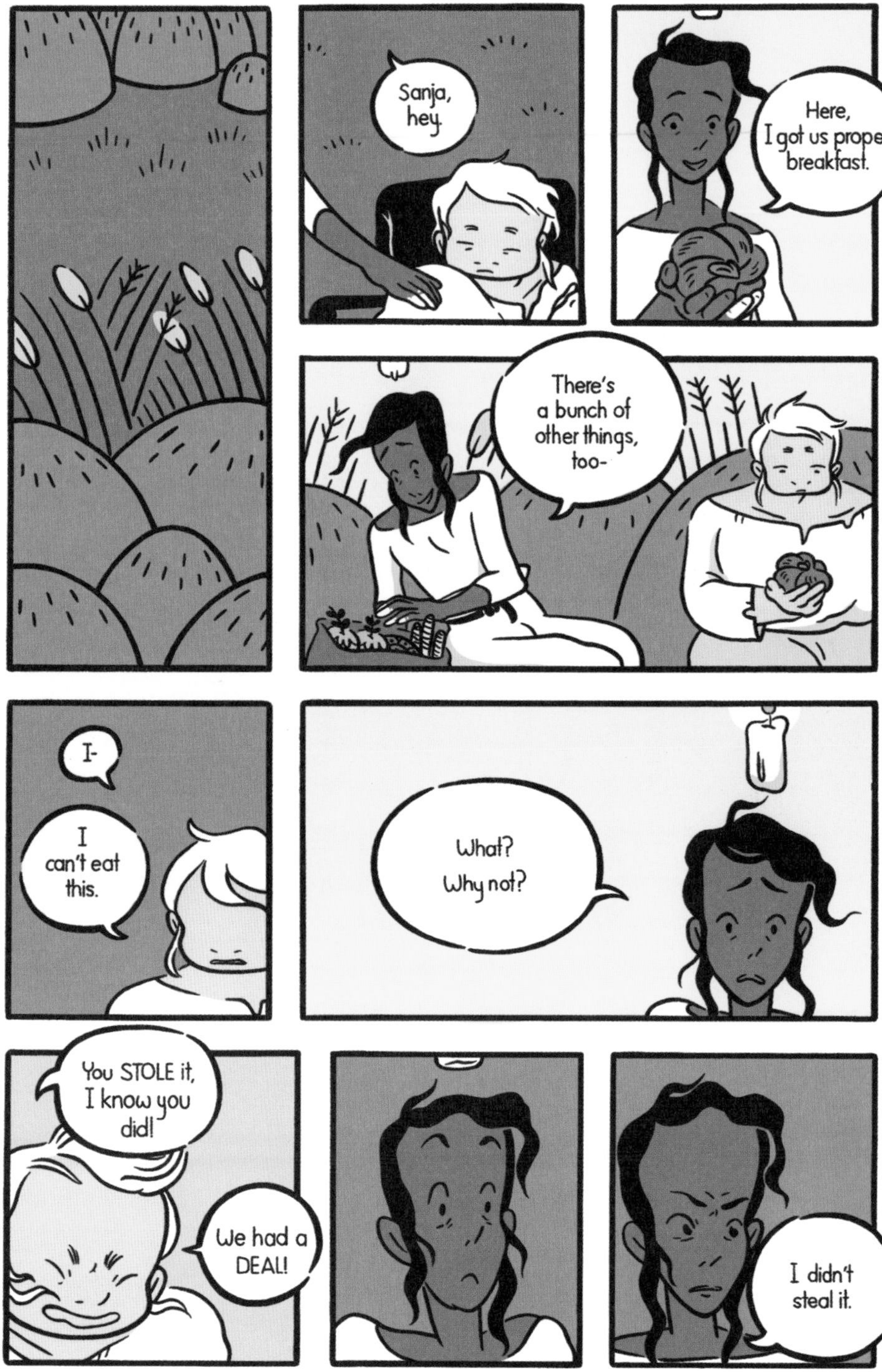
Sanja, hey.
Here, I got us proper breakfast.
There's a bunch of other things, too-
I-
I can't eat this.
What? Why not?
You STOLE it, I know you did!
We had a DEAL!
I didn't steal it.

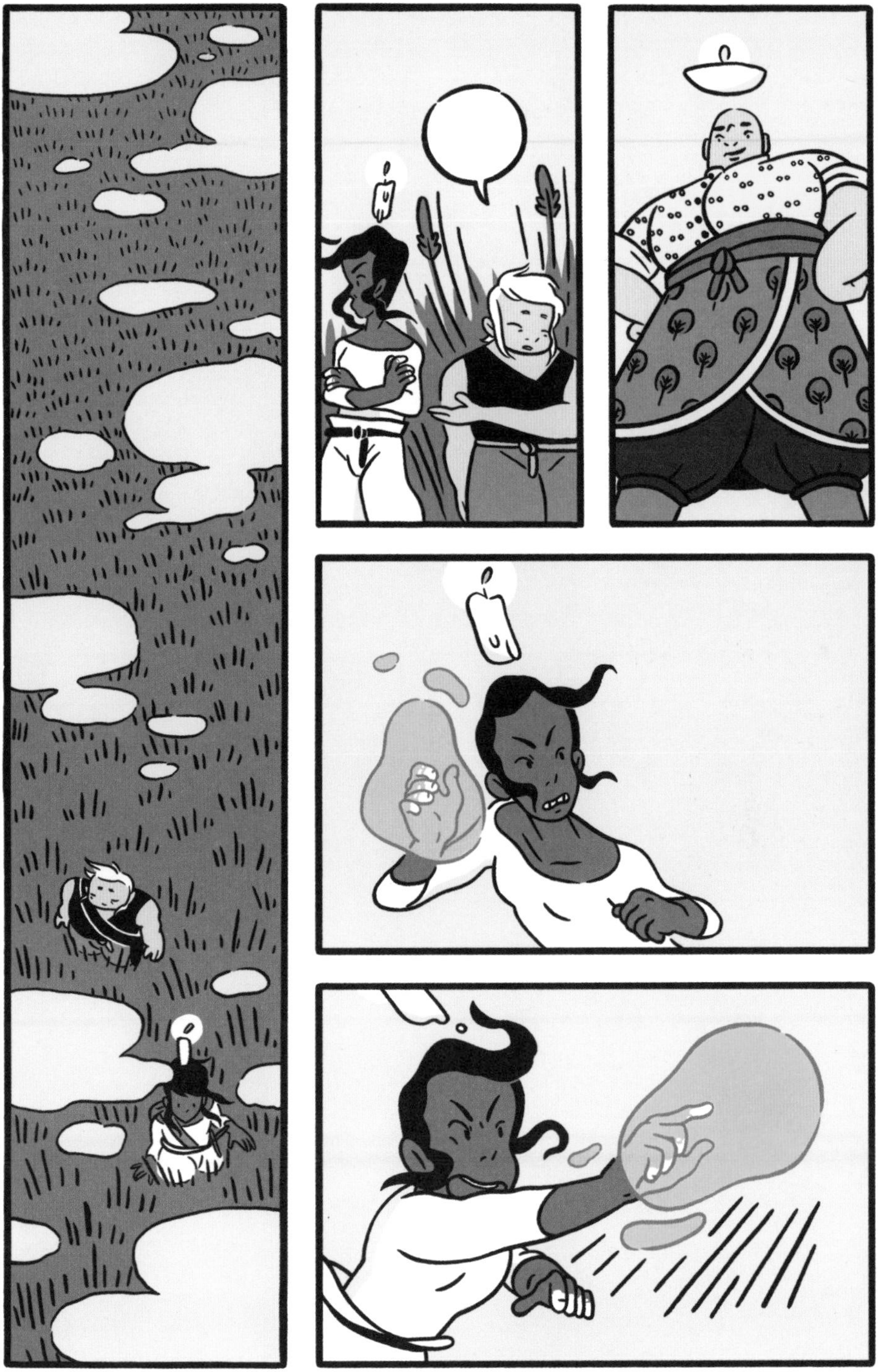

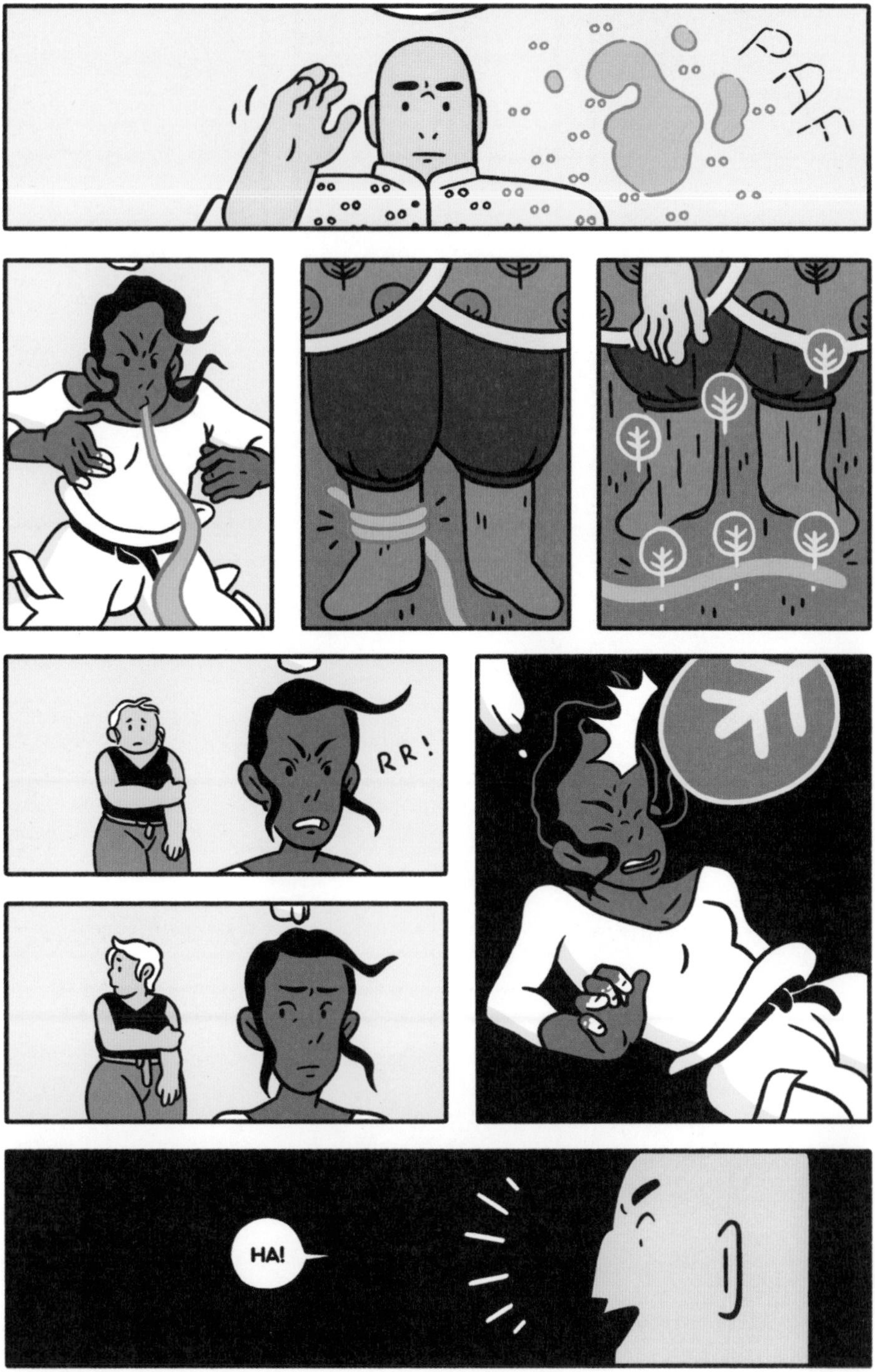
PAF
RR!
HA!

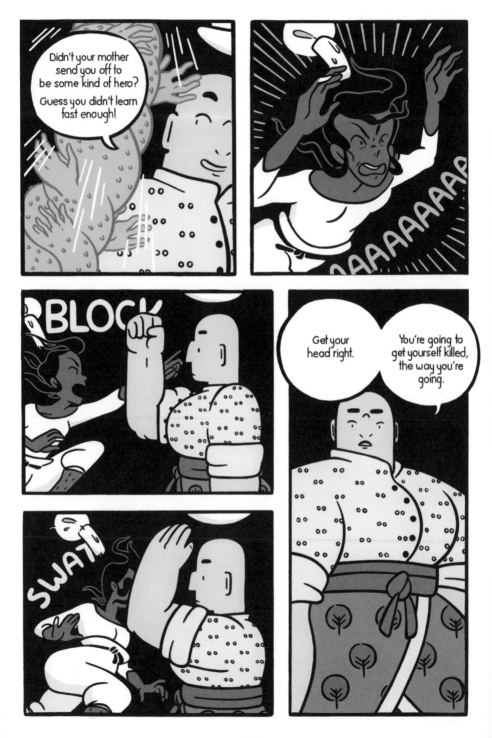

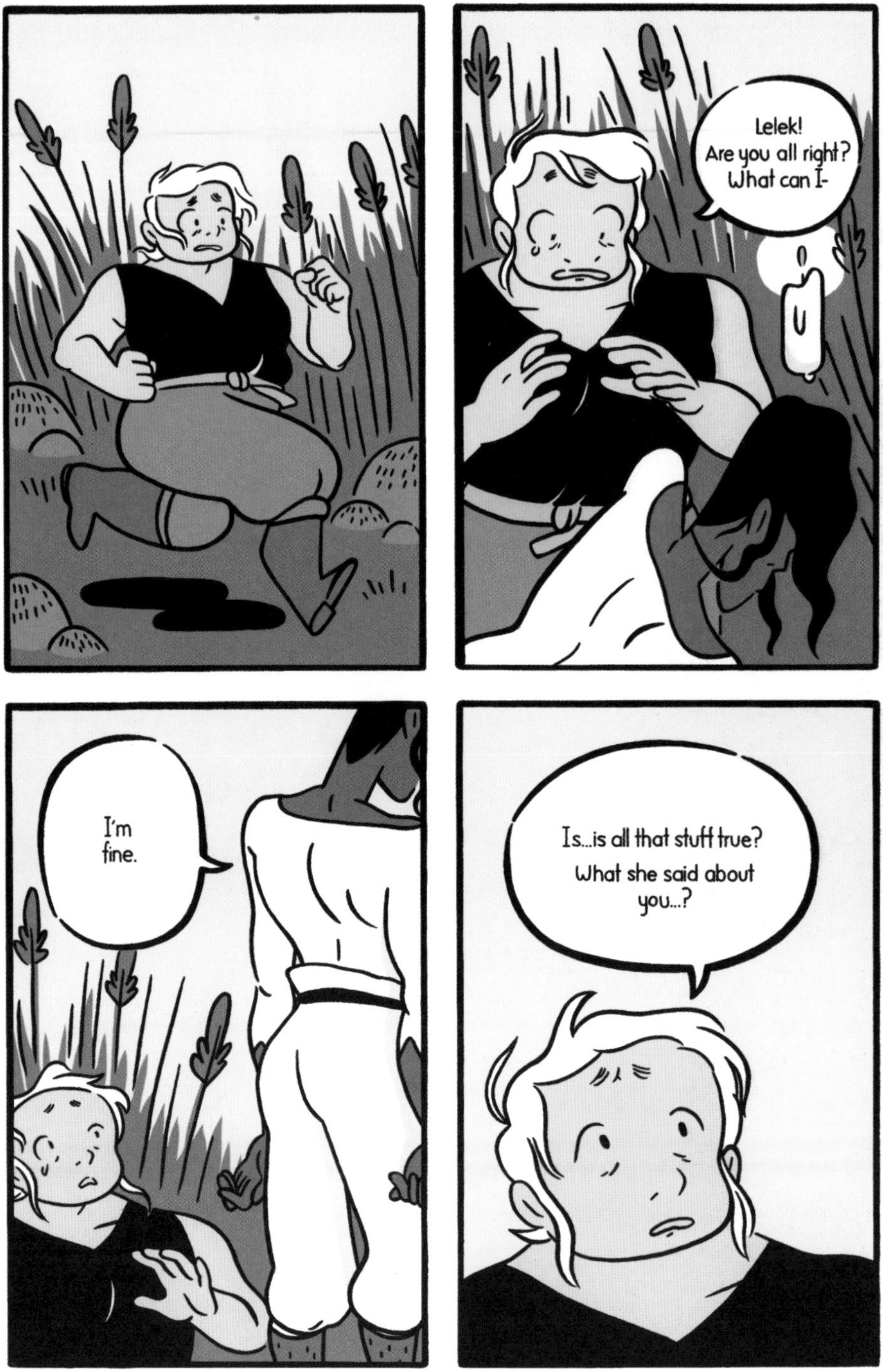
Lelek! Are you all right? What can I-
I'm fine.
Is...is all that stuff true? What she said about you...?

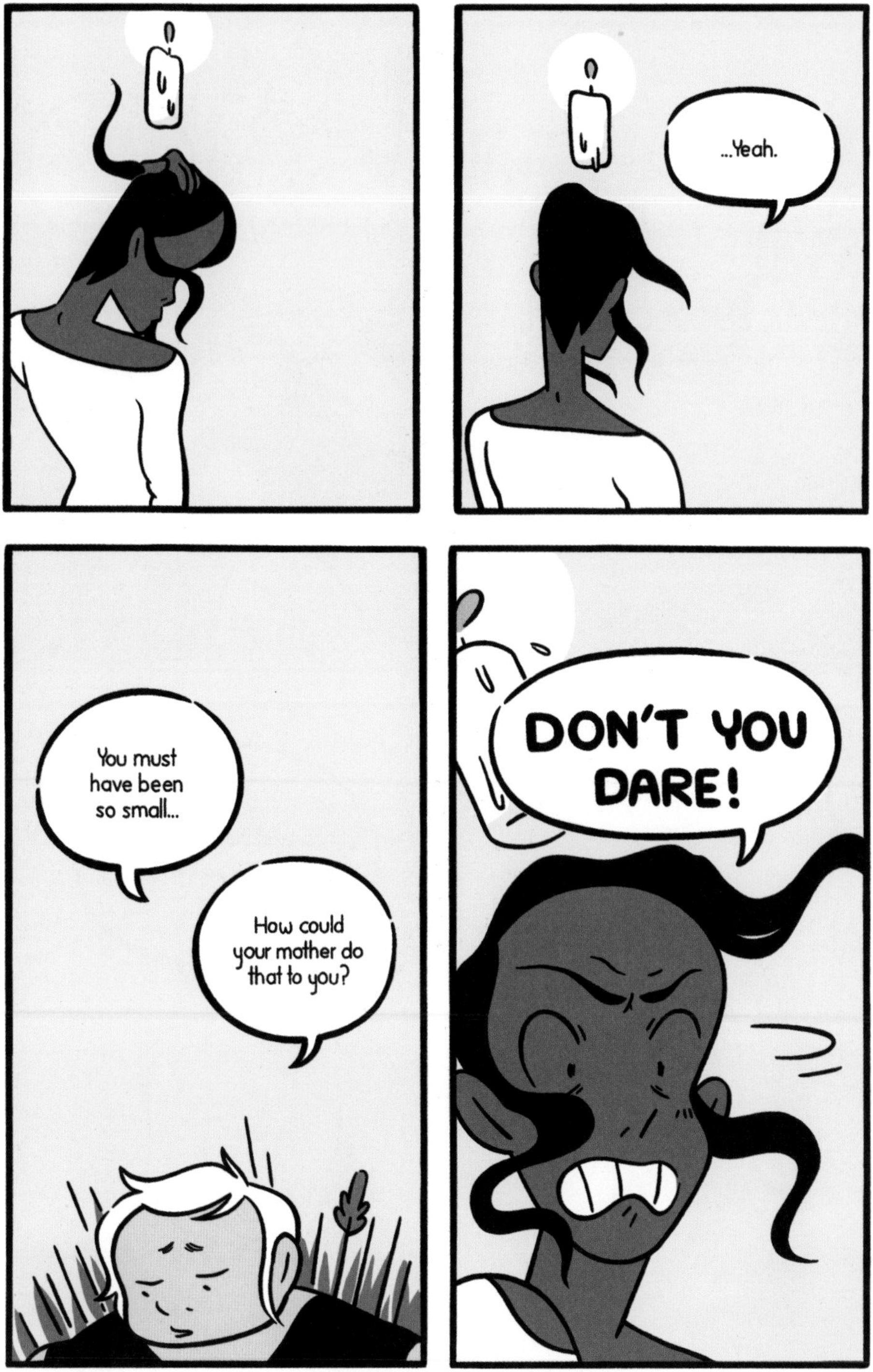
...Yeah.
You must have been so small...
How could your mother do that to you?
DON'T YOU DARE!

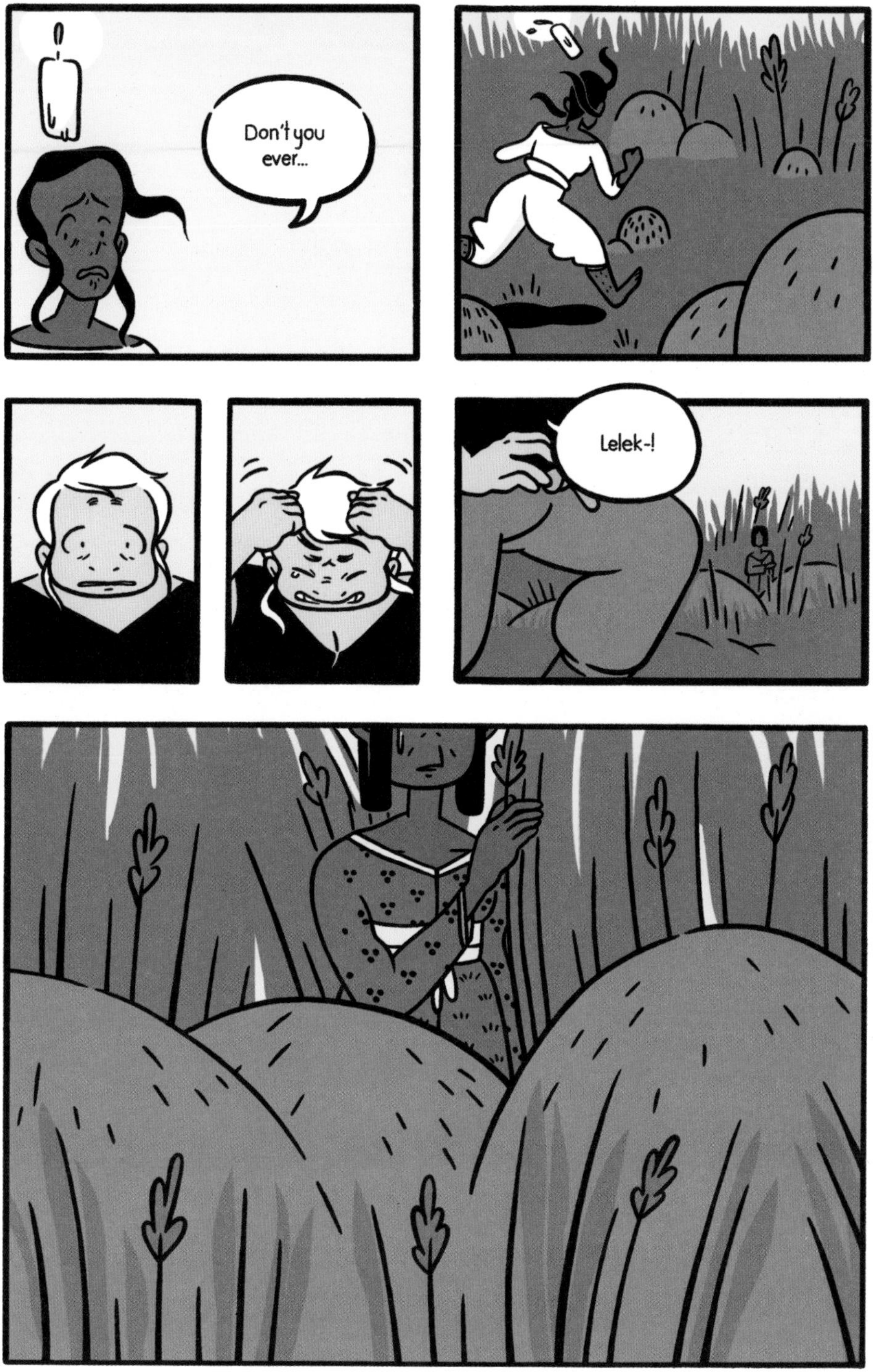
Don't you ever...
Lelek-!

Part 5

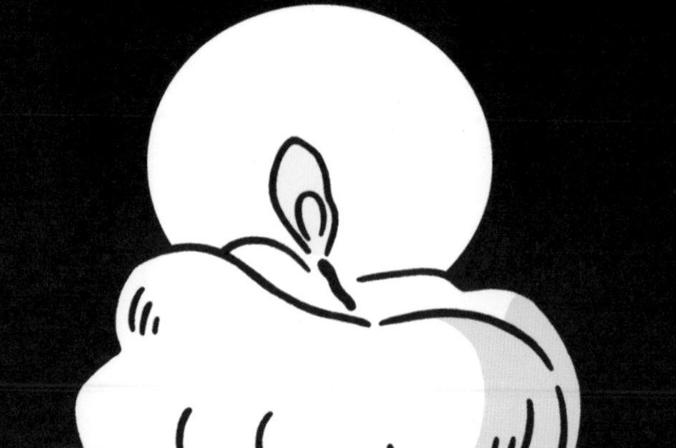

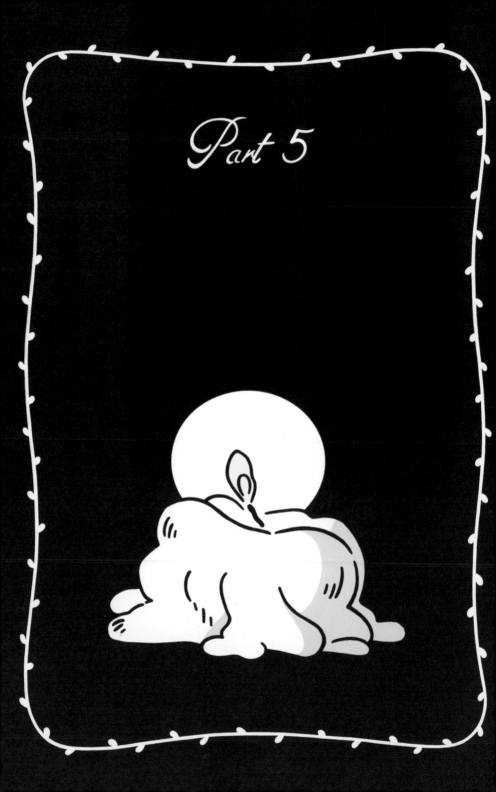

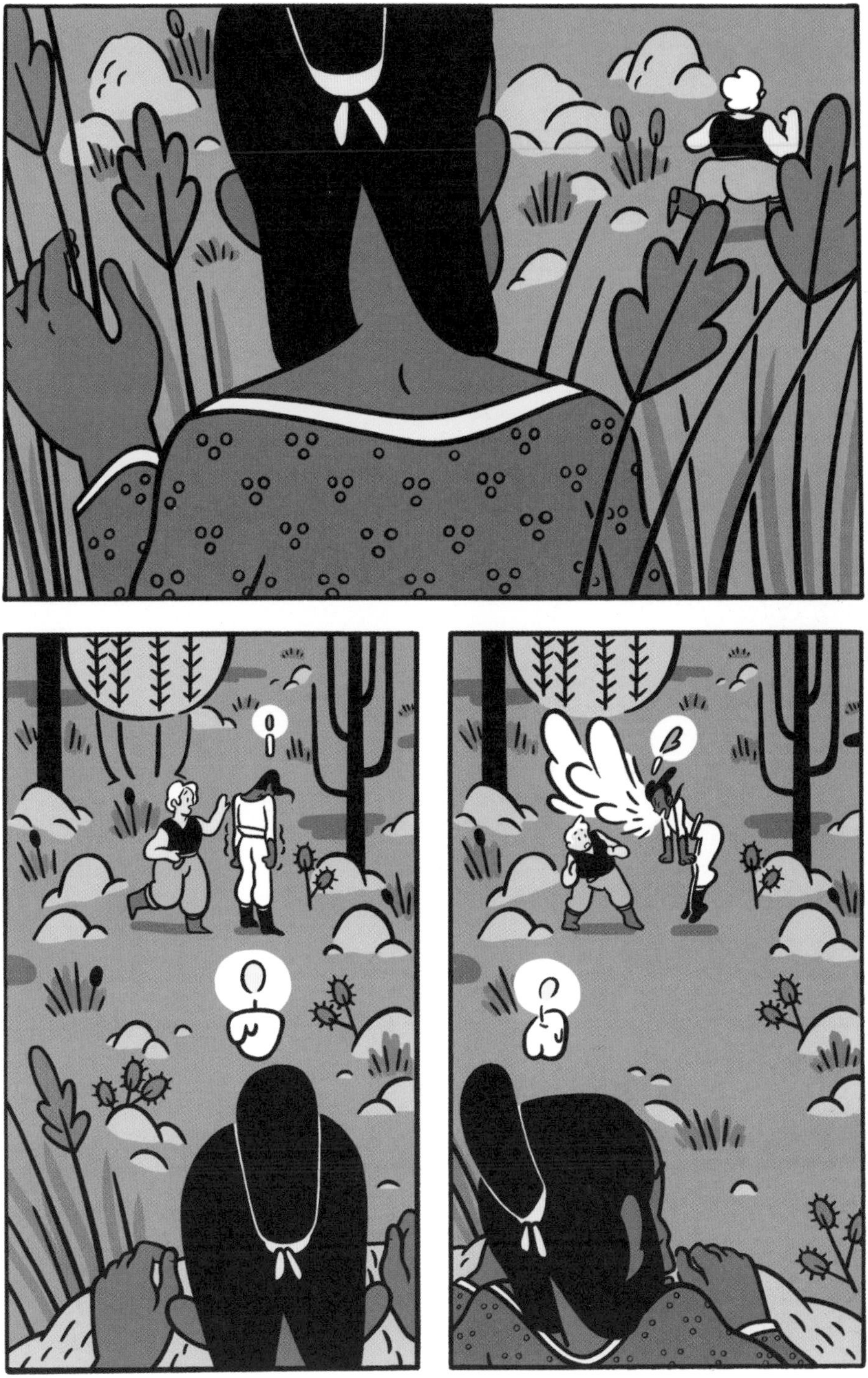
!
?
?

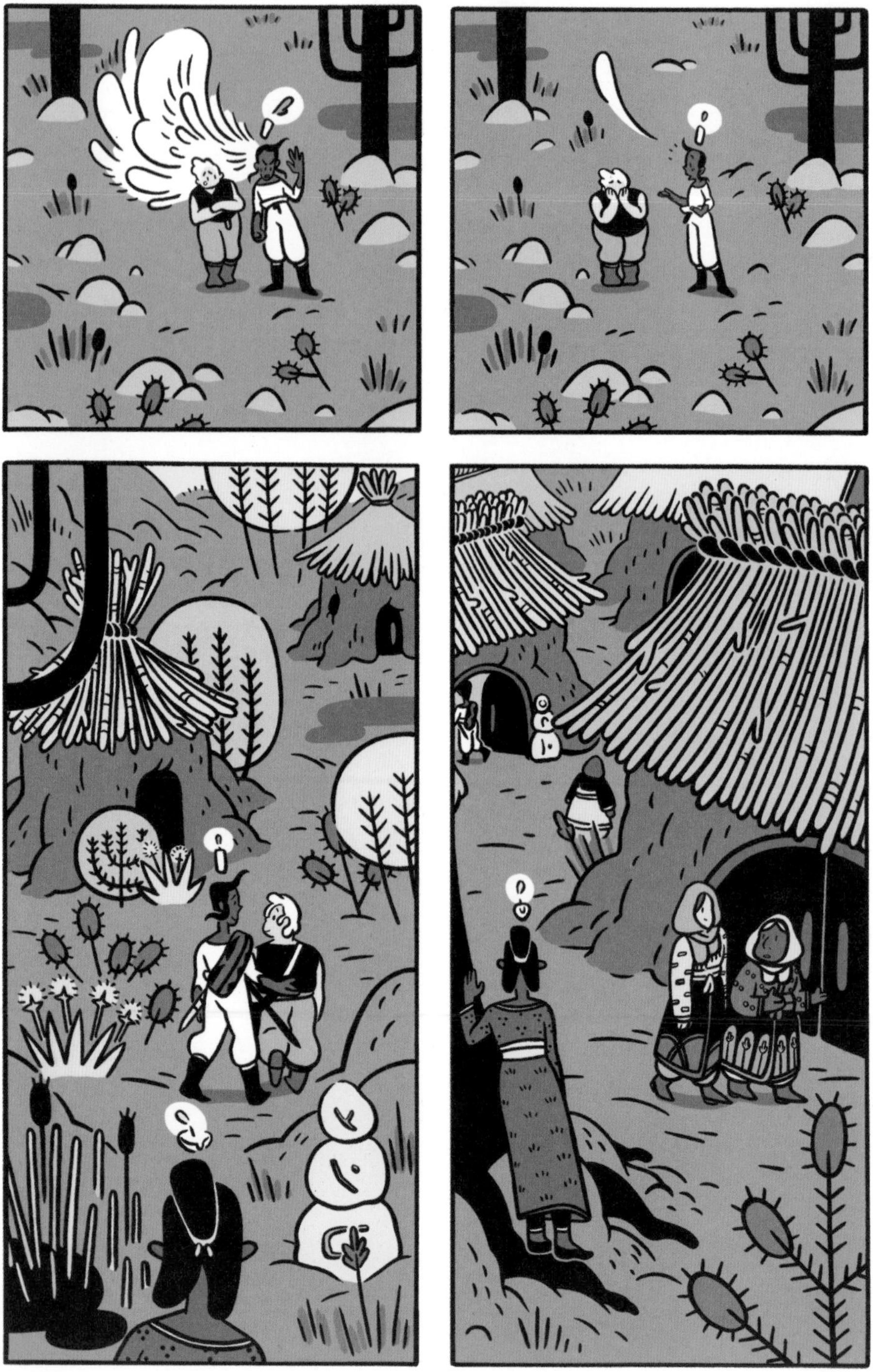

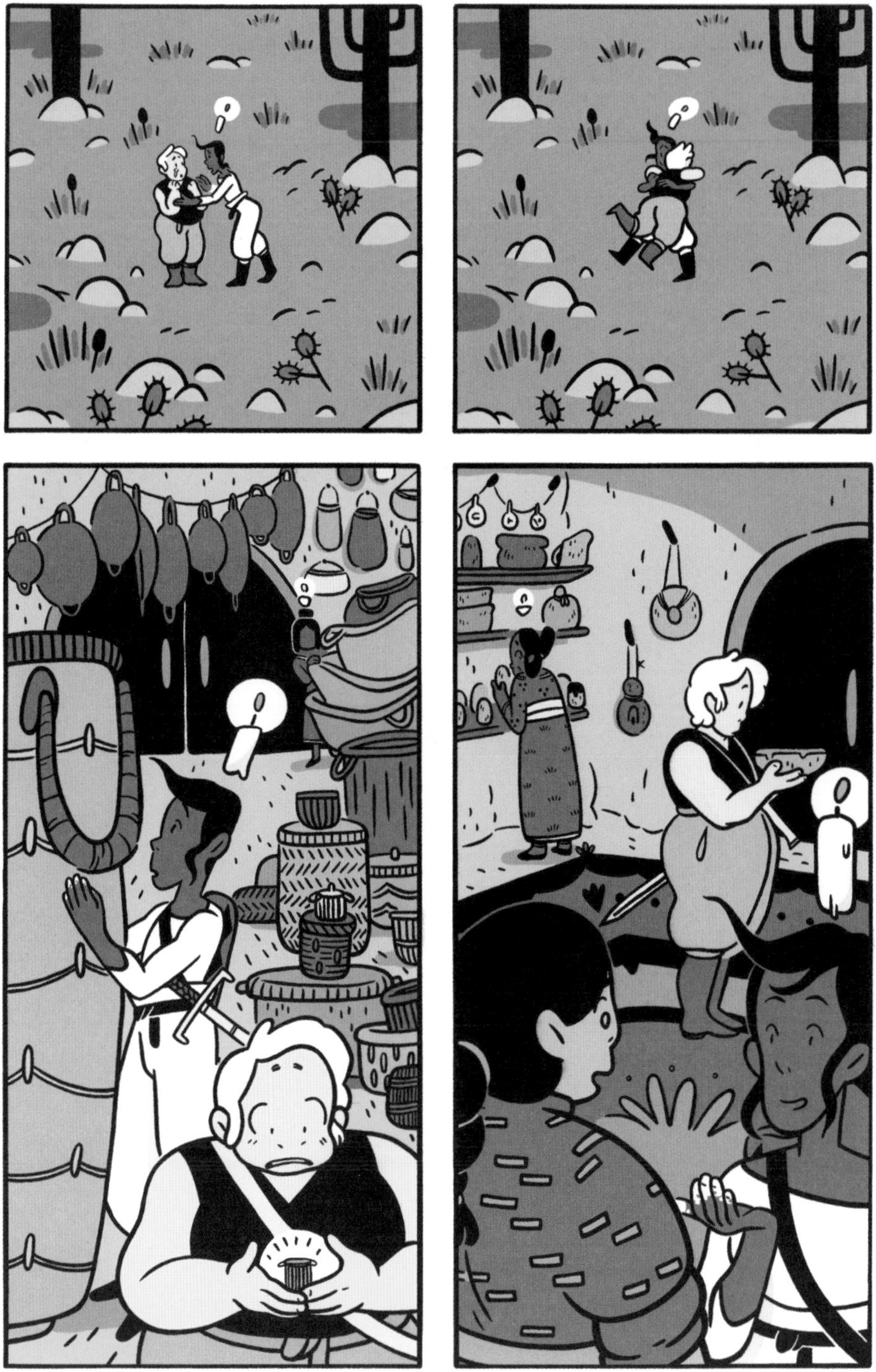

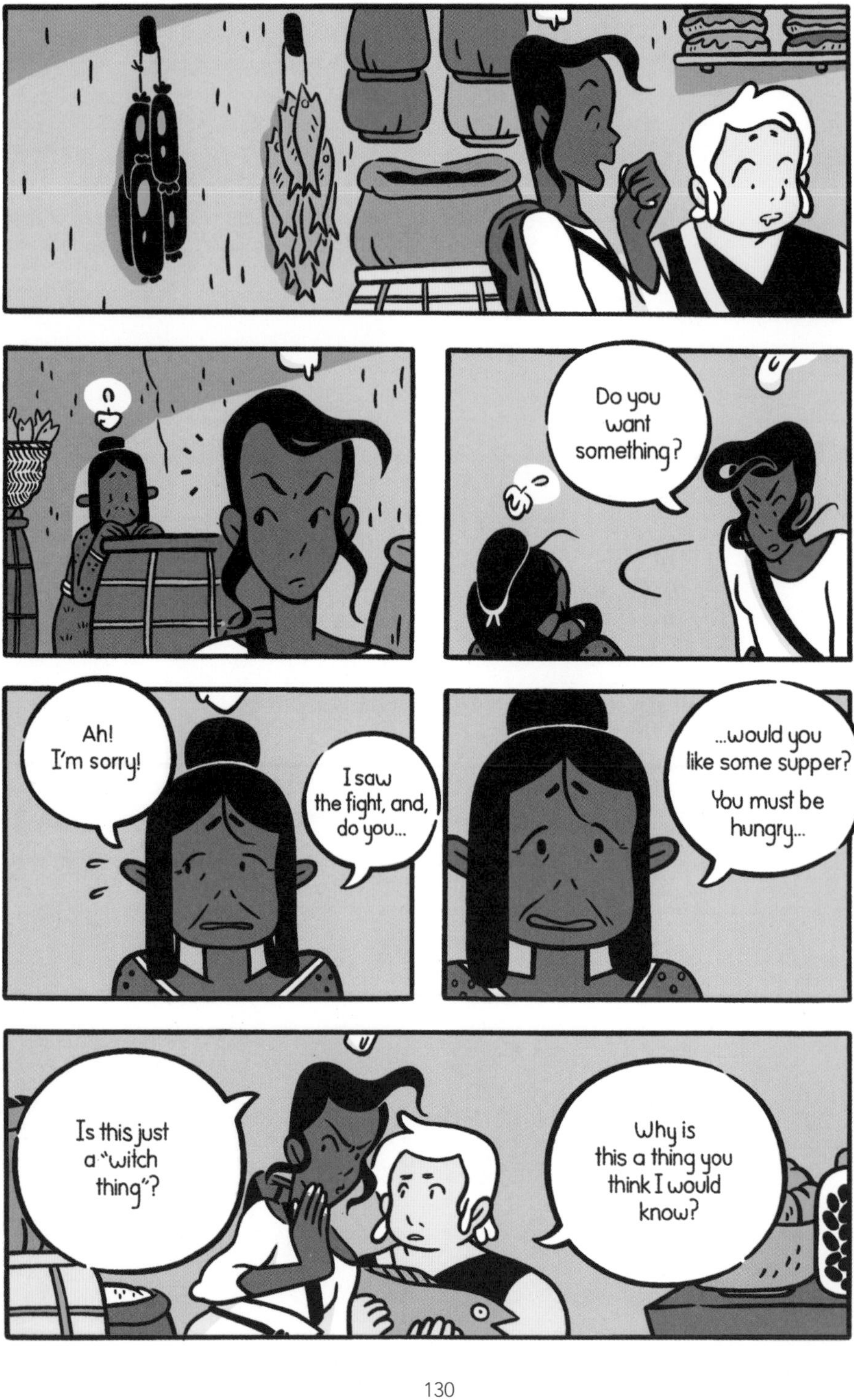
Do you want something?
Ah! I'm sorry!
I saw the fight, and, do you...
...would you like some supper?
You must be hungry...
Is this just a "witch thing"?
Why is this a thing you think I would know?

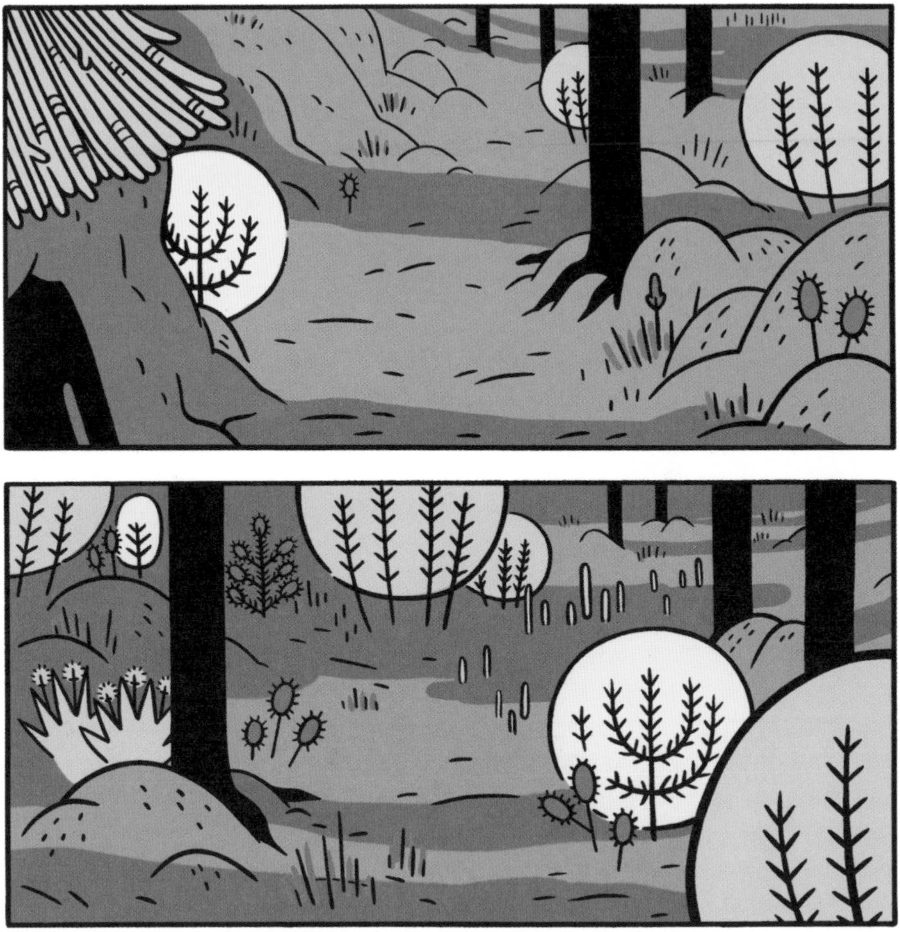

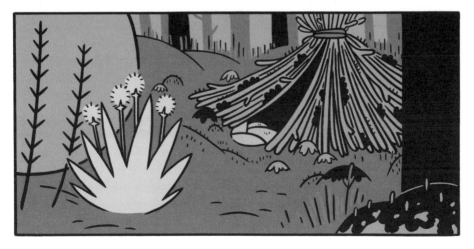

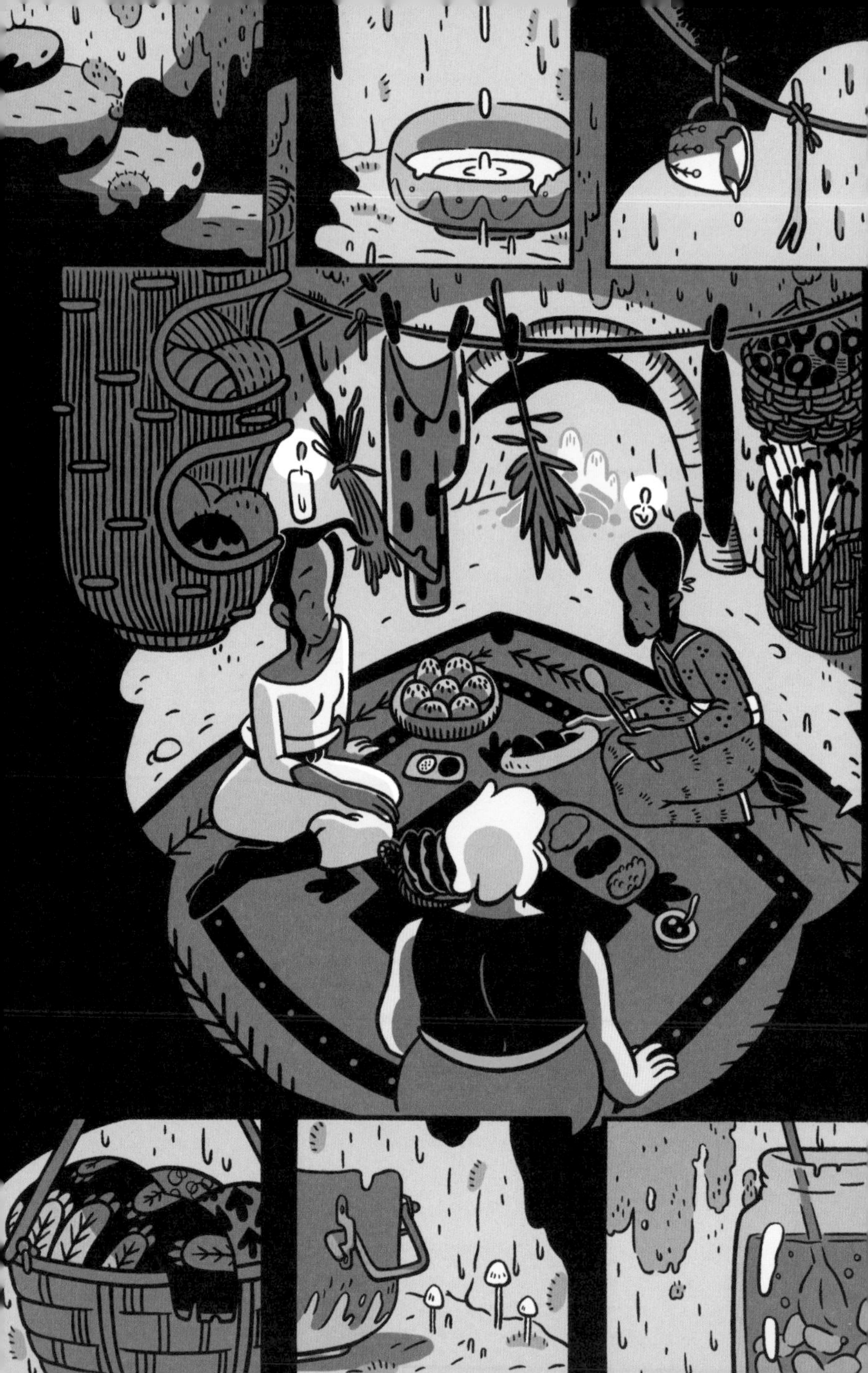

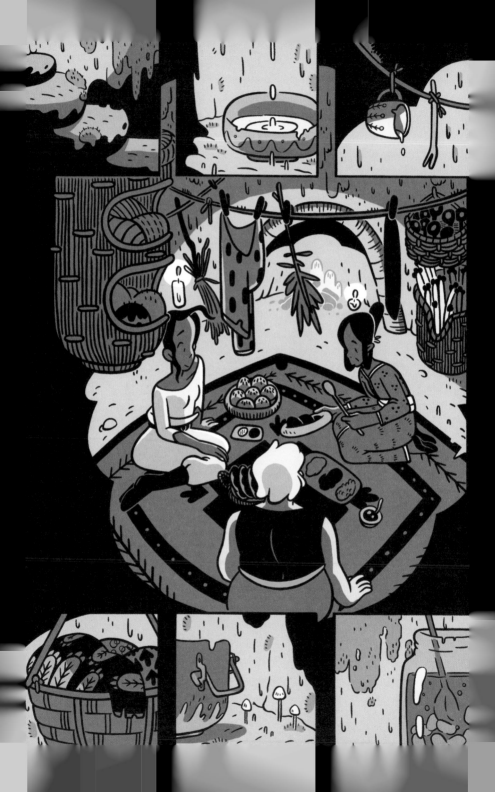

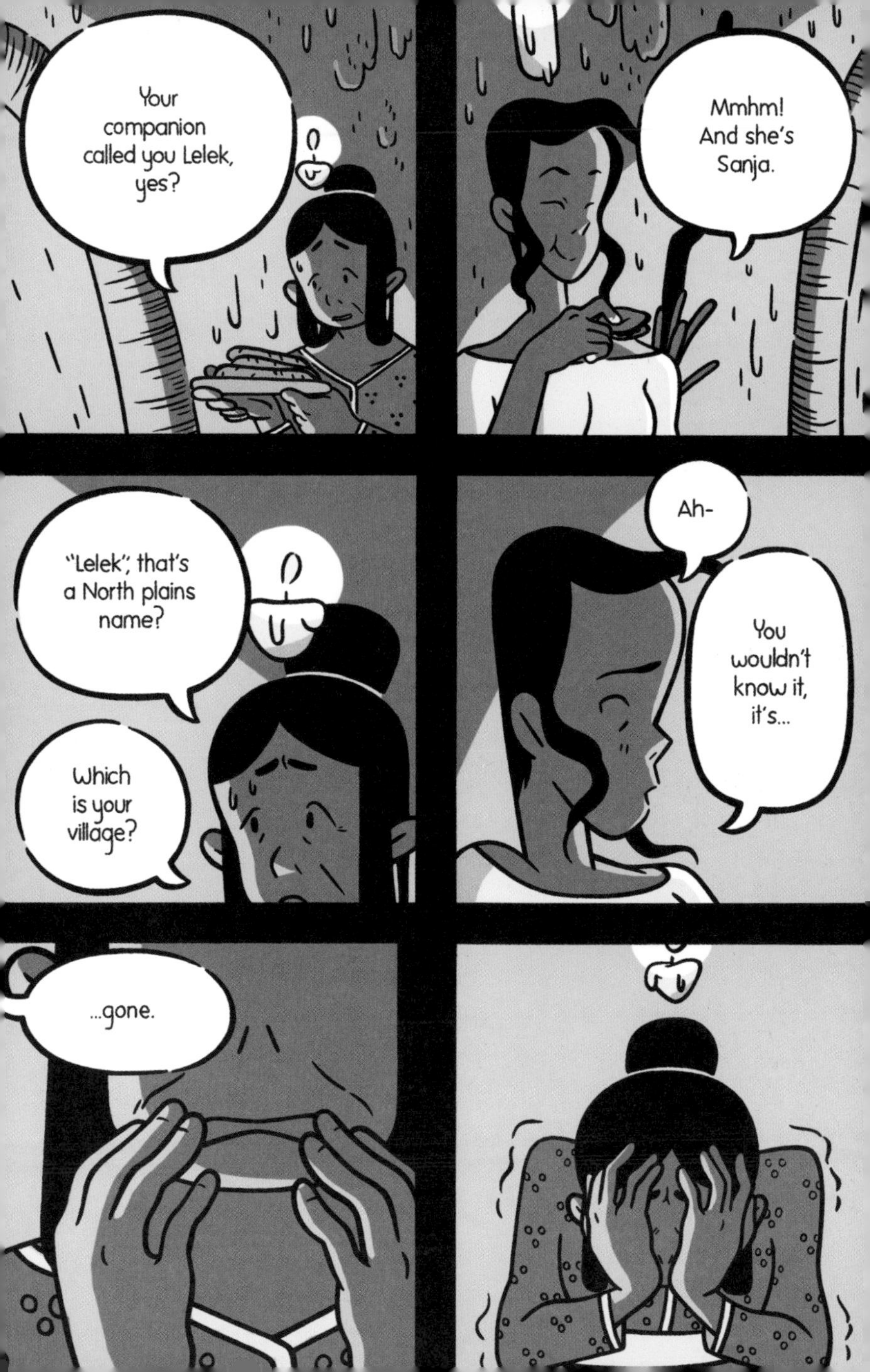
Your companion called you Lelek, yes?
Mmhm! And she's Sanja.
"Lelek"; that's a North plains name?
Which is your village?
Ah-
You wouldn't know it, it's...
...gone.

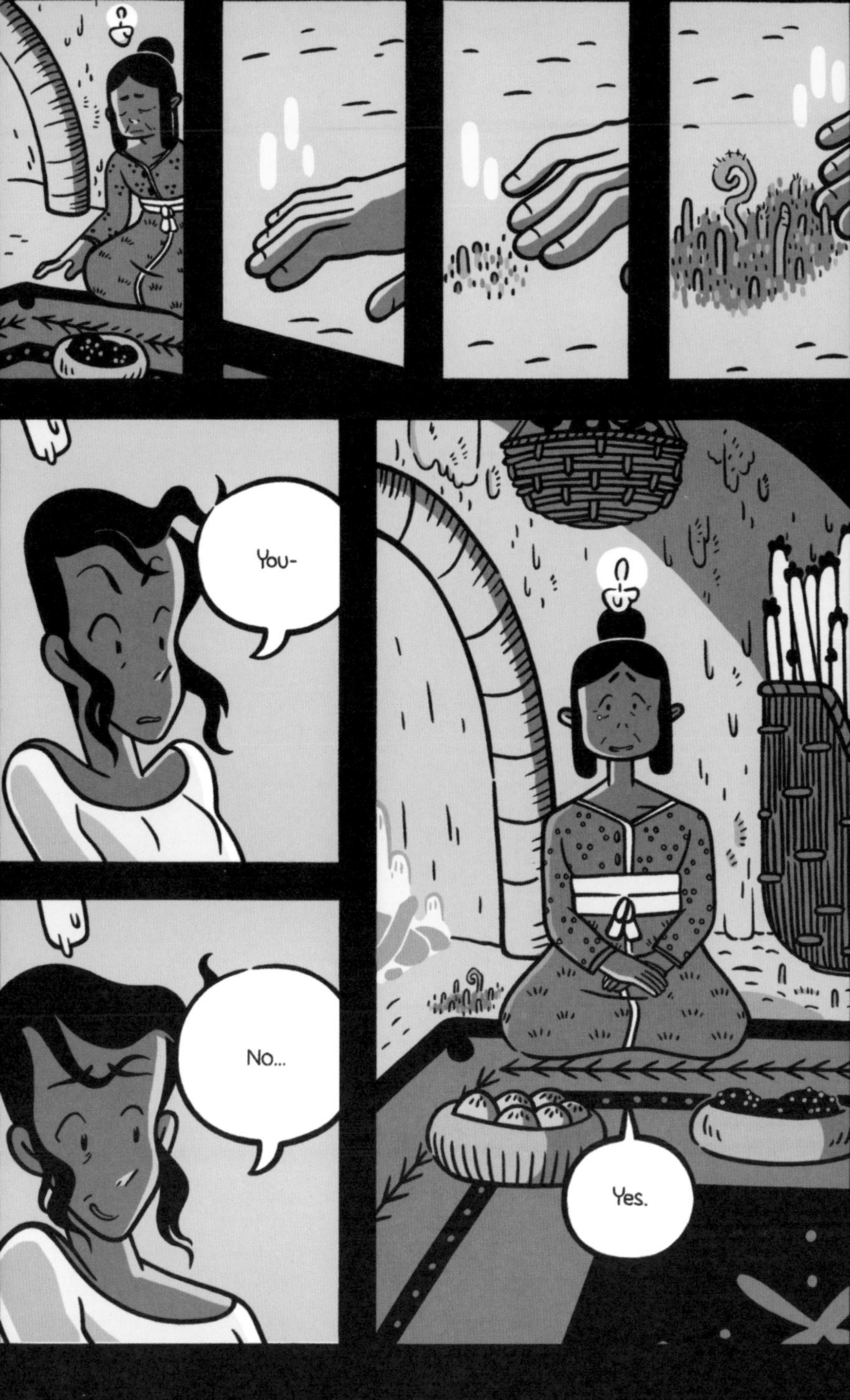
You-
No...
Yes.

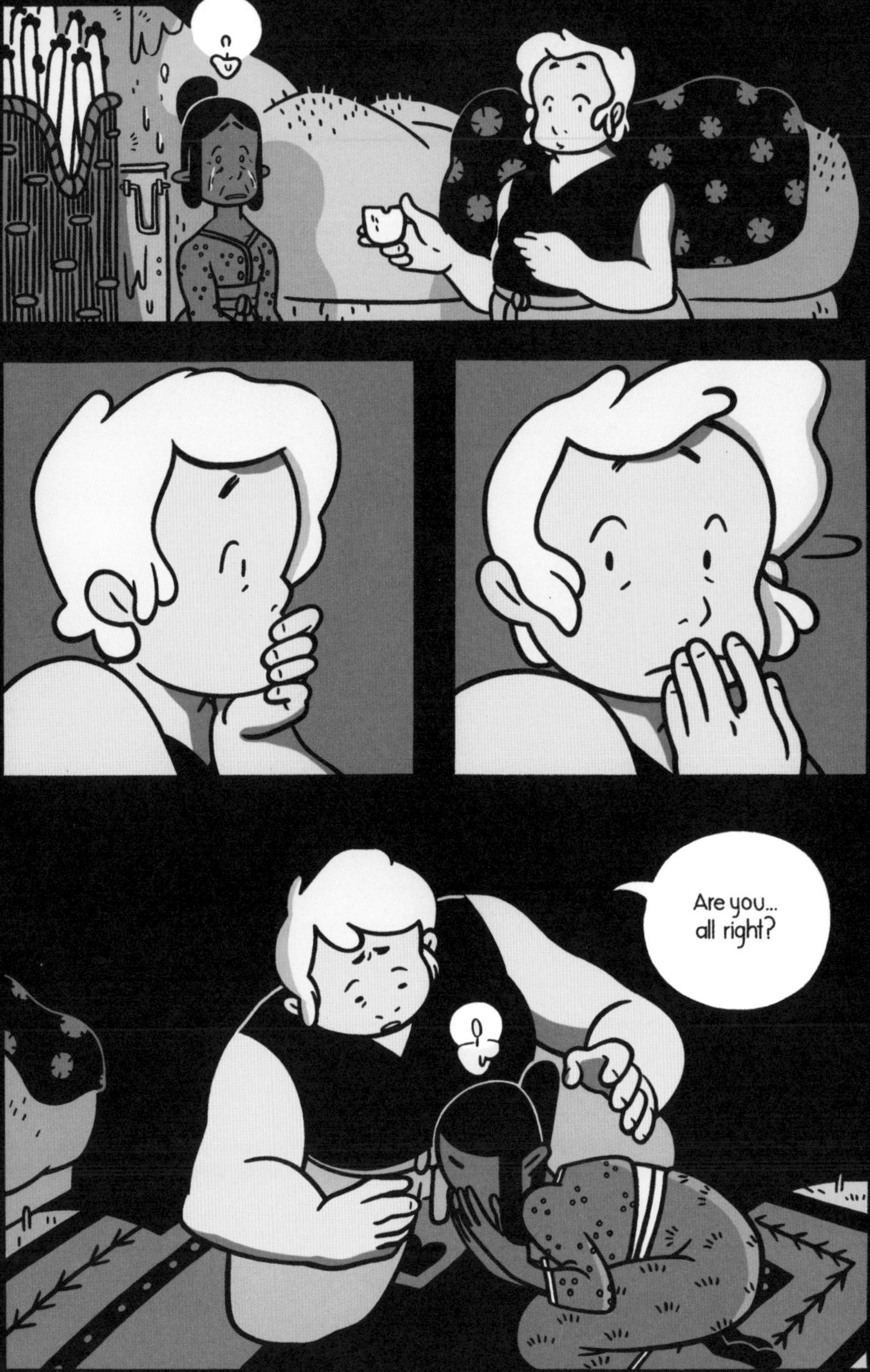
Are you...
all right?

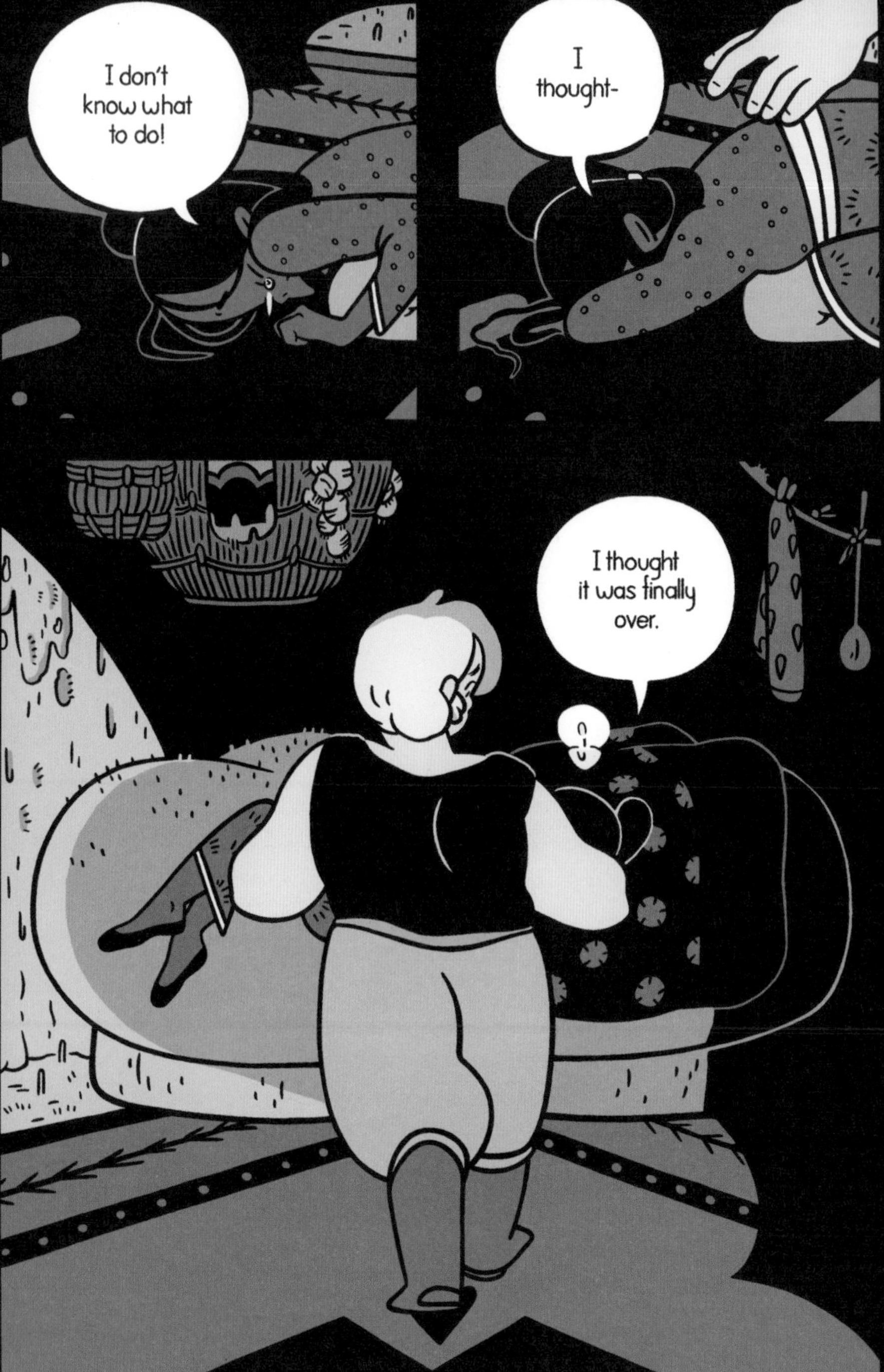
I don't know what to do!
I thought-
I thought it was finally over.

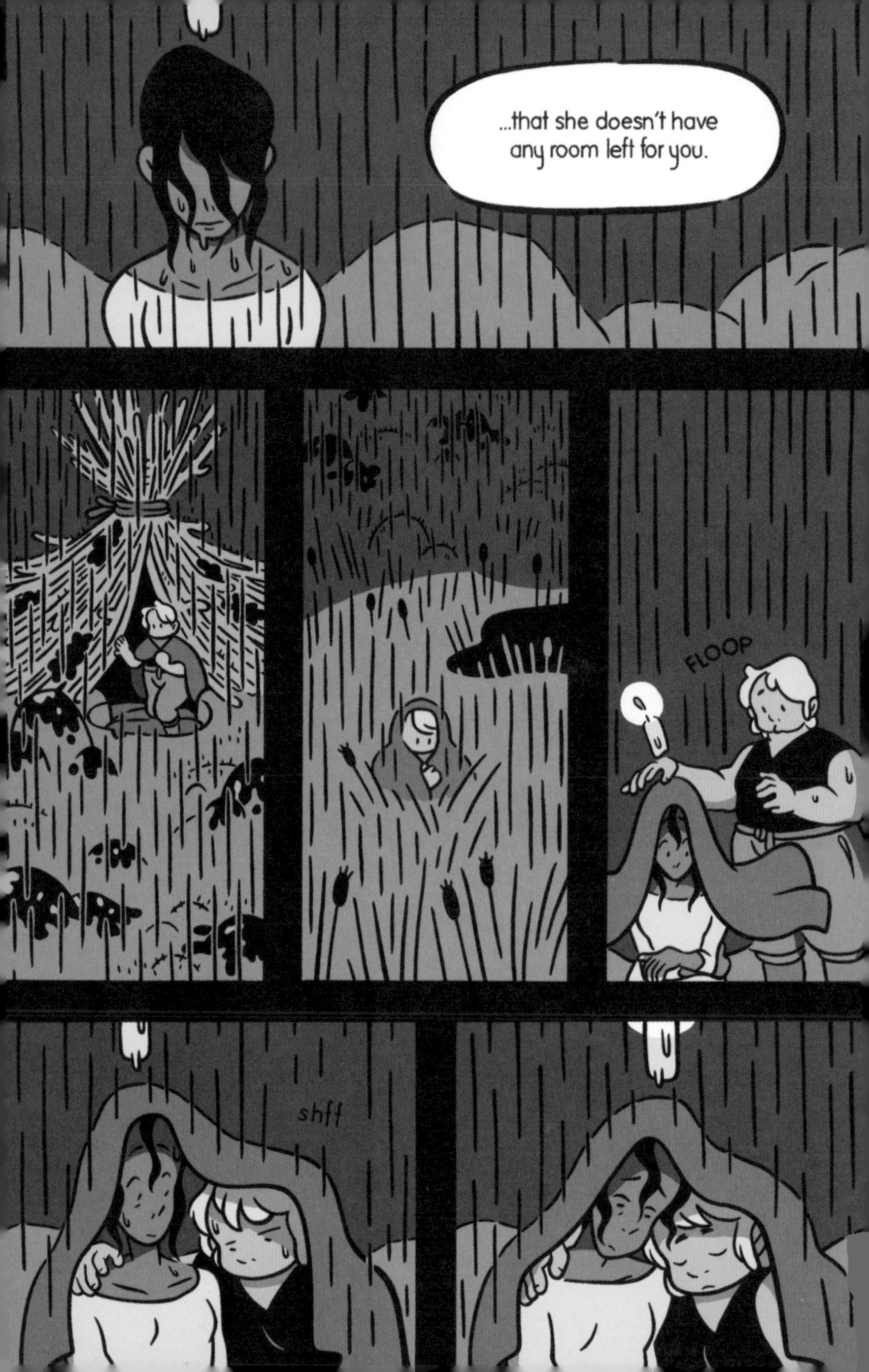
...that she doesn't have any room left for you.
FLOOP
shff

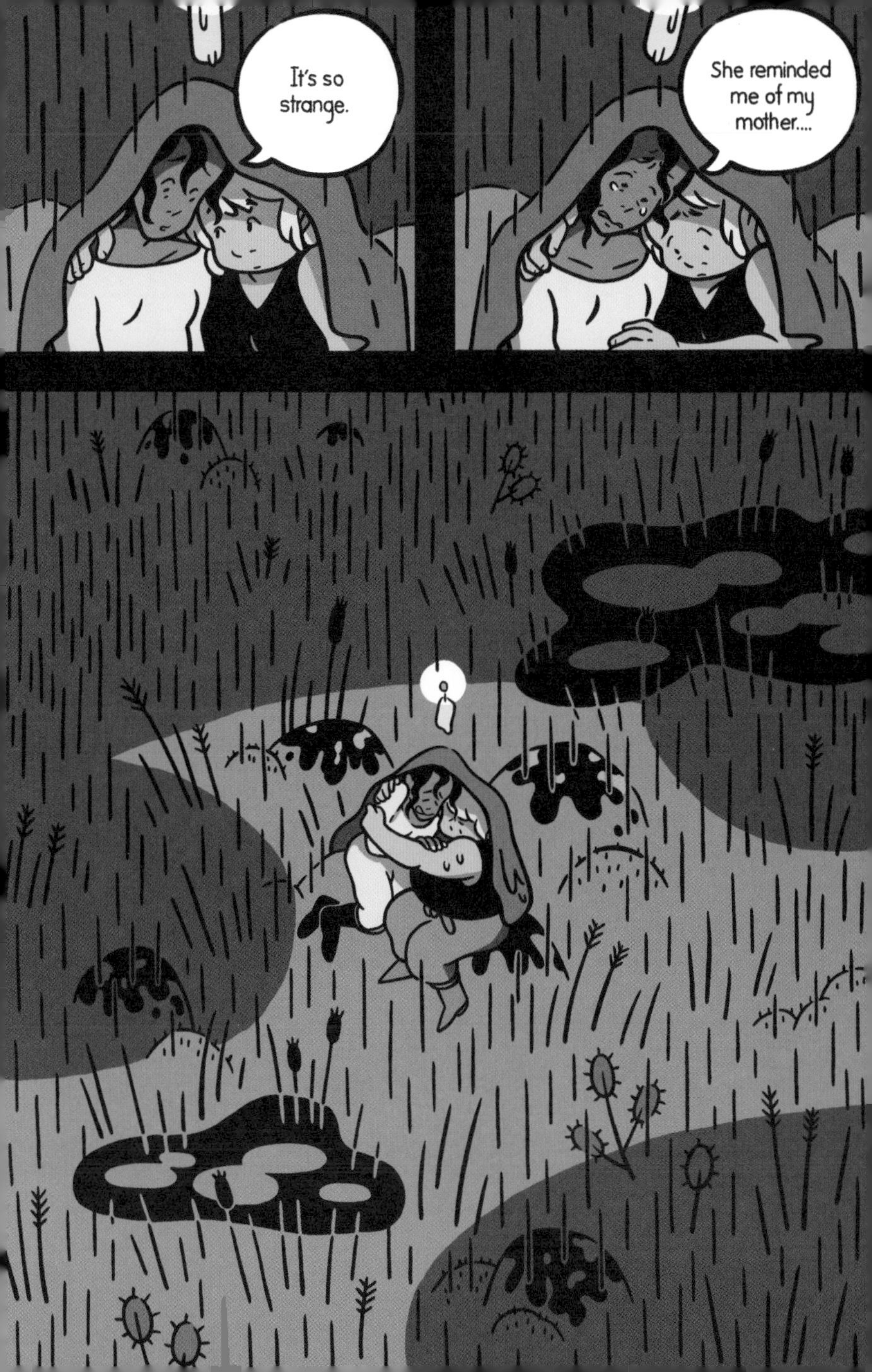
It's so strange.
She reminded me of my mother....

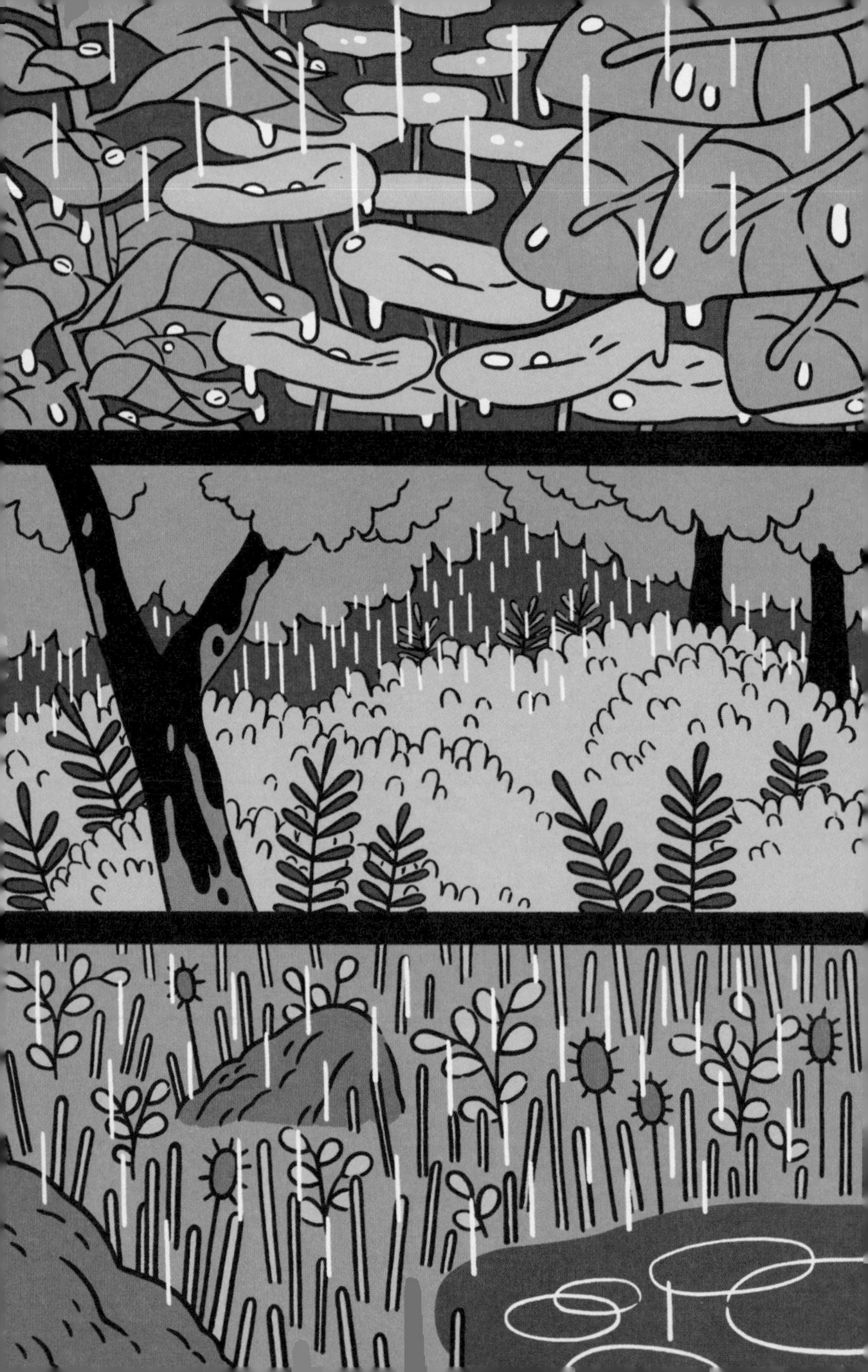

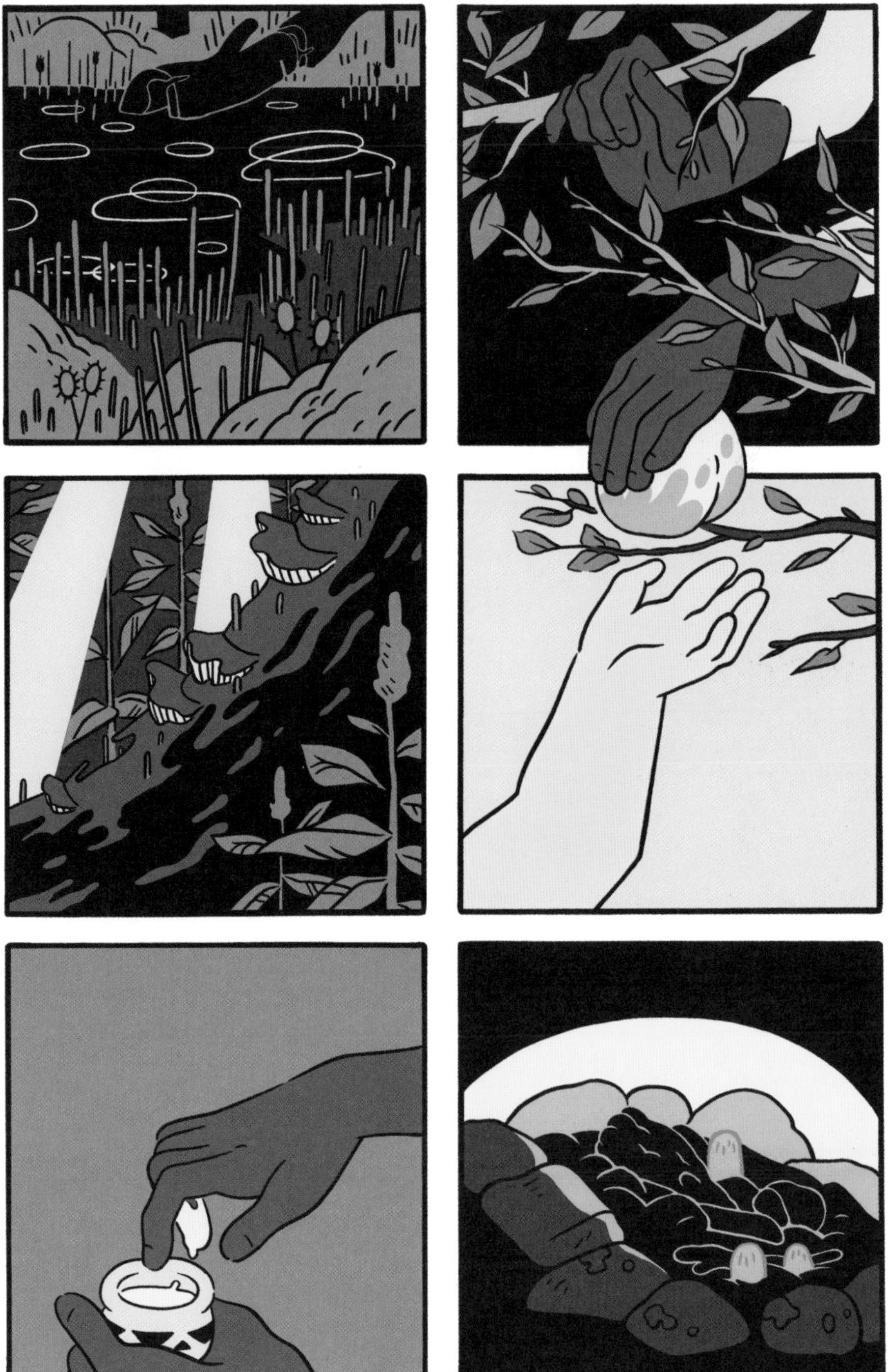

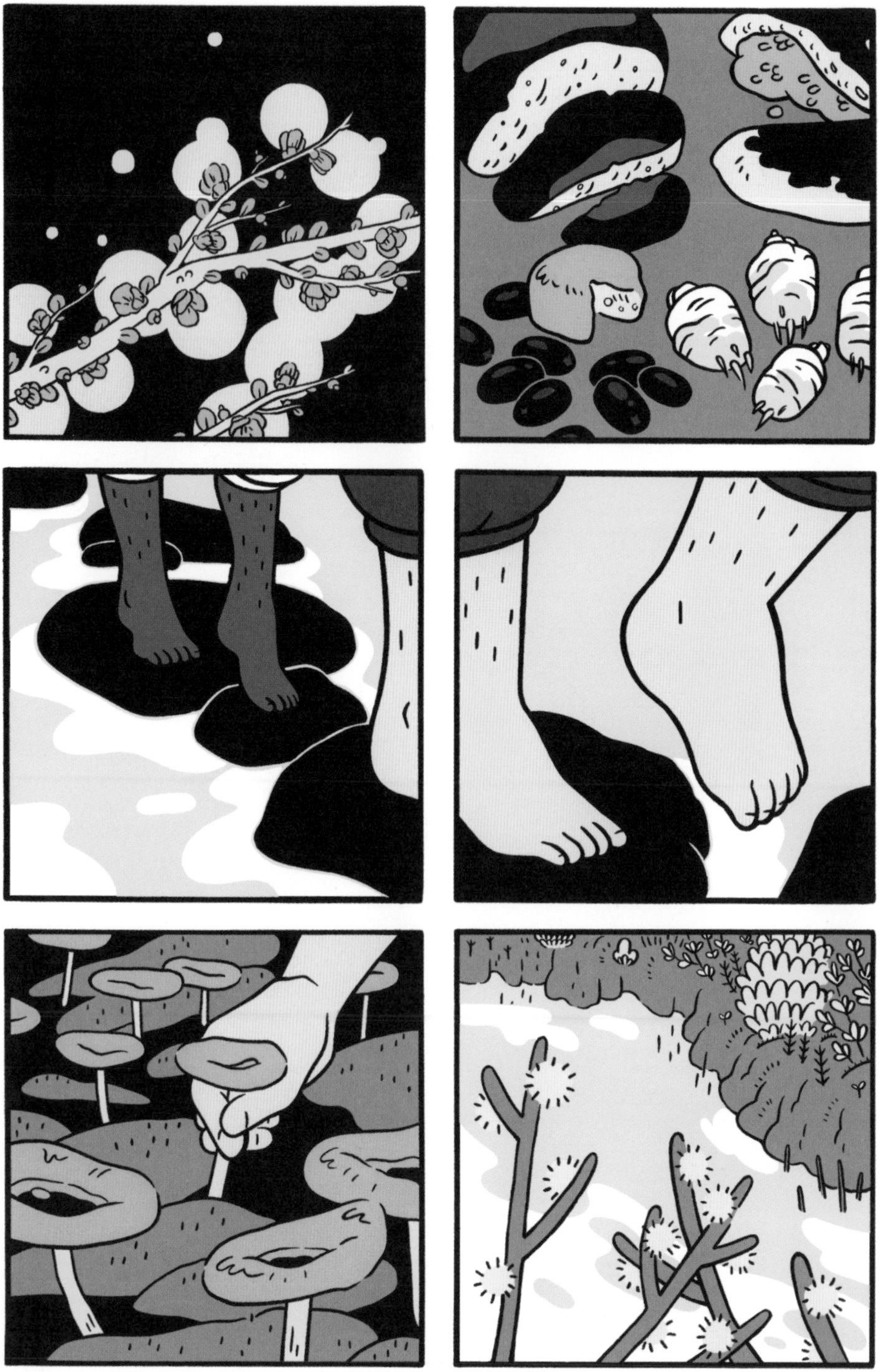

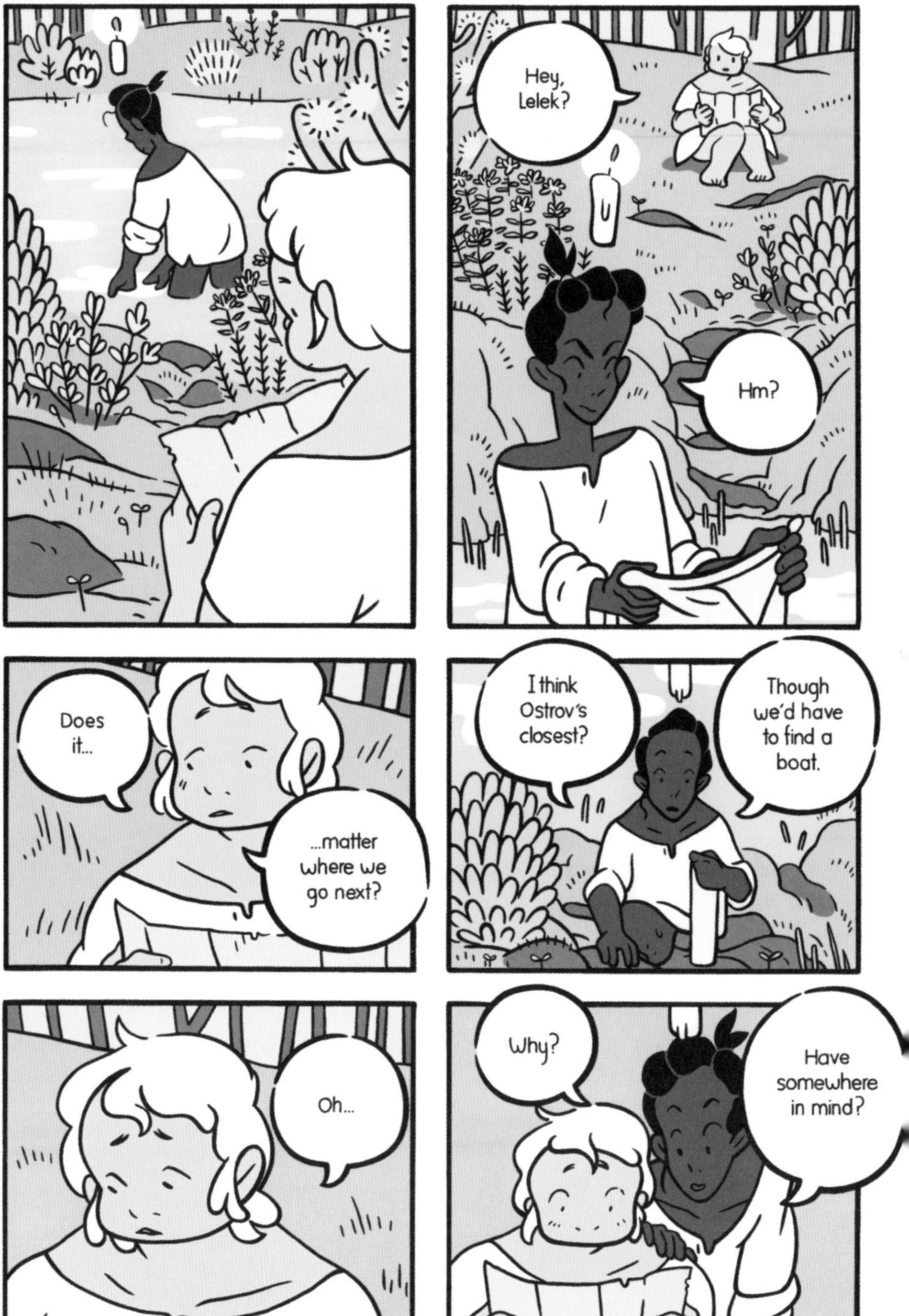
Hey, Lelek?
Hm?
Does it...
...matter where we go next?
I think Ostrov's closest?
Though we'd have to find a boat.
Oh...
Why?
Have somewhere in mind?

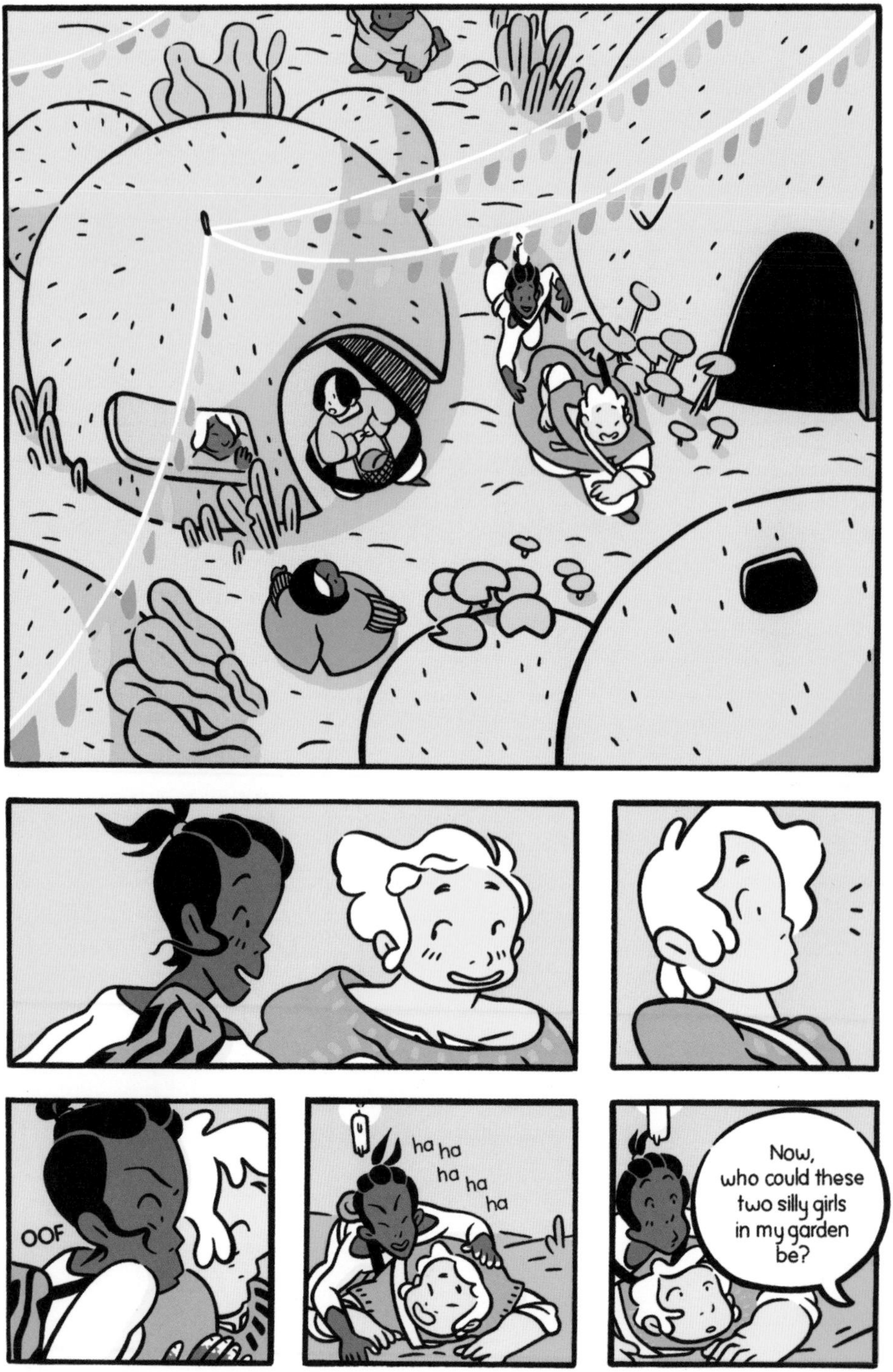
OOF
ha ha
ha ha
ha
Now, who could these two silly girls in my garden be?

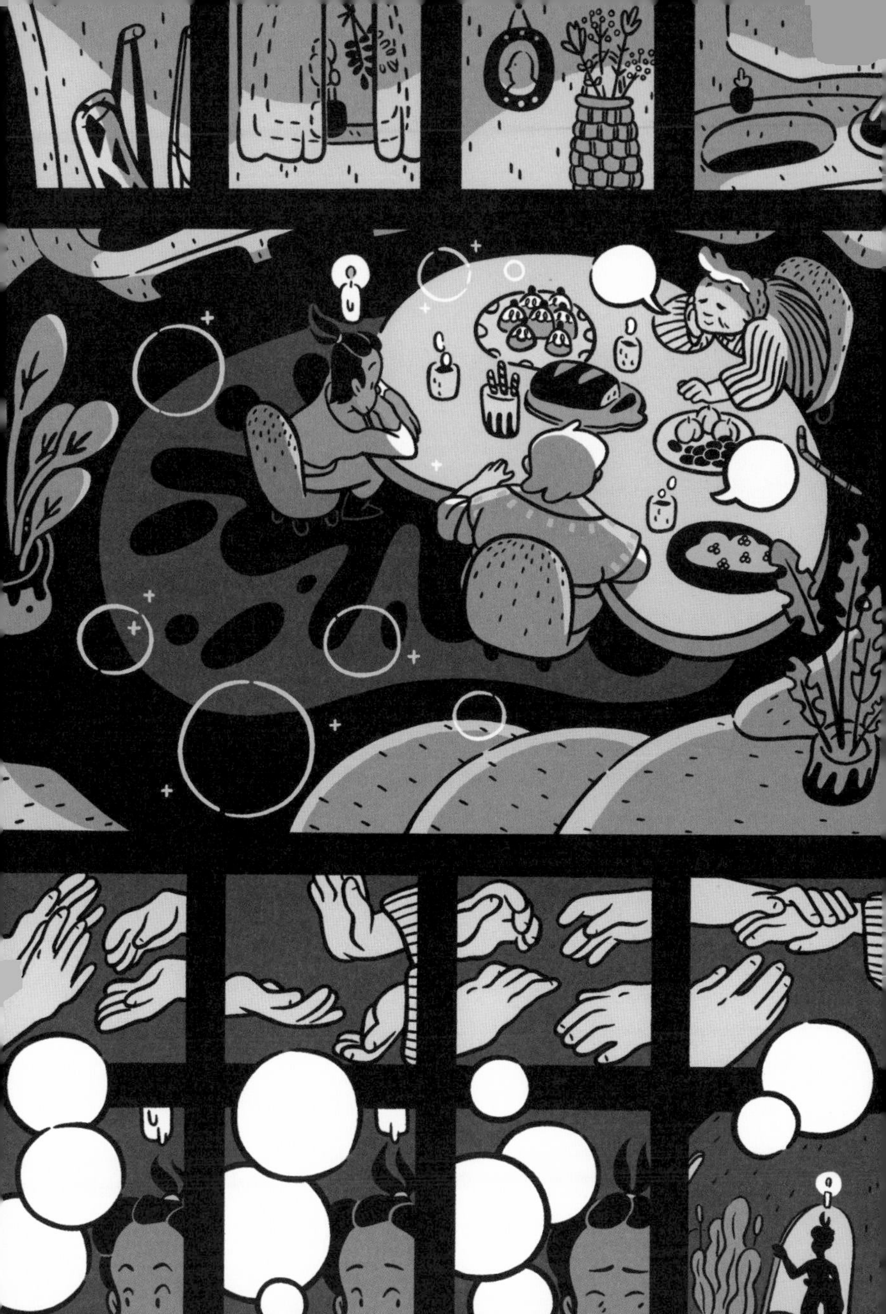

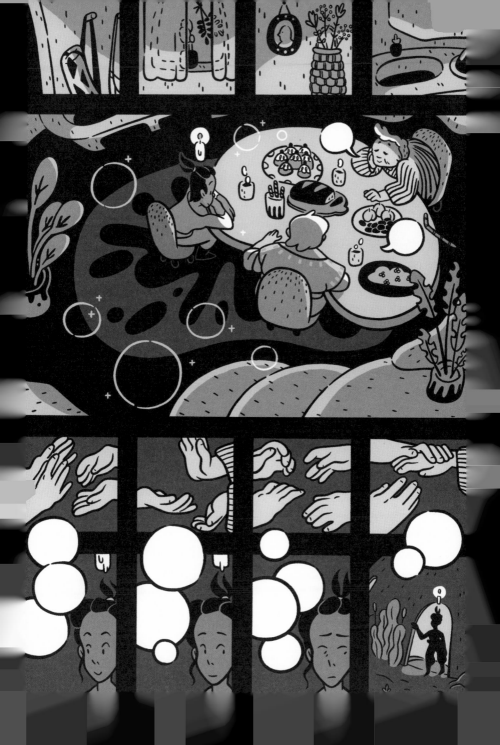

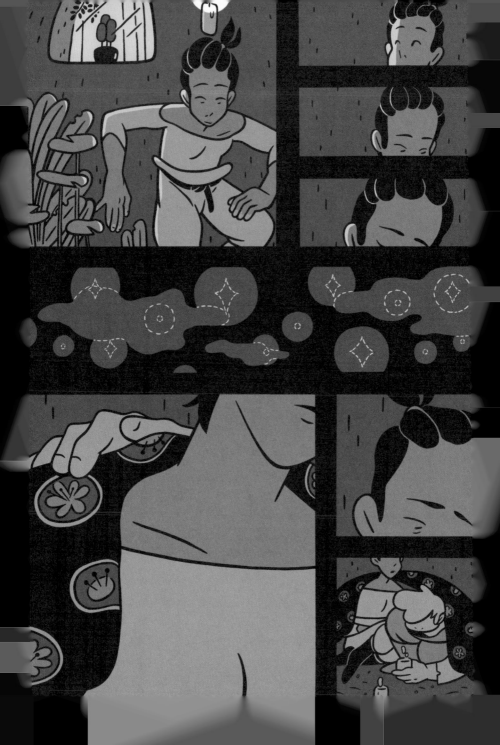

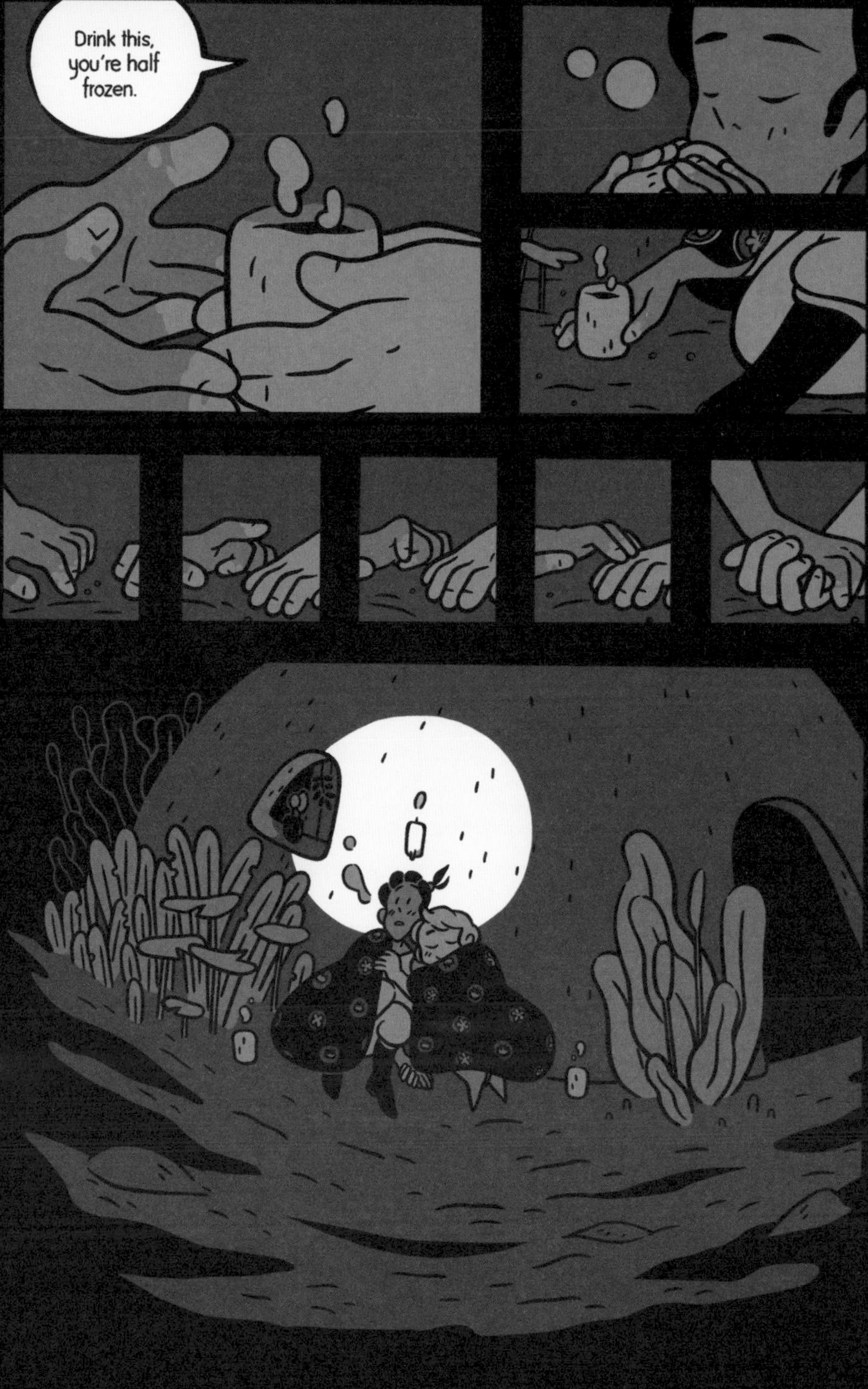
Drink this, you're half frozen.

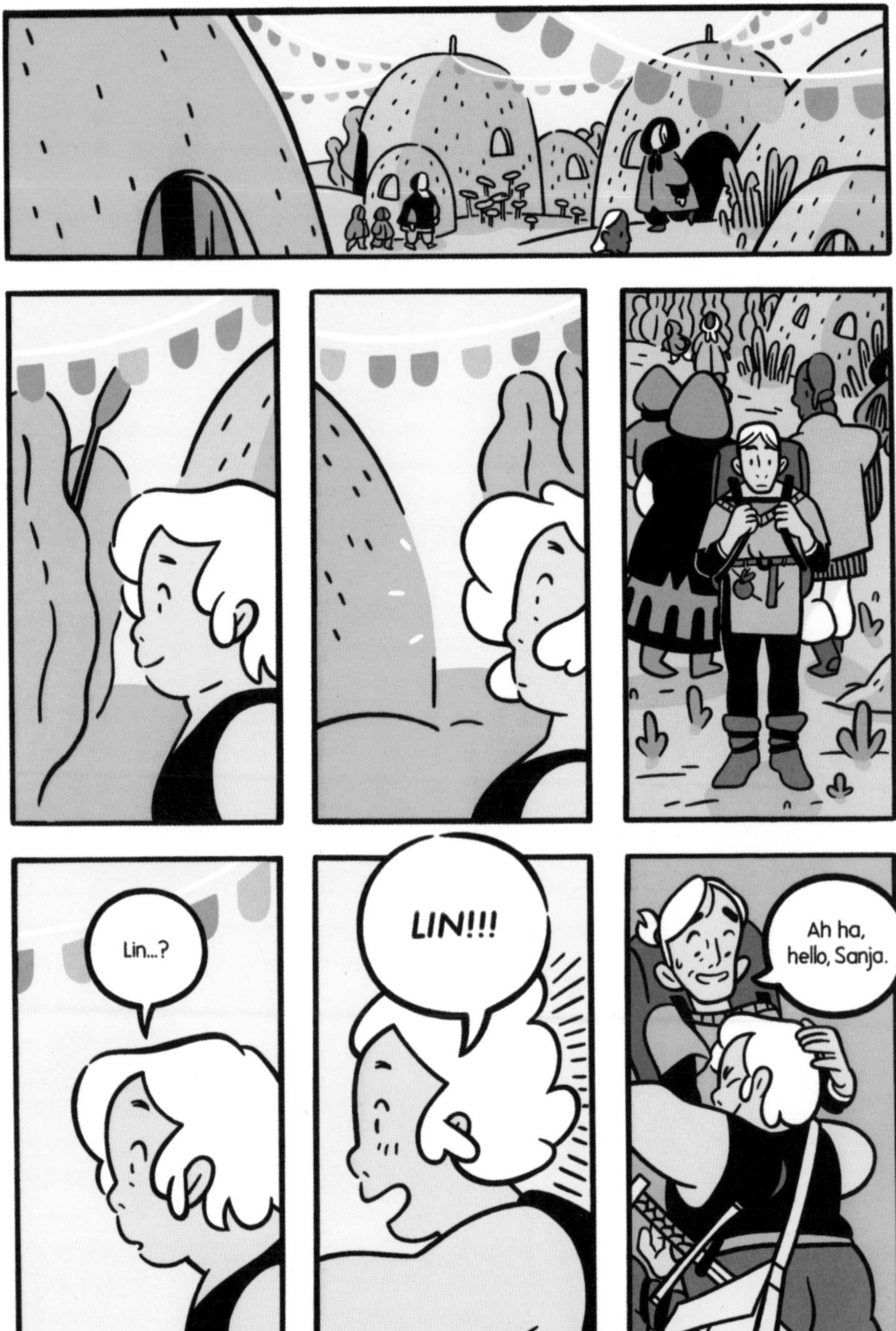

Lin...?
LIN!!!
Ah ha, hello, Sanja.

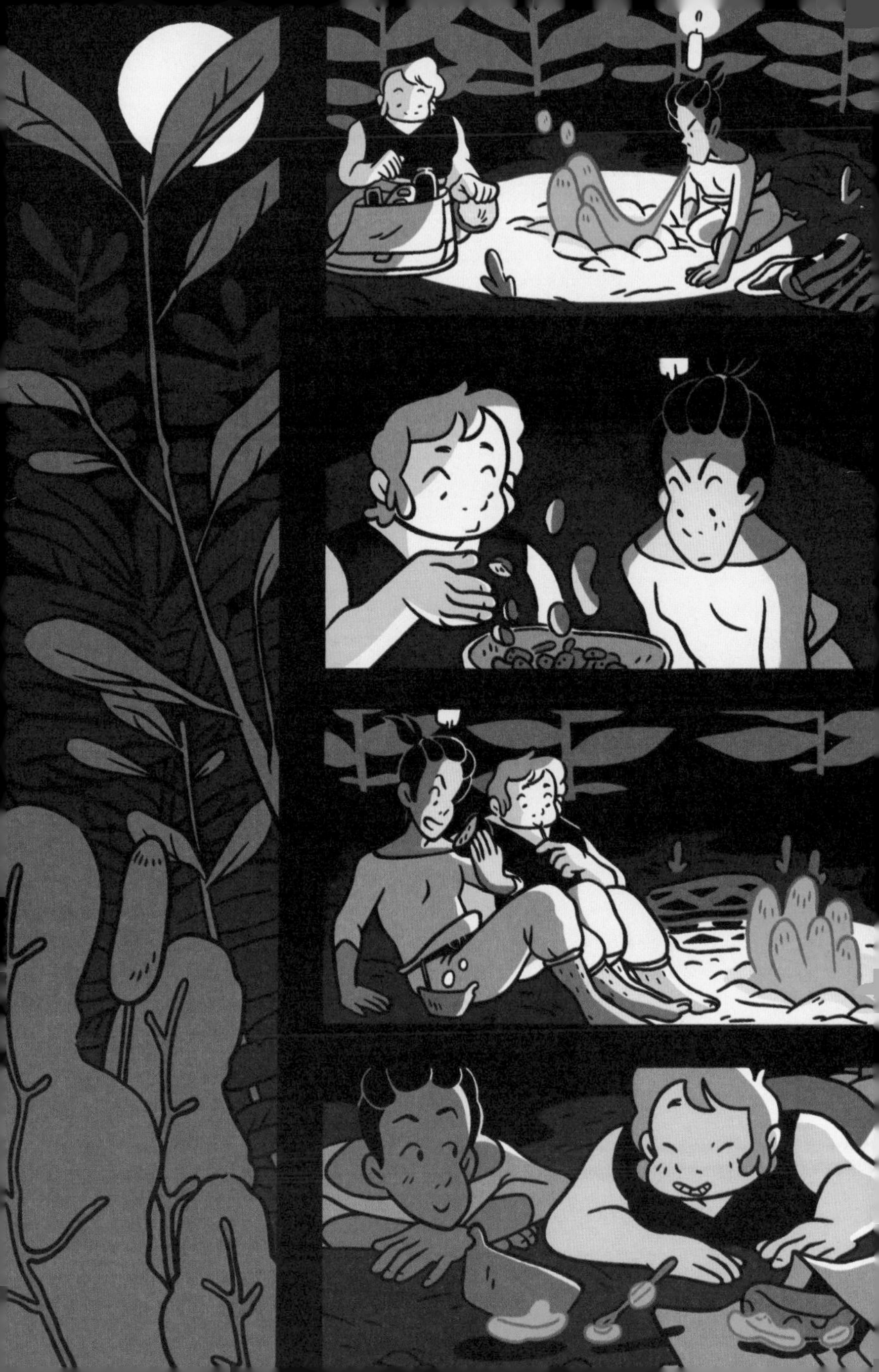

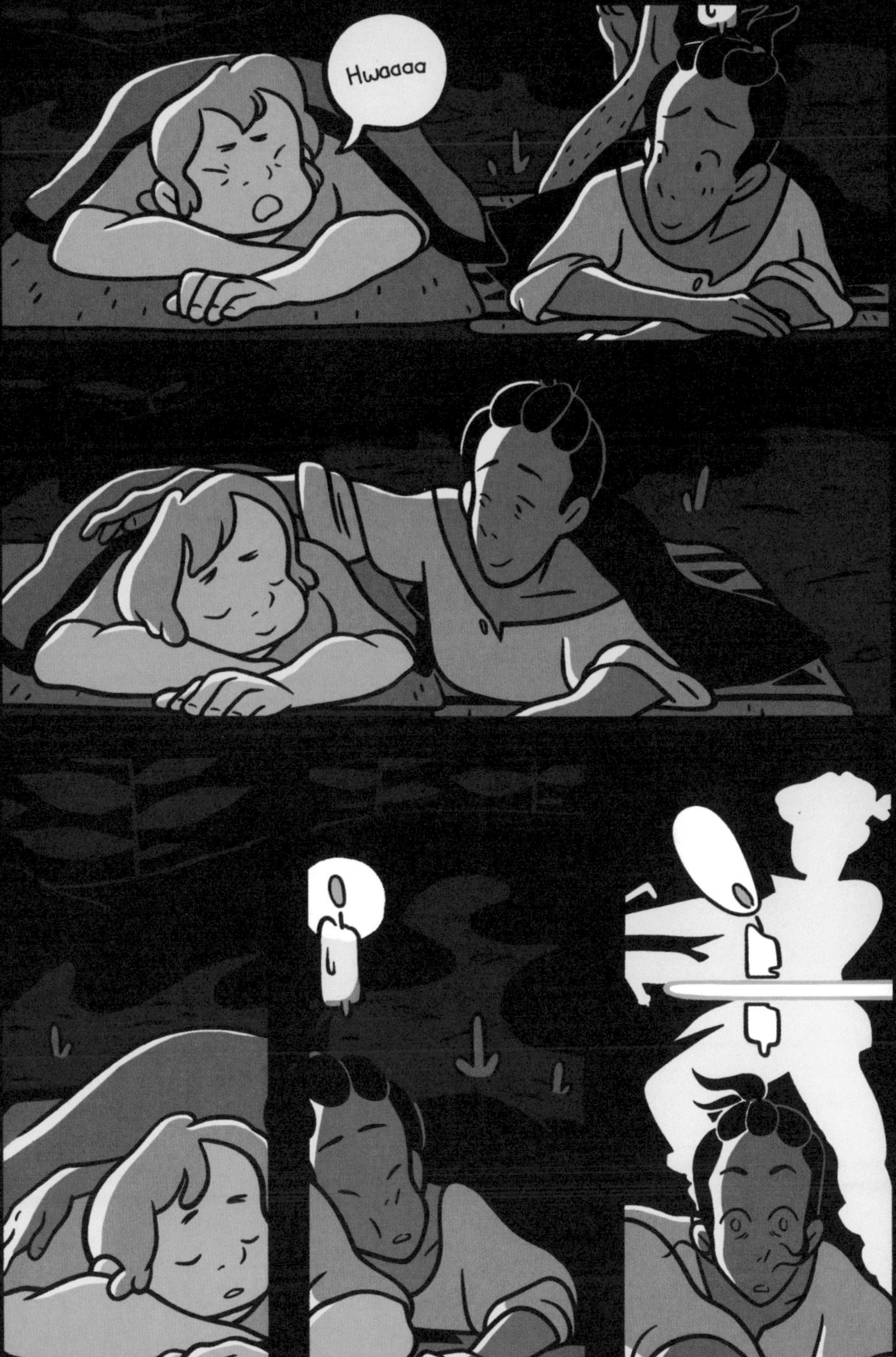
Hwaaaa

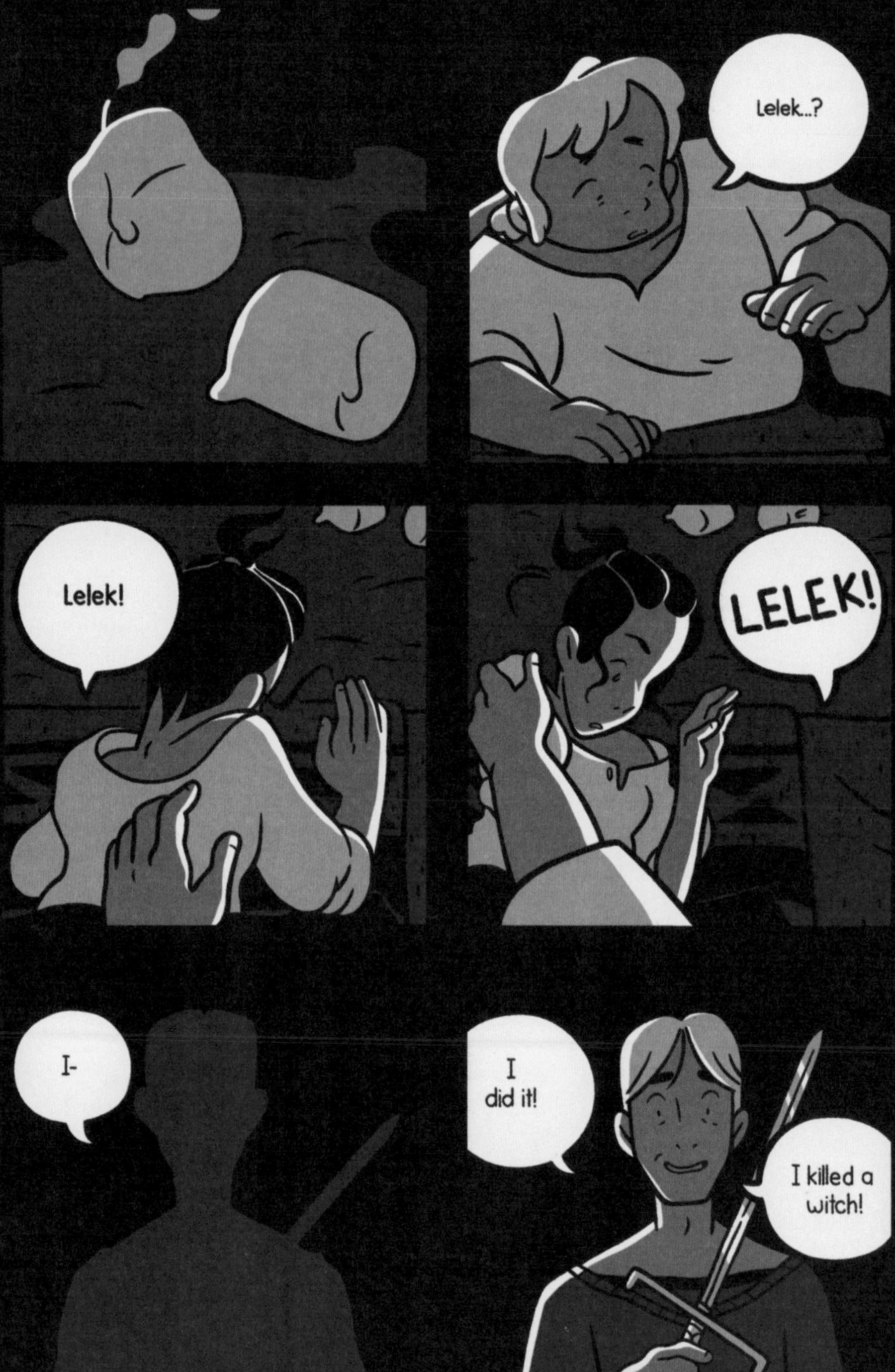
Lelek..?
Lelek!
LELEK!
I-
I did it!
I killed a witch!

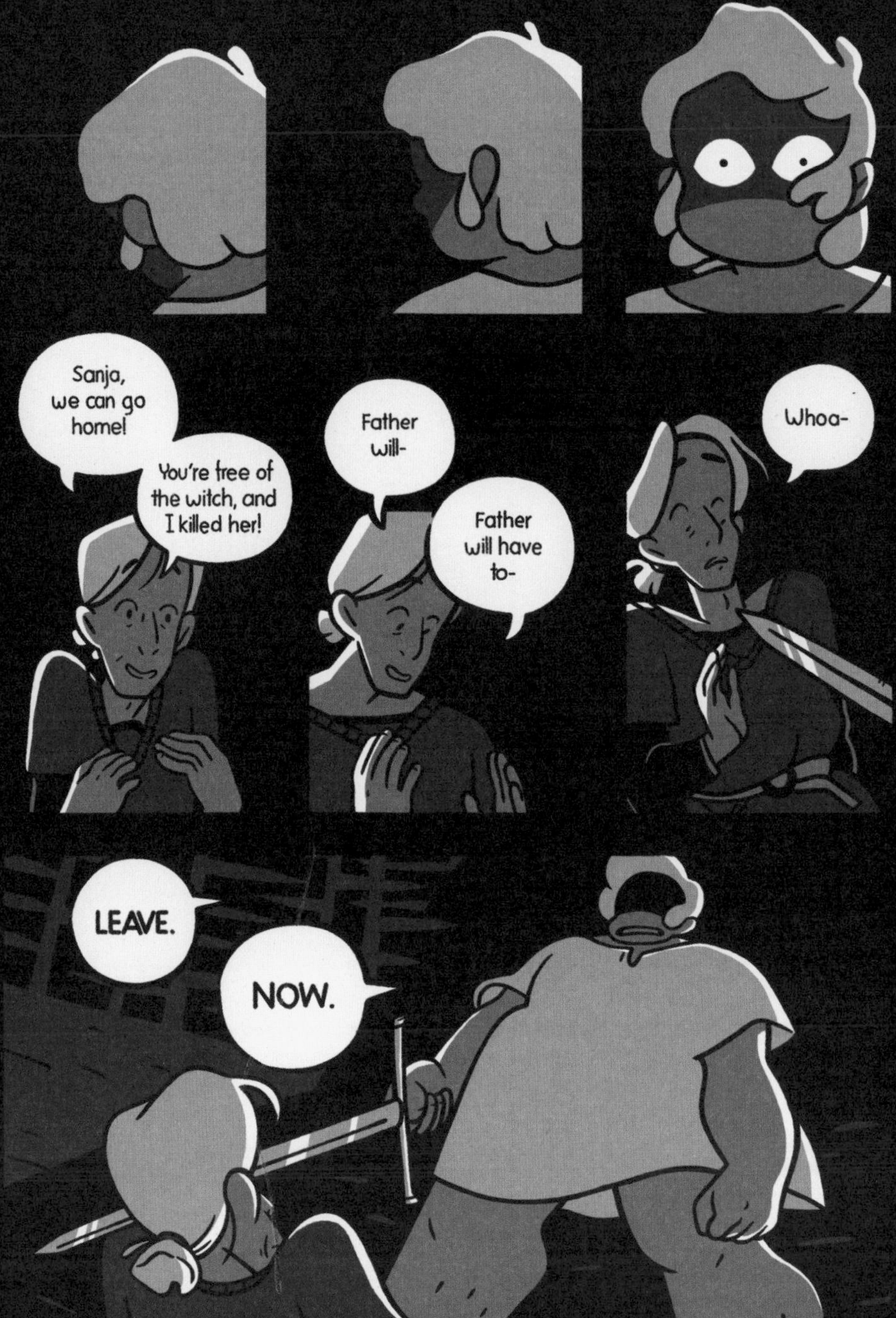
Sanja, we can go home!
You're free of the witch, and I killed her!
Father will-
Father will have to-
Whoa-
LEAVE.
NOW.

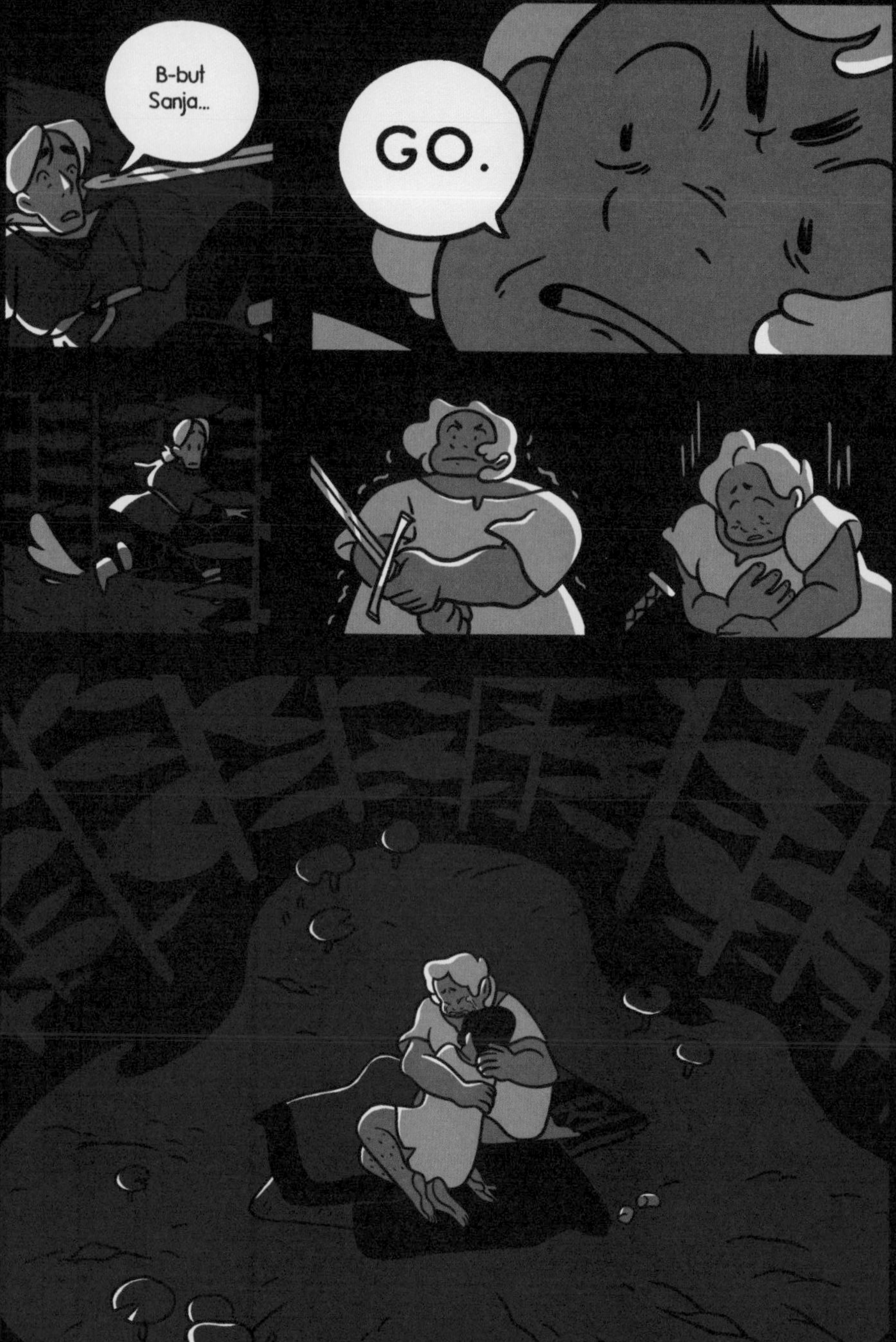
B-but Sanja...
GO.

Part 6

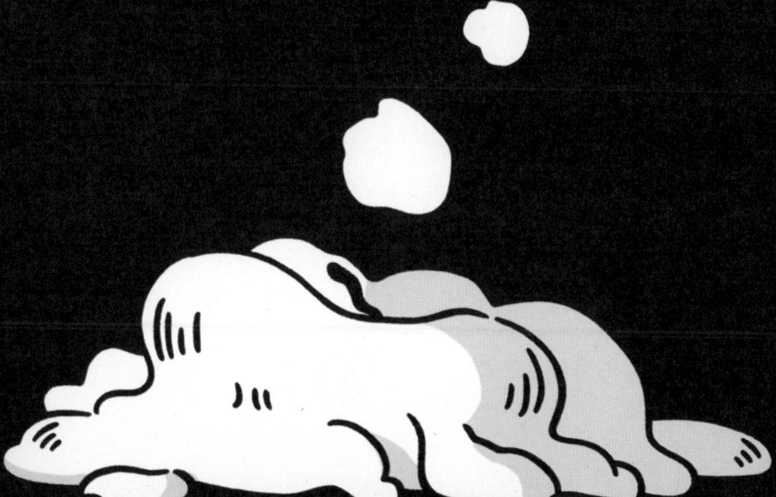

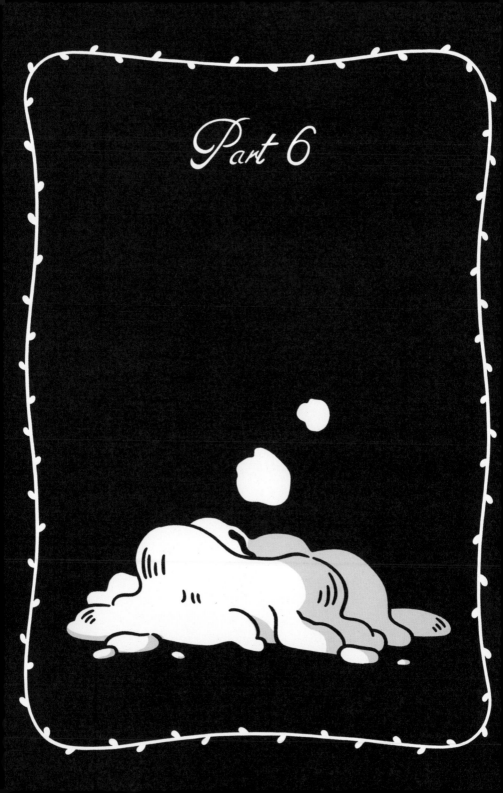

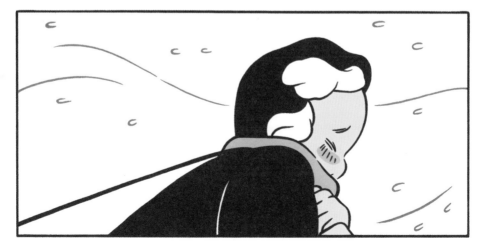

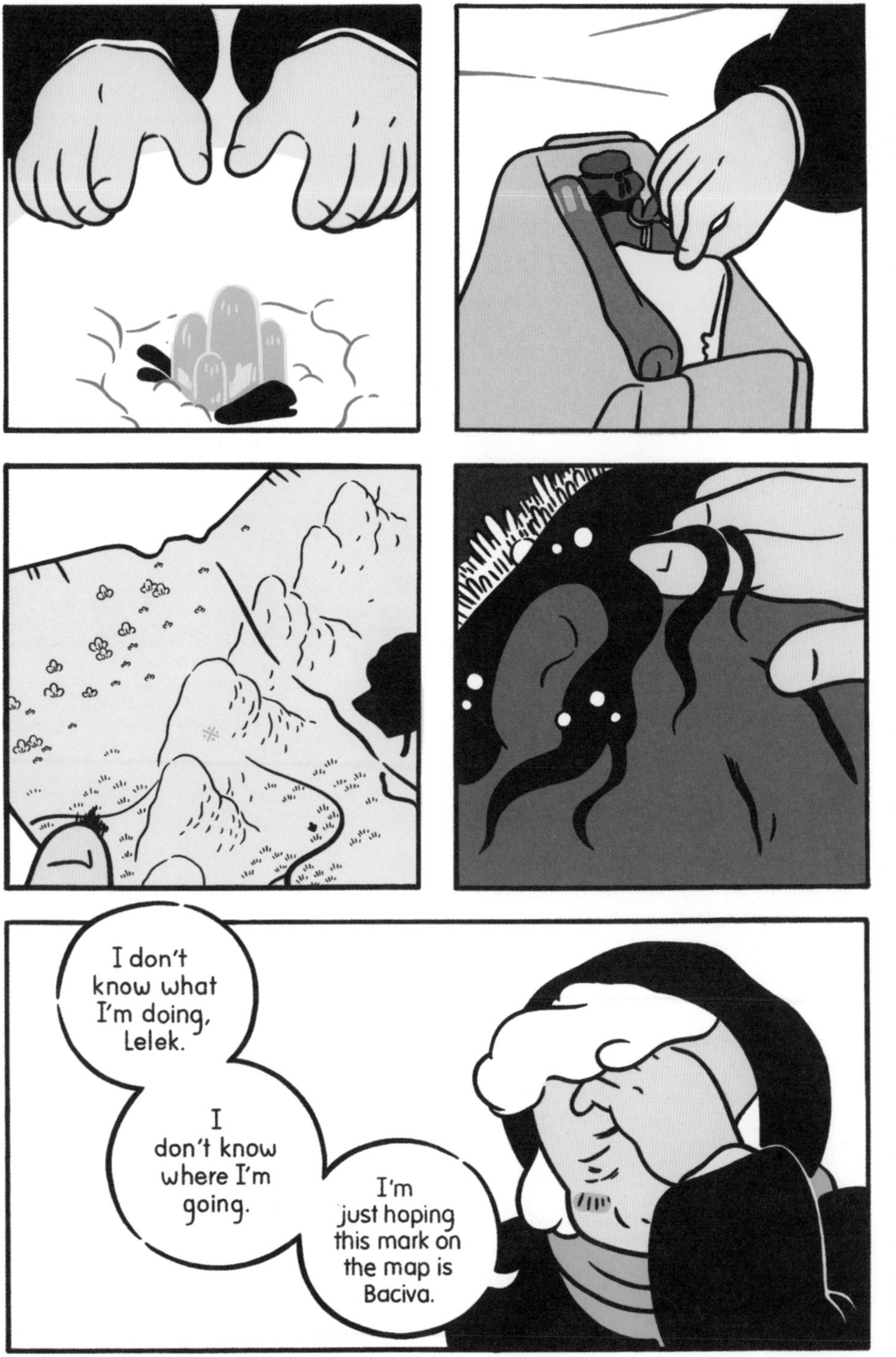
I don't know what I'm doing, Lelek.
I don't know where I'm going.
I'm just hoping this mark on the map is Baciva.

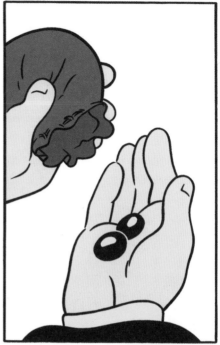

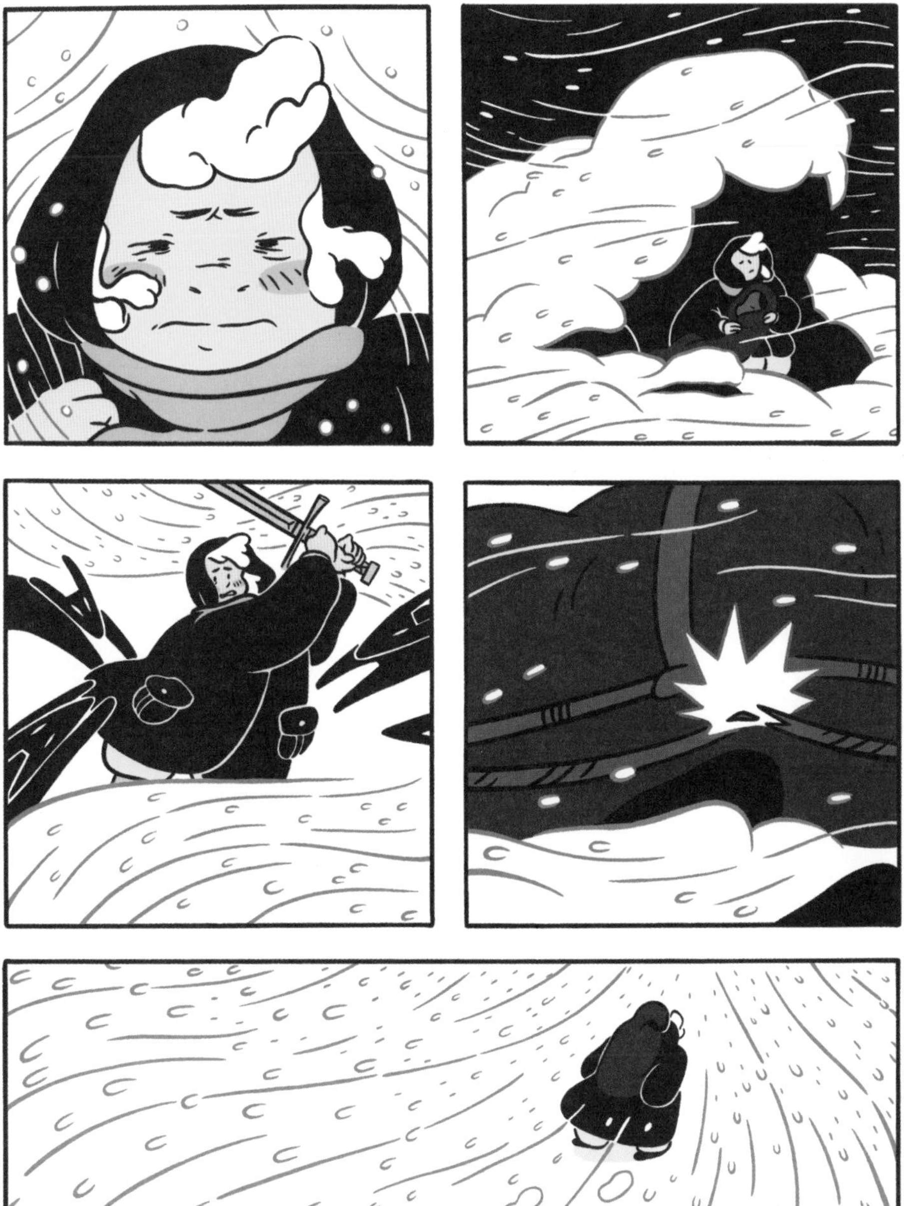

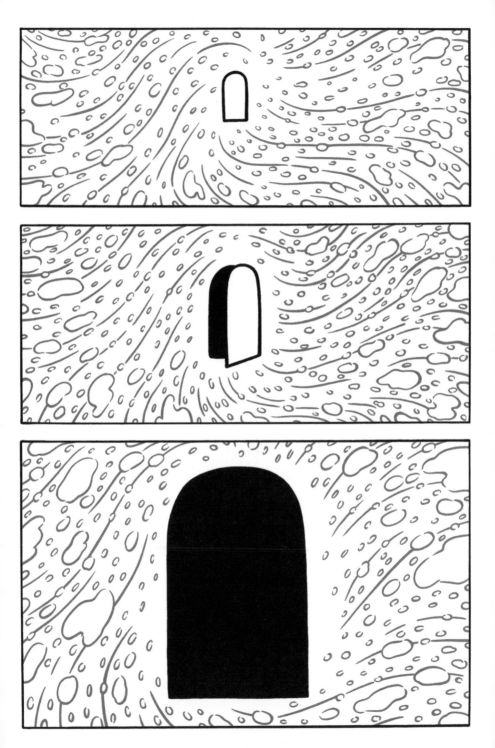

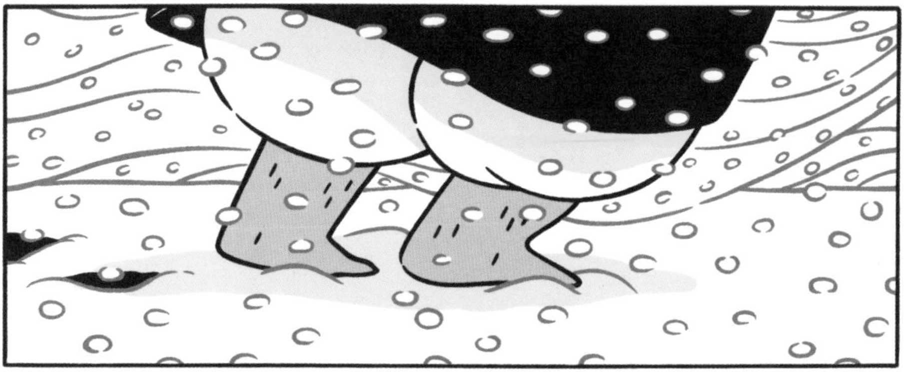

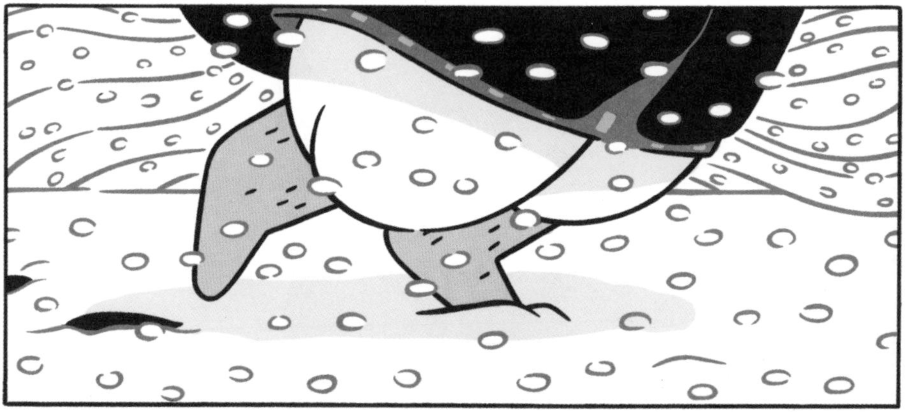

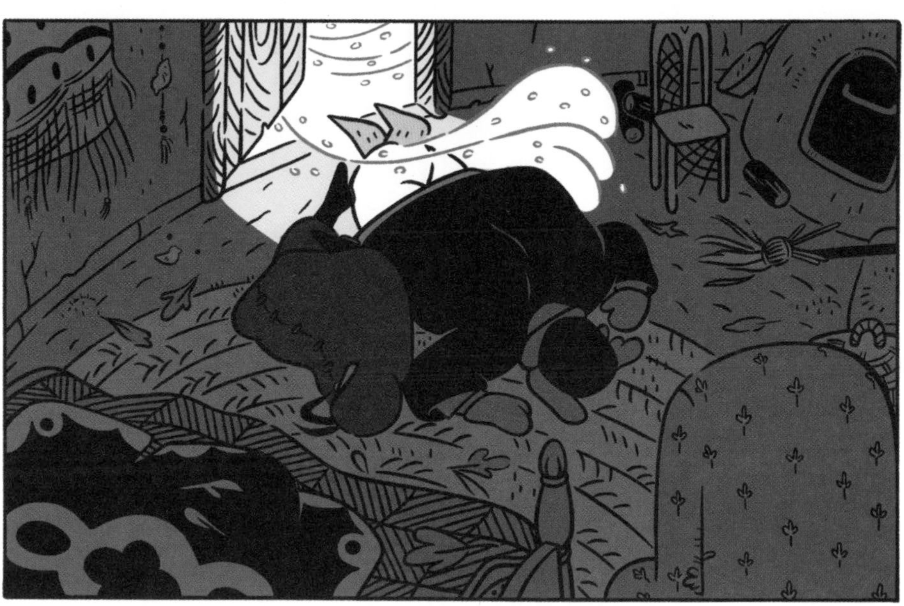

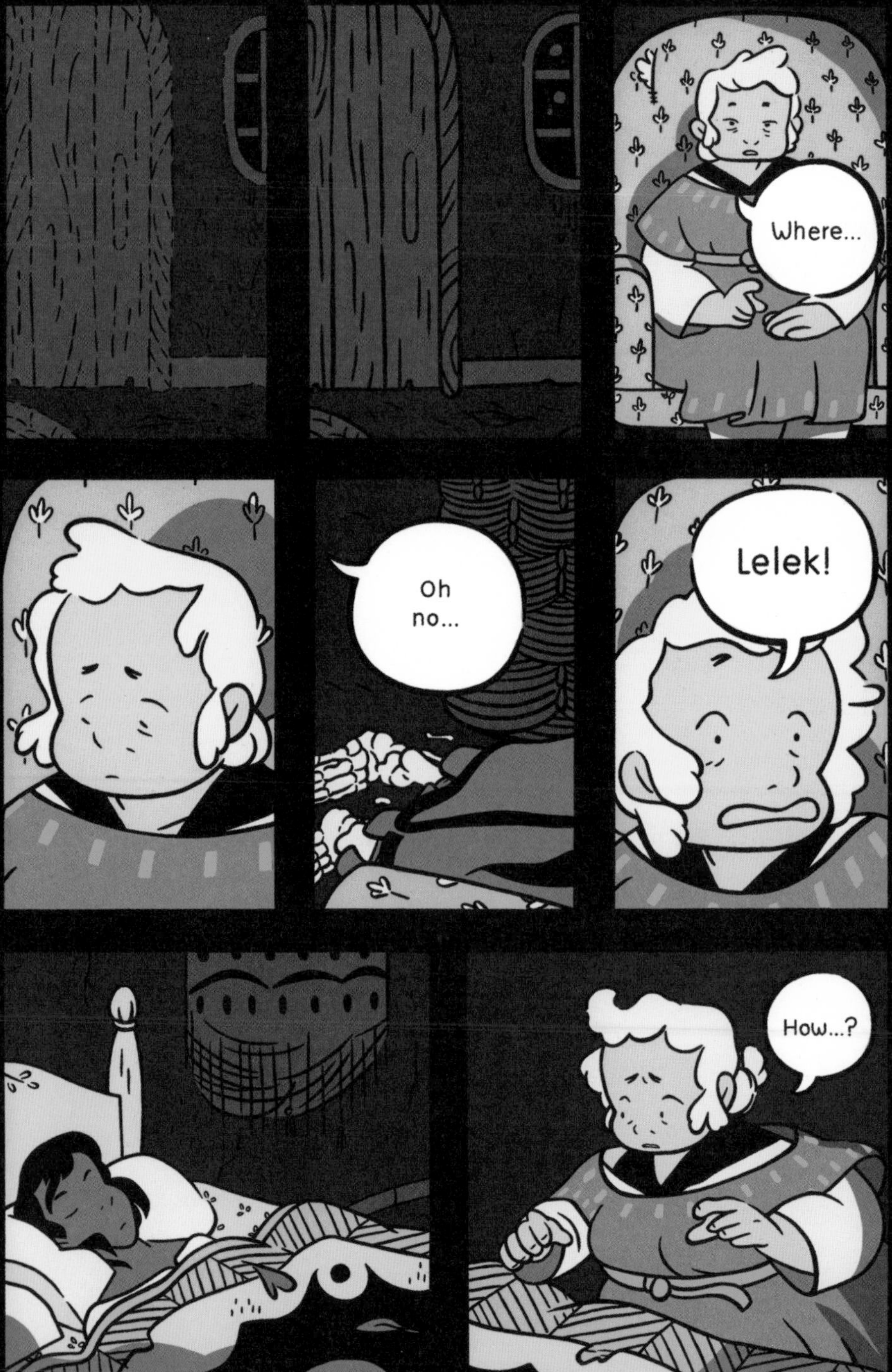
Where...
Oh no...
Lelek!
How...?

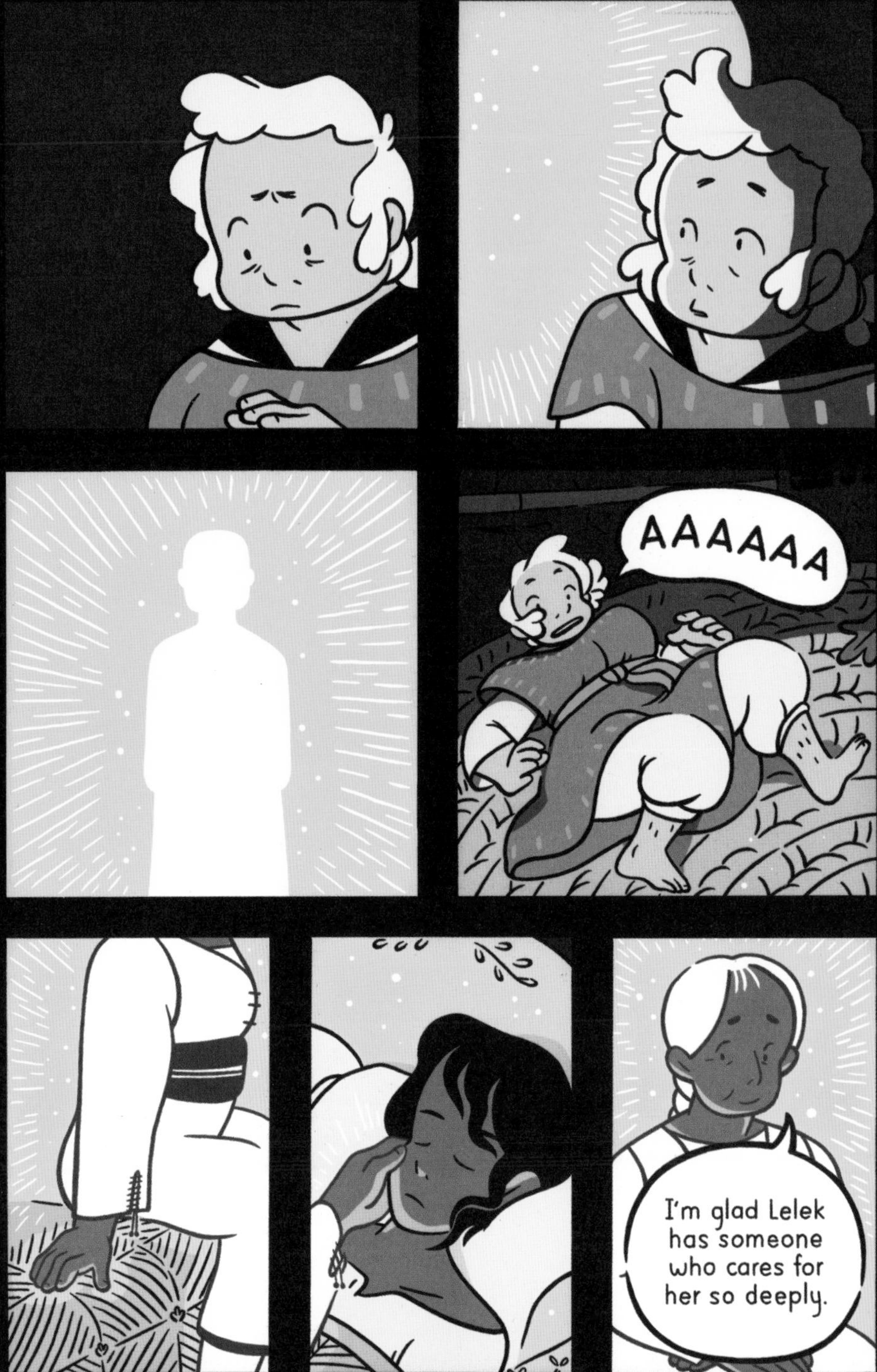
AAAAAA
I'm glad Lelek has someone who cares for her so deeply.

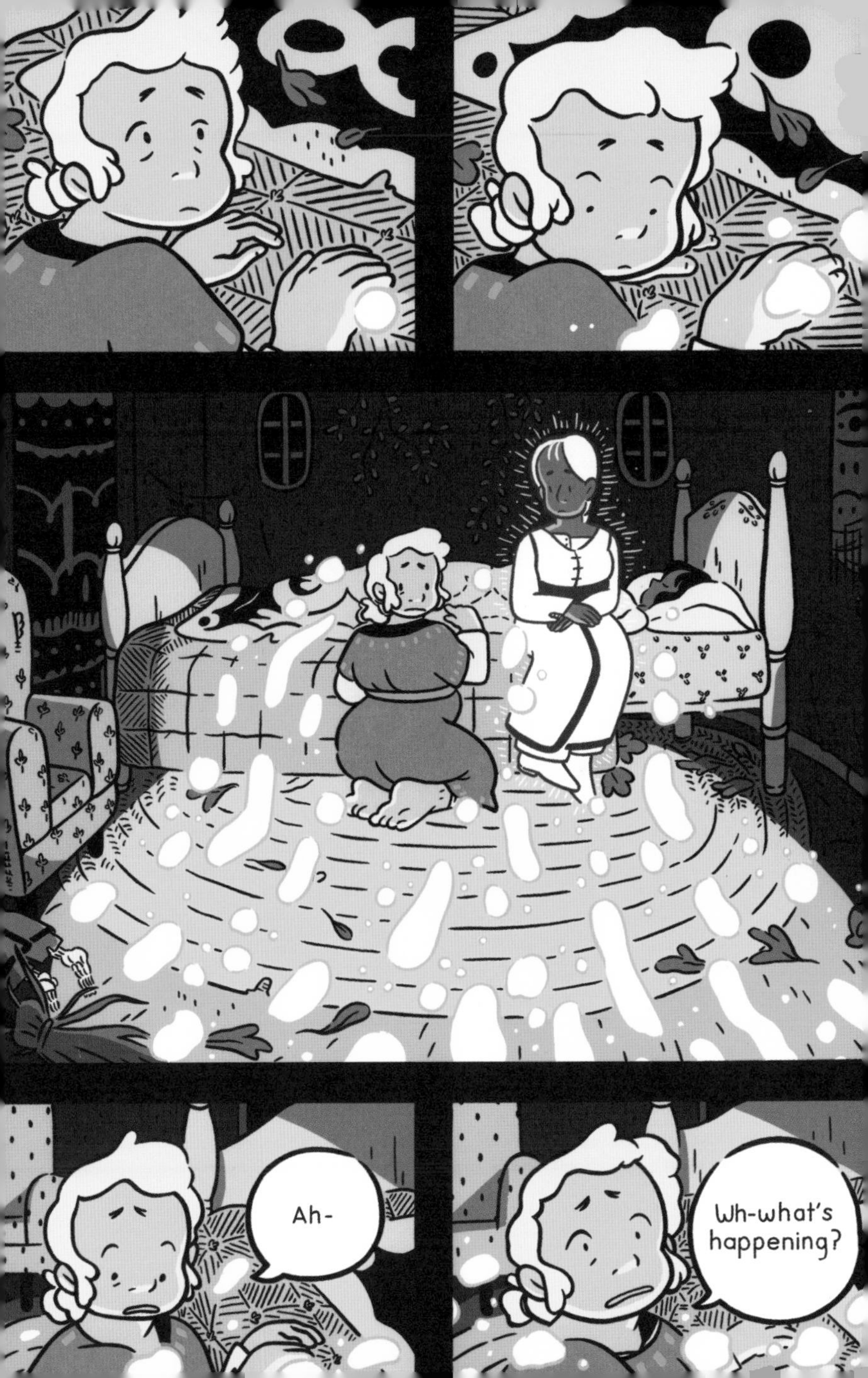
Ah-
Wh-what's happening?

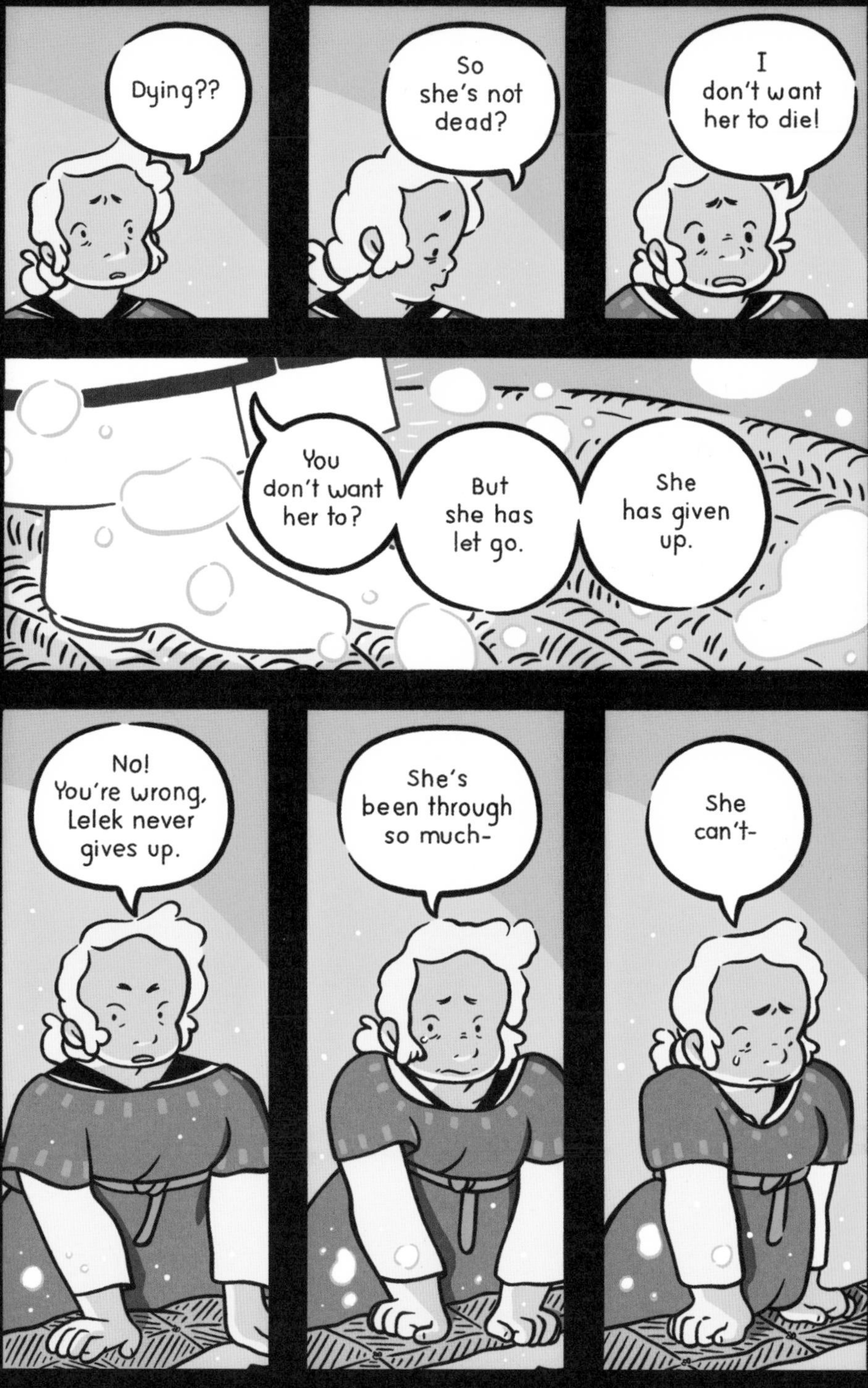
Dying??
So she's not dead?
I don't want her to die!
You don't want her to?
But she has let go.
She has given up.
No! You're wrong, Lelek never gives up.
She's been through so much-
She can't-

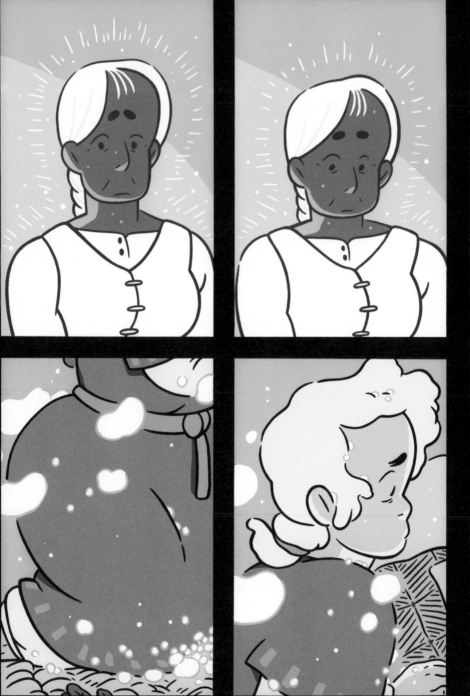

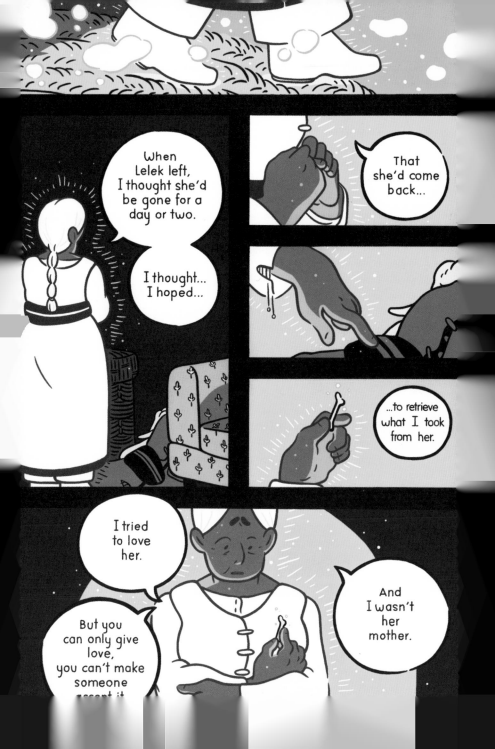

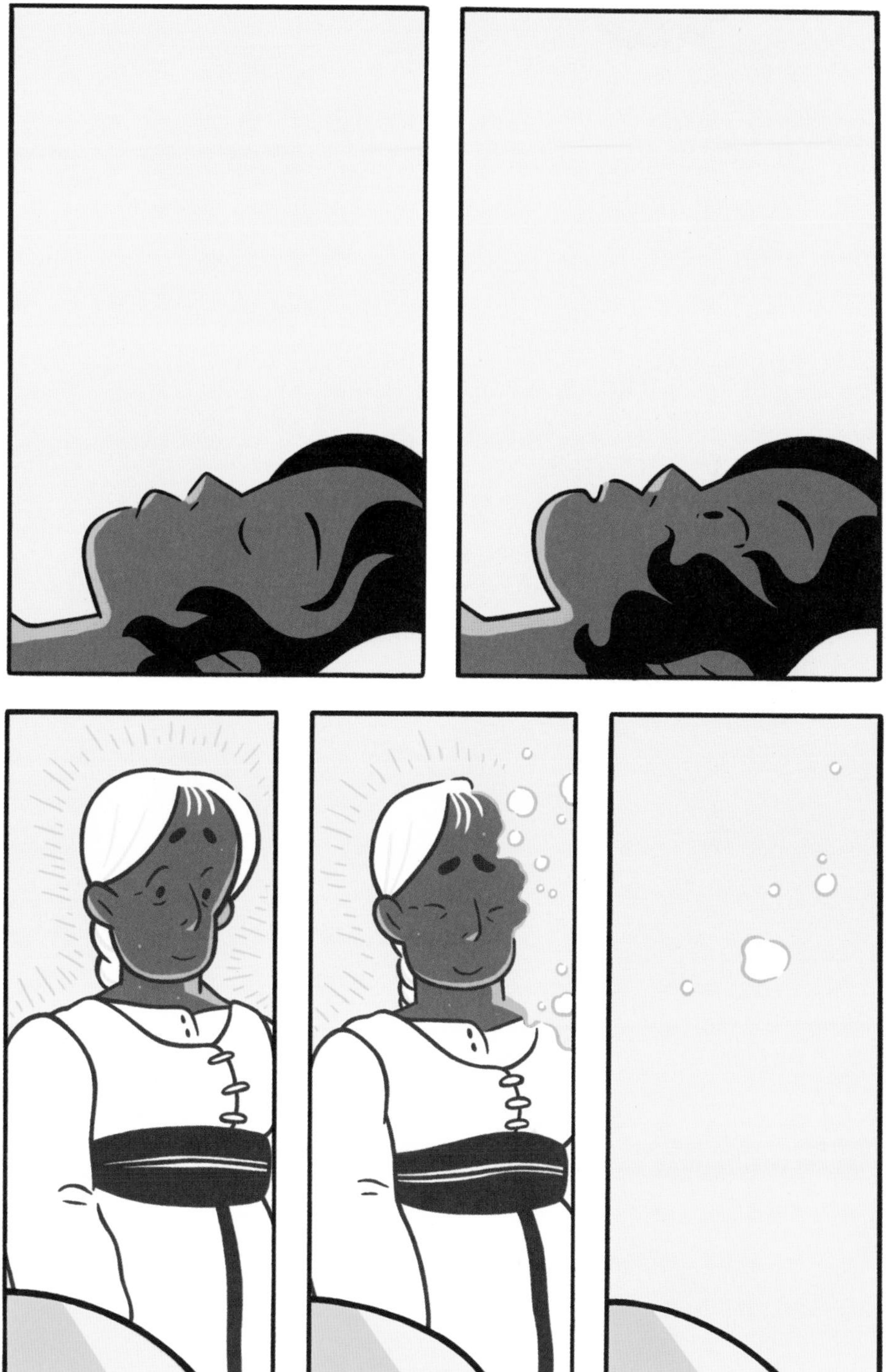

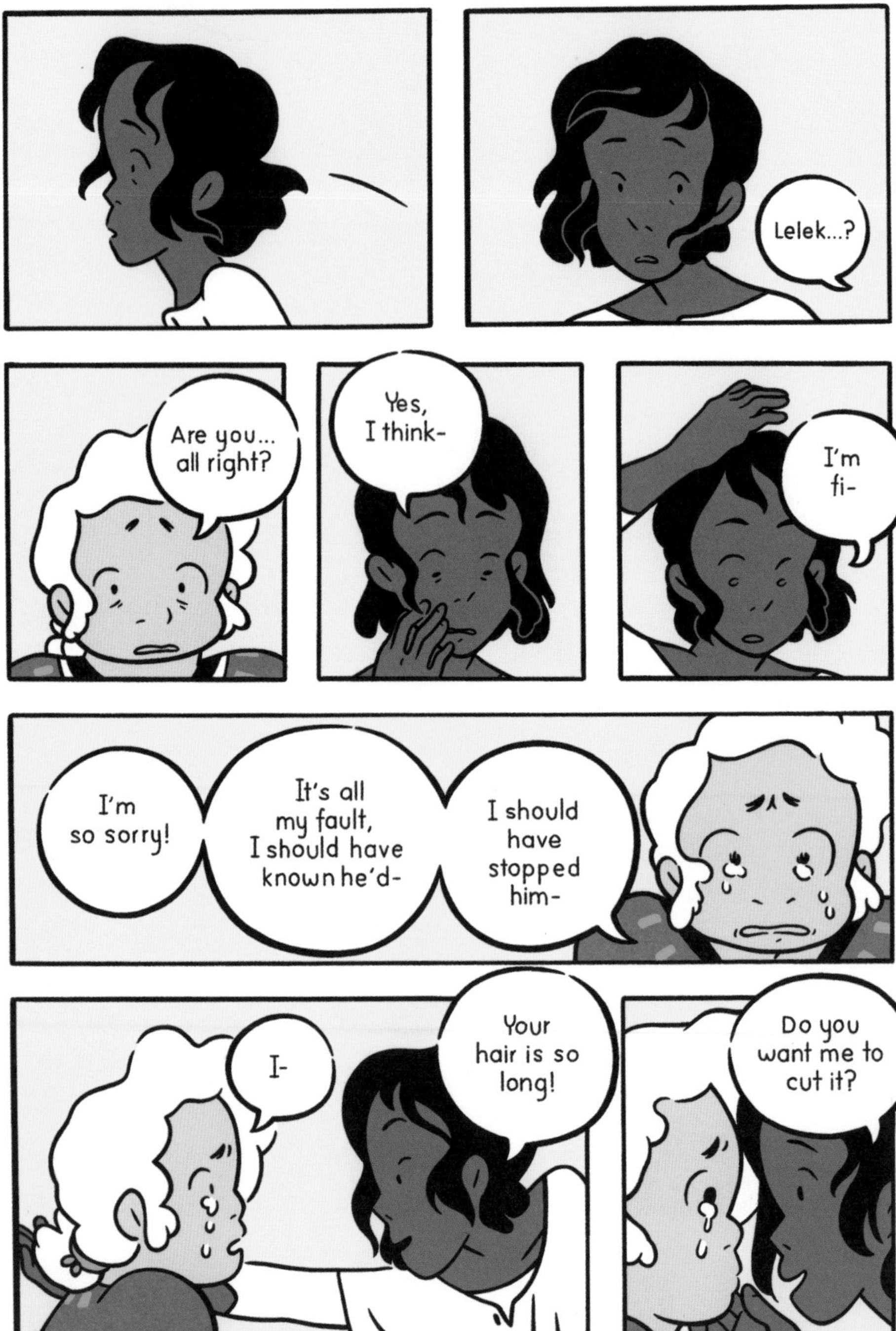
Lelek...?
Are you... all right?
Yes, I think-
I'm fi-
I'm so sorry!
It's all my fault, I should have known he'd-
I should have stopped him-
I-
Your hair is so long!
Do you want me to cut it?

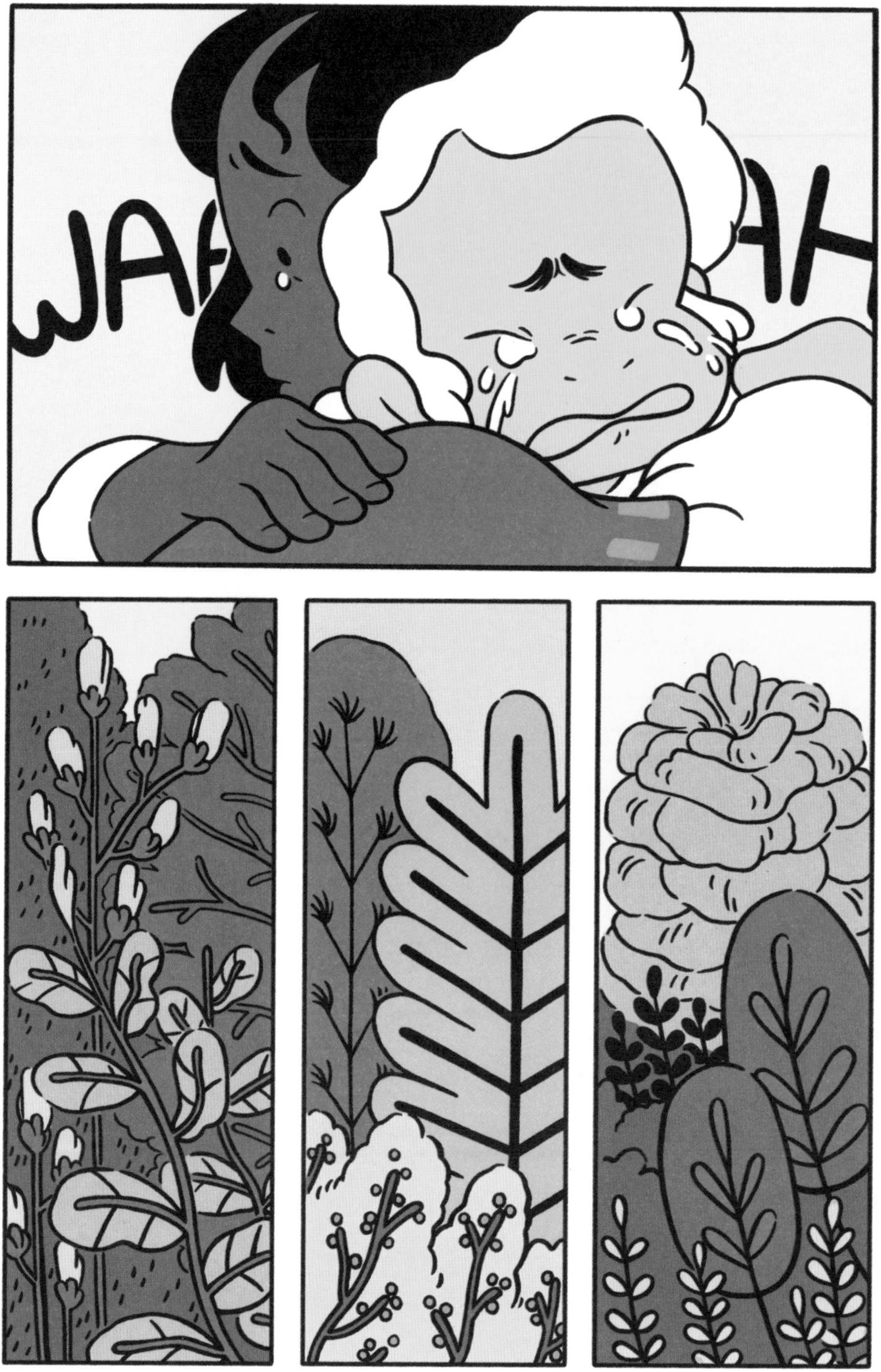

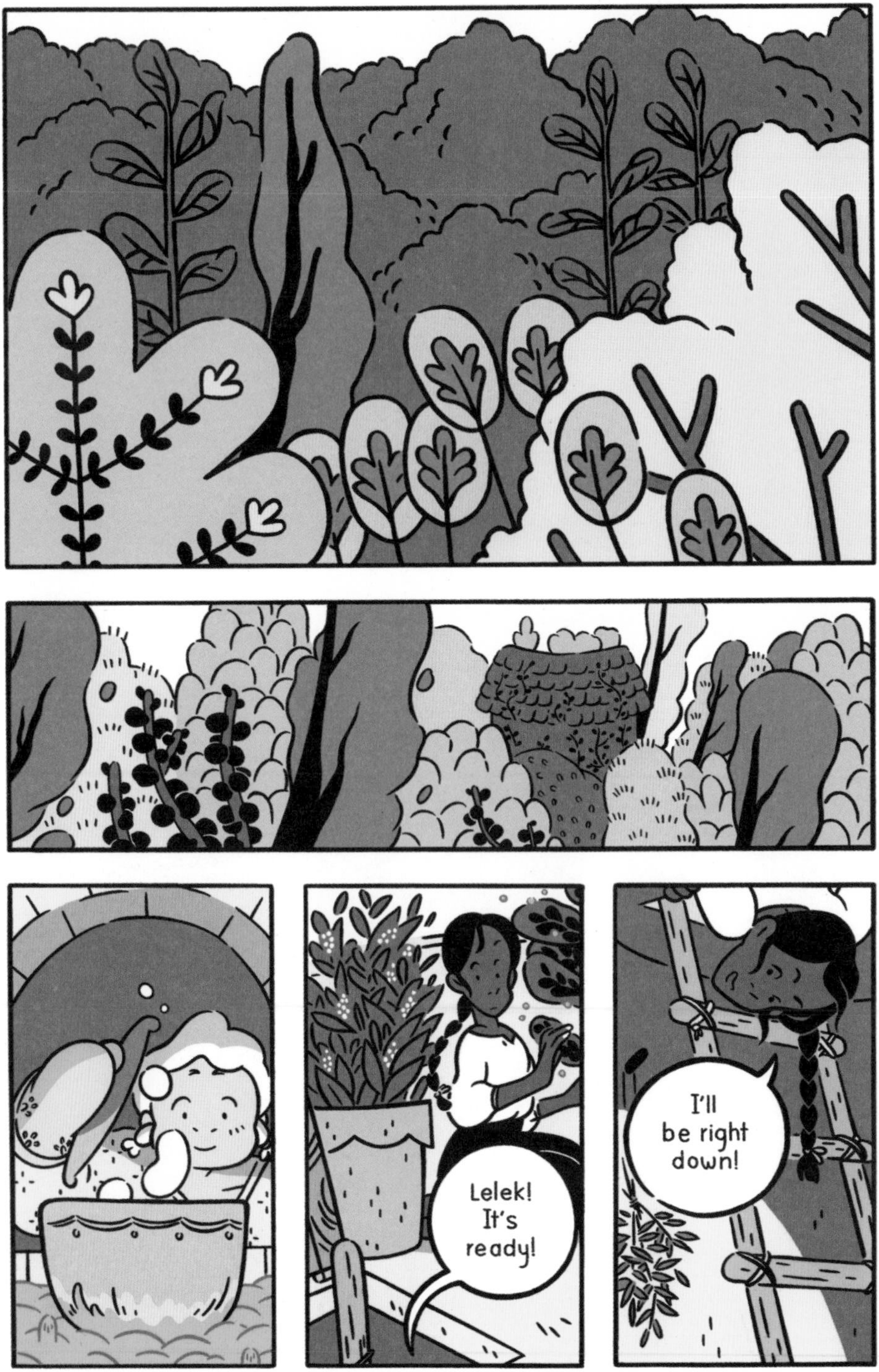
Lelek! It's ready!
I'll be right down!

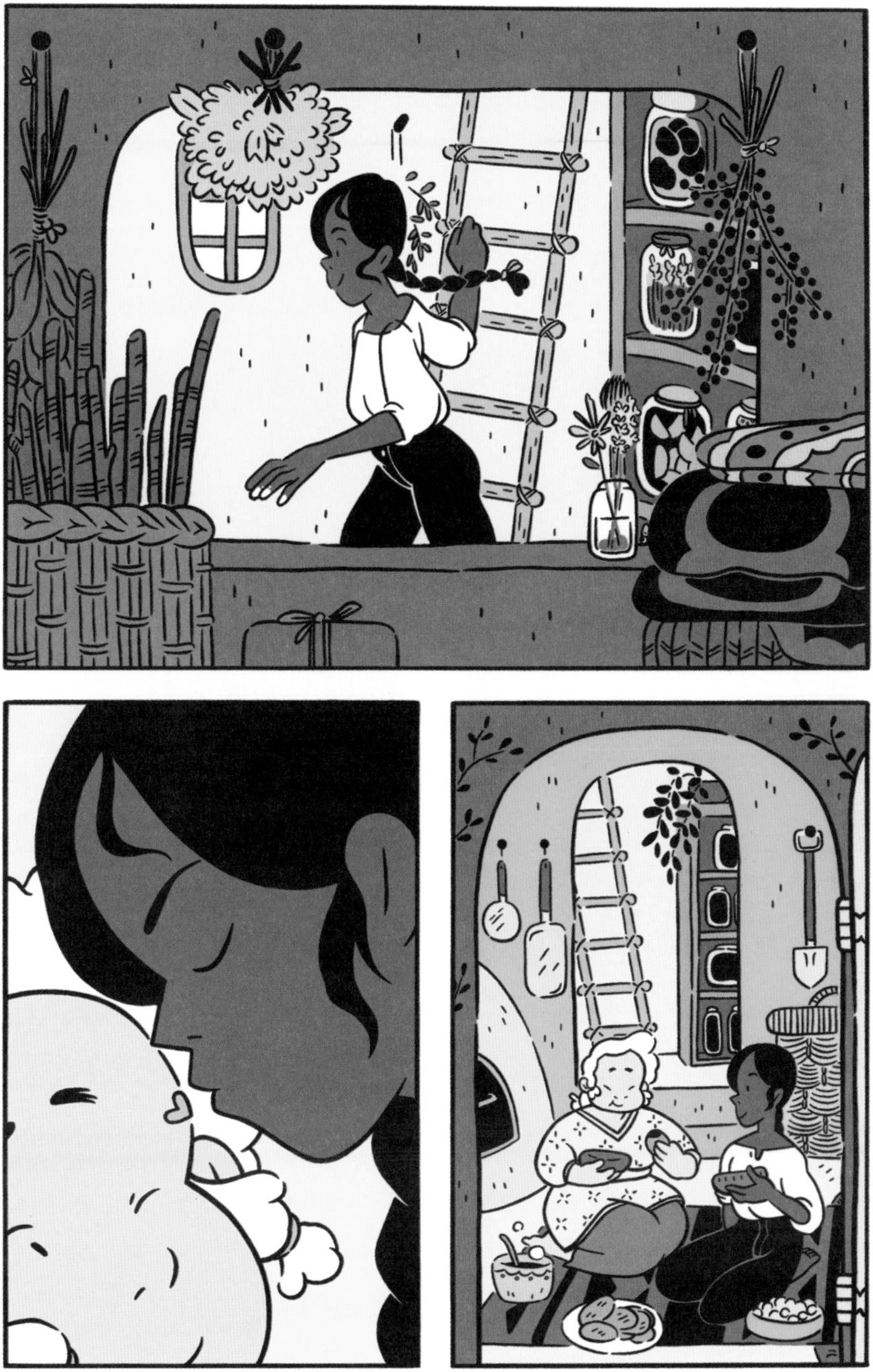

Epilogue

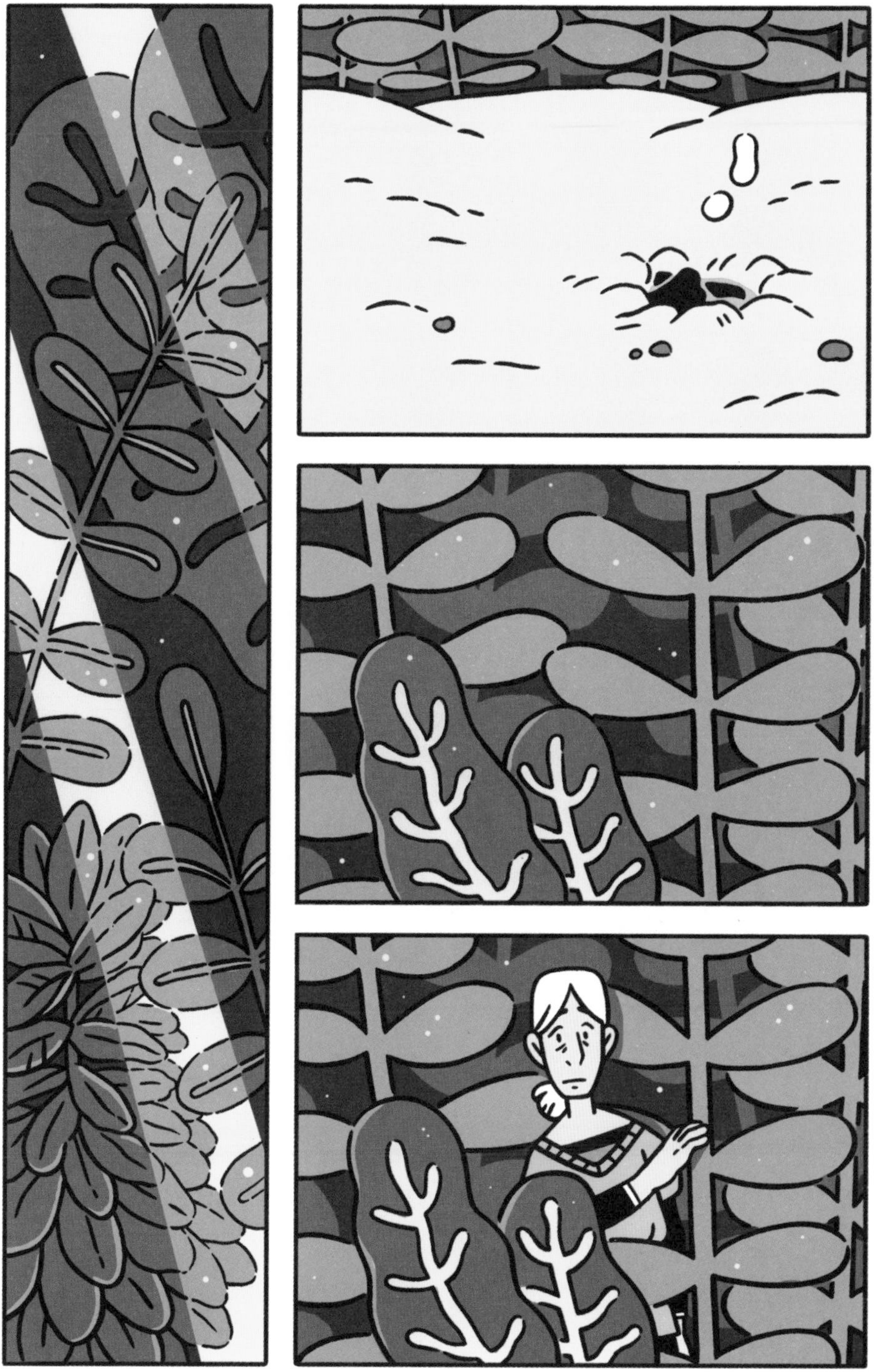

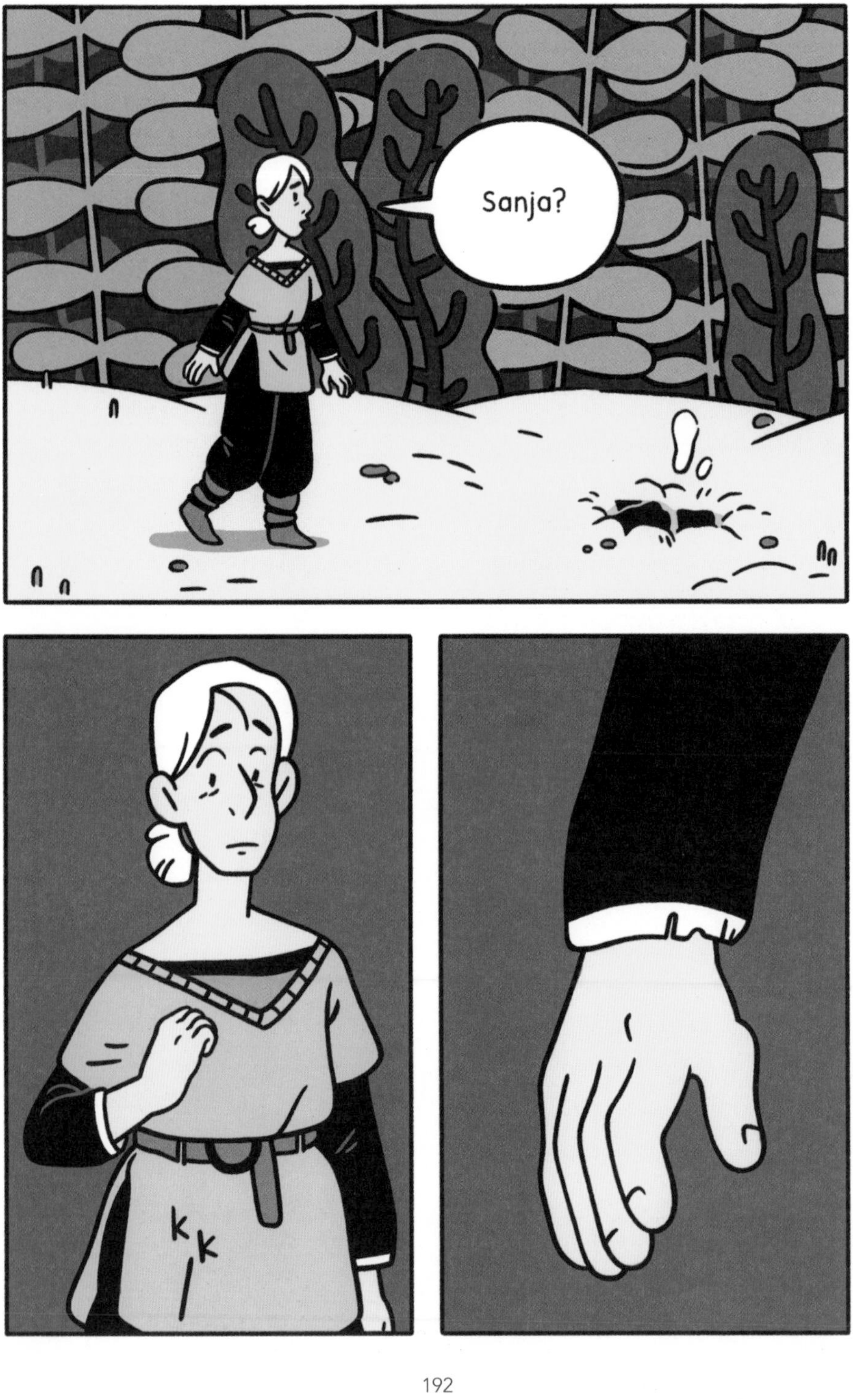
Sanja?
kk

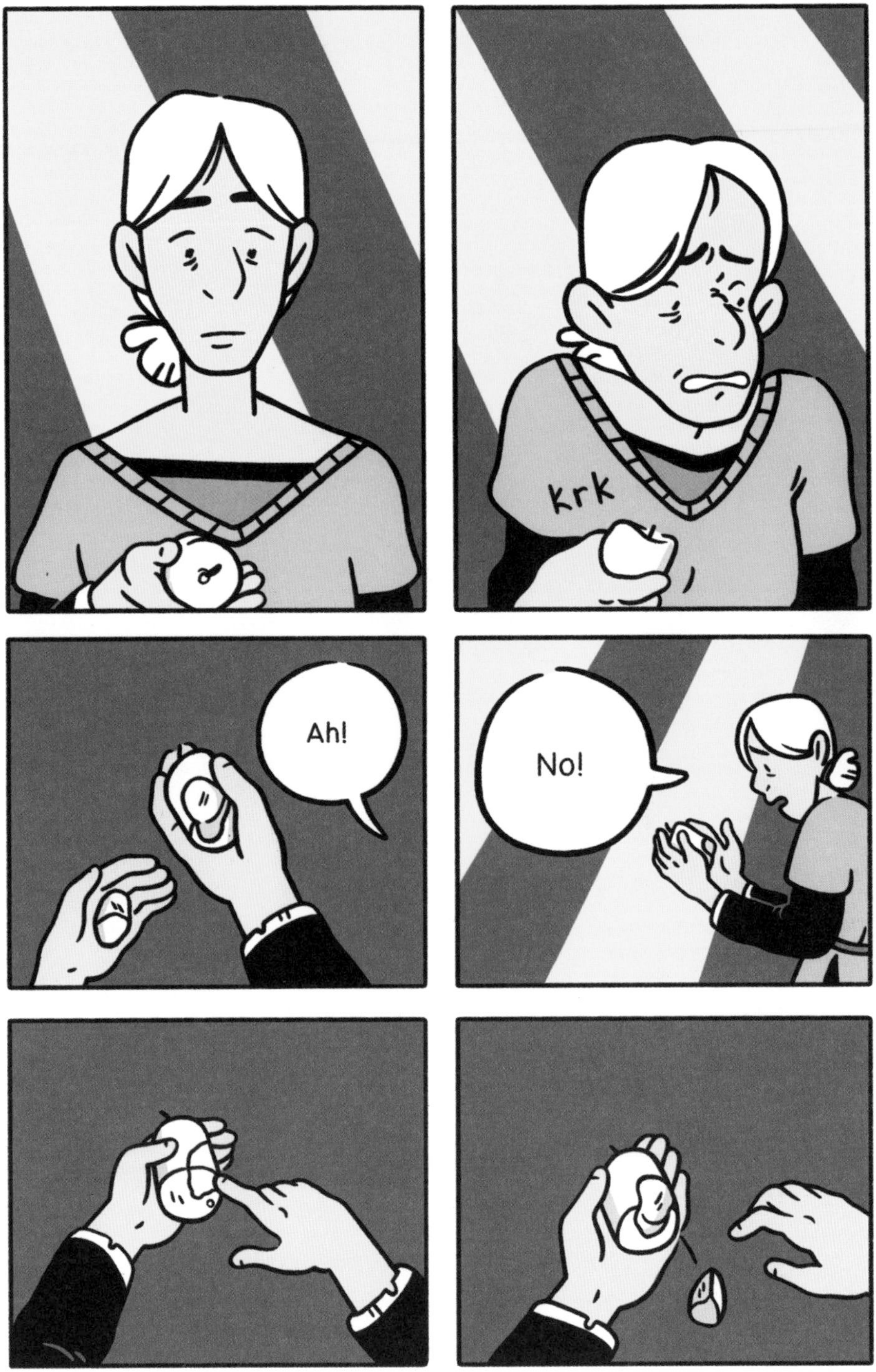
krk
Ah!
No!

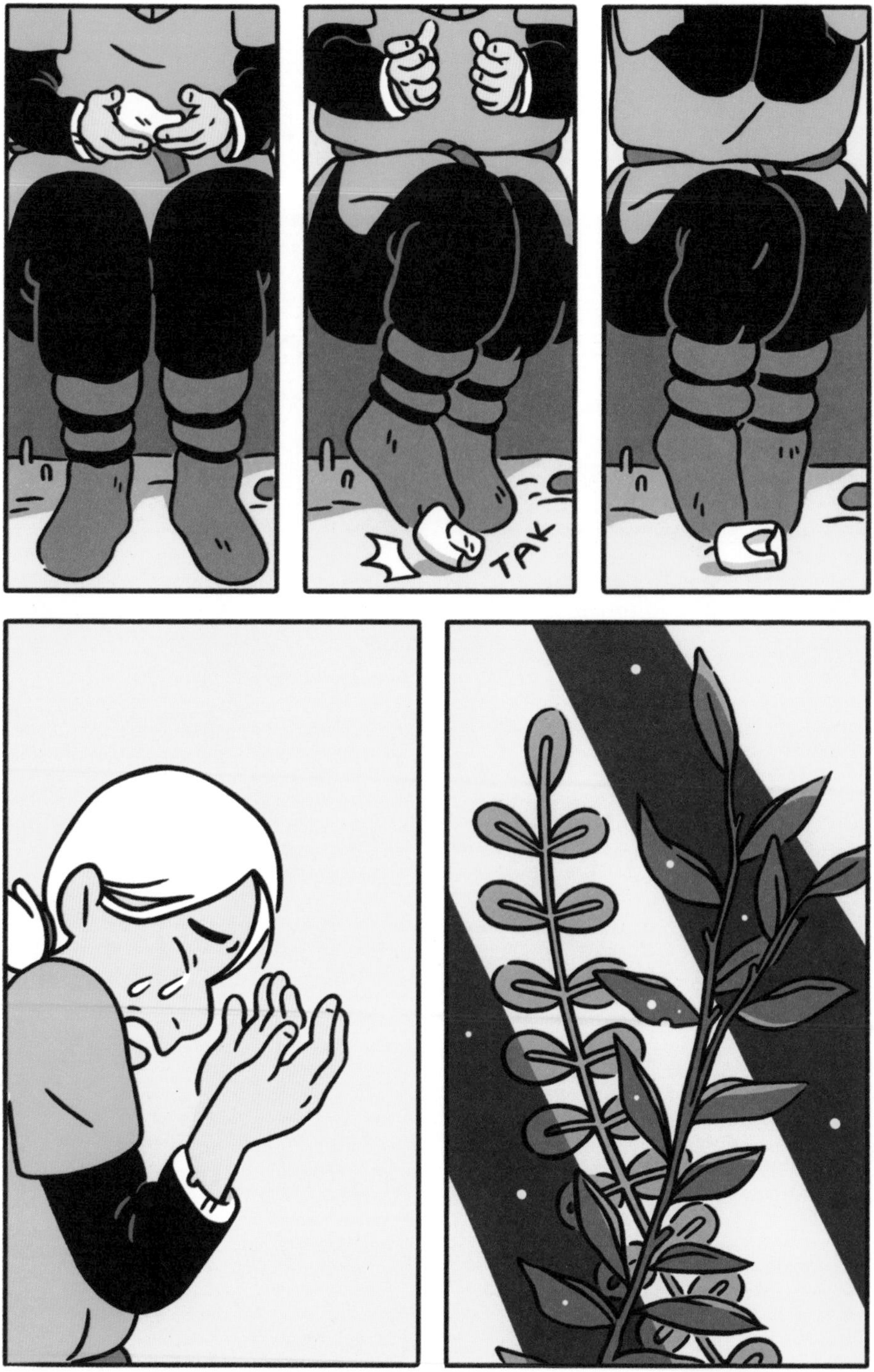
TAK

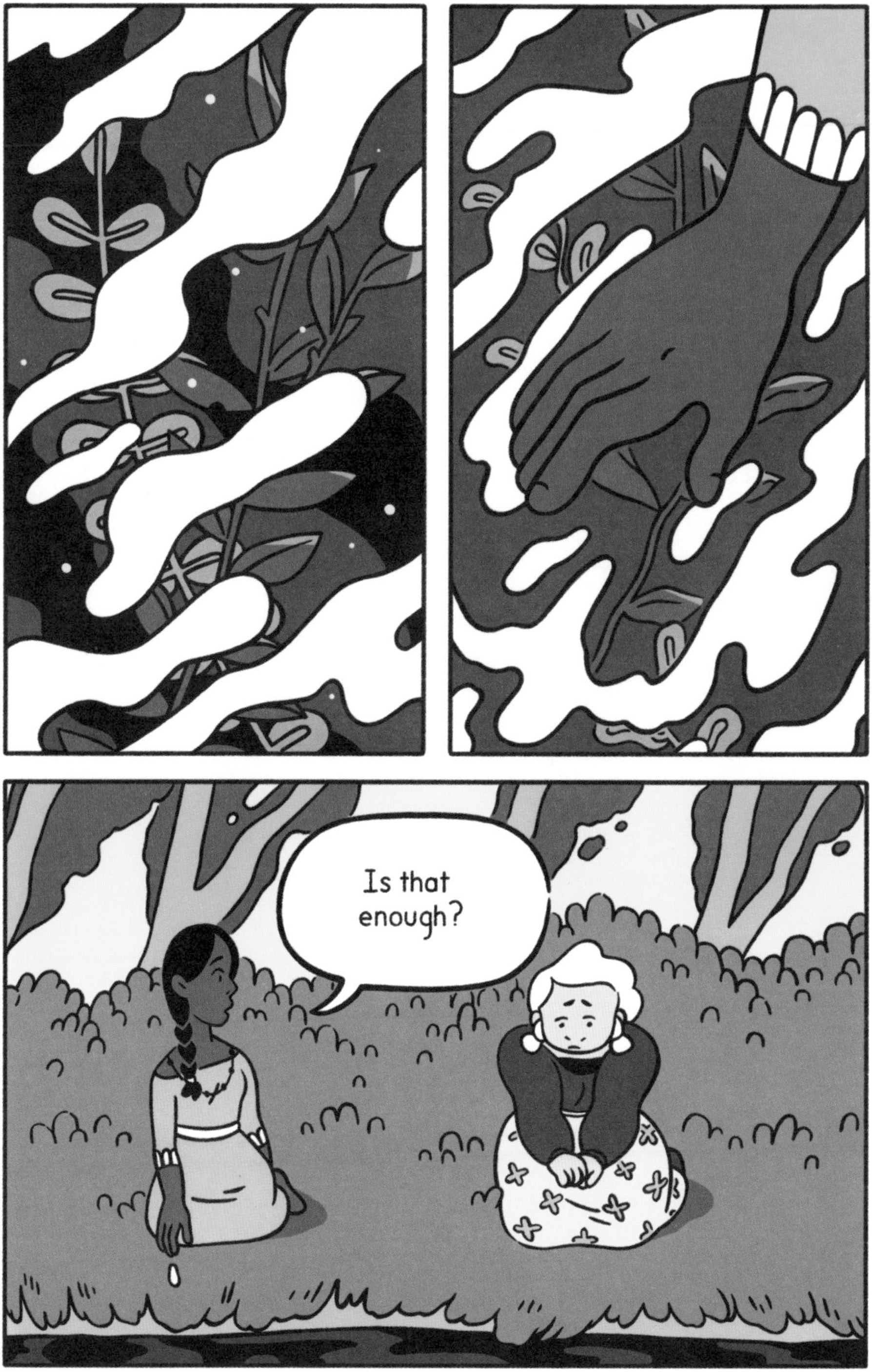
Is that enough?

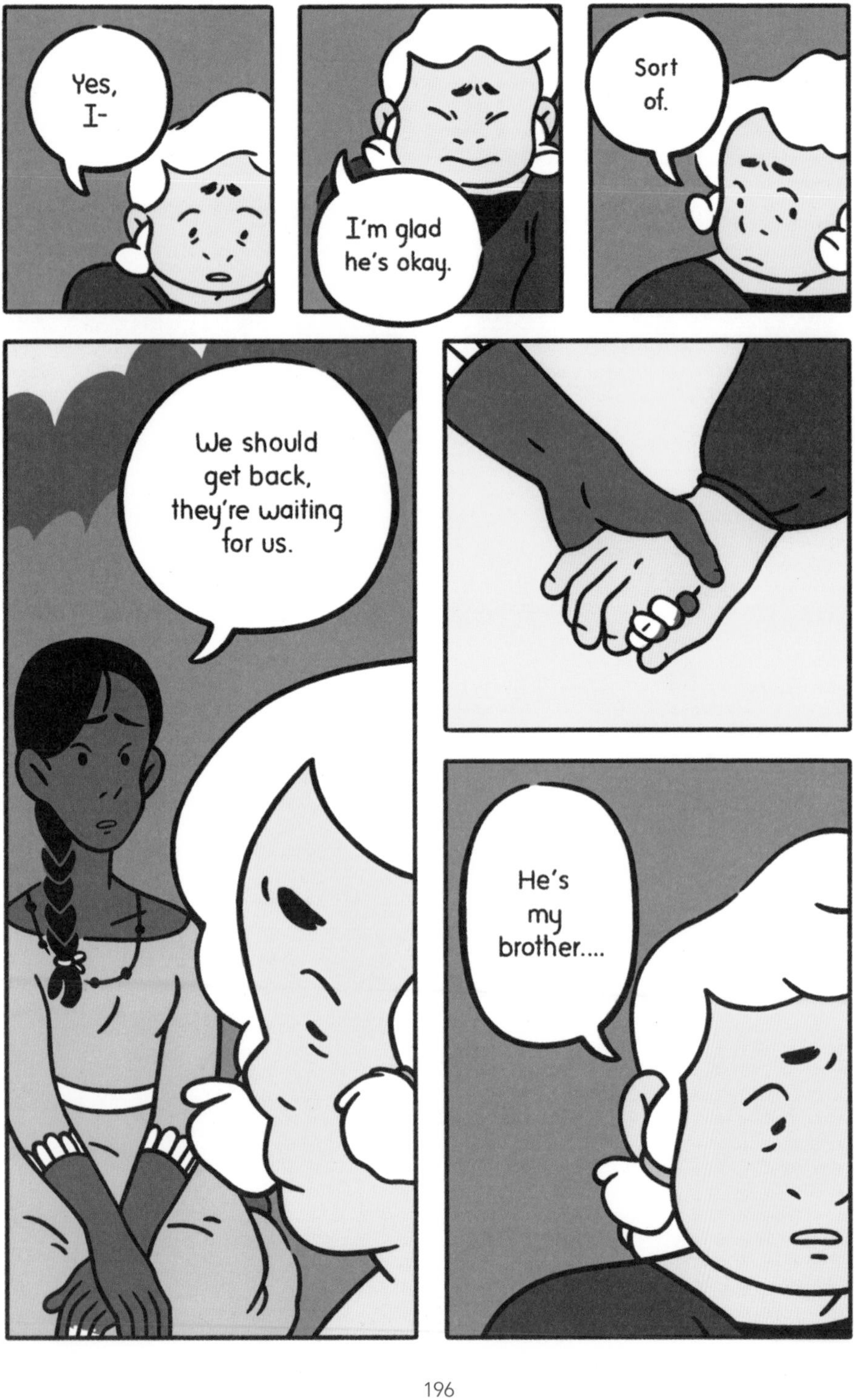
Yes, I-
I'm glad he's okay.
Sort of.
We should get back, they're waiting for us.
He's my brother....

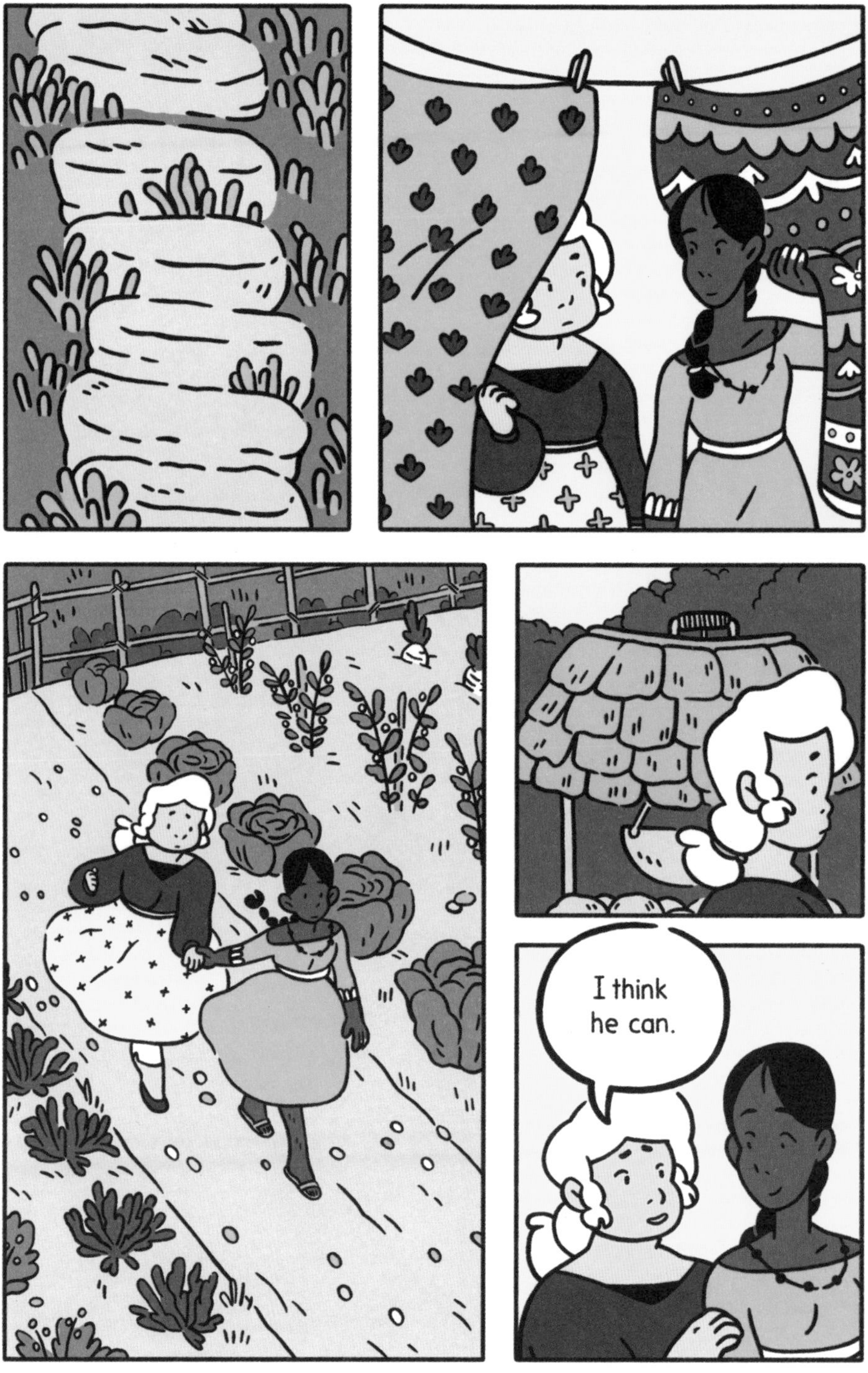
I think he can.

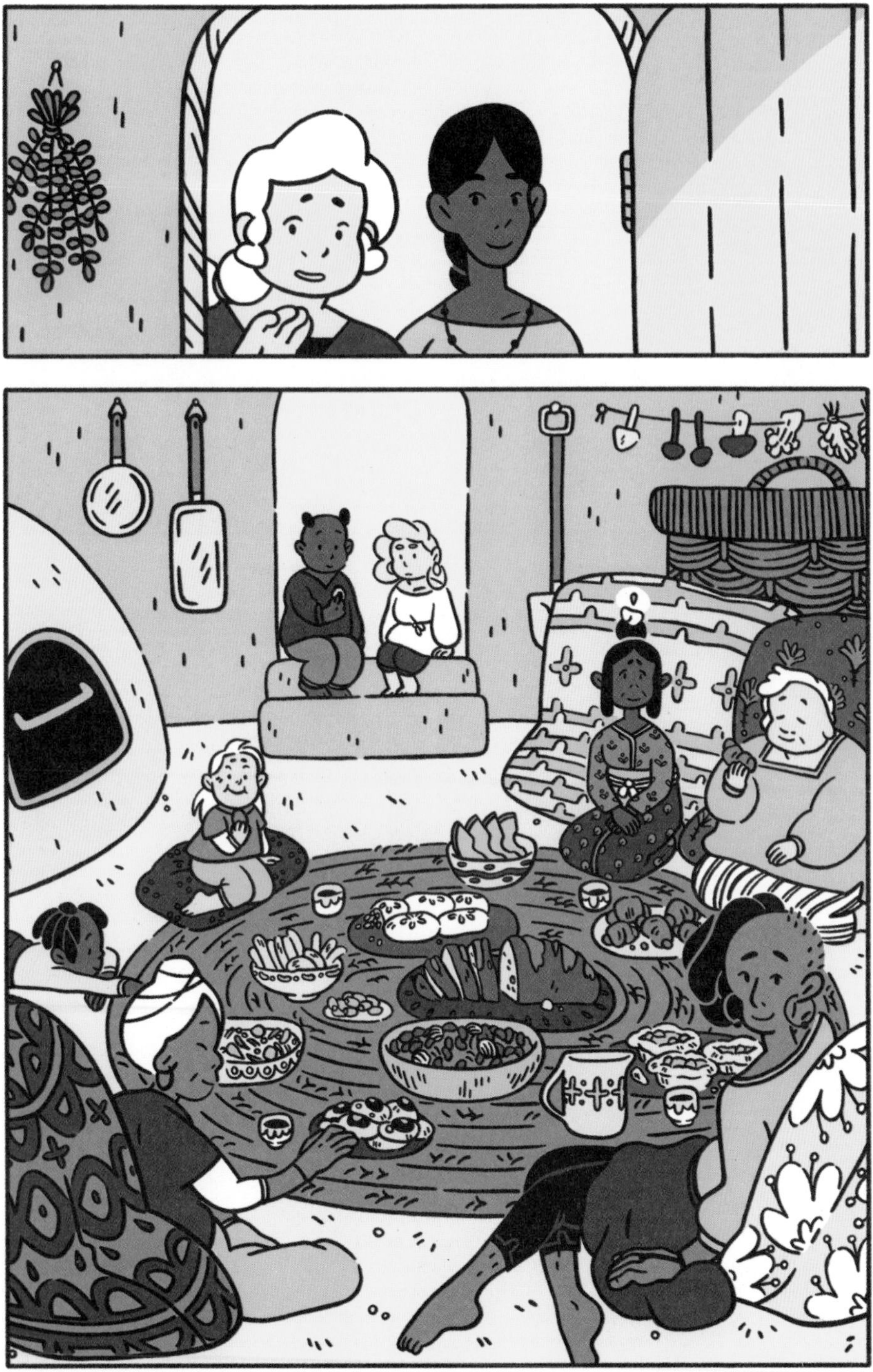

A note from the author:

From the start, *Witchlight* was an experiment in making exactly what I wanted to, and not worrying about what anyone thought it should be. I am incredibly grateful that so many people have embraced it.

A full half of *Witchlight* was made while listening to the podcast *Friends at the Table*, and I'm not sure how it could have gotten done otherwise. Their work has taught me so much about the joy and vulnerability at the core of all good storytelling. I am at heart a solitary and secretive creature, but their show makes me marvel at what can come out of true collaboration and trust.

Thank you to my parents for taking me to parks and museums and libraries, for teaching me how light works and the names of trees. Most of all, thank you for showing me how to tell stories for fun and taking the fear out of writing.

Thank you to Claire, for the good times. I hope we'll have more.

Above all others, thank you to Kevin Czap. When I first met them, I thought, "Who's this nerd?", one of many examples of my rude first impressions of the people who end up most dear to me. They were the first stranger to read my comics and say not just kind things, but insightful and true things about them. I am powered almost constantly by a brash and indestructible determination, but where that resolve stumbles, I keep going because I know Kevin believes I will.

RH GRAPHIC
THE DEBUT LIST

BUG BOYS
By Laura Knetzger

Bugs, friends, the world around us—this book has everything!
Come explore Bug Boys for the fun, thoughtful adventure about growing up and being yourself.

Chapter Book

THE RUNAWAY PRINCESS
By Johan Troïanowski

The castle is quiet.
And dull.
And boring.
Escape on a quest for excitement with our runaway princess, Robin!

Middle–Grade

ASTER AND THE ACCIDENTAL MAGIC
By Thom Pico & Karensac

Nothing fun ever happens in the middle of the country . . . except maybe . . . magic?
That's just the beginning of absolutely everything going wrong for Aster.

Middle–Grade

WITCHLIGHT
By Jessi Zabarsky

Lelek doesn't have any friends or family in the world. And then she meets Sanja. Swords, magic, falling in love . . these characters come together in a journey to heal the wounds of the past.

Young Adult